IMAGES OF TRAUMA

Images of Trauma

*From Hysteria
to Post-Traumatic Stress Disorder*

DAVID HEALY

faber and faber

LONDON · BOSTON

First published in 1993
by Faber and Faber Limited
3 Queen Square London WC1N 3AU

Phototypeset by Intype, London
Printed in England by Clays Ltd, St Ives plc

© David Healy, 1993

David Healy is hereby identified as author of this work in
accordance with Section 77 of the Copyright, Designs and
Patents Act 1988

A CIP record for this book is available from the British Library

ISBN 0–571–16326–2

2 4 6 8 10 9 7 5 3 1

Contents

for Rita and Tom

Acknowledgments

This book involves a joyride through a hundred years of psychiatric history. As with any joyride there is a certain disregard of convention. The reader, therefore, needs to be warned that a reviewer of my last book, while apparently enjoying the ride, complained about the cavalier approach to references and facts. As regards the references, the approach here may be less than a law-abiding Sunday driver might like. In parts of the book I have given references for entire sections rather than for specific points – unless a reference to a specific point has seemed necessary. But in a work of historical interpretation no one ever 'proves' things: points from one argument cannot be taken over as proven facts. It has seemed more appropriate to me in parts of this book to cite the works that have shaped the interpretation that I am offering.

While happy enough with the reviewer's qualms about my brushing up against the red reference cones on the edge of the motorway, I was less than happy about his concern at my treatment of facts, in large part because I had announced beforehand that some disregard for established facts seemed inevitable given the re-reading of events that was being undertaken. A similar re-reading is involved in this book, in which, as the reader will discover, the plot progresses as it were along a multi-laned motorway. Switching from lane to lane inevitably makes drivers who stick to one lane nervous. However as the thrust of this book is very much about the transience of scientific 'facts', especially the facts of psychological medicine, and about how certain lanes on the motorway stop abruptly – sometimes for no apparent reason – it is difficult to know what to make of appeals to stay in lane.

As in most cases of joyriding I have had passengers in the back. Some have been hijacked; these have included Ian Rickard and Ivor Browne. Others have been there before and have come along again for the ride, perhaps partly out of a fascination at the possibility of disaster; these include Justin Brophy, Helen Healy, Paula McKay and especially Roger Osborne of Faber and Faber. They have individually or collectively screamed from the back seat when it has looked as though I was going to hit something, and have as a consequence kept the car on the road, in better shape than would otherwise have been the case.

Another group of back-seat passengers have been the patients who have ended up being picked up on the edge of the motorway by this particular lift. Some may recognize themselves in the case histories. The book is in many ways an apology for my/our abiding inability to get them much further towards where they want to go than they could get under their own steam.

Coming from Dublin, where joyriding has been for many years an endemic menace, I know something about the folklore, or mythology, of the condition. One of the best known 'facts' of the genre has been a story about a policeman who stopped a fourteen-year-old joyrider only to find that he had his mother and sisters in the back seat. In keeping with this tradition, my parents and sisters have been in the back seat of this particular vehicle on occasion. It is almost certainly the case also that without their influence I would never have taken up joyriding.

The author and publisher wish to thank the following for permission to quote from copyright material:

Hackett Publishing Company for permission to quote from *The Passions of the Soul* by René Descartes; Sigmund Freud Copyrights, the Institute of Psycho-Analysis and the Hogarth Press for permission to quote from *The Standard Edition of the Complete Psychological Works of Sigmund Freud*, translated and edited by James Strachey; Penguin Books Ltd for permission to quote from *The Great Cat Massacre* by Robert Darnton; Faber and Faber Ltd for permission to quote from *The Four Quartets* by T. S. Eliot; and New Directions Publishing Corporation for permission to quote from *Collected Poems* by George Oppen.

Introduction

Consider the following clinical cases. A nineteen-year-old girl is admitted to a psychiatric unit. She seems miserable and depressed. Sustained and vigorous treatment with ECT, a variety of antidepressants and combinations of antidepressants, as well as treatment with neuroleptics, did nothing to alleviate her condition. Finally, after a year of treatment, despite little change and repeated suicide attempts, she was discharged from hospital.

It transpired that this girl had been multiply abused on two separate occasions, in what appeared to have been organized abuse. At no point during her stay in hospital was she questioned about sexual abuse. These aspects to her case were first stumbled on many years later by friends watching her nightmares. Subsequently under hypnosis, she gradually pieced together a story of considerable trauma, for which she had been amnesic for ten years.

Since childhood Steven had suffered from nightmares and sleepwalking. This became a particular problem when, in 1935, he was hospitalized because of an infection. To prevent him from sleepwalking about the ward in the middle of the night his hands were bound behind his back. On one such occasion he awoke and, in a half-conscious state, found himself tied down. Although he could not untie his hands he was still able to evade his bodyguard and escape into the surrounding countryside. He returned a few hours later.

Some ten years later, Steven was again admitted to a hospital – this time in an attempt to cure recurrent sleepwalking. One evening at about midnight the nurse saw him struggling violently on his bed, apparently having a nightmare. He was holding his hands behind his back and seemed to be trying to free them from some imaginary bond. After carrying on in this way for about an hour he crept out of bed still holding his hands behind his back and disappeared into the hospital grounds. He returned twenty minutes later, awake. As the nurse put him to bed she noted deep weals like rope marks on each arm, of which

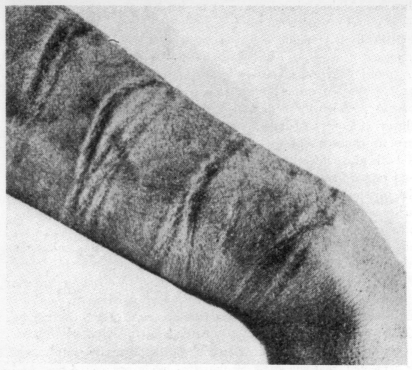

Fig. 1   Indentation marks appearing on patient's arm under hypnosis.

Steven, until then, seemed unaware. The next day the marks were still visible.

Steven's physician believed that the marks were stigmata caused by reliving the traumatic event of a decade earlier. To test this he caused Steven to relive that experience under a hypnotic drug. While reliving the experience Steven writhed violently on the couch for about three-quarters of an hour. After a few minutes weals appeared on both fore-arms. Gradually these became deeply indented and finally blood appeared along their course. Next morning the marks were still clearly visible; see Figure 1.[1]

A sixty-year-old woman was admitted to hospital following the death of her husband. She had many signs of depression – poor sleep, loss of appetite, loss of interest. But she was unlike most depressed subjects in that she did not know where she was and seemed to forget shortly after being told. She seemed not to know that her husband had recently died, claiming that he was alive somewhere – probably away doing some important business. That he had left her did not appear to bother her.

When her children visited she paid no heed to them. When she did engage others it was to tell them that the car park was sinking or that the main hospital building had burnt down or that the Red armies were coming.

A course of electroconvulsive therapy substantially improved her, but whenever she went out with her children for the weekend she came back worse. A meeting with the family indicated that, while they all appeared to love her, none was happy to have her come to live with them. Finally one of her children took her home for a month's trial period but brought her back after a week as her mother had begun to act bizarrely – wandering around claiming she had no head, and hiding in wardrobes.

Back in hospital her bizarre behaviour failed to resolve, and further courses of electroconvulsive therapy (ECT), antidepressants and neuroleptics had no beneficial effects. Her general disorientation led to her being transferred to a ward for demented women. There she could often be found standing up against the wall in a crucifixion posture for hours. She sometimes claimed she was blind, and indeed when walking around she often bumped into things. But on such occasions her eyes, typically, were closed. Despite all this, when taken out on ward outings to a nearby shopping centre, she, uniquely among the group, was apprehended for shoplifting. This and other incidents left ward staff certain that she was not demented, that she knew all that was going on around her. And indeed on occasional days she could be perfectly lucid and engage in conversation entirely appropriately. She has now been in hospital for several years.

A young boy of eight 'goes off his feet' abruptly. Later that day he is seen by a psychiatrist because his GP thinks the condition is probably hysterical. In discussion with the psychiatrist it turns out that the boy's father had promised to bring him to the cup final. He was not able to keep his promise but the final was drawn and there had to be a replay. Again the father promised to bring the son and again let him down. When faced with the prospect of telling his friends his legs gave way. He walked out of the psychiatric consultation.[2]

In contrast Estelle, aged twelve, while wearing a new dress one day got into an argument with a friend which ended in her being pushed over backwards. She fell and soiled her dress in a most embarrassing way. She came home and tried to conceal the shame. The following day she began to lose the power of her legs. She remained paralysed until healed by hypnosis eight years later.[3]

A fifty-five-year-old woman was in court to testify about a road accident. Having talked at great length when asked to she later interrupted further proceedings to let the court know about something she had just remembered. An irate magistrate ordered her to shut up. She did – for over a year. Why she later recovered was not very clear to subsequent therapists.

A man in his sixties due shortly to retire from a sales job loses his job because the business goes bankrupt. He has to sell his car. He could retire and supplement a rather meagre state pension with donations from his children. However he has always worked and feels obliged to keep on doing so. He finds factory work near by doing unskilled labouring in uncongenial surroundings. His family notice that he begins to become withdrawn and unhappy. After two years it becomes too much for him and he quits. Thereafter he sits at home all day doing nothing. This provokes anger and concern at home. His general practitioner refers him to a psychiatrist who diagnoses depression and tries him on anti-depressants, to no avail.

Shortly after this visit he begins to have difficulties walking. His gait becomes more and more peculiar, especially the left leg, which he drags after him while hopping forward on his right leg. His left arm sticks out at an odd angle. When asked what is wrong he complains of a pain in his knees. He has several falls which lead to hospitalization for suspected minor strokes or epilepsy. But no abnormality is discovered. He is sent home unchanged. His voice then begins to fail, at first slowly, but the failure is progressive so that after a few months it has almost completely disappeared. He can still communicate by writing. When asked why no one has been able to find anything wrong with him he writes, because they have not looked hard enough. The man has by now been almost aphonic for over a year. No one knows how to help him. He seems condemned to remain at home in this odd state until he dies.

Finally an attractive twenty-year-old girl is brought into hospital seriously depressed. She has stopped eating. She sleeps poorly, if at all. Her answers to all questions are that she has killed people, she is a murderer and she will be executed. She always looks distracted, at times appears to be having visions and on occasion is seen to walk backwards. Neither antidepressants in large doses nor neuroleptics make any differ-ence. ECT is considered, as she is seemingly delusionally depressed. However the nursing staff feel there is something different about this lunacy and suggest diazepam instead. She responds rapidly to a moderate dose of this and is normal within a few days. Subsequent discussions reveal that the episode began following an argument with her family about whether she should be going ahead with a marriage scheduled for a few weeks time.

Many such patients can be found in the back wards of psychiatric hospitals, where the staff will invariably feel that it should be possible to do something for them – that there is only a very small divide between a life inside the asylum and full and complete recovery. They represent some of the most difficult cases to be found in psychiatry. If asked to diagnose them, I would use the term hysteria. Many of my colleagues however would bridle at such a suggestion, claiming that there is no such thing. In part this is because the label hysteria gives no clear guidelines for specific treatment or indications about likely outcome. There is no consensus about how such states come about or how they should be treated. Whatever term is used to refer to them the individuals concerned appear now, and appeared to Freud and Breuer in 1895, to be suffering from a psychological problem. But what is a psychological problem? Why is there a dispute about what term to use for states such as these? Is the dispute at all responsible for our lack of progress as regards their therapy? These are the issues this book will deal with.

In 1980 the American Psychiatric Association (APA) created the category of post-traumatic stress disorder (PTSD). It also recognized for the first time that this or any 'psychological problem' could be precipitated *entirely* by external stress. The recognition of PTSD and a number of allied disorders has had legal and financial repercussions that were possibly not apparent when the change was first mooted.

Until 1980 what passed for the psyche was a curiously insubstantial thing. While artists may have believed in it, businessmen and lawyers ignored it. For the past hundred years one could seek legal redress or financial compensation for physical injuries resulting from negligence, but not for psychological suffering. All of this has changed since 1980. The potential consequences for the life sciences and for culture in general are immense. The impact on the practice of psychiatry, clinical psychology, psychiatric nursing and social work has been immense.

Since 1980 the face of mental health work has been changing rapidly as a host of neglected problems and their disturbing implications have surfaced. There are now serious questions being asked about whether we have too quickly written off reports of childhood abuse, physical violence or mental torture in the histories of individuals diagnosed as having schizophrenia, often, it now appears, on no better grounds than that they have been seriously disturbed.

Why should all this seem so new and produce a sense almost of panic when Freud surely discovered nearly a hundred years ago that the neuroses could be precipitated by environmental events? The answer to this is complex. In 1895 Freud claimed that childhood sexual seduction led to hysteria – effectively that hysteria was what would now be called PTSD (Chapter 3). In so doing he was one of the first, along with Pierre Janet, to claim that psychological problems could be precipitated by environmental stress. But more than this, he effectively discovered, along with Janet, the psyche and its disorders, the psychoneuroses (Chapter 2).

However along with the discovery of the psyche Freud became entangled in the hazards of psychodynamic interpretations; he became increasingly uncertain whether accounts of abuse in childhood could be believed. Within a year he was to revise his view of the neuroses and claim that environmental factors played a minimal part in their precipitation. Unlike Janet he began to view the aspects of the psyche he had recently discovered as superficial and set about creating a new method of analysing the psyche that would avoid the hazards of interpretation that had misled him in 1895 (Chapter 4).

This sea change has had a number of consequences. One has been a tendency on the part of both psychiatrists and psychologists to rule out of court the evidence from their patients' mouths. In great part this stems from Freud, whose post-1895 theory about why we behave the way we do had extensive recourse to the notions of repression and symbolic representation (Chapter 4). In postulating a repressive agency that keeps the most important things out of consciousness, and out of the social domain, and permits their expression only through the veil of symbols, he subverted our confidence in ourselves, producing a sense of helplessness in the face of psychological distress. Living with our fantasies and daydreams and experiencing the effects of anxiety does not, it would seem, give any of us much confidence about what to do for others who are disturbed by internal demons. In part this must surely be because of Freud's legacy that there are depths to the psyche that the ordinary individual cannot plumb and that tinkering around on the surface is at best worthless and may even be dangerous. In contrast to Freud I will argue that, in order to understand our psyche and its disturbances, we would do well to focus on the images in our mind's eye and to pay closer heed to the voices that ring in our inner ears or the thoughts that flit through our heads. These have in the past been dismissed as superficial. But far from worrying about any deeper meaning current work suggests that these images and events can profitably be taken at face value (Chapter 7). What is required is often a good description of what really is in the mind's eye rather than any interpretation of it.

Freud's change of opinion also affected cultural notions of psychological distress. In 1895 hysteria was the commonest psychiatric disorder, yet now it is apparently extinct (Chapter 6). Both psychiatrists and anti-psychiatrists have joined forces in dismissing it as a mythical disorder. Social historians have used the example of hysteria as evidence in favour of the thesis that mental disorders are merely socially sanctioned avenues for the expression of distress. For example in Elaine Showalter's marvellous book *The Female Malady*[4] the author describes in detail the constraints of the female role and indicates the pressure on women to become hysterical. But while describing the role from within at no point does she describe the resulting disorder from within. A truly psychological account of hysteria does not exist.

I will further argue that hysteria can neither be reduced to nervous malfunctioning nor be understood simply in social terms. By a psychological account I mean something close to what Freud was offering in 1895 – an account that focuses primarily on the internal images and dialogues of an affected individual, as opposed to an account of what may be happening to their neurotransmitters or of the social pressures that may shape their distress. My aim is to give an account of the imagery and emotions that seem to get out of control in neurotic disorders and of the *psycho*-dynamics that may govern entries and exits on this internal stage.

In linking particular psychological states with specific historical events involving sexual abuse, about which there must necessarily always be a certain amount of uncertainty, Freud almost fatally compromised the development of dynamic psychology. The same problems confront us today when we are faced with stories of satanic abuse of children. Can we ever be certain that we are not being deceived by accounts of past happenings that rest primarily on images and memories accessible to one individual only? The spectre of uncertainty thrown up by this problem has, more than any other, dogged psychology from its inception. It was in an effort to attain the supposed certainties of true science that Freud created psychoanalysis (Chapters 4, 9). In contrast behaviourists claimed that the demons within the cranial box are no more than insubstantial wraiths, that have no positive existence and hence are not amenable to scientific investigation. The appeal of this claim led to behaviourists supplanting psychoanalysts in the halls of scientific orthodoxy during the middle years of this century (Chapter 4).

While Freud struggled with these issues Pierre Janet also linked hysteria to trauma. Janet's psychology was a psychology of consciousness, as opposed to the focus of psychoanalysis on a dynamic unconscious and that of behaviourism on the external appearances of behaviour only. However from being the foremost investigator of the emerging science of dynamic psychology during the 1890s Janet was eclipsed by Freud, and his psychology of consciousness withered on the vine (Chapter 5). Strangely, however, the 1980s have seen both the rediscovery of Janet and the notion of a psychology of consciousness as well as the apparent comprehensive demise of both psychoanalysis and behaviourism as intellectual forces in psychology. Between 1890 and 1980 lies a story that concerns the nature of science.

The first six chapters of this book consider the question raised by Freud and Janet as to whether hysteria is precipitated by environmental events. They come down in favour of the argument that, broadly speaking, hysteria is precipitated by trauma, but that trying to interpret what has actually happened may be hazardous, and trying to intervene to put things right far from easy. But if this were all that was involved the significance of the creation of PTSD would be minimal. Hysteria today is after all but one of many neuroses that are recognized, and an uncommonly diagnosed one at that. Does the recognition of PTSD have implications for the other neuroses or for the larger notion of mental illness?

To tackle these questions the scope of the book needs to be broadened. In Chapter 7 recent developments in neurobiology and in the computer modelling of the psyche are outlined, focusing in particular on current research on the nature of internal imagery, the emotions and consciousness and in particular on the question of what distinctions can be drawn between conscious and unconscious psychological processes and how disturbances of these processes may contribute to psychological disorders. Chapter 8 takes these issues further and considers what makes the unconscious dynamic and what dynamics govern entrances and exits on the conscious stage. These issues are taken up against the background question of whether depression is a post-traumatic neurosis. In answering this negatively, and going against the grain of common assumption, I hope to make clear just how hazardous it may be to make interpretations about any relationship between past trauma and present distress. This chapter will also indicate how the management of uncertainty is central to the operations of both consciousness and the unconscious, a theme that will resurface in Chapter 10.

Chapters 2–8 focus on the images and dialogues that form what we term the stream of consciousness. Attempting to interpret these makes psychotherapy a hazardous enterprise, but one whose hazards can potentially be managed scientifically. However psychotherapy also attempts to do something altogether more mysterious: it attempts to discern the movements of the emotions. This has always been viewed at one and the same time as the greatest ability of the healer but also as a potentially subversive activity. Chapter 9 takes up this problem, charting the attempts of the psychotherapists from Mesmer through to Freud to deal with this issue and noting how such attempts have tended to derail into messianism and to meet with medical resistance.

Why this should be is taken up in Chapter 10. In essence the answer given is that the healer, as traditionally conceived, stands opposed to Descartes' vision of man as divided into a mechanical body and a spiritual mind. This division was of central importance to the development of modern science but it has made of modern science a mechanical enterprise. The existence of internal imagery and emotions and our increasing appreciation of the role of uncertainty in psychological functioning poses a gathering challenge to this mechanical approach.

It is against this background that the neuroses (psychological problems) are invested with significance. They straddle several divides – the brain–mind divide, the mechanical–holistic divide and the genetic–environmental divide. In so doing they reveal much of what it is to be human and point up a number of radical tensions in contemporary medicine. One such tension centres on the implication that individual psychological breakdowns are the fault, or fate, of those so afflicted, rather than a consequence of the social or political systems within which we live. Another lies in the implication that psychological disorder as an instance of mechanical breakdown is appropriately corrected by mechanical means – such as drug therapy. A welter of legal and financial interests hinges on these issues. Given the interests at stake it is not clear what the consequences of the creation of PTSD will be.

1　The Historical Origins of Hysteria[1–3]

If a woman becomes suddenly voiceless you will find her legs cold, as well as her knees and hands. If you palpate her uterus, you will find it is not in its proper place. You will also find that her heart palpitates, that she gnashes her teeth, that there is copious sweat and all the other features characteristic of those who suffer from sacred disease (epilepsy). Such women may do all sorts of unheard-of things. Hippocrates.[4]

The matrix is an animal which longs to generate children. When it remains barren too long beyond puberty, it gets discontented and angry and it wanders about the whole body, closing the issues for air, obstructing respiration and putting the whole body into extreme danger, causing all variety of disease, until at length desire and love bringing a man and a woman together make a fruit and as it were plucking the fruit from the tree, sow in the womb, as in a field animals unseen by reason of their smallness and without form. Plato.[5]

Sigmund Freud first entered the scientific limelight with his *Studies on Hysteria*, co-authored with Joseph Breuer in 1895. The central contention of their book, that hysteria was a disorder of reminiscences, a disorder predicated on traumatic memories, a psychological disorder rather than a properly nervous disorder, would not appear controversial now; then however nothing comparable had ever been claimed before, although Pierre Janet in Paris put forward similar ideas at much the same time. We are so accustomed now to considering this possibility in some form or other that the momentous nature of the breakthrough can only be recaptured by attempting to reconstruct the pre-1890 orthodox point of view concerning the origins of hysteria. It is such a reconstruction that Chapter 1 attempts.

However, as the rest of this book will reveal, there is more than simply the historical reconstruction of a vanished world-view involved in this exercise. The forces that shaped pre-1890s' orthodoxy, leading to a conception of hysteria as an endogenous disorder arising in a degenerate nervous system, did not simply dissipate with the first rays of the new psychodynamic dawn. Rather the influence of those forces remains potent, and perhaps even dominant, in both psychology and medicine to this day.

Etymologically the term 'hysteria' means a disorder stemming from the womb. From antiquity the cardinal features of the disorder included both convulsions and a feeling of suffocation, as though something were pushing into the chest from below. As these symptoms were much commoner in women than in men, and as the idea that the uterus was immovably fixed in the pelvis did not become established until the seventeenth century, it is not totally surprising that many saw the illness as resulting from a migration of the uterus upwards. Migration upwards might be caused by deprivation of intercouse, which would lead to the uterus drying up, losing weight and hence rising. In turn this view inevitably meant that neither men nor children could be properly hysterical.

Not everyone accepted the migrating uterus view. As early as AD 200 Galen preferred the idea that hysteria was caused by the emanation of vapours from the womb. Because of Galen's enormous influence this was the dominant paradigm until at least the end of the seventeenth century. The vapours, it was argued, arose from the retention of menstrual blood, or of female semen, or as a result of the toxic effects of *fluor albicans* (thrush).[6] In the case of the first two marriage and pregnancy were the obvious long-term solutions; tickling the cervix to release the toxins was an immediate hygienic manoeuvre that might also be undertaken.

Galen's theories of disease also implicated sexuality in the origins of hysteria in another way. This followed from his view that health involved a balance of humours in the body,[7, 8] which led to the common practice of bleeding in an attempt to restore a supposed balance and to attempts to treat diseases by blistering – raising blisters so that noxious vapours could escape. The sexual faculties provided a regular source of imbalance – once a month in the case of menstrual discharges – and an irregular but frequent source of imbalance in the case of masturbation.

The first clear shift away from the uterus came in 1667, when Willis referred to hysteria as the 'so-called uterine disease'. He classified it instead as primarily a convulsive disease caused by an alteration of the nerves and brain. By means of the nervous system, he wrote, 'are revealed the true and genuine reasons for very many actions and passions that take place in our body that would otherwise seem most difficult to explain: and from this fountain, no less than the hidden causes of diseases and symptoms, which are commonly ascribed to the incantations of witches, may be discovered'.[9]

In 1682 Sydenham commented that hysteria was the commonest *chronic* disease. He proposed that it affected females (hysteria *sensu strictu*) *and* males (hypochondria), and argued that it was caused by some ataxia or faulty disposition of the animal spirits (nerves). But it took a hundred years for the nervous origins of hysteria to become a clear possibility.

THE PASSIONS OF THE SOUL[10-13]

The defectiveness of the sciences we inherit from the ancients is nowhere more apparent than in what they wrote about the Passions. This is a topic about which knowledge has always been vigorously sought and though it does not seem to be one of the most difficult – because, as everyone feels them in himself, one need not borrow any observation from elsewhere to discover their nature – nevertheless what the Ancients taught about them is so little and for the most part so unbelievable, that I cannot hope to approach the truth unless I forsake the paths they followed. Descartes, *The Passions of the Soul*: Article 1.[14]

As early as AD 200, while emphasizing the humours and the uterus, Galen had noted, at post mortem, thin white 'tubes' that ran from the spine and brain to the heart, lungs and other organs, and hypothesized that these carried the 'sympathies', which were responsible for the intimate involvement of our bodies in emotional states – the excited flutter of the heart, the sinking of the gut or the terrified constriction of breathing. It nevertheless took until the end of the seventeenth century for any detailed work on the nervous system to be undertaken.

Neurosis

It took a further hundred years for this work to begin to influence thinking about behaviour. The notion of a neurosis crystallized between 1765 and 1785. The term was formally introduced by William Cullen in 1785, although the idea that general lassitude or suboptimal behaviour of obscure origin could be put down to 'nerves' had been mooted a few years earlier by Robert Whytt. Cullen defined the neuroses as disorders that involved disturbances of nervous functioning, without any obvious lesion or inflammation being apparent at post mortem. (In much the same way the word nephrosis had been coined to categorize functional disorders of the kidney in the absence of demonstrable abnormality or inflammation, as occurred in nephritis.) For Cullen hysteria was one subdivision of the spasmodic neuroses – all of which involved abnormal movement of muscles or muscle fibres. This group also included tetanus, epilepsy, colic, diabetes, palpitations and whooping cough.

Given contemporary views of the nervous system, in which nerve cells had not been recognized and the idea that nerve fibres conducted impulses between cells was a long way distant, it is not clear what Cullen meant by the term neurosis. Since he could not have meant actual faulty nerves it seems likely that he saw the neuroses as malfunctions of the system as a whole, with no definite, localized disturbance. These generalized disturbances of function displayed themselves in the production of pain, increased or decreased sensitivity to internal or external stimuli, spasms and general disorders of muscular movement, and in weakness.

The contemporary view was that the nervous system was of a piece, permeated in some unspecifiable way by an immaterial spirit. Therefore this early notion of a neurosis should probably not be taken to refer to a disorder of what we now understand as nerves or to an entirely physical disorder. Pinel for example saw the neuroses as being caused by the passions of the soul. An alternative explanation was that they resulted from the effects of sympathetic influences on the brain arising from malfunctioning of the stomach, womb or other parts of the body.

With Cullen and Pinel the notion of a neurosis became fashionable and there was a huge expansion in the number of diseases that were considered neurotic. However shortly afterwards one of the so-called neuroses, apoplexy (stroke), was discovered to have a very real and demonstrable cause in loss of brain tissue. By 1840 it was clear that many of the disorders that Pinel and Cullen had described as neuroses had either a localizable basis in nerve cell destruction, or indeed had nothing to do with nerves at all. For the remainder, who had 'neurotic' behaviour in the absence of a localizable lesion, the notion of a reflex was to provide a possible basis for explanation.

Reflex[15-18]

The machine of our body is composed in such a way that all the changes taking place in the motion of the spirits can make them open some of the brain's pores more than others . . . All the movements we make without our will contributing (as happens when we breathe, walk, eat and in short do all the actions common to us and beasts) depend only on the arrangement of our members . . . in the same way in which a watch's movement is produced by sheer force of its spring and the shape of its wheels. Descartes, *The Passions of the Soul*: Article 16.

René Descartes, in the mid-seventeenth century, introduced the notion that men and animals might function in many respects like automata.

4

This view required physical and mental operations to take place by means of tugs and pulls using some equivalent of ropes and pulleys and springs, or else by a hydraulic process involving fluid and valves. The obvious candidates for such threads or pipes were the nerves.

Descartes suggested that on stimulation by pain, for example, delicate threads lying in the nerve bundles are moved, which open valves within the brain and release animal spirits (particularly sensitive and irritable substances) which then lead to muscular movement. However Descartes did not mean that this should be an automatic and unconscious reaction, of the kind that we now mean when we use the term 'reflex'. Such an automatic and unconscious process might account for strictly vegetative functions but not for behaviour proper. For example the physical sight of fire would be associated with a mental image of flames. Animal spirits in the brain on catching a glimpse of such an image would be *reflected* in fright towards the muscles, disposing them for flight. Until about 1830 the primary meaning of the term reflex connoted some form of reflection, in the sense of judgment. Although some actions may seemingly occur beneath the level of conscious awareness, as in mechanically removing one's foot from a flame that one is not looking at, or in knee-jerks, these, Descartes argues, did not happen without the reflection of the soul. Such acts were after all invariably wise.

However Descartes, and Robert Whytt after him, argued that reflex actions might be governed by some lower faculty of the soul. The case of anencephalic infants, who were nevertheless capable of movements, was a strong pointer towards the possibility of such unconscious knowledge – a troubling one for those who believed that such acts had to be governed by some wisdom of the soul. So also were experiments on removing the brains of animals, which did not necessarily lead to complete passivity of the animal. Such findings greatly troubled scientists and philosophers, who saw the nervous system as a piece, not as a system composed of millions of individual cells organized in various hierarchies.

While Descartes, it seems, was prepared to envisage the nervous system as a machine with the soul localized to the pineal gland, for the most part the soul was thought to inhabit the nervous system as a whole, as there were no subdivisions to the system. The notion that the nervous system was organized in layers was introduced by Gall in 1810. The potential autonomy of the different layers that this view pointed towards caused a problem, in that it seemed to indicate that things could happen outside the control of the soul.

Gall's work on the internal hierarchy of the nervous system made it less likely that there could be one overall disturbance of functioning, and more likely that there could be localized pathologies within a stratified system. This view was reinforced by the work of Magendie and Hall, who separately demonstrated that the spinal column was not just a system for carrying messages from the brain, but contained systems that could operate independently of the brain.

This demonstration transformed the entire situation. It became possible to conceive of actions being automatic and unconscious. And when Hall introduced the term 'reflex' for such automatic and unconscious acts he stood the original notion upside down. This was one of the key acts of the emerging neuroscientific revolution of the nineteenth century.

The other major development, although one little remarked upon, was the notion of the unconscious that was implied in this formulation. Whytt, in a comprehensive review,[19] has shown that an idea of an unconscious had been around since the Greeks – Freud did not discover it. But essentially this earlier unconsciousness took the form of depths to the soul, some of which might be effectively impenetrable. The emerging idea of an unconscious, automatic reflex was radically different. This was not a localized piece of the soul but simply a piece of machinery, and one for whose operation there was no need to postulate the operations of either a soul or consciousness. As Laycock put it, 'researches of this kind whether instituted on the insane, the somnambulist, the dreamer or the delirious must be considered like researches on analytical chemistry'.[20] As Laycock, Carpenter and others began, during the middle years of the century, to postulate and discover reflexes at ever higher levels of the spinal cord the view of man that was implied was steadily beginning to look radically different to anything conceived by previous generations.

The notion of a reflex gave substance to the idea of the nervous system becoming disturbed in sympathy with disturbances in other organs such as the kidneys, teeth or uterus by a reflex mechanism operating outside consciousness. For example inflamed kidneys might be expected to lead to spinal irritation and thereby reflexly disturb the function of other organs or lead to generalized nervous irritability. This was not just an armchair theory of the neuroses. It led to the removal of kidneys and teeth in patients who, far from having specific renal or dental problems, had presented with complaints of being generally unwell.

Where hysteria was concerned the notion of a reflex overcame the implausibilities that resulted from an exclusive reliance on a uterine pathology. Rather than have the uterus migrate it was now possible to have nervous impulses from the uterus diffuse upwards, bringing abnormal sensations to other areas of the body. One obvious treatment for such a condition was hysterectomy – a treatment undertaken enthusiastically it would appear.

Associations[21-3]

When introducing the idea of a mechanical and unconscious reflex Hall had in mind something that played a part in the functioning of the spinal cord. He did not envisage its extension to the central nervous system. However, progressively over the following thirty years, Griesenger, Laycock, Jackson and others extended the idea of the reflex up into the central nervous system to account for increasingly more complicated behaviours.

As reflexes happened automatically and unconsciously this research programme raised for the first time the idea that consciousness might be an unimportant spectator of human activity rather than its guiding focus. This point of view was dramatically put forward by Thomas Huxley, who in defending Darwin suggested that consciousness was no more important to human functioning than the whistle of a locomotive was to the running of a train. He also compared conscious awareness to the mist or steam that hovers over machines while they work.

However there was another possibility. This lay in an associative model of the mind. This model argued that all there was to mental functioning was the associative bringing into consciousness of mental images. One image or thought would automatically lead to another. Association theories had begun with David Hume in 1750, who argued that we remember things because of associations between what is in our mind or what we see and what is then remembered. The theory was taken further by John Stuart Mill, who added the notion that we begin life with a *tabula rasa*, on which later impressions are inscribed. The associationist model suggested that certain images or memories could lie dormant in the mind, if no associative connections were made between them and other ideas or feelings. They could effectively be subconscious.

Subsequently, in 1855, Alexander Bain argued that a simple associative theory could not possibly explain the complexity of human functioning or the efficiency of learning. He argued that there must be some pleasure–pain mechanism involved. Thus associations would be built up in certain ways because of the pleasure that pattern offered. It was not just simply trial and error learning but trial and error stabilized by pleasure or pain. His best-known example was drawn from the birth of lambs. After birth they thresh about, get up and stumble around. But

7

once they find their mother's teat their behaviour becomes goal-directed very quickly.

It seemed plausible around 1850 that one central nerve cell might contain one association, image or thought. Associations might therefore operate reflexly. This marriage of associative theories of the mind to reflex models from physiology effectively led to the birth of scientific psychology. In 1855 Herman von Helmholtz had demonstrated that impulses travelled along nerves at a specifiable speed of forty metres per second. This opened the way for an experimental psychology that aimed at investigating associative reflexes by computing reaction times – how long it takes for a word or an image to conjure up another. This was undertaken by Wundt, one of Helmholtz's research assistants, who from 1875 began the systematic investigation of mental life using the reaction time as his principal experimental probe. For this work Wundt is commonly cited as the first true psychologist – as opposed to physiologist or philosopher dabbling in psychology.

The marriage of associative theories and reflex models also led directly to Freud's early formulations, and later to the key notions of behaviourism.

DEGENERATION[24–7]

One of the most important consequences of Descartes' division of individuals into a mechanical body and a non-mechanical mind was the effective elimination of the psyche. Before Descartes it had been commonplace to view the soul as having three divisions: the highest involving the rational faculty; the intermediate involving memory, the emotions and consciousness; and the lowest involving the passions and appetites. Faced with the problem of where the soul was located in the body Descartes proposed that the animal faculties resided in an essentially mechanical brain and the higher faculties hovered therein, being located if anywhere in the pineal gland. Since there is no obvious place in such a schema for any of the intermediate faculties of the soul this led to most of these being assumed into the mind, and to the disappearance of a distinctive psyche composed of memory, the emotions and consciousness.

Under Descartes' influence it was not possible to have a psychological problem – there could only be either spiritual or mechanical problems. If a subject had breathing difficulties, convulsions, paralyses, hallucinations or any other manifestation of hysteria, these *had* to involve some physical pathology of the organ in question. This might be a minimal disorder not visible at post mortem, which could lead to a sympathetic disturbance of the nervous system, which might in turn be aggravated by an emotional state. But some physical disturbance there had to be. Dysfunction without a pathology could only point to a *spiritual* problem. As serious disorders of the spirit implied damnation every effort was made to find a physical pathology.

As the notion of the reflex was extended to ever more complex behaviours, and in particular when it linked up with the associationist model of the mind, there came a further development. The notion that the nervous system consisted of a hierarchy of reflexes opened up an irresistible possibility – that at some point in the chain of reflexes there was a fault leading to a *degeneration* from optimal functioning. Some of the reflexes might be degenerate.

The term degeneration was introduced by Morel in 1857. By 1860 it was well on its way to being the central tenet of psychological medicine. Degenerate reflexes, it was thought, were something that might be inherited. Indeed, as demonstrating an acquired degeneration of nervous functioning was effectively beyond the resources of the day, the idea of hereditary degeneracy was almost inevitable. Time and again the authors of the period, from Briquet through to Freud, when discussing individual case histories note that their client came from degenerate or neuropathic stock. This it was assumed laid the basis for the abnormal nervous reflex that was hysteria (see pp.11–14). With the notion that a degenerate reflex might underlie their physical presentation the neuroses became for the first time an unequivocally physical illness.

In the hands of concerned physicians the use of the term degenerate did not have the implications that it might seem to have now. It implied a mechanical breakdown of function, which was some improvement on the belief that behavioural disorders were in some way a lingering manifestation of original sin. However degeneracy quickly became a broad notion – just as neurosis had eighty years earlier. All sorts of imbecility, antisocial behaviour such as alcoholism, drug abuse and criminality, as well as the neuroses were put down to degeneracy, which in this manner became one of the first theories to attempt to account for social problems in terms of biological disorder. Allied to an associationist psychology the notion of a degenerate reflex was invoked to explain perversity and disturbing behaviour of all sorts. The reflexes that would normally conjure up 'normal/acceptable' associations and mental contents might be expected, if degenerate, to lead to abnormal associations, some of which would be perverse or antisocial. It was also conceded that such aberrant reflexes might have creative outcomes on some occasions – which led to a widespread association between being an artist and being degenerate.

Given the supposed heritability of degeneracy, and the generally higher birth rates among the lower social orders, there were serious concerns that civilization would inevitably become extinct. The breeding of the perverse and neurotic rather than the brightest and the best would lead to an increasing enfeeblement of social life – signs of which every generation seems to see in those who come after them.

The notion of degeneracy, therefore, was never simply a biological or socially neutral one. This lengthy attempt to establish the historical pedigree of the concept of degeneracy has been undertaken for a purpose. One of my central contentions will be that all theories of the neuroses, until very recently, have been essentially variations on this early notion of degeneracy. The neurotic has been always thought to be in some way weak or flawed. For a brief period around 1895 Freud challenged this notion. But in developing psychoanalysis, I will argue, he moved back to one of the most radically degenerate theories of neurosis that there have been.

THE EXPLORATION OF HYSTERICAL NEUROSIS[28-33]

In 1859 Briquet published a treatise on hysteria which became the seminal study of the subject. To this day Briquet's syndrome refers to a clinical picture, usually affecting women, of having something physically wrong with oneself most of the time. It leads to repeated visits to family doctors. Once it has been 'proven' that the particular presenting complaint does not indicate serious illness another takes its place. In some severe cases the syndrome is diagnosed only after successive unnecessary operations. In extreme cases individuals end up with abdomens crisscrossed by surgical scars. Some recent estimates suggest that milder varieties of the syndrome may exist in up to 10 per cent of the adult female population. Such cases would formerly have been diagnosed as hysteria, but as there is a great reluctance to use this term today Briquet's syndrome is used instead.

The significance of Briquet's work, in the 1860s, was that it helped to establish anaesthesia as one of the hallmarks of hysteria. Ninety-three of his collection of 400 cases of hysteria had a relatively pure hemi-anaesthesia (one half of their body was less sensitive to stimuli than the other) and many more had a variety of other anaesthesiae. Briquet and others proposed that this anaesthesia was linked by a *reflex* mechanism to ovarian morbidity on the same side as the anaesthesia.

Another syndrome, neurasthenia, was first put forward in 1869 by George Miller Beard. This term literally means weakness of the nerves. It tended to be applied to a middle-class clientele, with hysteria being reserved for more demonstrative working-class behaviour. The typical neurasthenic felt weak and tired and lacking in will-power but rarely had convulsions, paralyses or crises. The cure was to travel, to take rests, to put on weight or some combination of all of these. It was supposed that the stress of fatigue or loss of weight uncovered a degenerate link in the nervous system. (The term neurasthenia has, like Briquet's syndrome, also come back into vogue today.)

A further indication of how the neuroses, and hysteria in particular, were viewed at the time comes from the response to metallotherapy when it was stumbled upon by Victor Burq around 1847. Burq found that copper appeared to reverse hypnosis. In so doing it also seemingly dissolved hypnotic anaesthesia. Based on this he argued that anaesthesia must form the actual basis for hypnosis. As hysteria typically also involved anaesthesia a formal link between hypnosis and hysteria was established. Burq claimed good results using metals to treat hysterics.[34]

It took a number of applications to the Société de Biologie in Paris before Burq's request for independent assessment of his findings was finally noted. Finally, in 1876, the Société's director, Claude Bernard, at the time perhaps France's most prestigious scientist, agreed to investigate. He appointed three of the best-known physicians of the day, Jean-Martin Charcot, Amedée Dumontpallier and Jules Bernard Luys, to conduct the investigation. They came down in favour of the scientific importance of metallotherapy. Some indication as to why they did may be gleaned from an incident from one of Charcot's ward rounds. Apparently one day while talking about hysterical anaesthesia, in the presence of some visiting English physicians, Charcot pin-pricked the arm of one of his patients. He expected her to be anaesthetic but she reacted with pain. Irritated, he asked afterwards what had happened and was told that Burq had earlier in the day applied his metal plates to the patient.

Charcot and hysteria

The effect of metals on the anaesthesia found in hysteria was of immense significance for Charcot. Working from the Salpêtrière in Paris, he was the foremost neurologist of the day. He had earlier risked clinical ostracism in arguing that hysteria involved real nervous disordering, with degenerate nervous reflexes as its basis.

For Charcot the clinical stigmata of hysteria involved anaesthesia, convulsions and paralyses. He argued that in its prototypical form, in individuals with *grande hystérie*, there were four distinguishable stages – epileptoid states, violent movement, hallucinations and finally a confusional state. Typically the attack would start with the patient falling backwards, becoming rigid and adopting strange arched postures. So unnatural were these postures, and so seemingly beyond the capability of normal people, they almost certainly constituted one good reason why most observers thought that there must be some physical disturbance involved.

Charcot became a principal proponent of the degeneracy theory of the neuroses. He collected medieval paintings and accounts of states of possession and of the trials of witches and took pains to illustrate how the unfortuante victims, who were often burnt at the stake, were hysterical (physically ill) rather than evil. He noted that one of the medieval tests to determine whether a subject was a witch or possessed was to search for an area of anaesthesia (the devil's claw) on the skin; by 1860 of course this seemed to be the cardinal clinical feature of hysteria.

In the case of hysteria Charcot initially thought that the degenerate reflex could be mobilized by fixing the subject's eye. Intense concentration, it seemed, led into the hysterical state. However this was a rather subjective and indefinable procedure. In contrast applying Burq's metals could, it seemed, disrupt the state. Further unusual things occurred. While the metals might restore sensibility in an affected area, Charcot noted that very often the opposite side of the body became anaesthetic. Not only that, but after the metals were removed the anaesthesia would oscillate back and forth from side to side of the body.

Subsequent clinical investigation added further details to the mystery. Another common hysterical symptom at the time was unilateral blindness. Sight it seemed could be restored in eyes that had been blind, but the restoration often led to the opposite eye going blind. More uncommon was unilateral loss of colour vision. The application of the metals led to the restoration of colour vision. But interestingly the colours appeared in one eye and disappeared in the other in precisely the order that the latest physiological experiments on colour vision had suggested they should if the phenomenon was real.

Workers at the Salpêtrière set about explaining what was happening. They noted that electrical currents and magnets could produce similar effects. They inferred that the metals, coming into contact with moist skin, were setting up minute electrical currents but that this was enough to have large knock-on reflex effects within the system. The experimental work done was very sophisticated given the available laboratory resources. Electrical differences were found in the skin around the site of the metal and inverse differences were detected on the opposite side of the body. (Similar changes can be shown today.) Such findings were also demonstrated on healthy volunteers and in laboratory animals.

For Charcot and colleagues the importance of these findings lay in their pointing to the nervous reality of hysteria. A variety of the most eminent scientists from around Europe came to see for themselves. Few demurred. Criticism tended to be from a distance and took the form of suggestions that all the effects involved were produced by expectant attention. The Salpêtrière response to the criticism of expectant attention was – if so, why do we find the same effects in animals?

Despite this support the Salpêtrière edifice began to topple during the 1880s, under challenge from Hippolyte Bernheim in Nancy. When he ensured that his subjects were unaware of the presence of the metal Bernheim was unable to reproduce the Salpêtrière findings. Given some hint of what was expected of them however all the symptoms in the world could be produced. Nevertheless, even while putting the effects of metallotherapy down to suggestion, Bernheim did not deny the existence of hysteria. It was he said an altered state often brought about by trauma. According to Bernheim it was not necessary for actual trauma to have occurred to an hysteric; such was their suggestibility, merely to have conceived of some accident was enough – in the act of conceiving the accident was effectively realized. This was a groping towards a psychological conception of hysteria but it is not clear what mix of physical, spiritual or psychological factors Bernheim saw in hysteria.

Charcot had taken his stand on the fact that the disorder that was hysteria was a genuine one, that patients were not feigning their illness. At the time hysterics were often dismissed as liars. But if they were lying, Charcot argued, they did so reflexly rather than deliberately. The question of feigning was raised in a particularly acute form when Bernheim argued that hysteria involved suggestion and not the induction of a nervous reflex as had been proposed by Charcot. This question, as we shall see in Chapter 3, was later to be the rock on which Freud's first attempt to formulate a dynamic psychology perished. It was also a burning issue in the First and Second World Wars. It has become one again today with stories of ritual satanic abuse of children. In the confusion, individuals with hysteria have all too often been caught between being seen as either degenerate or malingering.

Traumatic hysteria[35-7]

There is one further important aspect of Charcot's work on hysteria – a demonstration of the possibility of a traumatic neurosis. Using clinical cases Charcot illustrated that shocks – such as witnessing accidents, or coming close to being involved in them – sometimes led to paralyses, to losses of voice or of vision or to amnesia. These states were all but indistinguishable from the paralyses, blindness or amnesias brought about by physical disease. Charcot however, by restoring function under hypnosis and by reproducing similar conditions in hypnotic subjects, was able to show that they owed their origin to trauma, rather than to physical destruction.

However even this did not lead to a fully psychological or environmentally determined conception of the neuroses. Charcot saw the traumatic neuroses as arising through the action of trauma on a weakened nervous system to produce the effects by reflex, rather than through the production of an altered psychological state. Similarly Briquet and Bernheim also endorsed the notion that trauma might precipitate hysteria, but again both saw the trauma as acting on either a weakened nervous system or a feeble mind.

An association between hysteria and sexual trauma first began about this time. In 1857 Ambroise Tardieu published a medico-legal study of assaults on decency. He drew attention to the frequency of sexual assaults on children. Between 1858 and 1869 in France there were 9,125 persons accused of the rape or attempted rape of children, especially of girls between the ages of four and twelve. Tardieu was solely concerned with the physical effects of such abuse; he did not consider that there might be specific psychological effects.

While Tardieu appears to have believed that these assaults took place, orthodox medical response tended to deny their reality. Fournier in 1880 and Brouardel in 1883 argued for 'the simulation of sexual attacks on young children' and speculated on 'the causes of error in expert opinions with respect to sexual assaults'. 'Hysteria plays a considerable role in the genesis of these false accusations, either because of genital hallucinations which stem from the great neurosis or because hysterics do not hesitate to invent mendacious stories with the sole purpose of attracting attention to themselves.'[38] In addition, as we have noted, it was held that for hysterics lying was often the result of a degenerate reflex rather than an intentional act.

HYSTERIA IN 1890

What seems totally lacking in the notion of hysteria up to 1890 was any feeling or concern for the internal psychodynamics of patients who were being labelled hysterical. With the discovery of the traumatic neuroses the scene was set for the discovery of the psychological aspects of the disorder and its potential precipitation by environmental factors.

However a number of obstacles stood in the way of this discovery – or perhaps more precisely of its incorporation into the existing body of science. One was that the notion of a psychological disorder had yet to be discovered. Another was the need for a clear distinction between psyche and mind – a distinction that I would argue we still have not fully established. These conceptual issues would inevitably have taken a great deal of time to work through. The difficulties involved however have been compounded by the fact that these discoveries and their associated conceptual implications have taken place against a background of powerful vested interests. These interests have, broadly speaking, been hostile to the idea of an environmentally determined psychological disorder.

2   The Emergence of the Psyche

The clear discovery of the idea of a psychological disorder was inter-linked with the discoveries of the psychological nature of hysteria and of the possible precipitation of psychological disorder by environmental events. This complex of ideas was discovered simultaneously by Pierre Janet in Paris and by Breuer and Freud in Vienna. Exactly who made the most complete breakthrough is a matter of debate. All three got hold of the idea that neurotic patients had images in their mind's eye and that the nature and origin of these images rather than any physical pathology or moral failings should be the focus of concern. I will begin with Janet, as strictly speaking his *L'automatisme psychologique*, pub-lished in 1889, was the first footprint in the sand.

JANET ON HYSTERIA[1-4]

Working from the Salpêtrière in Paris, Janet began publishing on hysteria in 1887. From the start he characterized it as an illness of fixed ideas. In a foreshadowing of current community psychiatry arguments he argued that Salpêtrière thinking on hysteria had been overinfluenced by the population of hysterics within its walls. As a hospital with a strong neurological tradition it inevitably attracted subjects with convulsions, paralyses, anaesthesiae. Equally its doctors were predisposed to think in terms of nervous reflexes. These he argued were the accidents rather than the essentials of hysteria.

In 1907 Janet listed the major symptoms of hysteria as somnambulism, fugues, multiple personalities, convulsions, paralyses, blindness and loss of speech, as well as digestive and respiratory difficulties. While anaes-thesia was a common accompaniment of any of these states, for Janet it was not invariably present as it had been for Charcot. In all these cases, he argued, there was a disturbance of consciousness rather than an abnormality of reflexes. However while emphasizing the psychological nature of hysteria Janet appears to have believed that it most often occurred in neuropaths (individuals with some degeneracy of their nervous system). He also, on occasion, refers to it as a moral disorder. This oscillation between neuropathy and morality indicates that even in 1907 the notion of the psyche had not achieved an identity clearly distinguishable from both brain and mind.

The term somnambulism refers to a state of altered consciousness in which a subject may think and act in a distracted or absent fashion. In its extreme form it amounted to sleepwalking. But it was far commoner in forms where the subject was apparently wide awake but not fully aware. Janet accounted for it in terms of subjects acting under the influence of an idea or an imagination. For example one of his patients had a beloved niece who threw herself out of an upstairs window and was killed. Subsequently the lady would have turns in which she would seem to alter consciousness, begin to mutter about the niece and would start moving toward the nearest window, leaving her relatives and friends afraid that she would throw herself out.

Another patient, who nursed her mother during a terminal illness, began, after her funeral, episodically to re-enact in great detail the events surrounding her mother's death. The somnambulism included hallucinating the presence of her mother and making ready for her own suicide by lying down on what appeared to be an imagined train-line. After seeing, with horror on her face, the train come towards her she usually came to, just after it should have run over her. She then resumed daily living as if nothing had happened. Typically she and other subjects were amnesic afterwards for what had happened to them during the period of altered consciousness.

Nowhere was this amnesia better demonstrated than in fugue states. A fugue is an extended somnambulism, in which the subject may appear normally conscious to outside observers. Typically they wander away from their present circumstances and end up elsewhere, having apparently no idea how they got there, or in some cases even who they are. This has led to a number of celebrated cases, such as that of the Rev. Ansell Bourne, described by William James, who left home and lived elsewhere for several months before suddenly switching one day to being able to remember who he was, but having no idea of how he had come to be where he was. Janet has left many descriptions of such fugue states. In general they seem to happen in states of stress, especially mounting stress. They are not uncommon in students in the weeks before exams.

In such cases, Janet argued, subjects act under the influence of an idea that has become dominant, relegating other concerns, even details of personal identity, to the very margin of awareness. In the case of convulsions there was invariably a trauma of some sort, the remembering of which threw the subject into a paroxysm. It would often take only some significant word to trigger off the paroxysm, without a memory of the trauma coming clearly to consciousness. The same was true for the paralyses, of which the case of Estelle in the Introduction is a good instance. Often it appeared that the trauma need not actually have happened. Thus someone whose leg narrowly missed being run over by a train might be left with a paralysed leg afterwards. The giving way of both legs was particularly commonly noted. Janet pointed out that hysterical paralyses are usually far more complete than the corresponding organic paralyses. Where a stroke patient can usually move their affected limb to some degree the hysterical patient is often totally incapable of movement.

While arguing that anaesthesia was not invariably present in hysteria Janet found it in up to 66 per cent of his cases. It also appeared to persist in milder forms in a number of cases after recovery. It had/has the unusual character of conforming not to the accepted distribution of nerves but to a lay person's idea of what a nervous lesion should give. Thus the whole of a hand might be without sensibility, whereas actually only one half of the hand should be affected as different nerves supply each side. Furthermore, despite this loss of pain and other sensations, he noted that hysterical patients do not end up with severe burning of a limb because of accidental unnoticed contact with something hot – as happens to patients with an organic loss of pain sense.

Looking closely at this phenomenon Janet came to the conclusion that what was involved was a loss of memory for the paralysed or anaesthetized limb. He suggested that affected subjects were not able to *imagine* their paralysed hand being lifted up to touch their nose, for example. The representation of the limb did not appear to enter consciousness. Close observation of paralytics indicated that they could move their legs normally when they were lying down, bend them, twist them, sometimes even get up and hop awkwardly on them, but the *idea* of walking seemed to be lost.

Janet also described a number of hysterical problems of vision – subjects who were blind in one eye or had restricted fields of vision or who had lost colour vision. The interesting thing about these difficulties was that it seemed the subjects must be perceiving normally in some sense. For example in the case of blindness involving one field of vision only it was possible by using a system of mirrors to induce subjects into seeing what they otherwise seemingly couldn't. From such experiments Janet concluded that hysterical subjects could sense normally but were unaware of their own perceptions. *They seemed unable to attend to their own internal imagery.*

In trying to put these findings together Janet rejected Bernheim's idea that all that is involved in hysteria is suggestion. His conclusion was that the highest functions of the individual, their will, is suspended, and that personal consciousness is contracted. In this state things can happen and be processed by consciousness without entering *personal* consciousness, leaving an amnesia afterwards as a result. None of this, he argued, can be explained in terms of suggestion. The indifference and absent-mindedness of hysterics were never suggested to them. Rather it was, he thought, because subjects ended up in a state in which they forgot all else that they were suggestible to a most extreme degree.

In line with the then dominant associative models of the mind Janet suggested that in hysteria, owing to a paralysis of personal consciousness, suggested ideas are not inhibited by associations that would normally interfere with their full development. In the normal course of events, if the idea of doing something novel or outrageous comes to mind, we will pretty quickly run through the likely consequences in our mind's eye. Thus we imagine ourselves having a passionate affair only to have the reverie interrupted by images of our children wondering why we have left them. Without such inhibitory associations we would be at the mercy of every passing fancy or suggestion – as he believed hysterics to be. When normal subjects imagine a scene such as a dance, he argued, their legs tense or move imperceptibly; they may even half hear the music or begin to yearn for the excitement of daring to ask a stranger to dance. However such imaginings can be contained. In hysterics the normal process of reflecting and deciding is somehow bypassed and the image leads on to action – imagined vomiting to real vomiting, imagined diarrhoea to real diarrhoea. As such hysteria is a psychological disorder. But as impulsive fancies and suggestions do not have this effect in all subjects Janet did not entirely abandon the idea that there was something about the nervous system of hysterics that was necessary to the development of the condition. However the primary root of the disorder he felt lay in the nature of consciousness.

If consciousness is, as it seems on the surface to be, some pure indivisible function, it is difficult to see why inhibitory associations should not form normally, other than because of some degenerate nervous reflex. But if consciousness were a complex entity composed of multiple sub-units, which are in turn conscious, and had somehow to integrate ideas of self and systems of social belief, then it becomes conceivable that it might under certain circumstances 'split' into component parts. Hysteria he felt was a malady of personal synthesis, in which ideas and functions that constituted the model of the self split – dis-associate.

It is not clear where Janet saw the dissociated elements of the self being located. He introduced the term 'subconscious', but by this seems to have meant something akin to the older ideas about the depths of the soul. In contrast Breuer and, more particularly, Freud were to argue for a subconscious that was a distinctly different layer to the rest of consciousness – something subterranean rather than just split off from awareness.

BREUER ON HYSTERIA[5-7]

In 1880, at the age of twenty-one, a young girl known to psychology as Anna O. began to suffer a series of complaints. These included paralysis and loss of sensation, especially on her right-hand side, sporadic loss of vision and of hearing, a seeming inability to speak her native German although she could still converse in English, and periods of 'absence' for which she showed no recollection afterwards. Her absence appeared to involve a change of personality, confusion and hallucinations. These afflictions began when she was nursing her father who was terminally ill.

For almost two years afterwards Anna O. was treated by Josef Breuer, who saw her virtually every day for increasing lengths of time. She fascinated him. He diagnosed hysterical double personality disorder in a girl from neuropathic stock. What was particularly interesting was that Anna O. under hypnosis began to tell Breuer about the history of each of her symptoms – when they had appeared and how they affected her – in reverse chronological order. For hearing alone she could recall 303 separate occasions of difficulty. Each of them appeared to have begun in a moment of conflict about or fright because of her father. When she worked her way back through all occasions of difficulty to the point of origin of each symptom it disappeared.

Some years later Breuer and Freud became close colleagues and Breuer's account of the Anna O. case particularly intrigued Freud. In 1885 Freud went to Paris on a travelling fellowship to study under Charcot, who at the time was the pre-eminent authority on hysteria and hypnosis and who in 1885 was working on the question of the traumatic neuroses.

Freud subsquently went on to visit Bernheim, after which he returned keen to collaborate on the issues raised by Anna's case.

From 1889 to 1892 Freud saw a number of cases of hysteria. He persuaded Breuer to join him in writing up four of these: Emmy von N., Lucy R., Katherina and Elizabeth von R., along with the case of Anna O., and in formulating a theory of hysteria. This resulted in 1893 in the publication of 'On the Psychical Mechanism of Hysterical Phenomena: Preliminary Communication', and in 1895 of *Studies on Hysteria*, in which they concluded that hysterics suffered from reminiscences.

In the *Studies on Hysteria* the chapter attempting to outline a theory on the origin of hysteria was written by Breuer. He compared the self to an electrical grid in which the level of energy has to be kept relatively constant and evenly distributed. Like an electrical circuit faults are liable to develop if there is a weakness in a particular wire, whether through some toxin, some hereditary factor, some abnormal input (from a diseased organ for example) or because of malnutrition or exhaustion. Another possibility, if two adjacent wires were close together, is that there might be a short circuit. Faults he believed were particularly likely if excitation in the circuit was excessive. This could happen in cases of sexual or traumatic inputs. It could happen when excitation could not be discharged, as for example when anger is felt but cannot be expressed, or when there are two irreconcilable ideas present in the mind at any one time – for example when a married woman finds herself lusting after another man, or an adolescent thinking positively about dedicating his life to some high moral goal suddenly remembers that he was masturbating only half an hour before. Normally affects, ideas and vegetative functions such as digestion or respiration are kept apart, Breuer argued, but in some cases one could get an affect or idea short-circuiting into the digestive or other vegetative system, causing palpitations or nausea for example. Irreconcilable ideas cause these physical symptoms, Breuer felt, in much the way that being on a boat produces irreconcilable conflicts between optical and balance senses – and hence nausea.

However, Breuer argued that one further mechanism must also play a part in most cases of hysteria – dissociation. On this he was very close to Janet's position and was ultimately to differ profoundly from Freud. Breuer argued that typically we all have affects or ideas that are either incongruent with our self-conceptions or are in some way traumatic. Normally these wear away through a process of being gradually integrated in the network of other associations. For example the wedding night is often very traumatic for a woman. Regarding wedding nights and sexual assaults in general Breuer commented that physicians would be unwise to rule out the possibility of their causing subsequent problems as we have 'no idea what sort of symptoms an erection calls forth in women, because the younger ones refuse to say and the older ones have forgotten'. But as subsequent sexual relations build up a fund of benign associations and as anxiety subsides, letting prior associations surface during sexual contact, the woman is able to work through the potential block. This however cannot happen if the traumatic memory is isolated from the rest of our associations – if it cannot make associative contact. Freud argued that traumatic memories become isolated through repression: we do not want to remember. Breuer argued that they become isolated through dissociation: we cannot remember.

Any form of preoccupation, Breuer argued, can lead to absentmindedness, which is the basis of dissociation. For example when concentrating hard at work or being creatively imaginative individuals can be quite insensitive to what is going on around them. This, he argued, is healthy, as the energy being generated is utilized. So also are twilight reveries as there is little psychic energy involved. But if in the course of a reverie some worry or memory of a lover or some other emotional material should arise it might capture the mind, suck in all the surrounding psychic energy and be incapable of discharge other than through some short-circuit type of process. This is similar to what happens in hypnosis, where one idea becomes dominant; it is also what happens in anxiety, when a danger can flood the mind with just one idea, inhibiting all else; or equally in orgasm. In the case of orgasm Breuer suggested we see an extreme degree of emotion accompanied by a restriction of consciousness that is comparable to a self-induced hypnosis. When reverie is the origin, dissociation is liable to happen to those who are care-ridden – watching at a sick bed as in Anna O.'s case – or to those who are in love. Reverie in this case is quite comparable to an auto-hypnotic procedure. The effect of dissociation is to inhibit subsequent reminiscence, just as after hypnosis subjects are amnesic for what has happened to them.

Comparing this to Janet's model, and being even more community oriented than Janet, Breuer suggested that Janet's notion that splitting happened in weak individuals probably stemmed from his seeing too many patients who had been institutionalized. In contrast, Breuer and Freud's clientele were mainly young, well-educated women from the upper strata of Viennese society. Based on this sample Breuer felt sure that anyone could get the type of hysteria that he and Freud were seeing, and also that indeed many hysterics were more gifted than the average.

FREUD ON HYSTERIA[8-12]

Before 1890 Freud, like everyone else, saw all neuroses as arising from an *actual* disorder of the nerves. In common with many others he believed that the disorder was caused by a toxic effect of disturbed sexuality on nervous functioning – consequent on coitus interruptus or masturbation, for example. In the case of anxiety this was betrayed by the fact that the symptoms, such as palpitations, breathlessness and fatigue, were all concomitants of the sexual act. In neurasthenia, as the predominant symptom was lethargy, this pointed to excessive self-abuse. Dysmenorrhoea was also thought to arise from excessive masturbation. References to patients' masturbatory practices and methods of contraception pepper Freud's early works. Given the actual nature of the neurosis, and while hypnosis might be useful, the idea of catharsis under hypnosis would not be expected to be of much use.

In attempting to account for hysteria Freud's first difficulty was the close association between hysteria and hypnosis put forward in Paris, following the work of Briquet, Burq and Charcot, according to which hysterics were particularly susceptible to hypnosis. The *Studies on Hysteria* do not suggest that Freud was a particularly subtle hypnotist. Whether or not this was a fateful quirk of personal style, he found that not every hysteric was hypnotizable – by him. Accordingly the theory that hysteria arose by some sort of auto-hypnosis during states of altered consciousness, as proposed by Breuer, seemed less tenable. In addition it seemed that a number of non-hysterical patients, with obsessive-compulsive disorder for example, *were* hypnotizable. Furthermore he found that even under hypnosis many patients appeared able to defend themselves against remembering buried trauma.

This led to the idea that, far from an inability to remember a buried trauma, the issue was more one of reluctance to remember. From around 1892 Freud began to see hysteria, obsessive-compulsive disorder and paranoia as neuropsychoses. Unlike the actual neuroses, these neuropsychoses involved some buried memory. Catharsis was therefore the appropriate method of treatment. As in the actual neuroses he maintained that the origin of these disorders was sexual. In view of Breuer's remarks regarding the role of sexuality in hysteria, noted above, and the longstanding association with sexuality, this could not have been an unusual proposal for the time. But the precise nature of the sexual precipitation proposed by Freud for hysteria was highly controversial.

Aetiology of hysteria[13-15]

Freud claimed that the psychoneuroses all resulted from inappropriate sexual exposure of some sort during childhood. In his 'The Aetiology of Hysteria', he argued that the exposure was in the form of assaults, and that these assaults were most commonly perpetrated by the father: incest. These were events that involved shame or guilt, and accordingly the victims would not want to remember them. This distaste therefore would give rise to a defence against the memory. In other words the trauma or ideas that gave rise to hysteria did not do so simply because they were received while the subject was in a particular state of consciousness, as Breuer suggested. Rather it was the non-integratable nature of the event that lay behind the condition.

In distinguishing the psychoneuroses from the actual neuroses, a distinction based on the capacity of remembering to cure the psychoneuroses, Freud was left with the need to find an aetiology for hysteria. This necessitated a traumatic aetiology. But unlike Charcot's traumatic neuroses not all Freud's sample of eighteen patients had near-accidents. On delving deeper into their psyche however it seemed to him that all had sexual traumata dating from early childhood. Such an aetiology, in contrast to a more neutral trauma, such as a near-accident, suggested that the principal psychological dynamic leading to hysteria was a repression, owing to distaste rather than dissociation. What was repressed, he claimed, were the details of the incestuous assault.

This was a controversial position to take. No one else, it seems, was prepared to support Freud in this. But whether it was the claim regarding incest or the claim that *all* hysterics had been sexually abused that met with resistance has been the subject of much recent controversy. As mentioned in Chapter 1 the existence of child abuse, including sexual abuse, had been extensively documented by the forensic physician Ambroise Tardieu, in 1860. Freud, it is known, had copies of Tardieu's works. Furthermore it seems probable that while in Paris, with Charcot, he attended autopsies on children who were murdered by their parents or relatives having previously been chronically abused. It was possible therefore that a claim that some cases of hysteria had resulted from sexual abuse would not have caused problems. Freud, however, operating according to the scientific dictates of the day and taking a very medical approach, appears always to have thought that specific clinical syndromes required single specific aetiologies. Therefore, if there was clear evidence that some cases of hysteria arose in a particular way, and if what was involved was going to be a process governed by the iron laws of science, then all must do so.

In the case of hysteria he argued that the specific form of the sexual assault gave rise to the variations in the clinical picture. Thus pain on micturition or hysterical retention of urine arose directly because of an association with forced penetration. Hysterical diarrhoea or painful defecation resulted from anal penetration. Choking and vomiting were linked to oral sex. The hysterical crisis developed because of an awakening of associations recalling infantile scenes to consciousness and resulting in the most painful suffering and violent sensations.

The reproduction of the traumatic scene, Freud argued, should lead to a subsequent correction of the psychical course that events took at the time. Anticipating criticism, he pleaded that his findings did not result from his suggestions to patients because he had never yet succeeded in forcing on a patient by suggestion scenes he was expecting to find. Where he proposed possible sexual traumata that turned out to be incorrect the patient invariably told him so. Furthermore both he and Breuer had found that reawakening the memories of the traumata produced the re-enactment of events that were astonishingly intact, possessed remarkable sensory force and had the affective strength of new experience. This seemed more like a reliving than a remembering. During therapy patients would suddenly often switch from ordinary remembering to what seemed like a re-enacting of past scenes – in extreme cases, such as Steven in the Introduction to this book, down to reproducing physical stigmata. Both Breuer and Freud thought that such a reliving could not have been counterfeited. This finding was also consistent with what other therapists, such as Janet, were finding. It is also consistent with what happens to subjects after traumata today.

Freud argued that such effects could not be produced by suggestion. The findings, he claimed, pointed to the validity of the methods he was using. His method, which he had begun to claim differed from hypnosis, involved analysing the psyche by following threads of associations through the labyrinth of memory, to reveal a story that made sense. If he had simply suggested his own preconception to the patients their story would not make sense. Any alien material inserted by him would show clearly. In contrast, when the final story came out, following his procedures, it transpired that its details explained unequivocally why the patient had the symptoms they did. And if all this did not convince, in the final analysis the seduction theory was supported by a number of confirmed instances of childhood sexual trauma.

An Environmental Neurosis?

In carrying out this work we must of course keep free from the theoretical prejudice that we are dealing with the abnormal brains of *dégénérés* and *déséquilibres*, who are at liberty owing to a stigma to throw overboard the common psychological laws that govern the connection of ideas and in whom one chance idea may be exaggeratedly intense for no motive and another may remain indestructible for no psychological reason. Experience shows that the contrary is true for hysteria. Once we have discovered the concealed motives, which have often remained unconscious, and have taken them into account, nothing that is puzzling or contrary to rule remains in hysterical connections of thought any more than in normal ones. Freud, 'The Psychotherapy of Hysteria'.[16]

The seduction theory gave Freud clear grounds to reject the notion that some sort of degeneracy formed the basis of hysteria. While in one sense the clinical picture of an hysteric might be highly bizarre and on certain issues they might appear to act precipitately or injudiciously, appearances were deceptive. Once one was in possession of all the facts, typically the behaviour of these individuals made eminent sense. In other words the clinical picture told a story. Not being able to decipher the story pointed to the incompetence of the investigator rather than a failure of logic on the part of the story-teller.

While rejecting a model of the neuroses rooted in a degenerate biology, Freud thought that establishing the validity of his position depended on coming up with a *biological* theory that accounted for consciousness. What is mental life? Why are we aware of what we are aware of? We obviously have what is now termed a stream of consciousness, but what exactly is a stream of consciousness? Finding an answer to this offered the promise of indicating why we are aware of some things and not others – why certain things are blocked from consciousness or at least from conscious expression. It was in an effort to answer these questions that he wrote his Project for a Scientific Psychology.

Project for a Scientific Psychology[17–19]

This uncompleted document, written in 1895, was found, after his death, among Freud's correspondence to his then collaborator Wilhelm Fliess. In it he attempted to use all the current developments in neurophysiology and neurology to account for the psyche. It was only when we really understood how the nervous system worked, he believed, that we would understand how repression occurred. The notions he made most use of were the reflex and the then recently introduced notions of the neuron (1891) and the synapse.

Until about 1830 the brain was seen as an amorphous, sago-like mass containing granules of some sort, which some saw as the generators of electrical energy. This image fitted in with prevailing views of the brain, which believed it to be a single equipotential entity – something spiritual which did not have parts. The first suggestion that there might be a detailed structure to the mass came from Ehrenberg in 1833. After Schwann proposed that living tissues were made up of cells in 1839 the idea of nerve cells was extended to the nervous system. The fibres connecting nerve cells were then seen as electrical cables, which were continuous between cells. Messages could therefore simply flow freely from one cell to another. It was also believed that impulses could hop from one cable to another if the two cables ran closely together. Breuer's idea about dissociation depended on this kind of short-circuiting.

Wagner in 1846 was the first to suggest that there might be junctions between nerve cells. What exactly happened when cell processes met was uncertain, as the microscopes of the day where unable to detect such fine detail. From about 1870 there were two theories: one was that they were continuous, which effectively led to the concept that the nervous system was a unitary network; the other was that there were junctions between nerve cells, later to be called synapses by Sherrington in 1897. This latter view opened up the possibility that there might be resistances to the passage of nervous messages, which Freud postulated might be the basis of a cordoning off of some areas of the brain from easy access.

In attempting to account for how the nervous system works Freud supposed that it conserved energy – that is, the energy used must be generated somewhere. It could not be just conjured up out of the blue. The principal generators were internal needs, drives and appetites. These led to a build-up of energy levels in the system, which must be discharged in order to equilibrate the overall charge of the system. Failure to do so would be painful and unpleasant. Discharge, as in eating when hungry or copulating when so inclined, was in contrast pleasurable. However internal needs must be associated with external sources of gratification. It was with the entry of associative material into the system that the model became an 1890s (psychological science) rather than an 1860s (philosophical) one. Impressions from outside could travel along a number of pathways in the system. Why should they go one way rather than another? In particular why should certain associations issue in the symptoms of hysteria?

The answer Freud gave depended on the synapse. This he saw as a barrier to communication between neurones that could be worn down by the flow of nervous impulses through it. The differing strengths of various barriers to a particular impression determined, he argued, the path that would be taken by that stimulus. The strengths of the barriers would depend on the activity in surrounding neurones. In his system these neurones each represented an association, or memory. If the resistance to an impulse was high, it would be channelled off in some other direction, even to the point where its eventual discharge might be highly inappropriate.

The distinctive feature of the project compared to other neurologically based hypotheses of the time was that Freud did not turn to the concept of a degenerate reflex of any sort to extricate himself from difficulties. He attempted instead to provide a model whereby external events might lead logically to internal pathologies. Unfortunately such a project could not be sustained on the basis of the available knowledge of the day. It required, as Freud himself admitted, too much 'constructio ad hoc' and it collapsed unfinished under the weight of speculation.

The other significant feature of the project was the crucial biological reduction Freud effected – the equation of one nerve cell with one memory/emotion. This was a step Janet resisted, arguing that one psychological unit never simply correlates with one biological unit. Until quite recently Freud's position on this, which he never abandoned, would have been the more scientifically orthodox. Indeed in many ways it resembles some of the latterday behaviourist formulations. This sailing close to the headlands of biology gave him an advantage over Janet that has proved fateful for the development of psychological medicine.

3   The Hazards of Interpretation[1-4]

From 1893 to 1896 Freud's activity was extraordinary. During this time he wrote most of the studies on hysteria, articles on the neuropsychoses of defence and the aetiology of hysteria, as well as the Project; he was also seeing patients constantly and breaking new ground repeatedly, as the sheer enthusiasm of his writing suggests. He was at this time, according to Ferenczi, lying down on floors beside patients for hours on end chasing down therapeutic leads.[5]

The abandoning of degeneracy opened the way to the first formal psychodynamic paradigm. While Breuer and Janet were arguing for something very similar Freud was the first to make a clear break with the past and establish that certain traumatic events might have psychological rather than neurological or spiritual consequences. This is brought out most clearly in one of his contributions to the *Studies on Hysteria*, 'The Psychotherapy of Hysteria', which I believe now reads as the most modern of all his writings. In this he described the technique he was then using:

In these circumstances I make use in the first instance of a small technical device. I inform the patient that, a moment later, I shall apply pressure to his forehead, and I assure him that, all the time the pressure lasts, he will see before him a recollection in the form of a picture or will have it in his thoughts in the form of an idea occurring to him; and I pledge him to communicate this picture or idea to me, whatever it may be. He is not to keep it to himself because he may happen to think it is not what is wanted, not the right thing, or because it would be too disagreeable for him to say it. There is to be no criticism of it, no reticence, either for emotional reasons or because it is judged unimportant. Only in this manner can we find what we are in search of but in this manner we shall find it infallibly. Having said this, I press for a few seconds on the forehead of the patient as he lies in front of me; I then leave go and ask quietly, as though there were no question of a disappointment: 'What did you see?' or 'What occurred to you?'

This procedure has taught much and has also invariably achieved its aim.

29

Today I can no longer do without it. I am of course aware that a pressure on the forehead like this could be replaced by any other signal or by some other exercise of physical influence on the patient; but since the patient is lying in front of me, pressure on his forehead, or taking his head between my two hands, seems to be the most convenient way of applying suggestion for the purpose I have in view. It would be possible for me to say by way of explaining the efficacy of this device that it corresponded to a 'momentarily intensified hypnosis'; but the mechanism of hypnosis is so puzzling to me that I would rather not make use of it as an explanation. I am rather of the opinion that the advantage of the procedure lies in the fact that by means of it I dissociate the patient's attention from his conscious searching and reflecting – from everything, in short, on which he can employ his will – in the same sort of way in which this is effected by staring into a crystal ball, and so on. The conclusion which I draw from the fact that what I am looking for always appears under the pressure of my hand is as follows. The pathogenic idea which has ostensibly been forgotten is always lying ready 'close at hand' and can be reached by associations that are easily accessible. It is merely a question of getting some obstacle out of the way. This obstacle seems once again to be the subject's will, and different people can learn with different degrees of ease to free themselves from their intentional thinking and to adopt an attitude of completely objective observations towards the psychical processes taking place in them.

What emerges under the pressure of my hand is not always a 'forgotten' recollection; it is only in the rarest cases that the actual pathogenic recollections lie so easily to hand on the surface. It is much more frequent for an idea to emerge which is an intermediate link in the chain of associations between the idea from which we start and the pathogenic idea which we are in search of; or it may be an idea which forms the starting point of a new series of thoughts and recollections at the end of which the pathogenic idea will be found. It is true that where this happens my pressure has not revealed the pathogenic idea – which would in any case be incomprehensible, torn from its context and without being led up to – but it has pointed the way to it and has shown the direction in which further investigation is to be made. The idea that is first provoked by the pressure may in such cases be a familiar recollection which has never been repressed. If on our way to the pathogenic idea the thread is broken off once more, it only needs a repetition of the procedure, of the pressure, to give us fresh bearings and a fresh starting-point.

On yet other occasions the pressure of the hand provokes a memory which is familiar in itself to the patient, but the appearance of which astonishes him because he has forgotten its relation to the idea from which we started. This relation is then confirmed in the further course of the analysis. All these consequences of the pressure give one a deceptive impression of there being a superior intelligence outside the patient's consciousness which keeps a large amount of psychical material arranged for particular purposes and has fixed a planned order for its return to consciousness. I suspect, however, that this unconscious second intelligence is no more than an appearance.[6]

This instructing patients to tell him what they could see in their mind's eye, irrespective of whether it seemed appropriate or not or whether it was agreeable to do so or not, marks the critical discovery of the psyche. The issues are not simply historical, in that the difficulties his patients found are ones that every reader of this book will find if they try out the procedure on themselves or a friend. What you will see is someone who is obviously seeing more than they can say or are prepared to say (or who is hearing some internal monologue they are not happy to have overheard). It is just these difficulties that psychological medicine appears to have returned to in the course of the past decade.

While Freud's specific position on the aetiology of hysteria was never well received, the general impact of this work was extraordinary. It led to a complete revolution in the meaning of the term neurosis, which after 1895 came quickly to mean a disorder of the psyche, in the presence of a normal nervous system, with the terms neuropsychosis and psychoneurosis being abandoned as unnecessary.

The scale of the revolution can be judged by reference to one of the major textbooks on mental disorders in use at the time, Esquirol's *Mental Maladies*.[7] In this, the first authoritative textbook on mental disorders, published in 1845, Esquirol noted that 'the doctrine of crises is as ancient as observation in medicine – the cure of mental maladies is only deceitful or temporary, when it is not determined by some critical phenomenon – but the crises of insanity [have] been imperfectly understood or neglected'. The reader awaits a discussion of the issues of catharsis or abreaction at this point, of the role of resistance to insight being overcome in a moment of crisis. But instead Esquirol goes on to the cure of insanity following the outbreak of boils or shingles, the contracting of a fever, or after getting pregnant or giving birth. He notes that dentition can cause insanity.

Against this background, which was still the orthodox view in 1890, Freud and Breuer's discussion of the role of abreaction and catharsis in the termination of mental maladies marks a radical change. Equally, however, the term catharsis was being used in a novel way. It previously had been used to refer to the culmination of a tragic sequence of events or the resolution of a *moral* dilemma. Prior to Breuer and Freud it had never been used to indicate how a *psychological* problem might be resolved.

The abandoning of the psychodynamic paradigm

By 1897, just two years after publication of *Studies on Hysteria*, Freud had abandoned the seduction theory, which was the capstone of all his thinking at that point and which apparently also offered the experimental evidence in favour of the validity of his therapeutic methods. Why?

Furthermore, with the abandoning of the seduction theory, he was also to abandon the notion of an environmentally precipitated neurosis and to put in place of previous notions of a degenerate nervous system the idea of a degenerate psyche. Why?

PSYCHOANALYSIS AND THE TRANSFORMATION OF THE PSYCHE[8]

Some imaginations . . . differ in that our will is not employed in forming them . . . They only arise because the spirits agitated in various ways and coming upon the traces of various impressions which have preceded them in the brain, haphazardly take their course through certain of its pores rather than others. Such are the illusions of our dreams and likewise our waking reveries. Descartes, *The Passions of the Soul*: Article 21.

There were a number of problems with the seduction theory. In the first instance the neuroses rarely started in childhood. There was, Freud believed, little or no symptomatology in childhood itself in response to the proposed traumatic assaults. This, he argued, was because children were essentially non-sexual beings, which led to there being minimal immediate effects. The memory of the assault was stored, to be activated later by the sexual awakening of puberty or by further shocks; these latter did not have to be sexual. It was through his collaboration with Fliess, a pioneer in the field of infantile sexuality, that Freud became aware of the untenability of his position on the non-sexual nature of children.

Freud's second proposal had been that traumatic experiences gave rise to all the psychical neuroses – hysteria, obsessive-compulsive disorder and paranoia. But why should one act lead to three different outcomes? The reason Freud had offered was in terms of the stage of childhood development at which the provoking incident occurred. Thus sexual advances up to the age of four gave rise to hysteria, between four and eight to obsessive-compulsive disorder and between eight and twelve to paranoia. As the child aged it was less likely to be assaulted by a sexual encounter and more likely to take some degree of pleasure in it, which then had to be defended against, giving obsessive-compulsive disorder, or even to form an attachment to the perpetrator, leading to paranoia. These distinctions were not easily sustainable.

Thirdly, the theory implied a remarkable amount of child abuse in the community and even in Freud's own family – given what he saw as hysterical tendencies in his brothers and sisters. The question of the actual incidence of child abuse has resurfaced only recently. It now appears to be startlingly common, particularly in the childhood of individuals with nervous disorders.

Fourthly, Freud's success rate using the cathartic approach was not all that the seduction theory would have predicted. There were three problems, it would seem: not enough patients got well; too many left therapy; and of those who got well a number relapsed. This latter point touches on a number of key issues which will be taken up in more detail in Chapters 9 and 10.

Finally Freud began to be uncertain about the distinction between truth and fantasy in the material provided by some patients. This was an inevitable outcome of the technique of asking patients to tell him what they could see in their mind's eye. Simply recalling, for example, a stressful interview should bring home this point. Reseeing it in our mind's eye afterwards, all of us edit it, alter it radically, see ourselves saying what we wish we had said rather than what we did. This gets replayed many times and often leads later to an inability to be certain about what actually did happen.

But Freud was to put another interpretation on the phenomenon. One day one of his patients turned to him and embraced him. He later explained this away by arguing that she had been beginning to remember a former episode in which she had been talking to someone she desired and whom she was hoping at the time would turn to her and sweep her off her feet. The memory of the desire, Freud argued, returned stripped of historical context, which came later, leading to her advances towards him. So also, he argued, was it not possible that other deep wishes might emerge and attach themselves to the most convenient material – parents, especially fathers?

In this manner, Freud discovered fantasy. He later came to see indications of early exposure to sexual material as obscuring rather than illuminating the analytic picture. These indications first misled investigators into the nature and function of sexual fantasy, orienting them instead towards supposed real-life events. They also had made both Freud himself and many others overlook the true origin of the neuroses, which were more apparent, he later came to think, in non-traumatic cases.

Putting all of these elements together, Freud came to the conclusion that hysteria was a defence against an impulse rather than against a memory, and that the accounts of hysterics were fantasies rather than remembrances.

Emma Eckstein[9-10]

In a recent, highly controversial book, Jeffrey Masson has argued that this change in Freud's thinking can be charted through his changing attitudes to the statements of one particular patient of his, Emma Eckstein.

Emma came to Freud in the mid-1890s, shortly after he had become estranged from Breuer. The precise nature of her complaints is uncertain. Masson has argued that he saw Emma's problem as an actual neurosis – probably the result of too much masturbation. Freud's closest collaborator and friend after the split with Breuer was a Berlin otorhinolaryngologist, Wilhelm Fliess. Fliess believed that there was an intimate connection between the genital system and the nose. This led him to treat actual neuroses by applying a recently discovered local anaesthetic, cocaine, to certain key points of the nasal mucosa. Cocaine anaesthesia brought about temporary improvement. The improvements led Fliess to conceive of a more radical therapy involving removal of part of the turbinate bone of the nose. This, he thought, should lead to permanent rather than temporary cures. In March 1895 Freud volunteered Emma for the operation.

Post-operatively Emma began to bleed profusely. A local surgeon was called in and found that Fliess had left a considerable amount of gauze packing in the nose by accident (an accident that would then as now have led to claims for negligence). There followed a few weeks during which Emma bled episodically and, to judge by Freud's distressed letters to Fliess, quite torrentially. However, far from blaming Fliess for the mishap, over the course of a few months Freud worked the material around and came up with the explanation that Emma had been bleeding out of her longing to see and affect Freud himself. The first bleed had occurred with him there – the fact that gauze had just been removed was, he proposed, incidental. When she saw the effect this had on him, Freud argued, she later bled in order to bring him to her and to affect him similarly again. Therefore Emma herself was responsible for the bleeding.

Reading Freud's letters to Fliess at this time is highly embarrassing. It is almost impossible to have sympathy for him, except in so far as he seems to have been at the time very worried, isolated and somewhat naïve. This isolation would certainly have been mitigated by a change of position regarding incest and the sexual assault of children of the kind that he seemed able to manage in the case of Emma – that they, like Emma, were not simply innocent victims but somehow willed their own problems.

Fliess and infantile sexuality[11]

Freud was a later convert to the facts of infantile sexuality, rather than their discoverer. At the time that he was arguing for a seduction theory of hysteria, on the basis of the disruptive psychological effects of sexual assaults on prepubertal, essentially nonsexual children, both Albert Moll and Havelock Ellis were recording childhood manifestations of sexuality and its polymorphous character. Ellis in particular noted both oral and anal stages in sexual development. The facts of sexual perversity had also been pretty well established, in great part as a result of the pioneering work of Krafft-Ebbing and Havelock Ellis.

As regards infantile sexuality it was Fliess, later to be Freud's collaborator and friend after the rift with Breuer, who made the most novel observations. Fliess noted the presence of a sexuality that was not just the passive 'sexual' pleasure of sucking at the breast. Rather he recorded a more active sexual organization that displayed itself in the presence of erections from the first few weeks of life onwards. This sexuality appeared to develop insistently thereafter, in a way that posed constant fresh challenges to children. It was through Fliess that Freud came to realize that the sexuality of children was something quite different and more dynamic than he had hitherto thought.

Along with the notion of infantile sexuality Freud borrowed from Fliess the idea of dynamic development. Fliess had argued for the presence of a sexual dynamic in all children from birth. This dynamic was supposed to result from the operations of both a masculine and a feminine factor, the former having a period of twenty-three days and the latter one of twenty-eight days. All individuals were bisexual, he argued, but one or other of the sexual factors came to predominate, with the other being repressed to form the nucleus of the unconscious. The male factor was thought of as being the inherently active one and corresponds closely to what Freud thought of as libido – or sexual energy.

As Fliess saw it sexuality developed in a manner governed by the harmonics of a periodic system. This led to infants and children being propelled through developmental stages at the insistence of a burgeoning sexuality. In childhood, Fliess argued, the energy of this dynamic is not normally spent on sexual activity but is sublimated and converted by a process of reaction formation into the material from which higher cultural achievements are derived.

Although not endorsing all of these points Freud took on board many of Fliess's insights. In particular he realized that the handling of developing instincts was no less a potential source of later psychosexual disturbances than exposure to an act of seduction. In 1897 he formally abandoned his repressed trauma theory and replaced it with a psychology of repressed impulses. These impulses developed in a manner that was relatively independent of what was happening in the environment. Their development had to be integrated within the rest of the individual's personality, and their handling, he proposed, could have an even more pervasive effect on the psyche than memories.

In taking this step Freud moved from a position which stressed the overriding importance of environmental determinants in psychological problems to one which recognized a primary endogenous input to such problems. It was aberrations in the development of the sexual instincts, he held, that were the necessary and specific causes of the later generation of psychopathology, although environmental stressors or traumata might provide triggering or concurrent causes. This in effect was a turning back to a degeneracy model of the neuroses, in which the individual and their personal development was to be held responsible for their own disorder. Psychoanalysis became the study of the psychological management of instincts and of how this management governed the development of the personality. For example Freud developed a psychological explanation for the marked latency period that occurs between the ages of five and puberty, lying between periods of relative sexual turmoil, which seemed difficult to explain in purely biological terms. This lay in the genesis and resolution of the Oedipus complex. Given the unattainability of the desired sexual object (the mother) and the likelihood of castration in the event of trying, the natural resolution of an Oedipus complex would be for the child to identify with his father and to sublimate his libidinous impulses into other activities. Furthermore a reaction formation against things sexual would also be promoted. Where once there was interest and excitement there would develop an apparent lack of interest and disgust. These banks erected around the sexual tide would contain the problem until such time as the river rose much higher and burst its banks – as at puberty.

After 1897 the unconscious for Freud became the repository of innate sexual impulses which have been repressed because of their incompatibility with a normal adult psychosexual organization. Such an unconscious, it should be noted, is something quite different to the forgotten or partitioned off memories which he had formerly thought afflicted hysterical subjects. It is also something radically different to the depths of the soul model of the subconscious put forward by Janet. It was however quite congruent with the reflex models of nervous system functioning outlined in Chapter 1.

How these impulses have been managed determined, he argued, the future psychological normality of the individual. Several difficulties could arise. One was that a child might fixate at an inappropriate developmental stage. This Freud conceived as occurring in much the same way as cells during embryological development may fixate at the wrong place. Typically during intra-uterine life cells have to migrate over considerable distances to take up their final resting places. The introduction of a stressor or a toxin during this process, or a fault in the genetic programme, can lead to an incomplete migration, with the result that things grow in the wrong place or not at all. It was by this mechanism, he argued, that sexual perversions arise. In infancy everything can give sexual pleasure – the mouth, the anus, the entire skin. This undifferentiated sexuality is progressively given up as the child matures toward a genital sexuality. Under outside pressure however or the influence of hereditary factors combined with such pressures, the child could fixate at an earlier and, from the adult point of view, a perverse sexual stage. Alternatively sexual maturity might be attained but with one or two weak links left in the developmental chain. Under pressure, in such a case, the individual would be liable to regress. The regressive pull or intimations from an inadequately handled previous stage gave rise, he argued, to neurotic anxiety.

Before discussing the further development of psychoanalysis it should be noted that there *are* two sexes in each of us and that our sexualities do interact with stress responses. In the late 1890s adrenalin and cortisol were discovered and subsequently shown to be central to the stress response. In the late 1920s the urine of women was found to contain two substances, which varied in concentration periodically in line with menstruation – oestrogen and progesterone – and the urine of men to contain a male principle, testosterone. While Freud and Fliess might have been stumped by the existence of three sex hormones they would have felt vindicated by findings that both oestrogen and testosterone are present in substantial amounts in both men and women. These various hormones act to maintain the integrity and vitality of gonadal functions. They also act in concert with what is termed the autonomic nervous system – an unconscious, automatic system which meets many of the requirements of Freud's Id and is subject to the influence of an endogenous rhythmicity, which can legitimately be seen as a repository of unconscious knowledge. (See Chapters 7 and 8.)

Thus there is nothing inherently unscientific about concerning oneself with issues of an Id comprising instinctual forces, subject to periodic fluctuations. It must also be remembered that in postulating such an Id Freud did seem to offer an explanation for a number of puzzling psychological events – for example the *facts* of infantile sexuality, such as the obvious and frequent erections boys have around the ages of two and four. His theory plausibly linked these empirical events and the phenomenon of childhood amnesia – the fact that children seem unable to remember much if anything of what happened to them before the age of three or four. Indeed in 1900, when Freud was grappling with these issues, he was working at the forefront of the biological sciences of his day, just as he had been when constructing the Project for a Scientific Psychology. It was just this which so marked him out from Janet's and other psychodynamic approaches.

THE RECOURSE TO SYMBOLISM

Freud's volte-face from buried memories to unconscious impulses had profound effects when it came to interpreting the imagery we all see in our mind's eye. This becomes clear when we consider his psychoanalytic theories on the interpretation of dream imagery: whereas previously his concern had been to establish what exactly was in the mind's eye, the focus now switched to one of demonstrating how the imagery of dreams fulfilled unconscious wishes.

It is not immediately clear that dream imagery does reflect unconscious wishes or, if it does, just what those wishes are. Freud argued that dreams could fulfil multiple wishes from many stages of development. In response to this his critics questioned how the primary meaning was to be established. He replied that the true significance of dreams lay in the extent to which they re-enacted infantile wishes. The fulfilment of other wishes derived resonance from the primary wish fulfilment, or acted as a screen to distract from the primary activity of the dream. In order to maintain his point he was happy to interpret dreams forwards, backwards or sideways, or to let every element of a dream stand for its opposite, if such an interpretation would yield the expected result.

Even so some dreams did not yield up their sexual content, and it was in attempting to account for these cases that Freud took his most radical step. This was to argue that the irreducible material must stand in a *symbolic* relation with libidinal forces. This recourse to symbolism was to have the most profound effects on our understanding of the psyche.

It was, I believe, the step that more than any other has led to a profound alienation for many from their own psyches.

Summoning up the genie of symbolism from the interpretive bottle inevitably short-circuits the process of getting all the details of dream or any other imagery. Why spend hours or weeks trawling through a mass of detail when, with potential symbols lying all around, one can cut to the heart of what one knows, *a priori*, is the matter? Where abreaction had aimed at getting at the images that are lurking in the shadows and the full details of those images, the interpretation of symbols relegated concrete detail to a secondary place. If the reader dreams about pigs that fly, does it matter if the pigs have wings or if they, as it were, pass through the air rather than fly? A hundred books on dream symbolism pay no heed to distinctions such as these.

The central question here is, whence do symbols derive their meaning? If they are determined by the unconscious and all reduce pretty much to the same thing, an expression of erotic conflict, then details do not matter. If however symbols derive their reference from our social interactions with others, as I will argue in Chapter 7, then the details matter critically.

A number of cases may help clarify what is at stake. In a recent contribution to a symposium on psychodynamics Howard Shevrin described the case of A.M., who had had a blood phobia from the age of nine.[12] His phobia had displayed itself dramatically shortly before he sought help, when he went to see the film *One Flew Over the Cuckoo's Nest*. During the scene where one of the characters in the drama, Billy, a young, stammering weakling, loses out in a confrontation with the boss nurse on the ward and slits his wrists the sight of blood caused A.M. to flee the cinema.

Shevrin and colleagues decided that this episode and other details of A.M.'s history could best be interpreted in terms of difficulties with sadomasochistic impulses towards women, derived from a sadistic mother for whom he nevertheless yearned. The fear of blood, they argued, arose out of a conflict over sadistic wishes towards women and the need to defend against such wishes. It symbolized this conflict in a manner that led to the wished-for bloody attack being externalized, which allowed the patient to flee from a representation of his impulses and transformed him into a weakling. The scene in the film produced the behaviour it did by bringing his primal conflicts close to the surface.

This raises the central issue. Do the contents of our consciousness, the images in our mind's eye, have this particular kind of symbolic reference, whose meaning is ultimately to be derived from certain predetermined patterns? Psychoanalysts and the majority of practising psycho-dynamic therapists appear to believe they do. But this leads them often to ignore the full contents of what may be in my or your mind's eye, especially if they catch sight of some element of our imagery that might stand in an appropriate symbolic relation with the kind of interpretation they are programmed to make – even before they meet us.

The paradox that develops, at this point, is that, while what is in our mind's eye may never be what it seems to be, the process of interpretation is not for analysts today the hazardous enterprise it was for Freud in 1893–6. What for some of us is a marvellous diversity of social meanings and nuances, full of endless interpretive possibilities, reduces to a particular common denominator – for example, the Taj Mahal with its twin turrets and the strip of water in its forecourt becomes a representation of female sexuality.[13] This interpretation is confidently offered by Western analysts who may otherwise know nothing of Indian culture and social conventions.

The extension of analytic interpretations to art was inevitable, as taken to its logical conclusion there would seem no reasonable way to claim that neurotic imagery has a particular symbolic reference while denying the same underlying meaning to the imagery and symbolism of art. This extension of his theories was not one that Freud baulked at, and indeed much of the cultural force of psychoanalysis derived from making just such an extension. But taking the hazard out of interpretation in this way is in itself hazardous. For example Harold Klawans recently described the case of a girl who played the oboe, who found one day that she could no longer do so, although she could still sight-read music and could appreciate the playing of oboes and other musical instruments by others.[14] This perplexing complaint was deemed neurotic and led to her referral to an analyst, who discovered that at the time her difficulties started she was also having problems with her sexual relations. As an oboe can be seen as a rather obvious sexual *symbol*, this led to an interpretation of her difficulties in terms of a neurotic displacement of sexual conflicts on to an inappropriate area of her life. It also led to a very lengthy analysis – which did not restore her ability to play the oboe. This was not surprising as a later brain scan showed that her inability to play the oboe stemmed from a small and specific stroke affecting an area of her brain responsible for the execution of musical acts.

What this case demonstrates, I believe, is just how hazardous a recourse to interpretation in terms of symbolism can be. This is rarely conceded by analysts. But then again there is no hazard if one believes that the domain of reference of all symbols has been predetermined.

Little Red Riding Hood[15]

The issues can be brought home, and a glimpse of an alternative approach offered, if we consider the story of Little Red Riding Hood. Following Freud's line of interpreting myths a number of prominent psychoanalysts have offered analyses of the various fairy tales. Chief among these have been Bruno Bettelheim and Erich Fromm. Their analysis of Little Red Riding Hood has become in recent years, through the fiction of Angela Carter and Neil Jordan's film *The Company of Wolves*, one of the best-known and accepted of such interpretations.

Briefly, the red riding hood indicates a young girl on the verge of puberty; the sealed bottle she carries in her basket symbolizes her virginity; her mother's admonition not to stray from the path is an injunction against sexual intercourse; her visiting her grandmother is an Oedipal abolition of her mother. The wolf represents her Id and her father. The saving huntsman is her rational Ego and also, again, her father.

The analysts' contention is that interpreting this fairy story in these terms reveals the correct and timeless significance of the story. Their interpretations, like Shevrin's above, have some plausibility. The problem is that these interpretations cannot be correct. They are based on a fundamental inaccuracy, which is that the text used for these interpretations comes from the Grimm Brothers' version, which is a corruption of the version that came down through the oral traditions of French peasants. These latter are highly concordant and yield an 'original' version, assembled by Robert Darnton, as follows:

Once a little girl was told by her mother to bring some bread and milk to her grandmother. As the girl was walking through the forest, a wolf came up to her and asked where she was going.
'To Grandmother's house,' she replied.
'Which path are you taking, the path of the pins or the path of the needles?'
'The path of the needles.'
So the wolf took the path of the pins and arrived first at the house. He killed Grandmother, poured her blood into a bottle and sliced her flesh on to a platter. Then he got into her nightclothes and waited in bed.
'Knock, knock.'
'Come in, my dear.'
'Hello, Grandmother. I've brought you some bread and milk.'
'Have something yourself, my dear. There is meat and wine in the pantry.'

So the little girl ate what was offered. As she did, a little cat said, 'Slut to eat the flesh and drink the blood of your grandmother!'

Then the wolf said, 'Undress and get into bed with me.'

'Where shall I put my apron?'

'Throw it on the fire; you won't need it any more.'

For each garment – bodice, skirt, petticoat and stockings – the girl asked the same question; and each time the wolf answered, 'Throw it on the fire; you won't need it any more.'

When the girl got into bed, she said, 'Oh, Grandmother! How hairy you are!'

'It's to keep me warmer, my dear.'

'Oh, Grandmother! What big shoulders you have!'

'It's for better carrying firewood, my dear.'

'Oh, Grandmother! What long nails you have!'

'It's for scratching myself better, my dear!'

'Oh, Grandmother! What big teeth you have!'

'It's for eating you better, my dear.'

And he ate her.

The issue of establishing why this is the original version is a matter for historians and is beyond us here. The point that concerns us is that recent historical scholarship enables us to arrive at what is probably a good approximation to an original version. The significance of undertaking a proper historical investigation to establish what the original version probably was, as opposed to resorting to an interpretation of selected symbols and disregarding the difficulties in deciding just what the original version was, becomes clear in the case of Little Red Riding Hood, in that there are no red hoods, sealed bottles, admonitions or saving hunters in the original story. Interpretation of elements of a story in terms of its symbolic qualities may be justified (in my opinion quite infrequently), but if this is to be undertaken it would seem necessary to establish beforehand the correct version of the story to be interpreted.

Symbolism and hysteria

It was just this difficulty in establishing what the correct version of the original story was in the case of hysteria that the analytic recourse to symbolism sought to avoid. Where once Freud had interpreted physical symptoms as standing in a direct relation to traumatic assault, the abandoning of the seduction theory made this no longer an option. Instead symptoms came generally to be seen as standing in some symbolic relation to Oedipal conflicts. In contrast Janet and Breuer's dissociative hypothesis accounted for such symptoms in terms of either a removal of consciousness from, or a hyperawareness of, physical functions, as for example when soldiers in the heat of battle are unaware of wounds they have sustained – a matter of angling spotlights and drawing curtains on the stage of consciousness.

We have seen that Freud moved to a position of recognizing that the imagery of his analysands was a mixture of truth and fantasy and that these could not be distinguished. A moment's imagining should persuade the reader that reality-based and fantasy-based imagery is commonly closely mixed in all our minds. But in the particular case of incest the source of the interpretive problems is unlikely to lie in such a mingling. While a memory may blur with time, an outright fabrication of sexual assault during childhood is unlikely to be fantasized. The fantasies analysts appeal to in such cases are not 'seen' by the individual. They are rather inferred by the analyst from the ordinary imagery of the patient by a process of symbolic reference – the validity of which is determined by the analyst alone. As henceforth nothing was to be as it seemed, even clear statements of abuse based on the vivid remembering of actual seductions could be dismissed. There was therefore a sea change as regard seduction which reinforced the case *against* abused children. The question arises, whose truth and whose fantasies were being indistinguishably mixed?

The alternative interpretive approach, which will be developed further in Chapters 5, 7 and 9, is that what is in our mind's eye has no systematic ulterior symbolic reference. Things are what they seem to be, but for some reason we are seeing an incomplete picture. In some cases the spotlight of consciousness illuminates only a limited segment of the stage. The issue is, why do we have an incomplete set of images? Would abreaction reveal more? Would angling the spotlight into the wings of the stage reveal more?

Both the illuminated area of the stage and the shadowy wings are within consciousness. Actors lurking in the wings are not subterranean creatures whose existence can only be inferred symbolically. They are as much on the stage as those in the limelight and may even be heard moving about behind the curtain or be seen peeping out by some of the audience. When they enter on to the stage their manifest appearance can be taken at face value, although the interpretation of their role and significance may be hazardous as drama is an enterprise, redolent with latent social meanings, none of which has unequivocal priority.

In contrast the psychoanalytic approach to these issues has involved the claim that the true significance of what is happening on the stage lies in the manipulation of ciphers by some mechanism lying beneath the floorboards. And it takes several years of training to learn how to detect what is under the floorboards!

Psyches and minds[16]

In constructing a psychology of repressed instincts which sought conscious expression in symbols Freud moved beyond a psychopathological
theory about the origins of mental illness to a theory about personality.
He became more interested in the cultural significance of what he was
doing than in the mechanics of getting people well – more concerned
with the science of psychoanalysis than with dynamic therapy. He
appears to have had less and less interest in damaged people (patients)
and to have been less concerned with their lack of response to treatment.

One consequence of developing in this way was that Freud's previous
focus on getting an accurate description of the scene in the mind's eye
of a patient gave way to a more general analysis of all aspects of their
behaviour with a view to demonstrating what he, Freud, knew *a priori*
to be the case. Interpretation was no longer permitted to be a hazardous
enterprise. However unlike the analysis of imagery a full analysis of
behaviour inevitably involves accounting for cultural, social and religious
inputs to behaviour.

Psychoanalysis therefore had to aim at being comprehensive, a theory
of *everything*, rather than just a science of *psycho*-dynamics. It became
a theory of the mind rather than a theory of the psyche. This development has led, I would suggest, to a general loss of feel for what a
specifically psychological theory should look like. This point will be
developed further in the following chapter, in which I will attempt to
show just how inappropriate the extension of psychoanalysis into other
spheres of life has been, and also how contrary to our intuitive under-
standings of the psyche.

4   The Eclipse of the Psyche

All the struggles that people customarily imagine between the lower part of the soul, which is called sensitive, and the higher, which is rational, consist only in the opposition between the movements which the body by its spirits and the soul by its will tend to excite simultaneously . . . But there is only a single soul in us and this soul has within itself no diversity of parts. The error which has been committed in having it play different characters usually opposed to one another arises only from the fact that its functions have not rightly been distinguished from those of the body to which alone must be attributed everything to be found in us that is opposed to our reason. Descartes, *Passions of the Soul*: Article 47.

Freud's recourse to symbolism left him open to the criticism of arbitrariness. The only way to avoid such a criticism is to establish what the ultimate meaning of all symbols is – if there is one. This however involves creating a theory of the human mind rather than just a theory that accounts for the dynamics of consciousness. Freud embraced this challenge. As a consequence when one thinks of psychoanalysis today one thinks as much of a theory that attempts to account for culture as one that accounts for neuroses: a theory that offers answers on the nature of religion, the origins of creativity, the true meanings of both works of art and advertisements and a theory that has polarized the scientific community as no other.

This extension into the humanities is perhaps what at one and the same time drove a wedge between the 'science' of psychoanalysis and the remainder of the natural sciences, and equally imposed barriers between psychoanalysis and the interpretive sciences. The reason for this was that Freud, while aiming to account for culture, remained very much a biological psychologist. While the Project for a Scientific Psychology was not a degenerate psychology it was as biologically reductionist as it was possible to get. Far from moving away from such an orientation, in developing a psychology of instincts Freud remained

45

firmly in the biological camp, from which he drew support from the emerging theory of evolution.

Darwin[1-2]

Darwin did not simply develop a theory of evolution. In elaborating evolutionary theory he provided a new paradigm for biology, one that established it as an autonomous science able to generate its own scientific agenda. Before Darwin anatomy and physiology had been the only respectable biological subjects, as only they could be seen as investigating the organic components of a machine or the organic mechanisms by which the machine worked. It had not been respectable to touch on the issues of vitality or purposiveness: with the development of an evolutionary biology it became possible to study behaviour, especially instinctive behaviour and its vicissitudes.

In the Project for a Scientific Psychology, as a hardnosed, mechanically oriented scientist, Freud had attempted to construct an essentially physical/mechanical model of the mind but had run into insoluble problems. An evolutionary approach allowed him to ask the question, *why* did this behaviour appear? rather than just, of what mechanical operation does it consist? This approach bypassed the difficulties in a mechanical approach while remaining respectably scientific. It also specifically supported a consideration of the question of instincts and in particular the sexual instinct.

In evolutionary terms there are two particularly important instincts – the will to survive and the urge to reproduce. Of these the reproductive instinct is arguably the more important. While Darwinism is often portrayed as a doctrine of the survival of the fittest this is often misleadingly interpreted in terms of the acquisition of brute strength conferring an evolutionary advantage. In contrast Darwin himself pointed to the evolution of features such as the tail-feathers of the peacock, which far from promoting actual survival were much more likely to hamper it. However the function of a peacock's tail-feathers, he argued, was not to assist in any escape from predators but rather to attract the female. Survival of the fittest in evolutionary terms must mean the passing on of what we would now call genes and the survival of genotypes rather than the survival of any one individual: it will come down to sexual selection.

Under this selection pressure, Darwin argued, many 'mental' attributes could be expected to evolve – such as courage, perseverance, intelligence, cunning, as well as an appreciation of beauty (females appreciating a beautiful tail-feather display). Arguably it was this role for sex in evolution that led Freud to accord sexual libido a place of paramount importance in his theories, much to the mystification of others such as Jung and Adler who argued that sex could not be the ultimate determinant of human behaviour.

Freud was later called a Darwin of the mind by his biographer Ernest Jones. This was not just metaphorical. Freud saw the evolution of mental life as involving a struggle between instincts, affects and ideas for survival within the psyche. He even argued that the interplay of intellectual debate concealed a struggle between instinctual forces. He liked also to compare his achievement with that of Darwin, who had dethroned man from his exalted position within the animal kingdom, while he, Freud, in turn had dethroned the ego from mastery in its own house.

Haeckel and the biogenetic law[3]

Darwin published his *Origin of Species* in 1859, but it was the later adoption of 'Darwinism' by others rather than any wide reading of his book that led to the spread of his ideas. Indeed the arguments of others were often heeded more than those of Darwin himself. Chief among these others was Ernst Haeckel.

Haeckel's *General Morphology of Organisms* appeared in 1866 and was shortly after labelled by Huxley, one of the most ardent proponents of evolution, one of the greatest scientific works ever written. In Germany, and in Europe generally, Haeckel's reputation far outstripped that of Darwin. Writing the definitive history of biological thought in 1929 Nordenskiold commented that not only had Haeckel influenced more scientists than Darwin, but that 'there are not many personalities who have so powerfully influenced the development of human culture – and that too in many different spheres – than Haeckel'.

However while popularizing evolution Haeckel was actually advocating something quite different to Darwin. The essence of his belief was caught in the phrase '*ontogeny recapitulates phylogeny*'. This became known as the biogenetic law. It states that the development of individuals (ontogeny) proceeds by paths already mapped out by earlier members of the species, or even by earlier species in the evolutionary chain (phylogeny). Thus, individual development *remembers* ancestral development.

Haeckel argued that the evidence for this view lay firstly in the similarities between other species and human embryos at different developmental stages, and secondly in the supposed similarities between children and primitives. For example human fetuses have gill slits at one point during intra-uterine development; Haeckel asked why. According to biogenesis this was because they were passing through (recapitulating) earlier evolutionary stages as they developed. As one of these stages in human development was aquatic, so it could be expected that at some stage the human embryo should show some remembrance of this. Other analogies between embryonic development and evolution were proposed, including an analogy between the just fertilized ovum and the earliest single-celled organisms.

Far from being a fanciful idea the biogenetic law was the height of scientific orthodoxy in embryology and palaeontology during the latter half of the nineteenth century. It appeared, Ariadne-like, to offer a thread for a latterday scientific Theseus successfully to find a way through the labyrinth of prehistory. The hope was that by studying embryological stages and the developmental stages of children more of the secrets of the past would be revealed than through the unearthing of all the buried monuments of antiquity or fossils. These secrets might include insights on the animal ancestry of man, as well as the origin of his mental, social and ethical faculties.

The biogenetic law was also consonant with the evolutionary ideas of Jean Baptiste de Lamarck, who before Darwin had proposed a theory of evolution – but of a very different kind to Darwin's. Where Darwin had argued that the struggle for survival favours those who can adapt best to their environment and that thereby the appropriate adaptive mechanisms are passed on, Lamarck argued that organisms can acquire characteristics they need and that these can be passed on to their off-spring. How else could the giraffe's long neck arise other than by repeated stretching to eat leaves higher up? For Lamarck evolution was a process driven by the internal needs of the organism. Without this he felt evolution would be unintelligible. Darwin did not entirely reject this, although modern evolutionary theory does.

Haeckel and the Lamarckians argued that adaptations acquired during life were passed on by terminal addition – the latest adaptive gain was added on to the end of the developmental sequence. However this was liable to lead to developmental sequences that were inordinately long. It was therefore necessary that there should be some mechanism for condensing the sequence to a manageable length. Memory seemed to offer a suitable model for the kind of process that might be involved. Like memories, to-be-inherited characteristics were acquired in proportion to the intensity and duration of the originating stimulus. Like memories, less relevant details could be forgotten so that the overall outline of what needed to be remembered could stay roughly the same length. Like memories, what was once a conscious acquisition could become automatic and unconscious with repetition. In particular, it was argued, instincts are the unconscious remembrance of things once learned so strongly and impressed so indelibly into memory that the germ cells themselves were affected. They contain therefore the organism's memory of past history in unconscious organic form.

PSYCHOANALYSIS AND THE BIOGENETIC LAW[4-5]

It is at this point that biogenetic theory and the interests of Freudian psychology coincide. The general theory of evolution supported Freud's exclusive focus on sex. But the biogenetic law helped to provide a rationale for a number of the problems thrown up by this exclusive focus. I will deal with two of these, the question of repression and the development of the Oedipus complex.

In Chapter 2 we noted that Freud parted company with Janet and Breuer on the question of dissociation. He argued instead that repression was the mechanism responsible for the production of the signs and symptoms of hysteria. While distasteful traumatic events were the supposed aetiological factor this was quite plausible. But why repress pleasurable fantasies? On the other hand, what did human embryos do to their gill slits if not *repress* them? It was this latter meaning of the term that psychoanalysis adopted – confusingly so, for the rest of us. If repression operates in this way we obviously cannot know what we have repressed. We must depend on archaeologists of the mind digging down through earlier developmental layers to tell us. It was just such a shift in meaning that put the emerging science of psychodynamics beyond the reach of the average individual.

As regards the Oedipus complex, while it might plausibly be involved in the psychological make-up of some individuals, could it really be involved in all cases? Freud took up the question of the origins of the Oedipus complex in a series of publications from *Totem and Taboo* in 1913 to *Civilization and its Discontents* in 1930. In these he moved beyond a consideration of the dynamics within the individual psyche to a consideration of the problem on the level of the human species. Applying the biogenetic law to psychological development opened up the prospect that the developmental stages and conflicts that any one child passes through are predetermined by the prior experiences of the species. On this basis he argued that the Oedipus complex, of desiring one's mother and fearing one's father, stemmed from historical events.

In the primal human horde the older males would monopolize the females and restrict the access of younger males to them. This inevitably

would lead to revolt and parricide. Far from solving the problem parra-
cide would lead to conflict among the conspirators and fratricidal conflict, the outcome of which would be ambivalence about the original
murder. Therefore to solve the problem a compromise must have been
reached at some point whereby younger males emigrated to establish
their own hordes. This led to the creation of the incest taboo. Furthermore, as a consequence of remorse, the slain father would have been
installed as a totem godhead and lawgiver. Transgression against his
laws would give rise to guilt. This scenario gave rise to something
strongly resembling an Oedipus complex.

By virtue of the actual occurrence of such events on multiple occasions,
Freud argued, the Oedipus complex had been inherited as a species
memory. He also proposed that the development of totemism and the
incest taboo were the point at which the apes became human. They were
the first distinctively cultural acts set up to control animal impulses.

This line of thinking was developed further in *Civilization and its
Discontents*. Haeckel had proposed that sex was initially a function of
the entire body of single- or multi-celled organisms and that only later
did a specific genital organization develop. One of the later acquisitions
was the importance of smell in sexual attraction. This operated through
the release of chemoattractants in the environment.

Building on this Freud argued that the evolution to an upright posture
in man had inevitable mental consequences. In the first place vision
rather than smell would become the sensory modality of principal
importance for reproduction. But as vision became important so also
would it become apparent that the sexual organs were now exposed and
visible by virtue of the alteration in posture. This would lead to shame
and embarrassment. As smell became less important its associations
would undergo an organic repression (like gill slits) and smells that
formerly were pleasurable would now arouse disgust. These processes
of sexual development and reaction formation, Freud argued, could be
noted among both primitive people and developing children.

Fanciful though such arguments may now seem the incorporation of
such thinking into psychoanalysis perhaps did more than anything else
to make it the social force it later became. In the first place many thought
that it strengthened the clinical base of the theory. Now that instincts
were to be seen as ancestral memories, and the sexual instinct in particular as the engine of evolution, the developmental task of negotiating a
path, between the demands of instinct and the restrictions of modern
society, toward maturity could be seen as a truly dramatic one, prone
to aberrations.

In developing in this manner psychoanalysis acquired a cultural resonance that other theories of psychopathology lacked. Freud's formulations appeared rooted in the acceptable biological ideas of their day while accounting for many of the cultural myths of Judaeo-Christian civilization.

An important implication of these formulations was that civilization itself was a terminal addition to human evolution. Freud argued that, as we have become civilized, an increasingly large set of basic instincts have had to be repressed. Increasingly, therefore, there is the likelihood of inadequate repression or inappropriate fixation leading to the probable development of an increased incidence of neuroses and perversions in civilized man. Civilization therefore could be expected to lead to degeneration. This was a message in tune with the temper of the times.

The legacy of that message is still with us. It is common among psychologists to decry the medical claim that there is a genetic (degenerate) basis to the neurosis. But until quite recently the taking of childhood histories, even by dynamically oriented therapists, has in effect been an enquiry about the unfolding of psycho-genetic instructions in the life of this particular child rather than an investigation of potential environmental determinants of a neurosis.

Project for a Scientific Psychology[6]

Today Freud is liable to be characterized by his opponents as being impossibly vague, almost mystical, and certainly not scientific. Much of the above may seem to reinforce such claims. However we should remember that Freud was very concerned with the biological developments of his day. Sulloway has argued that much of his work can be properly understood only if its hidden biological assumptions are recognized. For a biologically trained and biologically oriented scientist around 1900 it would have been impossible to ignore the facts of evolution and the biogenetic law which appeared to account for it. The alternative would be to have one's scientific course run perilously close to philosophy and metaphysics.

In contrast to their psychological contemporaries operating within philosophy departments psychoanalysts at the start of this century could be distinguished by their willingness to grapple with the real phenomena of hunger, lust and fear and our animal inheritance. While anxious to maintain that there were distinctions between psychology and biology, that the two were independent sciences, Freud would never have been happy to develop a psychology that was lacking in biological relevance.

In modern parlance, he saw himself as erecting a theory of behaviour that had a fundamental ecological validity.

Nor was Freud arbitrary in his arguments, or anything short of logical. While his initial observations on hysterics were the primary empirical data he sought to explain, his subsequent theoretical developments arose out of attempts to pursue rigorously the logic of his early formulations and to deal systematically with their apparent flaws. Arguably the problem was that he was too logical and too systematic and that the methodical unfolding of his analytic presuppositions took precedence over any attempts to expand his clinical base with reliable observations. He failed to distinguish between science and logic. In doing this however he was being a scientist *par excellence*, as this was commonly then, and still is often now, understood. I have argued elsewhere that for Galileo, Newton and Descartes science involved the working out of the logical implications of an initial set of conjectures. Where a conflict arose between the consequences of a conjecture and observable data it was the data rather than the conjecture that was commonly sacrificed. This was exactly what analysts began to do (and all too often still do) in therapy. Far from allowing his patients to refute his proposals Freud used the material they offered him in one way or the other to support his argument. Free association became a process of waiting for the patient to 'slip' in the way that the theory dictated – all the rest of the details offered being ignored. Indeed as a number of his case histories demonstrate Freud was frequently unwilling to wait for the appropriate slip but dictated to his patients what was happening to them, whether or not the evidence supported him and whether or not they agreed – as the case of Dora clearly shows.[7]

There have until recently been two dominant philosophies of science. According to one science proceeds by setting up hypotheses and deducing consequences. This Freud did thoroughly. The apparent disfavour his deductions caused were, for him, a good indication of the scientific validity of his procedure rather than the reverse. After all had not all the great scientists – Copernicus, Darwin – incurred disfavour? According to the other, scientists make inductions strictly from the observable facts. But this too has its pitfalls. The biogenetic law was supremely scientific by this criterion: unlike most scientific laws it arose solely as an induction from empirical data. Although many exceptions to it were detailed, even by the Haeckelians and Lamarckians who supported biogenetic law, accessory arguments were developed to account for the exceptions. Furthermore at no point did the biogenetic law succumb to empirical disproof. It was, rather, bypassed by the rediscovery of Mendel's work, which implied a radically different mechanism for heredity.

It was not until the 1920s that this new proposition became clear in biology, and even then biologists were slow to give up a biogenetic view entirely. In great part this must be because of the intuitive plausibility of the idea. As Lamarck said it is difficult to see evolution making any sense without such a mechanism – a remark echoed by Freud toward the end of his life when, in 1937, in the course of writing *Moses and Monotheism*, which depended heavily on a recapitulatory mechanism, he was informed by Ernest Jones that such thinking had gone out of fashion in biology. Freud wrote in the final text that he realized that one difficulty in the way of accepting his proposal lay in its running counter to contemporary biological wisdom, which rejects the idea of acquired qualities being inherited. He decided however that he would stick to his guns, as he could not picture biological development proceeding without taking this factor into account.

INCEST REVISITED[8]

I have argued that instinct, inhibition and repression are biological terms which acquired a larger cultural resonance once dropped into the sounding box of psychoanalysis. Freud's efforts to incorporate these terms were often inspired. But working at the forefront of the biological sciences of his day he was liable to be mistaken. The biogenetic law provides an example of this, on a grand scale. However the issues involved were not just a matter of theory. The theory was significantly to influence the interpretations put on accounts of trauma in childhood and war and in particular on accounts of incest. It is in the handling of incest that some of the damaging practical consequences of psychoanalysis are revealed.

As we have seen, according to psychoanalysis incest is a primal fantasy and the incest taboo the origin of culture. Incest is supposedly the hallmark of our animal nature, something we have repressed. On this repression is built the human personality. But does incest indicate animality? And what are the psychological consequences of infringing the taboo? The latter was the question that faced Freud between 1893 and 1896. With the development of psychoanalysis he offered a theory about the origins and importance of the incest taboo but, perhaps amazingly, seemingly had no view any more as to what the consequences of infringement of this taboo might be.

Early anthropological writings on incest had been dominated by the notion of a previous stage of human history characterized by unbridled sexual behaviour. This may in part have made for a general acceptance of psychoanalysis. The idea of such a prehuman stage was first challenged by Westermack in 1894. Convinced that the basis of human behaviour must be consistent with the laws of evolution he argued that, if we do not resort to consanguineous sex, there must be some biological reason why not. In other words the propensity to mate outside one's blood relations must be a proclivity rather than a defence. This propensity would then be elaborated in custom and laws. In support of his findings he noted the relative absence of erotic feelings between siblings raised together.

Freud and others counter-attacked. If there was a proclivity to breed out, why erect laws to ensure that we avoid incest? Furthermore the lack of erotic impulses for family members was a surface phenomenon. Analysis revealed that the depths were an entirely different matter.

In reply to this Westermack pointed out that laws do not forbid what men wish. Is there then a natural inclination to murder? He also stuck to his guns on the absence of erotic feelings between siblings and turned to animal data for support. His own observations and subsequent studies by others have demonstrated quite conclusively that animals also have a propensity to outbreed. Incest does not normally happen in the animal kingdom. In the wild animals avoid incest, even when the consequences are loss of social status.

There have been a number of studies which have attempted to test the Westermack hypothesis in humans. Arens reports on one carried out on Israeli kibbutzim. The results indicated that where children are brought up together and no restrictions are put on childhood sexual experimentation and curiosity, and even where the wish of the parents is that the children marry within the community, there are rarely if ever any such marriages. Children brought up together seem not to find each other sexually attractive. Similar studies in China and Lebanon have led to essentially the same conclusions. Furthermore marriages contracted between individuals brought up in the same household, even where not related to each other, have a lower fertility rate and higher rates of dissolution.

Thus close contact during childhood appears to lessen sexual attraction. Not only does this apply between siblings but it also appears to hold between mother and siblings, which is particularly inconvenient for the Oedipal hypothesis. It would seem that there is a biologically determined period up to puberty where contact has a negative imprinting effect. The father of course is the one member of the family who is most likely to be out of the home for considerable periods of time, and a number of studies show that the fathers most likely to sexually abuse their daughters are those who are at home least often.[9]

Returning to the level of anthropological theory, Arens has pointed out that Freud completely misinterpreted the incest taboo.[10] A taboo is not a proscription so much as a reservation. In older societies with clear incest taboos the meaning of the taboo is not so much that individuals should refrain from incest as that certain people, the rulers, are obliged to marry within their own family. They *must* be incestuous; it is this that sets them apart from commoners. Furthermore, reviewing the fieldwork on incest, Arens has pointed out that a proscription of incest is not a cultural universal. In societies where children are brought up in close contact with siblings there is less likelihood of there being any injunction against incest. He has also noted, in addition, that there have been a number of well-documented instances where incest has been practised steadily, by virtue of unusual social arrangements rather than as a result of one individual forcing their will on another. In such situations the results have not been shame or undue psychological damage.

This evidence negates the notion of barely containable impulses seething beneath the surface, but far from making the subject of incest less of a problem Arens has argued that it makes it perhaps even more disturbing. It makes incest, rather than the incest taboo, the hallmark of the human. Social arrangements it would seem may make incest more likely – by having fathers away from home too much for example, a problem that social injunctions such as rules for exogamy attempt to mitigate.

The possession of culture therefore does not imply some superiority to animals but rather indicates that the human species has embarked on a hazardous enterprise. An enterprise that may generate incestuous attraction and produce participants who are uniquely capable of going against the grain of nature and forcing their will on another, even where no attraction exists.

It has recently become chillingly clear that the sexual abuse of children does lead to neurotic disturbances in later life. However, far from confirming the central importance of sexual libido in the psychic economy, the findings from sexual abuse suggest that issues of power and domination are more important: incest by virtue of aberrant social arrangements does not appear to have damaging psychological consequences, but physical abuse of children or mental cruelty leads to a very similar picture to that of sexual assault.

This problem is one that psychoanalysis, by concentrating on the origins of the incest taboo, managed entirely to avoid. In so doing it contributed to making the actual problem of incest invisible. As late as 1948, in his survey on sexual behaviour, Kinsey was to claim that incest existed more in the mind of clinicians and social workers than in actual performance. We now know that this is not the case.

PROJECT FOR A 'SCIENTIFIC' PSYCHOLOGY[11-13]

Another way out of Freud's 1895 impasse in attempting to frame a scientific psychology was to ignore consciousness. As noted in Chapter 1 the development of the notion of the reflex and its application to human behaviour pointed towards a possible sidelining of consciousness. While the idea of simply basing human behaviour on reflexes seemed far too crude to apply to the set of communicative acts that was dynamic psychotherapy, such an approach could offer results if a strict focus on the outer manifestations of behaviour was adopted. This approach, which came to be known as behavourism, was first propounded in 1913 by John Watson.

Watson was an experimental psychologist working on animals. As such internal imagery and introspection were of little interest to him. The central question was, what was the relevance of animal to human behaviour? He answered this by turning the question upside down. What was the difference between humans and animals? Typically the answer is along the lines of language and thought, to which Watson replied that language could be just a set of habits of the throat and thinking – a case of sub-vocal speech.

Watson argued that when it came to studying animals we are perfectly objective and scientific; we posit reflexes and habits which we then investigate experimentally. But when the reactions of humans display a complexity not found in animals we panic and introduce mystical concepts that probably can never be subjected to experimental proof or disproof. The fact that it seems that some knowledge remains latent (unused) is no proof that there is an unconscious, or a censor, an Ego or an Id.

His arguments won some support as, at the time, the experimental study of internal imagery was running into serious difficulties. Findings could not easily be reproduced. And in the absence of more detailed knowledge of brain function there seemed to be no easy way to test out competing views. Debates on the intensity of imagined colours and the issue of whether thought can be imageless or not, and if so what proportion is imageless, seemed insoluble and gave introspectionist psychology a faintly ludicrous halo. However while introspective psychology might have developed uncomfortable similarities to medieval metaphysics, there was equally little doubt for most people that internal imagery was a real phenomenon. Watson's arguments were therefore by no means compelling. His advantage lay in that working with rats he was clearly steering closer to physiology than to philosophy. Psychoanalysis had aimed at this initially but by 1913 was less clearly on target.

The dictates of the philosophies of science at the time, which were that science should be inductive and experimental, favoured Watson. Working with animal behaviour it was difficult to be anything other than inductive. One could only work from observable behaviour. The experimental subject was not open to persuasion or suggestion and prior beliefs and cultural biases did not come into the equation. Thus, in an area where there were so many possible variables, focusing on animals brought about a significant reduction in the possibility of having one's experimental results confounded by unanticipated events. This led to the observable data and nothing but the observable data becoming the focus of attention, never mind the fact that the data concerned issues that were trivial and of little obvious relevance to human concerns.

While the scientific legitimacy that behaviourism claimed was seemingly theoretically neutral, with Watson proclaiming that 'science endeavoured to understand the laws of nature and was indifferent to the uses that may be made of them', behaviourism also found favour with the rising liberalism of the times. Where Freud moved away from an environmental precipitation of the neuroses towards an endogenous aetiology, Watson's emphasis was on the environmental determinants of behaviour. He had little time for theories of inherited degeneration or the domination of behaviour by instincts. This was brought out by a memorable quote, when he said that he 'would feel perfectly confident in the ultimately favourable outcome of careful upbringing of a healthy well-formed baby born of a long line of crooks, murderers, thieves and prostitutes'.[14]

In considering the behaviour of animals there seemed to be little point in making a distinction between conscious and unconscious, but this did not stop Watson accounting for the genesis of the neuroses. He took an eleven-month-old infant who seemed to show little or no fear except of loud sounds and in particular showed no fear of animals brought close to him. Watson then proceeded to make him afraid of white rats by sounding a loud noise behind the child every time he reached out to stroke the rat. After a number of trials the child began to cry when he saw the rat. This experiment was later to be widely cited when behaviour therapy for the neuroses was developed during the 1960s.

However while Watson was a clear environmentalist, later behaviourism was as degenerate in its orientation as psychoanalysis. By the time behaviourism began to emerge into the mental health arena it was with the theoretical underpinning of B. F. Skinner rather than that of Watson. And for Skinner's operant behaviourism the issue with the neuroses was that the neurotic subject was getting something out of their predicament that was maintaining the state. Crudely put, they were enjoying their discomfort, in a manner that could only be seen as degenerate.

Skinner and Ryle[15-16]

While the rise to prominence of behaviourism has been the subject of many excellent investigations in recent years, what followed was in many ways even more surprising but has been less well investigated. As noted Watson's arguments were not compelling. So much was this the case that by the 1930s strict behaviourism seemed to be in terminal decline. Animal experimenters such as Tolman in California had shown that the behaviour of animals could not simply be explained in terms of stimuli-response reflexes.

When put into cages and required to escape, rats appeared to problem-solve their way out. Tolman's group also put rats into mazes and taught them to find their way through the maze to a food reward. The maze was then flooded so that the rats had to swim if they wanted the reward. According to orthodox behaviourism this should have put them back at square one, as learning to get to the reward had to be a matter of acquiring long chains of reflexes, among which joint position sense was thought to be one of the particularly important sets of stimuli. These latter cues however would all be altered if the rat had to swim. But it seemed that the rats did not have to relearn. They made their way fairly directly through the water to the food, from which Tolman concluded that they must have some internal map or image of the maze.

Tolman's findings had many similarities with work being done on primates by the emerging school of Gestalt psychology in Germany. In experiments based on Wolfgang Koehler's studies of chimpanzees Tolman's group trained monkeys to watch a banana being placed beneath a bucket. They were then taken away and distracted and later brought back to the bucket. At this point they invariably looked underneath for the banana. If, unbeknown to them, the banana had been replaced by a lettuce leaf they were typically indignant and looked around the room for the missing banana, suggesting that they had a clear *image* of what it was they expected to find.

Despite these findings Tolman's work and Gestalt psychology were eclipsed in the 1930s by the resurgence of a strict behaviourism. Neo-behavourism as espoused by Clark Hull in Yale and later radical behaviourism as propounded by Skinner arose to counter any softening of attitudes towards the exorcized ghosts of mental imagery and any attempt to draw distinctions between conscious and unconscious mental processes. One factor cited in this resurgence was an increase in research funding for psychologists in the 1930s, large amounts of which went to prestigious units such as that at Yale, whose directors just happened to be behaviourally oriented. Another factor was the rise of logical empiricism as a philosophy, and the strong endorsement philosophers such as Bertrand Russell and Gilbert Ryle gave to the behaviourist approach. As Ryle put it, people may object to the exclusion of introspections and dreams from attempts to account for human behaviour. It may seem like playing Hamlet without the prince. But on close inspection, 'the extruded prince . . . came to seem so bloodless and spineless a being that even opponents of [behavioural] theories began to feel shy of imposing heavy theoretical burdens on his spectral shoulders'. When one of the leading philosophers of the day argues with such a polemical flourish it takes a strong man to resist. Ryle noted that his own favourite author, Jane Austen, managed to convey intense drama and emotional subtlety and depth without ever having recourse to internal streams of consciousness or to dreams.[17]

I would argue however that it was primarily psychoanalysis that put paid to introspection and a psychology of consciousness. From 1910 onwards psychoanalysis increasingly deserted the arena of consciousness. The one bulwark against behaviourism would have been to take the self-reports of subjects at face value. This was dynamic psychology's starting point, the thinking behind Freud and Breuer's *Studies on Hysteria*. But the involvement of psychoanalysis in the interpretation of symbols appeared to have put it in the realm of the humanities rather than of science. And on this point psychoanalysis seemed incapable of reform from within. The only option open to 'scientific' psychologists in the face of the irrefutable theory of the mind that psychoanalysis had become seemed to be to abandon completely the notion of a dynamic unconscious, in much the way that Eastern Europe countries rebelling against Stalinism have seemed to need to throw out communism and even socialism as well. But in this case the fledgling psychology of consciousness went out with the murky bathwater of the unconscious.

Unfortunately Ryle's dramatic language and the increasing success of behaviourism in the 1960s in the treatment of phobic and obsessive-compulsive disorders only served to obscure the fact that orthodox behaviourism was of little use in cases of hysteria. Indeed behaviourism generated its own set of terms to malign hysterics. The idea arose that hysterical behaviour, even where it was utterly bizarre and seemingly uncomfortable to the subject affected, was maintained by secondary gain – subjects were supposedly getting something out of their behaviour that others had not noticed and put a stop to.

This kind of formulation is now parroted by every medical student when asked about hysteria and is found in a multitude of textbooks. Needless to say it does not make for a particularly helpful approach to the problem. Behavioural techniques based on these notions do not work for hysteria. Neither does behavioural theory readily account for the occurrence of incest or predict what its consequences should be. And in particular orthodox behaviour therapy has nothing to offer those who are the victims of child abuse, where, as we shall see, one of the sequelae is recurrent intrusive imagery.

EVOLUTION AND PSYCHOLOGY[18–19]

In 1866 a priest from a poor order in Brno published some results of work he had been doing since 1856.[20] The article has been described as a model scientific paper, not by virtue of the startling implications of the work reported, or the difficulties inherent in performing experiments that would solve current scientific difficulties, but rather because of its low-key and concise presentation of the relevant data and the sober formulation of its conclusions. Apart from this one publication Mendel did little to publicize his findings. He most certainly did not have the inspired presentational and political skills of a Freud. His story is a caution against doing science the way philosophers of science think it should be done.

Some romance goes out of the story perhaps when it is revealed that the same priest was a university trained physicist and chemist, and that one of his teachers, Franz Unger, had a theory of evolution that had close resemblances to the one Mendel's data later supported. The reason Mendel succeeded where others failed can, it seems, be put down in great part to the population analysis he undertook, in contrast to an analysis of single individuals. Taking tens of thousands of plants, and cross-fertilizing and analysing the results statistically, Mendel came up with probabilities that could be generalized. All things being equal, such and such a thing would happen. This statistical approach was in marked contrast to Freud, whose method lay in the intensive analysis of individual cases. Such a method as Freud's, I have argued, is appropriate for matters of historical fact, such as whether this individual was or was not abused thirty years ago by their father.[21] It is not however capable of being applied to the question of whether ontogeny recapitulates phylogeny.

Despite what now appears to be the clear success of his statistical method, in great part it was just this method that led to Mendel's being ignored. A statistical approach gave rise to a kind of law that was quite the opposite to the biogenetic law, which was seen as iron and invariant as Newton's laws were thought to be. In 1900, when the significance of Mendel's work was beginning to be appreciated, it was still iron and invariant laws that science was after, rather than relations between probabilities. These were thought of as an inferior sort of science. The irony of course was that only a few years later even Newton's laws would be seen to be relative, to hold only if other things are equal.

Another factor possibly conspiring against Mendel lay in the lack of a word for what investigators were trying to find. Different thinkers and experimenters toyed with the possibilities of what could be responsible for inheritance and came up with gemmules (Darwin), plastidules and plassons (Haeckel), colloids and crystalloids (Spenser). Very often a science does not get off the ground until a usable word with an appropriate amount of creative ambiguity gets drafted in to fill a central function. So it was with neurosis and psychosis.

The term gene, with its accompanying science of genetics, was not coined until 1906, by Bateson. The terms genotype and phenotype were not coined until 1909 by Johanssen. The launch of these various terms coincided with a switch to a Mendelian approach. With the launch of 'genetics' anything that did not conform to the Mendelian paradigm was soon shunted to the back-burner. This was the fate of the biogenetic law as it became clear that the units of inheritance were small and discrete and probably chemical – that it was a recipe that was inherited rather than a blueprint, a recipe for mixing environmental inputs rather than a blueprint that incorporated ancestral learnings.

The implications of the new genetics can be brought home by an example. In recapitulatory terms man is the inheritor of ancestral learnings. He is old even before he is born. However an emphasis on recapitulation led to an ignoring of evidence that, far from being old at birth, one of the characteristics of the human is their failure to grow up, their remaining young and flexible. For example human and chimpanzee babies show striking resemblances but human and chimpanzee adults do not. The adult human retains even in adulthood the shape of head that infant chimps and humans have, while the adult chimpanzee matures to a more 'ape-like' cranium. It is failure to mature which permits the brain expansion that distinguishes humans from other primate species. This phenomenon is called neoteny and is superficially in many ways the opposite of recapitulation – a clearcut case of humans not going through the stages traversed by other animals on their way to maturity.[22]

Nevertheless it took until the mid-1930s for probabilistic genetics to be definitively accepted and for its influence to spread beyond biology. Its acceptance in the end was probably influenced by the quantum revolution and the modern probabilistic physics that was rising from the ashes of Victorian certainty. All of a sudden it began to seem that even the interpretation of hard scientific laws was a hazardous enterprise.

Modern evolutionary psychology[23-4]

It is important to stress at this point that Freud's mixing of evolutionary biology and psychology was not, *a priori*, mistaken. His contemporaries William James and James Baldwin were evolutionary psychologists whose work is still acceptable today. Baldwin's influence gave rise to the developmental psychology of Piaget and to much current work on developmental neuropsychology.

Working from within a framework established by the work of James and Piaget, Jerome Bruner, one of the most notable of current cognitive psychologists, has taken issue with the Freudian picture of the child as being an egocentric, fantasy-dominated individual, responsive almost exclusively to inner needs.[25] The evidence, he argues, points rather convincingly in the opposite direction. Children from a very early age (less than twelve months) can take up the perspective of others. They appear to be innately social. This innate sociality finds its full development in human culture through an intimate co-operative interaction with others rather than through competition.

In further contrast to Freud, who relegated religion to the category of neurosis and who lost interest in the question of consciousness, William James went on to become the first serious explorer of the psychology of religious experience.[26] In this endeavour he drew heavily on orthodox Darwinian theory.

It is partly because of Freud's general cultural impact that it now seems inconceivable to most readers that a psychology of religious experience could emerge out of Darwinism. The struggle for survival and the notion of inherited instincts conjures up a vision of egoism that seems at odds with the world of religious vision and that seems to relegate the values of such visions to the realms of self-deceiving fantasy. However in a cogent revisionary view of evolutionary theory Robert Richards has recently argued that the central question that Darwin and his contemporaries attempted to answer was how evolution could lead to altruism. If evolutionary theory could *not* be shown to lead to a moral faculty, Darwin thought, it would fail. None of the proponents in the debates on the validity of evolution questioned the *existence* of altruism or morality in man. Thus, the implication was, if the theory could not explain these, then at some point God must have intervened, and accordingly at the end of the day evolutionary theory would really explain nothing very important.

This was the approach William James took. But in addition to developing a comprehensive psychology of religious experience James, along with Janet, was also a psychologist of consciousness.[27] Neither saw evolutionary theory as being a problem for such a psychology. And indeed the most recent trend in thinking on this subject has been to cite evolutionary theory in favour of consciousness, on the simple basis that we obviously have a consciousness and, if so, it must be important and of evolutionary advantage.[28-9] This position committed both Janet and James to locating psychopathology within the field of consciousness rather than in the interaction between consciousness and any dynamic unconscious. On this basis what is needed in psychotherapy are detailed explorations of consciousness, in the sense of attempting to get hold of all the images and words that are within consciousness, rather than attempts to make symbolic links with supposed biological processes.

Coda

The collapse of the biogenetic law fatally compromised psychoanalysis. It also compromised the basic mechanism that Freud postulated was responsible for the generation of the neuroses – a process of quasi-biological repression that operated outside of consciousness. But it was to take a further forty years before the Freudian notion of repression was to lose its grip on the psychodynamic imagination. What can take its place? So accustomed are we culturally to the idea of defending against our inner instincts that most readers will probably not readily be able to see an alternative. There are two that we will explore in the following chapters.

One is dissociation. As this concept has lain for so long outside the psychological mainstream we will have to work our way through a variety of seemingly esoteric disorders that have been termed the dissociative disorders to get some feel of the issues involved.

The other process is repression. But by this I mean something quite different to the kind of process proposed by Freud, which operated outside of consciousness and over which we have little or no control. Rather I mean something much closer to what Freud meant in 1895, when repression meant the suppression of traumatic memories. This is much closer to what the reader will probably intuitively understand by the term repression – that is, the pushing out of consciousness of disturbing material at least semi-purposefully. If this latter form of repression is operative in the neurotic disorders the implication is that we, the afflicted, know our own minds far more than we are usually given credit for, or indeed give ourselves credit for.

5   Consciousness and its Vicissitudes

In as much as we only have a single and simple thought of a given thing at a given time, there must necessarily be some place where the two images coming from the two eyes, or the two other impressions coming from a single object through the double organs of the other senses, can coalesce into one before they reach the soul so that they do not represent two objects to it instead of one. There is no place else in the body, where they can thus be united unless it is done in [the pineal] gland. Descartes, *Passions of the Soul*: Article 32.

Despite the obscurity of the Freudian notion of repression it was this rather than Janet's dissociation that won out as being the mechanism thought to be responsible for the psychoneuroses. Trying to decide just why this should have been the case is no easy matter. In this chapter I will try to pinpoint as closely as possible the point in time at which repression clearly gained the upper hand. The case of Sally Beauchamp will help us date this event to somewhere around 1915. In recent years dissociation has re-emerged to the point where it has replaced repression. This re-emergence is clearly visible from around 1975; this will be dealt with in Chapter 6.

So dominant has the Freudian concept of repression been, and so complete the neglect of consciousness as a consequence, that the notion of dissociation requires illustration. To get a better understanding of the issues I will look at a number of states that have been labelled as dissociative. The curious thing about some of these states is that they will, I believe, seem to the reader at the same time both esoteric and commonplace. This, I assume, is because such states are actually very common but our awareness of them has been marginalized owing to their inconsistency with what have until recently been the dominant conceptions governing psychological thinking.

The term dissociation was coined by Janet and literally meant dis-associated. It is usually taken to refer to the splitting apart of psychological functions that normally go together. Pain perception may become dissociated, for example, in the heat of battle or sport when serious injuries go unnoticed for lengthy periods of time. In Chapter 2 we listed the stigmata of hysteria, according to Janet, all of which he saw as involving dissociation. The prominent ones were fugue states, absences, somnambulisms and in particular amnesia. But there are a large number of other states first described around the end of the last century, and many others more recently described, that have been termed dissociative.

Depersonalization and derealization[1-3]

One of the most dramatic and yet common forms of dissociation occurs when self-perception dissociates. This leads to the experience of depersonalization – is this body, behaving seemingly automatically, really me? Such an experience was first formally noted by a French clinician, Krishaber, in 1873. The patient was a twenty-eight-year-old civil engineer who sought help out of distress at feeling he was double. He experienced one self that thought and one self that acted and he did not know which was him. He expressed this as a feeling that he had entered a dream of some sort.

Most readers will have experienced something similar at interviews or on other stressful occasions – a feeling that they are somehow looking on *at* themselves making a fool of themselves. It can also happen spontaneously, particularly when subjects are relaxed or relaxing. It may lead to the feeling that you should pinch yourself to make sure you are really there.

A converse phenomenon – derealization – was described after the First World War by Mayer-Gross. In this state the subject has the experience that real life has no more substance than a television programme. It has somehow become two-dimensional. Again most readers may have had this experience at interviews, when all may seem unreal. The interviewers may look strangely distant. Other derealization experiences are feelings that everything is being staged, or that there seems to be a haze or a fog between you and the world.

A central feature of such depersonalizations and derealizations is an awareness on the part of the experiencing subject that something abnormal has happened. Judgment is typically not impaired. However if marked the experience may provoke considerable anxiety and lay the basis for a full-blown anxiety state or may lead to the development of a phobia about going out or going into specific situations. This can be a vicious circle as anxiety itself is a potent trigger to dissociation. Attempts to express this and some of the more esoteric dissociative experiences, outlined below, have led until quite recently to subjects being labelled as schizophrenic. Typically these experiences start and end abruptly. They may also occur before a fit, in individuals who have temporal lobe epilepsy, or they can be produced by electrical stimulation of the temporal lobes.

Hypnoid dissociation[4]

While sleeping we all dissociate. Far from being unconscious to happenings around us we still process information, it seems, but we do not elaborate this processing into conscious percepts. This dissociation may be quite selective, as indicated by mothers who may awaken at the slightest sound from their children but not in the face of the din of traffic passing the bedroom window or the alarm clock. A dissociation of sorts appears to happen actually within sleep as well, when we may have the experience of watching ourselves dream – so-called lucid dreams.[5]

The relation of dissociation, hypnosis and hysteria has traditionally been close. The term hypnosis which was derived from the Greek for sleep, and the earliest hypnotists aimed for a state of somnambulism to mark the achievement of deep hypnosis. As we have noted Breuer used the term hypnoid dissociation to characterize a fundamental mechanism in many cases of hysteria. And for Janet and others somnambulism was one of the hallmarks of hysteria. Furthermore there are a host of unusual experiences that can occur in trances, meditation, deep relaxation and on the edge of sleep. Many people have the experience on falling asleep of hallucinating so vividly that they mistake what is happening for reality. For most of us the same phenomenon appears to give rise to what may be one's most vivid dreams, although these do not amount to hallucinations. This dreamy state which differs from the rest of sleep and in which dreams seem also to differ from those encountered otherwise in sleep has been noted from antiquity by observers such as Aristotle and Hobbes. The philosopher Swedenborg and others have been able to describe how such states can be induced and how in them imagination can slip the noose of mundanity.

These hypnoid experiences may also include sensations of leaving one's body, as outlined below. They may also occur in anxiety states as well as when we are deeply relaxed and on the edge of sleep. Thomas Kenneally in *A Family Madness* has recently given a compelling fictional account of the possibilities for disaster inherent in the combination of anxiety and some of the more esoteric of the dissociative experiences.[6]

OBEs and NDEs[7-9]

When falling asleep many people have the sensation of falling or moving. In relaxation this can be exaggerated so that one may feel oneself seemingly rise upwards to float somewhere just above the body. This out-of-body experience (OBE) may or may not be accompanied by an ability to apparently turn around and look at the body left below. Sometimes the floating self appears to have an experience of moving off which is typically described in terms of flying. Far from being mysterious such phenomena appear to be much the same kind of events as those that are happening in the visual or auditory systems at the onset of sleep, but occurring in this instance in the proprioceptive and kinaesthetic sensory systems. Their mysteriousness lies more in most people's lack of conscious awareness of possessing any such senses or sensations.

Closely related to OBEs and sharing many of their characteristics are near-death experiences (NDEs). Recent years have seen increasing interest in the complex of phenomena that may occur to some subjects close to death. This interest was focused by a book, *Life after Life*, by Raymond Moody. Frequently it appears the subject will hear themselves pronounced dead. They then find themselves moving along a tunnel after which they emerge in the light. They may stay for a while to watch resuscitation procedures. Or else they may move directly towards a source of light, perhaps accompanied by shadowy others. They come to a boundary at which they realize that they are not going to die and that they have to return to the body left behind.

Some experiences, especially near-death by drowning, may include having a panoramic vision of one's past life in which one appears to move backwards through time, seeing what appears to be everything in often quite minute detail. One of the best accounts of this was provided by Ambrose Bierce, in a short story entitled 'An Occurrence at Owl-Creek Bridge'.[10]

Such changes it seems cannot be put down simply to anoxia of the brain, as similar experiences have been recorded in subjects exposed to danger but not actually dying or undergoing catastrophic physical changes. They have also been reported from all cultures and from all recorded periods of history. An interesting feature about them is that there appears to be a basic core experience that is common but also a quite marked adaptation of the experience to the cultural situation of the individual. Thus if they meet anyone other than their relatives, for Hindus it will be Lord Krishna and for Christians Jesus.

Such experiences point to a further reason why the concept of dissociation has not been popular and a psychology of consciousness has been treated with caution. A perennial problem of such psychologies is their apparent propensity to derail into the praeternatural or parapsychological. This problem will be found to recur through this and subsequent chapters. In Chapter 10 I will look at some reasons for this and try to offer the outlines of a scientific handling of the issues raised.

Aside from these esoteric experiences there are a host of others that we all have at some point, which have in recent years come to be seen as dissociative (see Appendix). These include the experiences of *déjà vu* and its opposite, *jamais vu* – feelings that one has been somewhere before, or met someone before, when all the evidence points to the impossibility of this, or feelings that a place or person one should know is quite alien. Other experiences are not recognizing oneself in mirrors or being told by friends that you met them and didn't know them or meeting friends and not remembering it afterwards. Being unable to remember significant chunks of one's life also counts as a dissociative experience, as does having waves of emotion wash over one for no apparent reason.

MULTIPLE PERSONALITY c.1890[11-13]

By far the most dramatic dissociative state, and the one I propose to use to illustrate the rise and fall of the concept of dissociation and the associated interplay of psychology and biology, is that of multiple personality disorder (MPD).

In 1831 a Dr MacNish published a book entitled *Philosophy of Sleep* in which he recounted the story of a lady who lived earlier in the century and who has since become known as the Lady of MacNish. According to the account she was a healthy and well-bred lady who one day without warning fell into a profound sleep which lasted some hours longer than usual. On awakening her mind was a blank. She knew nothing of who she was, or where she was. She had to relearn everything including reading and writing. Some time later she fell into another deep sleep from which she awoke back to her old self and amnesic for all that had happened in the interim. For four years she oscillated between one state and the other. This same case was later described, apparently in the belief that it was someone else, by Dr Weir Mitchell in 1888.

In 1860 a Dr Azam, a physician from Bordeaux, reported the case of Felida to the French Académie de Médecine. Azam first encountered Felida in 1858, when she was fifteen. At this time she had apparently been ill constantly since the onset of puberty. The symptoms were attacks of motor agitation, disturbed eating, aches and pains, and she had become morose and withdrawn. She also began to develop swooning spells from which she would awake gay, active and healthy. Unlike the Lady of MacNish she did not have to relearn anything in these states and she could clearly remember her melancholy state. Her gay state usually lasted only two or three hours. On returning to her melancholy state she could remember nothing of her happier interlude.

Over a few months Felida's gay spells grew more frequent. During one of them she became pregnant. She first consulted Azam in a melancholy state because of her concern about her swelling abdomen, apparently not realizing she was pregnant. She returned gaily a few days later laughing at the discomfiture to which she had put him. This oscillation occurred until she was a middle-aged lady, when the happier self took over, almost completely.

Between 1882 and 1889 a number of eminent French physicians published studies of the case of Louis Vivet. He had six different existences, some of which appeared to be younger versions of the same person. Some of his personalities knew of others but were unknown by them, others were in contact with each other, others knew nothing of each other. His various states had quite different personalities, one being gentle and industrious for example, another lazy and irascible. In one state he had a left-sided paralysis, in another a right-sided one and in a third he was paralysed from the waist down. Curing the paralysis by hypnosis also brought about a change of personality to one of the others that were not paralysed.

These different cases, Janet argued, typify three different forms of MPD. In the Lady of MacNish there is a total disconnection between the two states. In the case of Felida there is partial awareness between the states. In Louis Vivet there was a great number of personalities that changed place quite regularly every few hours.

In 1887 Janet introduced a further aspect to the subject. He had recently taken into his care a twenty-year-old girl called Marceline. She had not eaten for months. She vomited if force-fed. She had retention of urine and generally appeared to be in the last stage of emaciation. She lay in bed seemingly insensible to the outside world. Nevertheless Janet succeeded in hypnotizing her. Under hypnosis she became alert, ate, urinated and defecated normally and appeared perfectly normal. On being taken out of hypnosis however she reverted to her former state. Eventually he decided to leave her permanently hypnotized. Her parents on visiting and finding her normal took her home, where things were all right until she menstruated. This plunged her back into the original state. Returning to hospital she was restored by hypnosis, and over the course of the following years she got by in this way – living normally under the influence of hypnosis for some weeks until some event precipitated a return of the former state, which was then relieved again by hypnosis. Based on this case it seemed that personalities could be created through hypnosis.

Allied to the issue of personality creation through hypnosis was the phenomenon of seances. These began in the 1860s and involved the contacting of departed spirits through mediums. To observers like Janet and James what appeared to be happening was a case of autohypnosis, as the medium often appeared to take on characteristics of someone else at the point of contact. The voice might change, the things said might become coarse and disturbing and the facial features distort. These observations were typically supported by the mediums, who reported being penetrated by another being so that they had the impression that they became someone else.

Writing in 1907 Janet estimated that there were between twenty and thirty well-known cases of MPD – most of which had been reported from the United States. However the issue was larger than this handful of cases might suggest. Through the nineteenth century there was growing interest in the phenomenon of double consciousness. This was well illustrated by Robert Louis Stevenson's fictional creation, Jekyll and Hyde. The interest aroused by such fictions was supplemented by some of the cases listed above being reproduced widely in the major textbooks so that they became public knowledge.

The biology of dissociation[14]

As outlined in Chapter 1, what was to be psychology was in the mid-nineteenth century split between an essentially spiritualist view of man and the emerging physiological and mechanical view. There was a great deal of scientific interest in the project of reducing spiritual phenomena to mechanical operations. Despite the esoteric quality of the dissociative experiences they were seen as appropriate for scientific investigation because the facts of biology seemed, initially at least, to hold out hope for a mechanical explanation.

As a consequence of the popularity of the idea of double personality the idea developed that mental problems might be the result of two minds struggling against each other. This it was thought might explain apparent abrupt changes of mood, or episodic outbursts of rage and aggression. It also seemed that such a disorder might explain why mental patients could be found talking to hallucinated others. The phenomena of multiple personalities, *déjà vu* and *jamais vu*, as well as the experience of depersonalization, in which the subject can have the experience of looking at themself from outside as it were, appeared to confirm these notions.

The main stimulus to the development of such ideas, however, came from contemporary investigations of brain functioning. The location of the mind within the brain had been a problem since Descartes. On close examination the brain appeared to have two lobes and four ventricles. How could an indivisible soul reside in any one of these? Intuition suggested it must be in a single and unique organ. The only such within the skull is the pineal. This was one of the principal reasons for Descartes' belief that 'even though the soul is joined to the whole body, there is nevertheless one part in which the soul exercises its functions in a more particular way'. Ironically, although within the skull, the pineal gland is not even part of the brain.

The other option was that, as the brain parts were all double, there might be more than one mind within the skull and that these minds might compete. The doubling of the cerebral hemispheres could in this way be seen as laying the basis for a phylogenetic origin for madness and neurosis – evolution predisposed to madness. One of the first speculations in the area came from Herbert Spenser. He suggested that just as two eyes produced binocular vision, allowing us to perceive in three rather than just two dimensions, so also human knowing was probably analogously bicerebral. This view however received a setback with the demonstration that each eye sent information to both cerebral hemispheres.

In 1845 Arthur Wigan published a book, *Duality of the Mind*,[15] in which he proposed an alternative view – that, rather than the two hemispheres of the brain combining to produce the final product, they were independent and capable of sustaining separate personalities. Double consciousness therefore could be explained in terms of switching from functioning on one side to functioning based on the opposite side. Madness and confusions could be accounted for in terms of an imbalance between the two hemispheres or a mismatching of their outputs. The neurological data at the time were ambiguous, in that while it had begun to seem that the left half of the brain controlled the right half of the body and vice versa, a number of studies revealed that there was some input from the left side of the body to the left brain and similarly on the right. This led some neurologists to claim that we all have, potentially at least, two full brains. Furthermore in a number of cases it seemed that one could lose a hemisphere and still function adequately.

In 1863 Paul Broca and Gustav Dax independently reported to the Académie de Médecine findings that were to be central to this debate, and to many subsequently. These were that strokes, which involved loss of speech, at post mortem were found to have *unilateral* destruction of brain tissue – on the left side. Broca reported on eight cases, saying, 'I dare draw no conclusions.' But he challenged his colleagues to find cases of right-sided lesions.

The reason for being so hesitant was almost spiritual. With the abandonment of the pineal as the seat of the soul and the growing acceptance of a brain localization for the mind, investigators it seemed yearned for a spiritual order of sorts. This was crystallized in Bichat's laws of symmetry in 1805. The brain, as the highest organ, must be symmetrical – and on superficial inspection it appears to be. When Broca's findings challenged this paradigm the immediate response was shock. Briquet argued that it was patently absurd that there should be asymmetry. Were Broca and colleagues proposing that the right eye might see blue, black and red for example while the left one saw green, yellow and blue? Defenders noted that there were many examples of asymmetry if one but looked. Our right and left hands for example differ markedly in function if not in form. Equally one of the two eyes was invariably dominant over the other.

The initial solution to the problem was something of a compromise. Broca argued in 1865 that both hemispheres were symmetrical, that there were no innate functional differences, but that in early brain development the left hemisphere grew slightly quicker than the right. When it came to mastering complex tasks, such as language acquisition, we tended to fall back on our more developed hemisphere.

This started another hare running. The implication that education and civilization might avail itself of asymmetries quickly led to a concern to discover as much asymmetry as possible, in contrast to previous attempts to ignore it. Such asymmetries, it was thought, might explain the differences between men and women, between civilized and savage races and between the sane and insane. Studies soon appeared finding that women had less developed asymmetry than men and that savages were less asymmetrical than Europeans. As it was believed at the time that the effects of education and civilization to foster asymmetry could lead to the inheriting of an even greater tendency towards asymmetry, the whole formed a heady cocktail.

Further developments followed. In 1874 Karl Wernicke localized what has become known as Wernicke's speech area. Where Broca had appeared to correlate an inability to produce speech with a left-sided anterior lesion, Wernicke found that a left-sided posterior lesion could impair the ability to interpret speech. Localization flowered after this. Far from being symmetrical it seemed, as in the case of language, that the highest functions all lay on the left.

This led to a personalizing of the two hemispheres. The left came to be seen as intellectual, male, objective, oriented towards the world, whereas the right was emotional, vegetative, female and subjective. The difference between the two hemispheres seemed to be supported by findings from hysteria, which was typically associated with left-sided paralyses and anaesthesiae, supporting the idea that it might result from a pathology of the right side of the brain. Not only this, but Janet found that, in cases of hysterical loss of speech, paralyses and anaesthesiae if they occurred did so on the right side of the body. All of this seemed to fit the emerging anatomical data rather well.

When it came to the phenomenon of double personality the temptation to ascribe a personality to each of the hemispheres was naturally all but irresistible. A good deal of evidence began to accumulate giving apparent support to the idea. Charcot and colleagues, experimenting with the use of metals in hysteria, had found that when the application of metals to one side of the body restored sensation or motor function on that side it was invariably lost on the other side. This suggested that some functional lesion was being transferred from one side of the body to the other. In the same way it was found that pain could be transferred from one side of the body to the other and presumably ultimately from one side of the brain to the other. One of the patients to whom this was done reported her experience in terms of doors banging between two sides of her brain. Not only anaesthesia and paralysis but behaviour also could be transferred.

It seemed possible to hypnotize one half of the body only, with the implication that only one half of the brain was also hypnotized. This seemed to leave patients feeling cut in two. It also seemed possible to induce quite different experiences in each hemisphere. For example Dumontpallier induced a hypnotized subject to hallucinate an attack by dogs on her right and a country fête on her left. To observers it appeared that the right side of her face showed horror and the left contentment. Thus, along with the example of Janet's Marceline, it appeared possible to divide the personality by hypnosis and that this divide seemed facilitated by the presence of two cerebral hemispheres.

This pointed to the possibility that each of the personalities in dual personality inhabited their own side of the brain. However there were a number of problems that were not easily reconciled with such a view.

One, which became apparent during the late 1880s as no cases of right-localized speech were recorded, was the fact that each of the dual personalities appeared to be able to speak – although some of the intervening personalities appeared to have to be retaught. More problematic were cases such as Louis Vivet in which there were more than two personalities. These inconsistencies between psychological phenomena and the apparent biological possibilities set the scene for increasing disfavour with the idea of dissociation. This was sealed by the emergence of an alternative biological model of the mind that appeared to be more consistent with the idea of repression.

Repression and inhibition[16–19]

As noted in Chapter 1 researchers proceeding up the nervous system from the spinal cord began to outline a nervous organization composed of a hierarchy of reflexes. Within this hierarchy one way of conceiving of mental activity was the associationist way. This of necessity made mental life dynamic, in that one memory tended to call up another depending on the strength of the connections between them. But the model seemed far too simplistic to account for much. Greater complexity was introduced by a further set of developments.

Working with the vagus nerve of the frog Weber found that stimulating this nerve led to a slowing of the frog's heartbeat. This finding remained neglected for some time probably by virtue of its counter-intuitive nature – stimulation by nerves was expected to lead to some increase in vitality, not a decrease. But it was later developed in two ways. Sherrington and others in Britain went on to develop the modern version of the spinal reflex. This depended critically on the notion of reciprocal inhibition, by which is meant that when nerves organize an activity they must simultaneously turn on and turn off various component elements of the activity. For example moving my arm to lift a cup of tea does not just involve a nervous command to my biceps to contract but also one to my triceps to relax. Without a relaxation of the triceps, biceps activity would lead to one or other muscle being torn from the bone. This simultaneous relaxation and contraction requires organization. Sherrington's achievement was to show that this degree of organization all took place in the spinal cord, without the need to import some 'soul' into the process.

However a quite different demonstration of the phenomenon of inhibition by Ivan Sechenov was of greater importance for psychological thinking. The demonstrations of inhibition since Weber were all of muscle or gut activity being inhibited by nervous impulses, not of nerves being inhibited by nerves. Starting from an interest in the phenomenon that we can block a sneeze or resist the temptation to scratch Sechenov also noted that the spinal reflexes of frogs who had been decapitated were often brisker than those of intact frogs. This led him in 1862 to investigate the possibility that the brain might generally inhibit spinal activity. He went on to demonstrate that this was the case.

This provided a major extension to Descartes' reflex theory. Since Descartes it had been assumed that there was some relationship between the intensity of the stimulus and the intensity of the reaction. But Sechenov's work opened up the possibility of stimuli that could elicit variable responses. The possibility of such flexibility led Sechenov to postulate the decidedly Freudian notion that the development of a hierarchy of inhibitory influences underlay the evolution of man and the development of civilization.

This line of thinking was taken to its ultimate conclusion in the 1880s by Hughlings Jackson. Where Sechenov had demonstrated an inhibitory influence of the brain stem on spinal reflexes, subsequent work extended this up through the mid-brain. Working from clinical cases Jackson extended the notion up to the cortex in man and especially to the frontal cortex. The clinical sequelae of strokes illustrate his position quite well. As a result of strokes affecting the cortex of the brain the ability to move an arm or a leg may be lost. But there is also an increase in the tone of and strength of the reflexes in the affected limb. This hypertonicity and hyperreflexia, Jackson argued, is normally inhibited by the cortex and it is that inhibition that enables us to use our limbs in the flexible way we do.

A natural experiment, in 1875, appeared to support Jackson's view. This involved a railway worker, Phineas Gage, who in the course of an explosion had an iron bar propelled through the frontal lobes of his brain. Remarkably, he was up and about only an hour later. He suffered little by way of intellectual or memory deficits. But his behaviour was transformed. He became 'disinhibited'. Specifically he was coarser than before, more distractible, impatient and unable to co-operate with others.

Jackson's belief that the frontal lobes were the ultimate inhibitor was a widely shared one. Even Broca agreed with it; he was more struck by the frontal location of his so-called speech area than by the fact that it was lateralized to the left side of the brain. Loosening of frontal lobe inhibition, under the influence of alcohol or cannabis for example, could therefore be expected to yield a regression to behaviour more appropriate to an earlier evolutionary state.

Jackson's views, with their notion of higher conscious areas inhibiting lower unconscious ones, were tailor-made for adoption by Freud. They included the idea that it was the process of evolution that built repression into the system. Jackson even postulated that in sleeping, dreaming and insanity conscious inhibition was loosened, and primitive thinking and emotions could come bubbling up to the surface. Hence, he argued, knowing all about dreams should reveal all about insanity.

Sally Beauchamp[20]

The triumph of the hierarchical model of the brain loaded the biological scales in favour of a repressive rather than a dissociative model of the neuroses. The significance of this biological loading and the time of its triumph become clear in what was to be the most celebrated case of MPD.

In 1905 the Boston physician Morton Prince published the story of Sally Beauchamp in a book entitled *The Dissociation of a Personality*. This individual had it would seem four personalities and perhaps twelve or thirteen other states that might have evolved into personalities. Of the main personalities one was impossibly proper and refined, another was flirtatious and extrovert and a third angry and brooding. She became the most celebrated case of MPD, perhaps partly because of the racy quality of Prince's account, not far removed from the suspense of Jekyll and Hyde. Prince's mastery of when to throw in the next telling detail or the next unexpected twist in the plot adds to the undeniable suspense of waiting for the inevitable 'murder' of the most appealing personality – Sally.

Most of the features of the case map accurately on to the model of hysteria outlined by Janet. This was no accident since Prince was in close contact with Janet, whose 1906 lectures on the major symptoms of hysteria were delivered in Boston. Furthermore, along with William James and other Boston psychologists, Prince was actively interested in the nature of consciousness and dissociation. A number of other cases of notable fugue states or MPD were also reported by the Bostonians. A possible criticism of his study was that Miss Beauchamp mapped all too well on to the notions of the disorder that had been worked out before she presented.

Despite great interest in this case, by the time Prince gave details of a further twelve cases a few years later the issue was almost dead. Psychoanalysis had taken over as the dominant dynamic psychology – particularly in America. From an analytic point of the view the inevitable erotic interplay between Prince and Miss Beauchamp had been naïvely ignored. Miss Beauchamp, an attractive twenty-six-year-old, had been coming to see Prince for over four years, sometimes several times a week and sometimes for entire afternoons, and he appeared more than willing to be called out to her apartment and elsewhere on emergencies, even late at night. Recasting the story it was argued that Miss Beauchamp had settled her Oedipal difficulties of the need to both please and defy her father all too well in establishing separate personalities to take on each of these functions.

Although splitting of personalities was noted during the war in individuals who were shellshocked there were after that few clear-cut cases reported until 1957, when Thigpen and Cleckley published details of a case under the title *The Three Faces of Eve*. They found themselves flooded thereafter with referrals. But of thousands of other individuals seen there was only one other case that they were happy to accept as MPD. The reason for this dearth of cases is usually attributed to Prince having come off worse in the argument with Freud over what was going on in multiple personality. Like Breuer, Prince had opted for a simple hypnoid splitting. However Miss Beauchamp's *four* personalities did not give Prince any anatomical protection to fall back on and his book came to be regarded as a curiosity – until quite recently.

MULTIPLE PERSONALITY c.1980[21-4]

Writing in 1975 in perhaps the most authoritative psychiatric textbook, the *Comprehensive Textbook of Psychiatry*, John Nemiah noted that the prevalent view was that multiple personality disorders had become extinct, at least in Western civilization.[25] He demurred, but did agree that the condition seemed relatively rare in 1975 compared with the situation at the turn of the century. This view was articulated as late as 1978 by the prominent psychoanalyst Charles Rycroft.[26] He felt that such conditions could occur only where the mind was idealized at the expense of the body, and that this could not now happen, in great part because of the irreversible influence of Freud.

However even as Rycroft wrote the ground was shifting. Periodically psychiatrists worldwide review the diagnostic systems they use. The categories of disorder that emerge from these reviews represent consensus views of the profession as to what pathological conditions are being seen. Once established, practitioners are strongly encouraged to use the consensus categories in order to facilitate research and communication.

There are two systems: one is worldwide, the International Classification of Diseases (ICD); the other is American and is laid out in a *Diagnostic and Statistics Manual (DSM)* of which there had been two prior to 1980. *DSM* III was drawn up during the latter half of the 1970s. One of the central aims of its authors was to ensure that it did not embody any Freudian preconceptions, as both *DSM* I and II had done.[27] It was hoped that a framework could be adopted that would be neutral regarding competing ideologies.

DSM III established several new diagnostic categories on the basis that, although they were at odds with prevailing theories, common experience suggested they occurred, if infrequently. In 1974 Schreiber had described the sixteen personalities in Sybil, and Davis and Osherson reported on Julie-Jenny-Jerrie. Eugene Bliss in 1980 reported on a series of fourteen cases. This handful of reports constituted the grounds for a diagnostic category of Multiple Personality Disorder. The exclusion of MPD from previous classifications had been the result of their psycho-analytic orientation.

The following criteria were laid down for MPD: (1) the existence within an individual of two or more distinct personalities, one of which is dominant at any particular time; (2) the personality that is dominant at any particular time determines the individual's behaviour; (3) each individual personality is complex and integrated with its own unique behaviour patterns and social relationships.

The authors of *DSM* III appear to have had no awareness of just what was going to happen in response to the creation of the new category. Almost immediately afterwards several series of cases of MPD were reported, with one group claiming to have a hundred subjects. Whereas pre-1980 textbooks were talking about a rare and exotic syndrome which classically displayed double personalities, a rush of recent studies suggest a disorder in which there are typically four personalities but in which there may be up to twenty.

Up to 1980 around 200 cases of MPD had been reported worldwide. By 1984, 1,000 were known to be in treatment. As of 1988, 4,000 were in treatment and there were estimates of up to 20,000 cases in the USA alone. In part some of these are likely to be simply cases being rediag-nosed, using the criteria laid down by *DSM* III. However it is striking that at present such cases come almost exclusively from the USA.

Subjects currently being diagnosed as having MPD turn out already to have been to the psychiatric services and usually to have received some other diagnosis, either personality disorder or schizophrenia. Herein lies the rub. This explosion of interest has given rise to heated controversy, in part presumably because it involves some physicians rediagnosing patients previously seen by others. Many of the psychiatrists claiming to have patients with MPD have themselves been diagnosed by sceptical colleagues as suffering from a *folie à deux*. The sceptics in turn get diagnosed as having single personality disorder. So vehement has been the reaction that now there is even research being done on why reactions should be so vehement.

On top of these clinical difficulties the multiple personality phenomenon ran into a murder trial that left many feeling that for legal reasons it would be just as well if there were no such thing as MPD. The trial in question was that of Kenneth Bianchi, known as the Hillside Strangler. In Los Angeles, in the winter of 1977, ten young women were murdered and their bodies were left displayed on Los Angeles hillsides. Two other women were murdered in Washington a year later and similarly displayed. Kenneth Bianchi was arrested. He protested innocence. An examining psychiatrist hypnotized him and was confronted by Steve, who acknowledged the murders and described them in sadistic detail. Kenneth denied knowing Steve. Was he guilty?

Based on expert opinion, the court thought he was. One of the crucial pieces of evidence was that shortly after it was suggested to Bianchi that he must be faking, as real multiple personality disorders came in threes rather than twos, a third character, Billy, appeared. However as research on MPD has progressed it has seemed to a number of observers that many of the personalities of the condition do appear during the course of therapeutic engagement and seemingly in response to suggestion. Therefore one might question whether the timely appearance of Billy really was evidence against a diagnosis of MPD.

Quite apart from such controversial cases recent research on the disorder has thrown up an interesting profile of the typical individual who suffers MPD. The vast majority are female. They typically have been sexually assaulted in childhood, although simple physical abuse is also common, and the onset of the disorder dates from the assault. From childhood onwards they show evidence of amnesic periods. Depression is common. So also is the hearing of voices, particularly voices coming from within the head. Fifty per cent have what are termed somatization features – Briquet's syndrome or more classic hysterical conversion reactions. However far from patients switching personality at the drop of a hat switching seems to happen only during periods of conflict and is often associated with headaches.

This clinical picture has strong resemblances to Breuer's portrait of Anna O. and is almost identical to that of Sally Beauchamp. In just the same way as cases being diagnosed today several of Miss Beauchamp's personalities put in their first appearance while she was under hypnosis. Just as in current cases her switching between personalities was liable to happen at times of conflict or great emotion. Just as now certain stimuli evocative of past experiences would trigger a switch between her personalities. However on the issue of possible precipitation Prince was ambivalent. Miss Beauchamp claimed to have been in some way 'double' as a child and to have spent considerable time day-dreaming and fantasizing. She came from a home where her father was apparently quite violent and where she adored but was unloved by her mother. This is quite typical of today's cases. But whether there was sexual abuse or childhood trauma, as invariably appears to be the case today, is unclear. The disorder appears to have taken deeper root at the time of her mother's death, when Sally was thirteen. The night her mother died a baby sibling also died – in Sally's arms. (Prince appears not to have considered the possibility of manslaughter here.) Her condition was further aggravated by an ambiguous sexual encounter at the age of twenty – was she raped? There are no clear answers from Prince.[28]

This consistency in accounts across almost a century is impressive. When subjects who will ultimately be labelled MPD are first seen now they typically are not aware that they have a number of different personalities. Even after coming to therapy, if they are being treated by someone who does not believe in MPD or who does not recognize the possibility in this particular case, personalities do not emerge. Different personalities often emerge only when they are first suspected by a therapist. Therapist suspicion is alerted by a history of amnesic episodes, or by hearing that the patient's wardrobe contains clothes that they cannot account for or by asking them to keep a diary and finding that it contains differing hand-writing styles. The existence of the personalities can usually be demonstrated only by hypnotizing the patient and asking for their hidden self, the part the therapist has not met, to come forward. This it does. Very frequently the therapist then spends a great deal of time with their prize patient – much as Breuer did with Anna O. and Prince with Sally Beauchamp. During the course of this time further personalities appear. Initially these are all very fleeting and undeveloped but with time they appear to establish a greater resonance. Janet had argued that naming the personality gives it a focus around which to crystallize.

It is usual to designate one personality as the host and the others as alters. The alters typically have different names, different tastes, often different voices and accents as well as different interests. The personalities may be variably amnesic for each other, although general knowledge is usually shared between them. There are some indications of physiological changes concomitant with changes in personality. For example cases have been reported where one of the personalities was heavily sedated by 5 mg of diazepam (valium) but others could tolerate up to 50 mg. Interesting and indeed surprising as this is, readers should not be persuaded that this implies the personalities are fundamentally different entities. Many readers would be sedated by 5 mg of diazepam but if faced with the stress of an interview or having to deliver a speech could tolerate 50 mg without much if any sedative effects. It differs little from the situation of Miss Beauchamp, one of whose personalities got drunk on one glass of wine whereas another could take six to eight without apparent effect. Other physiological changes have been reports of altered thyroid function and allergy pattern between personalities.

The physiological data seem to support the 'reality' of MPD. However there are also a number of oddities of the condition that give rise to concern. Firstly, both today and at the end of the last century, it has been found predominantly in the USA. And secondly, several years ago, there appeared to be a distinct fashion for there to have been abuse, which occurred as part of a satanic ritual – a fashion that seems now to have arrived in the UK. A more recent fashion in the USA appears to be that the abuse occurs on spaceships following abduction by aliens. In both the satanic ritual and spaceship abduction scenarios the abuse has been described in great and vivid detail by subjects, with apparent reliving rather than just remembering being demonstrated in some. A clear-cut case surely of the mixing of truth and fantasy noted by Freud! While such cases certainly do point to the hazards of psychodynamic interpretation it must also be noted that the truth and fantasy being mixed do not derive from any degenerate *endogenous* source. Rather the spaceships and the rituals clearly have their origins in environmental inputs of some sort.

What causes MPD? The current view (among those who believe in the existence of the condition) is that children, especially between the ages of four and ten, dissociate readily and spend quite a bit of time talking to imaginary companions anyway. The occurrence of trauma at this time, it is argued, somehow makes subjects subsequently more liable to dissociate than others. In the course of some abuse or trauma the original personality dissociates into a subject who lives in a world where abuse happens and a subject who is unaware of the abuse or the traumatic event. This is made a more clearly multiple personality picture if the perpetrator of the abuse, as they often appear to do, suggests that they have two little girls or boys, one of whom shares a secret with them and the other of whom knows nothing of what is going on – in effect a creation of personalities by a form of hypnosis. This explanation closely resembles the one offered by Breuer to account for the features of the Anna O. case.

Neo-dissociation[29]

There was another development during the 1970s that favoured an explanation of the origins of MPD in terms of childhood trauma. This came from research on hypnosis. Reviewing, in 1973, the dominant proposals regarding the mechanism of action of hypnosis, which were based essentially on psychoanalytic or behavioural notions, Ernest Hilgard had proposed an alternative view, which he termed the neo-dissociation hypothesis. Neo-dissociation was in 1973, and still is, a rather vague proposal, the principal merit of which seemed to lie in the fact that the competing theories at the time were so obviously even less adequately able to account for the features of hypnosis. Its creative vagueness however must have been in tune with the zeitgeist, as it very quickly took over as the dominant theory of hypnosis.

The neo-dissociative hypothesis did produce one piece of experimental evidence directly relevant to MPD. It had been known since Janet that most people and certainly most hypnotizable individuals show a phenomenon called automatic writing. If, while holding a pen over a piece of paper, attention is distracted in a way that leaves the pen in close proximity with the paper, many individuals will find on looking back at the paper that they have doodled or made marks on it. If this is done often enough some subjects can produce coherent sentences, seemingly unbeknown to themselves.

While studying the phenomenon of analgesia under hypnosis Hilgard tapped into something similar to automatic writing. He asked subjects being subjected to a variety of experimental pains but who seemed indifferent to the pain to indicate if some part of them was registering the pain nevertheless. The outcome was that subjects were able to indicate by a variety of means, including writing, that they were in pain, while at the same time verbally reporting that they felt little or no pain. On the basis of these findings he postulated that in hypnosis a 'hidden observer' remains in touch with 'reality' in some fashion. The notion of a hidden observer fits in well with the proposal that MPD may derive from the mobilization of a dissociative mechanism in response to trauma. It will become clear in Chapter 9 however that there are serious problems with the idea that a hidden observer may remain in some way in contact with reality while the rest of us dissociates.

Comparing his neo-dissociation theory with Janet's concept of dissociation Hilgard suggested that neo-dissociation, as he envisaged it, occurred strictly within consciousness, and implied a model of consciousness in which there are overlapping compartments. Janet, in contrast, had proposed a layered model of consciousness in which there was both conscious and subconscious processing. Both however involve mechanisms that lie within consciousness, in contrast to the Freudian model of the psyche which postulated a radical unconscious.

While Freudian views were dominant dissociation remained a dubious concept. But with the endorsement of a number of dissociative disorders in *DSM* III researchers have felt freer to explore the empirical occurrence of dissociative states, as opposed to the artificial creation of dissociation in laboratory settings. This has led to the development of a number of scales aimed at assessing the frequency of dissociation and giving an index of individual dissociability. It seems certain that significant numbers of dissociative states will be found to occur widely and frequently, which raises the question of how such widespread occurrence could have been so completely ignored.

Before attempting to answer this there is one further state to consider in which consciousness splits and in which seemingly hidden observers can record events that conscious selves are unaware of: anaesthesia.

CONSCIOUSNESS AND ANAESTHESIA[30-1]

The first point to be made is that just as there is no well worked out definition of dissociation, so also there is no good working definition of anaesthesia. This may appear to be a startling claim but it is literally the case. Anaesthesia is what happens when a subject being operated on does not complain. While it has been termed the therapeutic sleep, anaesthesia is not the same thing as sleep. It can be induced in subjects who are apparently fully awake. It can be induced by hypnosis or by drugs and the hypnotic procedures to be used or the amount of drugs needed for induction are well known. But as to what it is that these techniques actually do, apart from stopping a subject being distressed, no one can clearly say.

Until recently there was little interest in this issue, partly because anaesthetics so obviously work. Until a few years ago patients who reported post-operatively that they had been aware of events happening during their operation were treated to the full weight of medical disdain. In a typical case of awareness under anaesthesia the experience is one of being quite lucid, although mercifully not in pain. There is no way of communicating this state to the observing anaesthetist, as muscle relaxants are usually also given so that the subject is incapable of any movement, even that of blinking an eye. They can simply stare helplessly out as their anaesthetist stares in while checking for pupillary responsiveness to light. A minority of cases in this state are however aware and in pain, often of an excruciating kind. It has been through the efforts of these subjects to receive redress that the phenomenon of awareness under anaesthesia has been slowly coming to light.

Some very curious findings have been trickling out. In 1965 a South African psychologist called Leavinson arranged to have ten volunteer subjects going to surgery anaesthetized more heavily than usual – close to the limits of safety. These subjects were not consciously aware of anything. During the procedure a mock crisis was staged in which the theatre staff acted as though the patient's responses indicated some serious internal problem with potential loss of life. This was brief, and afterwards the anaesthesia was brought back to normal levels and surgery continued. Post-operatively the patients remembered nothing of the operation – until they were hypnotized. Under hypnosis four of the ten were able to repeat the precise words used by the various actors in the crisis and four others were able to give a good account of what had happened.

This report was not taken up at the time of first publication. But more recently a number of studies have shown that suggestions under anaesthesia that the operation is proceeding smoothly and that there are unlikely to be post-operative complications have led to reduced requirements for post-operative analgesia and a shorter stay in hospital. These issues all return us to the question of what is consciousness. It seems that we process far more information than we are ever aware of. What is it that restricts entry into awareness?

There is no simple answer. Many of the agents which suppress awareness and are used accordingly for anaesthesia, such as the barbiturates and benzodiazepines, are also amnestic agents: they bring about forgetfulness. But the very same agents have been used extensively during two world wars and in other traumatic situations for abreaction – to recover memories. Often under the influence of these drugs soldiers during the war could be induced to relive traumatic events with all the verisimilitude that characterized the reliving of sexual assaults under hypnosis for Freud or Janet.

Dissociative anaesthesia[32–4]

There is another phenomenon that is pertinent here, which is the issue of what are now called the consciousness expanding or psychedelic drugs. A variety of such compounds have been used by various peoples throughout history for the induction of trance states. The best known of these was mescal, used by some Native Americans, but there have been scores of such drugs in use worldwide, including magic mushrooms and hashish. The use of these drugs was brought to Western attention in the nineteenth century by the members of the Parisian Club des Hachichis, who included Baudelaire and Gautier. William James in his *Varieties of Religious Experience* came out in favour of there being a possible overlap between the states induced by these drugs and certain mystical experiences.[35]

The story developed in pace and complexity with the discovery of LSD in 1948 and subsequently other compounds. In 1957 Humphrey Osmond coined the term psychedelic (mind-manifesting) to convey some idea of the effects of this class of drugs of which LSD had become the prototype. He also laid down the marker that these drugs were of 'more than medical significance'. Aldous Huxley's *The Doors of Perception* and *Heaven and Hell* led to a widespread awareness of and interest in the new class of compounds.[36]

The properties of the psychedelic drugs have proved difficult to pin down. It seems that one of the effects of LSD is to induce a state of suggestibility. The effects that are produced depend to some extent on the setting in which the drug is taken. With the right setting – dim lights and music and the company of others – the experiences may be profound. The subject may find buried material from their past life re-emerges into consciousness. In some cases subjects seem to relive rather than simply remember past episodes, especially past traumata. Sometimes this will involve reliving their birth. In other cases the experience may be of being one with the universe. Also found are transpersonal experiences, in which subjects seemingly become someone else from some other time and place or in which they may even become an animal. Intense depersonalization, derealization, *déjà vu, jamais vu* and out-of-body experiences are common.*

LSD was quickly pressed into therapeutic use. It gained acceptance as

---

*However in a laboratory setting with sober investigators the effects primarily involve sensory distortion. This became clear in the course of military research on the possible use of LSD in drinking water to disorient civilian populations if necessary. When taken by sober scientists in research settings the predominant finding was nausea and perceptual instability.

an abreactive agent, which investigators in the 1950s and 1960s thought would allow them to penetrate incisively into the subconscious. The word psycholytic was used to describe its effects – this literally means a cutting into the psyche. It was used in the treatment of alcoholics, with the stated therapeutic goal of taking apart the Ego of the addict in the hope that when it reassembled itself their dependence on the addiction might be lessened. This approach was seen as mobilizing the inner resources of the patient rather than the more orthodox approach of highlighting the weaknesses of the alcoholic and attempting to shame them into abstinence. A great number of studies were reported in the pages of the *American Journal of Psychiatry* during the 1960s in support of the efficacy of this treatment.

The peculiar relevance of all this to our subject matter is that LSD was also used as an anaesthetic agent for surgery. It was excellent as such but its duration of action, between eight and sixteen hours, was a serious drawback. Another agent, introduced by Parke-Davis in 1957, phenylcyclidine (PCP), proved better in this regard. In many respects PCP was almost the ideal anaesthetic in that it had few adverse effects on cardiac or respiratory function – unlike the other agents in use, then and now. Its effects on the psyche were also quite different in that subjects were not put to sleep so much as dissociated and indifferent to surgical procedures. PCP however had a serious drawback in that up to a third of those taking it were quite disoriented post-operatively. In such states a number of patients seemed not to know who or where they were. Some became violent. Others were seemingly awake but hallucinating. PCP was withdrawn from the market. It has since gone underground and is widely abused in the USA.

PCP has been replaced in anaesthetic practice by ketamine, which has minimal emergence side-effects, most of which can be abolished by diazepam, and which also has the advantage of a short duration of activity – one to two hours. Like PCP, ketamine dissociates rather than sedates. Subjects who have not been given muscular relaxants, so that they can move an arm for example to indicate awareness of the location and quality of their pain, are able to do so while at the same time remaining indifferent to it.

In surgical situations the subjective effects of ketamine have not been well characterized, owing it would seem to the almost startling lack of interest in such effects on the part of anaesthetists and surgeons. But when taken in laboratory settings the effects are similar to those of LSD. These include feeling light, experiences of altered body consistency, shape or size, an awareness of some bright light on the edge of consciousness, feelings of timelessness, radiant visions, insight on the riddles of existence, out-of-body experiences and dissolution experiences.[37]

What does ketamine do? In a recent volume on consciousness in contemporary science, to which cognitive neuropsychologists and philosophers contributed, Richard Gregory has noted that the philosophical debate about consciousness could potentially go on for ever without coming to a resolution.[38] He suggested one way out of the impasse would be for those concerned with the issue of consciousness to take a variety of anaesthetics, which after all affect consciousness in some way, following which attempts to produce models of consciousness might be more dynamic. He himself took ketamine and reported on its effects. In a laboratory setting, in which he was closely monitored and required to attempt to complete a set of psychological tests at regular intervals, the principal effect seems to have been perceptual instability. Sensation, in the sense of colour vision, visual acuity and auditory recognition, was normal. But when it came to putting sensations together into percepts, the percepts were unstable. Alarmingly and uncomfortably so.

Commenting on consciousness, informed by his experience under ketamine, Gregory suggested that we become conscious in the face of novelty. For example, when we have put on our clothes we may be aware of them for a brief period afterwards, or a longer period in the case of new shoes for instance, but pretty soon owing to a lack of novelty we stop being conscious of them. In general he suggested that when our representations of the world fail to account for what is happening we become aware of the discrepancy: 'consciousness is always associated with some surprise'. On this basis an agent like ketamine, which interfered with perceptual stability, is highly likely to alter consciousness. The surprising thing about producing an altered state of consciousness, as opposed to simply sedating or alerting someone, is how easy it is to do. Hyperventilating for several minutes will produce many of the effects of ketamine, as will its opposite, breathing in carbon dioxide. Sensory deprivation also produces a very similar picture. Fevers alter consciousness. Deep relaxation will do so as well, as does high anxiety. Relatively abrupt changes in sensory input or physiological conditions therefore seem capable of disrupting the normal state of consciousness.

If we add to this Janet's contention, that there is no such thing as a neutral consciousness – no consciousness that is not in some way shaped by personal concerns and prior knowledge – we get an equation in which relatively small physiological changes may produce a radically different awareness of the self.

There are two issues of pertinence here to the dilemmas that faced

Breuer, Janet and Freud. The first is that subjects on ketamine or in altered states of consciousness often seemingly vividly relive their past. This became clear in the late 1950s, as scenes of childhood trauma emerged under LSD. Under the influence of psychoanalytic theories these were invariably dismissed as childhood fantasy at the time. More recently this effect has led to the use of ketamine and hyperventilation as abreactive agents in place of LSD in a few centres.

Although the balance has now swung back towards believing the evidence pointing toward trauma that emerges from such sessions, there is a problem. Individuals on ketamine or LSD not only relive episodes from childhood, but they may also seemingly relive their birth or experience themselves as someone else from a different time or place. This first became disconcertingly clear in clinical work using LSD in the 1960s. Far from simply penetrating the unconscious, psycholytically, and uncovering the expected erotic impulses and Oedipal conflicts, investigators found that subjects were far more likely to 'go transcendental'.

Is this a mixing of truth and fantasy? What controls entry into consciousness – is it unconscious fantasies or something else? The common explanation given by subjects, on ketamine or LSD, is that they have somehow contacted the transcendent ground of being and that therefore their experiences derive from some supraconscious source. This is obviously quite problematic for a scientific psychology, aiming at probing the mechanical workings of the psyche. But despite these transcendental difficulties the exploration of awareness under anaesthesia and the neuropsychology of dissociative agents means that once again it has become possible to talk about a biology of dissociation, so that dissociative theories of the neuroses are no longer disadvantaged compared to psychoanalysis or behaviourism. But before tackling further the question of consciousness and the role of altered states of consciousness in the neuroses, we have one further set of dissociative phenomena to consider.

6 The Traumatic Neuroses

On 15 September 1830 the world's first passenger railway line opened between Liverpool and Manchester. Shortly after the opening the first train crashes occurred. A growing number of accidents left victims who were significantly disabled – paralysed, blind, deaf or anaesthetic – but who did not have clear-cut organic lesions. Insurance claims against the railway companies focused attention on these conditions, which were called traumatic neuroses. At the same time other traumatic neuroses were being noted arising from accidents at work. From 1880 onwards various European countries enacted legislation to provide compensation for traumatically injured workers.

Many prominent physicians believed that potential access to insurance moneys or to compensation from the state could not but lead some citizens to 'set out on a broad road of imposture and dissimulation'.[1] Others concluded that these conditions were the result of the psychological shock of the accident, given 'the vastness of the destructive forces, the magnitude of the results and the imminent danger to the lives of a number of human beings and the hopelessness of escape'.[2] (Freud it can be noted was train phobic.)[3] Against both of these possibilities, it is probable that a proportion of such cases had whiplash type injuries.

In Chapter 1 Charcot's work on the traumatic neuroses was noted. He was the first to demonstrate that many of these could be alleviated by hypnosis, and conversely that hypnotized subjects could produce the symptomatology found in the traumatic disorders. He also noted that these conditions shared many symptoms in common with hysteria, such as hemianaesthesia. Both he and Janet accordingly saw the traumatic neuroses as variants of hysteria. Charcot however considered that what was involved was the mobilization of a degenerate reflex by the traumatic event. Janet in contrast was more clearly aware of the psychological after-effects of trauma. Others argued that there were differences to hysteria, especially in the relative intractability of the traumatic neuroses to treatment.

While the European railways threw up the first cases of post-traumatic neurosis the American Civil War provided another important milestone in the development of the problem. In the *American Journal of the Military Sciences*, in 1871, Jacob Mendes Da Costa reported a condition he called irritable heart.[4] He described the case of William Henry H. who had enlisted in the army in 1862. He appeared to be in good health then and was a hard worker. He admitted to being anxious before the Battle of Fredericksberg. But after the battle he had severe pains in his chest and palpitations. Between the pains and the palpitations he was unable to move. Subsequently the symptoms recurred during military duties, especially while on the march. After being wounded in the battle of Gettysburg he was so incapacitated that he was confined to bed.

Da Costa could find no evidence of a structural change in the heart – there were no murmurs of the type that might result from the valves not working, and no irregularities of the pulse. He concluded that the disorder might be functional in the sense of arising from an irritability conveyed to the heart by the action of the recently discovered sympathetic nerves. Irritable heart or Da Costa's syndrome was later diagnosed in soldiers following the Franco-Prussian War of 1870 and the Boer Wars of the 1890s.

Da Costa's syndrome is a term still in use today, for chest pains in men without an obvious cardiac cause – it is the commonest cause of cardiac investigations, a male version of Briquet's syndrome. Another term for it is a cardiac neurosis, which Freud admitted to having, although at a time when its implication was decidedly physical rather psychological.[5] It might also be called an anxiety neurosis. But there was no such term as anxiety neurosis in 1870. Westphal had described agoraphobia in 1871 and obsessive-compulsive disorder in 1878. In 1893 Hecker had distinguished a state corresponding to Da Costa's syndrome and called it anxiety neurosis but meant by this, like Da Costa, a state in which the nerves to the heart were somehow physically disturbed. In contrast Wernicke in 1894 described an anxiety psychosis – a state closer to the modern notion of an anxiety neurosis.

In 1895 Freud distinguished between neurasthenia, which he still saw as an actual neurosis caused by excessive masturbation, and anxiety neurosis, which was a psycho-neurosis whose form was determined by the psychological effects of failing to complete the sexual act properly – as in coitus interruptus.[6] This he held was even the case where the condition came on, for example, in a man who had just received news of his father's death. Close questioning he argued would reveal that such a man would perhaps have been practising coitus interruptus for several years and that the news was only the final precipitant of the disturbance. Unlike Da Costa's syndrome, which came to be reserved for conditions that affected the heart predominantly, the term anxiety neurosis came to be applied to states where there might be fainting today, chest pains tomorrow and diarrhoea the day after.

THE CRUCIBLE OF WAR[7]

These developments in the understanding of anxiety and hysteria laid the seeds for a conflict between the medical view that the neuroses involved an hereditary degeneration; an environmentalist view as espoused by Janet (and originally by Freud); and the subsequently developed psychoanalytic views. The First World War was to provide the first important testing ground.

However one conceives of the problem, what we can term for the moment 'battle neuroses' were not new. Herodotus giving an account of the battle of Marathon in 490 BC described the case of Epizelus, the son of Cuphagorus:

[This] Athenian soldier was fighting bravely when he suddenly lost the sight of both eyes, though nothing had touched him anywhere – neither sword, spear nor missile. From that moment, he continued to be blinded as long as he lived. I am told that in speaking about what had happened to him he used to say that he fancied he was opposed by a man of great stature in heavy armour whose beard overshadowed his shield, but the phantom passed him by and killed the man at his side.[8]

Unlike in previous wars, from early in the First World War a remarkably large number of soldiers succumbed to traumatic neuroses. The condition was popularly termed shellshock. The stigmata of shellshock were amnesia, loss of sight or of hearing, aphonia, paralyses and contractures. These are essentially Janet's symptoms of hysteria. Da Costa's syndrome and a range of anxiety neuroses were also found. The number of soldiers affected steadily increased during the course of the war. It is estimated that over a quarter of a million from the British ranks alone were affected. Of these a greater proportion were from among the officer ranks. This posed a problem for degeneracy theory. Could so many have hereditary degeneration? Could hereditary degeneration afflict the ruling classes even more than the working classes? How was such a problem to be managed?

Shellshock appears to have been far more common during the First World War than in any previous war, which might argue against a psychological interpretation. Medical authorities opposed to the idea of a psychological disorder offered one possibility – the shells from which it got its name. These were deployed for the first time on a large scale in the First World War. There were several cases of individuals who had been killed by shells exploding nearby but who seemed superficially uninjured. A handful of these at post mortem were found to have minor tears and haemorrhages in their spinal cords. This is not dissimilar to the effects of concussion, which can kill and leave similar sequelae – or to those of whiplash. It was argued that these blast effects might give rise to shellshock.[9] There was even some speculation that the bullet-wind of machine-guns might potentially bring about similar damage. Another concept invoked was diachisis, which involved a supposed alteration of physiological connections between areas of the brain consequent on an insult, whether a stroke or trauma of either physical or psychological origin.[10]

The issue was important as there seemed to the medical establishment to be only two options. One was that there was a genuine neurological disorder, in which case the soldier might be invalided home and would be entitled to a pension. (Da Costa, as befits a military surgeon, had solved this problem as regards cardiac conditions by postulating that the sympathetic nerves were actually genuinely disordered and affecting the heart as a consequence.) The other option was malingering/cowardice. In this case court martial was a strong possibility, as was execution. The numbers involved may well have been the only thing that prevented mass execution. Sufficient courts martial could not have been held, whatever the logistics of organizing the executions. Many it seems felt that executions might be called for, if only as a discouragement to others, given the proportions of the problem and the risk of mass defections from the front line. An alternative solution would have been possible if psychologists could reliably distinguish shellshock from malingering. They couldn't, but despite difficulties in making the distinction it was nevertheless widely accepted that the two were different conditions. The arguments offered were a variation on the theme of: although I may not be able to tell you what the difference is between a pony and a donkey, I usually know it when I see it.

If the physical effects of shells impacting did not cause shellshock in other than a small proportion of cases, was there anything unique about the First World War that could account for the disorder? A consensus of opinion points toward one further possibility. In this, as in no previous war, troops were unskilled and the technologies with which the war was fought were frighteningly impersonal. The role of the average soldier and officer was simply to stay in trenches while subjected to aerial bombardments, and to go over the top to provide cannon fodder when ordered. There was no scope for individual skill in the art of combat, no scope for strategic cutting and running, as in previous wars, and no scope therefore for exerting an element of personal control over one's fate. More than in any other war there was a clash between duty and likely survival. This, I will argue later, provides just the kind of stimulus liable to produce a psychological as opposed to a mental or neurological disorder.

Alienists and analysts[11]

Martin Stone notes that in both the popular and academic minds the influence of Freud is credited with the transformation of psychiatry in our times from a pessimistic, asylum-based discipline to a community-oriented, relatively optimistic science. In the popular view psychoanalysis supposedly emphasized the environmental determinants of mental illness and posited common links between normal mental functioning and abnormal psychological states. However we have seen that the belief that psychoanalysis supported an environmentally determined view of mental illness seems rather to have been an after-glow from the original seduction hypothesis.

Nowhere is this more clear than in analysts' views about shellshock. In seeking to tackle the problem the army turned not to asylum-based alienists (the old term for psychiatrist), who appeared to have little to offer, but rather to psychologists, who were quick to offer their services. A wide variety of psychodynamic therapists took part in the war effort. It was found by many that cures could be achieved by enabling the individual to remember trauma that had happened to them. To those therapists who were not analysts it seemed impossible to believe that pre-existent sexual problems could be at the heart of the condition. It seemed much more obvious to talk in terms of purely environmentally determined fear.[12-14]

Far from accepting this view the psychoanalysts saw what was happening as a magnificent confirmation of their beliefs. In war, they argued, the repressions of civilized life were dropped and barbarism rose to the surface. Commanding officers were literally father-figures, or older brothers, furnishing the affected victims with a rerun of infantile situations and arousing primal sadistic and homosexual impulses. The outer war reflected the primal war of infancy. Shellshock was merely the environmental trigger that brought about collapse. In favour of this they noted that many cases arose that were not the consequence of involve-

ment in a shocking situation. Commenting on the war neuroses consequent on the Second World War Otto Fenichel was later to remark that
'trauma that upset the entire economy of the mental energy also of
necessity upsets the equilibrium between the repressed impulses and the
repressing forces'.[15] Or as Freud himself put it, repression, which lies at
the basis of all neuroses, involves a reaction to primal trauma.[16] Indeed
the very war itself, he argued, represented a demonstration of the basic
truths of psychoanalysis, showing that so-called civilization rested on a
basis of repressed primal impulses. Men in war do not sink so low as
people think; rather it is people in peace who have not risen so high as
they believe.[17]

Despite losing much of its scientific legitimacy in the eyes of many as
a result of such views, psychoanalysis, as the best organized, most coher-
ently formulated and most vehemently proselytizing psychotherapy was
well placed at the end of the First World War to take advantage of the
drastic institutional and legislative changes forced on asylum psychiatry
by the war. Paradoxically the other group well placed were the asylum
psychiatrists.

Ever since the asylum-building movement in the nineteenth century
there had been a tension between medical and social approaches to a
number of the mental disorders. In the absence of reliably demonstrable
medical lesions, social theorists argued that the medical establishment
had commandeered a range of problems that it had no real expertise in
treating and from which it had no right to exclude other interested
parties. In reply the medical establishment argued that, while no lesions
could be offered at present, the stigmata of the various conditions suggested that one would be found – besides which medical treatment saved
patients from misguided morality, which was often their lot under social
régimes. While hereditary degeneration as opposed to environmental
determinants could be invoked, asylum doctors got away with their
claims.

With shellshock the fragile hegemony of the alienists was compromised. Drastic changes were necessitated by the sheer size of the population of victims of shellshock. It was necessary to provide a range of
non-asylum based treatment facilities after the war for their management. The first outpatient clinics were opened and these provided the
nucleus of a new psychiatric service. In addition the spectacle of so many
of the finest and apparently most stable men developing shellshock put
a serious dent in the notion of degeneracy.

However while the war threatened traditional psychiatric beliefs it
also provided an opportunity for the extension of psychiatric power and

influence and paradoxically was *de facto* responsible for an increasing medicalization of social problems. Broadening public perceptions of what constituted mental problems was one thing but who was to treat them? Those who were already handling mental problems were inevitably best placed to continue in power.

A political compromise was arrived at, in which professions other than the medical profession were introduced into the mental health arena, as part of the mental health team, under the medical aegis. Effective political power therefore remained concentrated in the hands of a group whose private sympathies were often still with the degeneracy view and whose professional commitment was to finding the biological faults or failings at the heart of the neuroses. A degeneracy view therefore survived in both medical and psychological camps, despite the evidence of the war and in the face of an increasing public consensus. And as the Second World War was to show, medical and psychoanalytic views were to prove compatible bedfellows.

The Second World War[18–21]

The Second World War provided a second round in the contest between medical, analytic and environmental establishments. Knowing something of what to expect, the medico-political response to shellshock was more sophisticated this time around.

Discharges from battle for battle neuroses were to be without pensions as, it was thought, the possibility of obtaining pensions would be conducive to such reactions. More important, a clear decision was taken on all sides to suppress information about the possibility of war neuroses. It was held that public interest in neurotic reactions was a good breeding ground for the manifestation of symptoms in potential neurotics. Where information was disseminated it was to the effect that there was an almost unlimited human resistance to stress and that breakdown implied that the subject must have something else wrong with them. While a stressful precipitant was not denied, it was argued in Europe that there had to be a constitutional predisposition to neurotic reactions before the effects of shock could be seen as neuroses. The appeal to a neurotic constitution was an updating of nineteenth-century degeneracy theories. This was advocated most forcefully by William Sargant and Eliot Slater, who were to be among the most eminent of British psychiatrists after the war. The evidence for the supposed neurotic constitution was almost entirely lacking.

In America poor parenting was held to be the cause. One American study cited as evidence the fact that 66 per cent of war neurotics had been nail-biters at some time. In the same study it was claimed that the fathers of typical war neurotics were sadistic and alcoholic while the mothers were nervous and over-solicitous.

Sargant and Slater argued that the mechanism behind shellshock was similar to what had happened to Pavlov's dogs after a flood in his Leningrad laboratory. Pavlov had been working on the conditioning of reflexes as the basis of behaviour. Dogs trained to associate feeding with the ringing of a bell came to salivate when a bell was rung. After a flood in his laboratory Pavlov had claimed that those dogs with the weakest constitutions came off worse and were often untrainable afterwards. In contrast the shock was sometimes beneficial to dogs with better constitutions. There is no record of what constituted a good or a bad constitution other than Pavlov's opinion. Sargant and Slater argued that those suffering from war neuroses were 'emotionally immature, constitutionally anxious or had personalities that were otherwise feeble, fragile or unstable . . . Many such men if permitted to live out their life in peace would never have known what it was to shake, sweat, tremble and be woken by nightmares.'[22] Added to this were observations that individuals rarely showed signs of collapse if they had not also lost considerable amounts of weight. This observation stemmed directly from the observations of Weir Mitchell on neurasthenia in the 1870s. He argued that potentially aberrant nervous functioning was laid bare by weight loss, and treated the condition by the famous rest cure. This involved rest but also a concerted effort to get the patient to gain weight – two or three stone if possible. In the Second World War an updated form of this involved the use of insulin to promote weight gain.

Sargant and Slater also invoked the evidence of a seemingly successful physical treatment. Heavy sedation with barbiturates, it was claimed, would often reverse the effects of shellshock if the individual was treated shortly after its onset – but not if the condition had become chronic. Towards the end of the war ECT came into clinical use and also appeared to be useful in many cases. This at the time was thought to be useful in shellshock by virtue of a 'depatterning' effect which would interrupt recent learning.

In America it was argued that the constitutional basis of the war neuroses lay in fundamental Freudian dynamics. As Grinker and Spiegel put it the subsequent nightmares of past battles in distant lands took the place of nightmares about the subject's real fears – pilots who had dreams of planes exploding in mid-air were actually displaying their fears of a first sexual encounter. There was debate as to whether the war neuroses were real neuroses, in that they often occurred in apparently normal characters and often appeared to clear up completely. Grinker and Spiegel argued for their neurotic reality on the basis of their sharing common mechanisms with real neuroses – regression, repression etc. Recovery, they argued, came about because a temporary retreat from reality allowed the Ego to gain much needed gratification and hence strength to regroup and continue. After draining themselves by giving their all such soldiers needed replenishment, which would happen by the natural developmental mechanism supposedly found in children – that of demanding constantly and not giving anything. When their officers or authority figures were not forthcoming this could, as in the case of children, call forth sullenness and rebelliousness.

Grinker and Spiegel argued strongly for the use of brief focused psychotherapies for such conditions. Thus a soldier who had lost a comrade and felt guilty about the loss but also guilty at feeling some antagonism to the dead comrade might be shown to have really been reacting to the potential loss of a brother or father. The comrade perhaps could be shown to be someone with whom the soldier was competing in some way – to kill the greater number of the enemy for example – in a manner similar to the way he had competed previously with a brother. The 'irrational' emotions towards the dead comrade could then be attributed to the earlier relationship. Such insights apparently solved the problem.

Chemical abreaction

Stemming from the experience of both the British and the Americans during the war a further development took place. It was found that under sedation abreactions could be successfully conducted. And as sedation with barbiturates was much easier to produce than hypnosis it increasingly took over. Amphetamines were sometimes added to the barbiturate to excite the individual emotionally in the hope that if sedation did not knock out his censor then it might be overwhelmed by a combination of psychic excitement and physical immobility. There were modest successes with this line of treatment.

Forty years ago such chemical abreactions were a regular part of practice in psychiatric hospitals. As they have completely gone out of vogue now one can only assume that the gains were relatively modest. But one consequence of this form of treatment was that abreaction (the quintessential psychological treatment) was medicalized, as only medically trained individuals were to be entrusted with these potent psychoactive agents. Furthermore, while disappearing from hospital practice, the influence of such approaches did not disappear. Arguably a further consequence of this approach was the widespread chemical tranquillization of anxiety that began developing during the 1960s, ending up in the 1970s and 1980s as a major iatrogenic problem. Only now does the tide seem to be turning.

THE SUPPRESSION OF HYSTERIA

Once the Second World War was over orthodox academic interest in the traumatic neuroses appears to have dissipated very quickly. Within a few years the textbooks no longer had a separate section on them; even Slater and Roth's classic *Clinical Psychiatry*,[23] perhaps the most authoritative of the British textbooks, dropped its separate section on these disorders. They were subsumed under the section on hysteria. Hysteria itself shrank progressively in size in textbooks and became an increasingly rare diagnosis. This, I hope to show, was not the consequence of medical advances but rather medical suppression.

Slater[24-7]

In 1965 Eliot Slater administered what is widely seen, among an older generation of psychiatrists, as the *coup de grâce* to hysteria, in an article carried in the *British Medical Journal*. With caveats, he was prepared to accept the use of 'hysterical' as an adjective to describe certain reactions a subject might have. But he firmly set his sights against the notion of hysteria as an entity in its own right. It was never diagnosed, he said, other than as an assertion of a universal negative – that is, if the subject had no physical illness and was not depressed or schizophrenic then in the absence of anything else they were diagnosed as hysterical. There were no true features that hysteria had that might not be produced by other illnesses. Even dissociation, he argued, was entirely normal; anyone who looks through a microscope dissociates from what the unused eye might be seeing. A diagnosis of hysteria rested on the absence of any other diseases and typically also, he wrote, on dislike of a patient or on the bizarre quality of their presentation.

Taking a sample of ninety-nine patients seen during the 1950s in the National Hospital and given the diagnosis of hysteria, Slater could not satisfy himself that they possessed any common features. Many, he claimed, had been misdiagnosed as they later showed up with real conditions. Many others failed to get well and appear to have been excluded as a result of their chronicity. Others presented again later with different clinical features for which again no diagnosis could be found. This he noted was the common experience of many of the follow-up studies done on subjects who had been labelled as having hysteria.

In the face of this broadside it quickly became almost impossible to make a diagnosis of hysteria in Britain. Anyone doing so was liable to end up with egg on their face, as it was assumed that Slater's data proved that the patient would later turn up with a real disorder that retrospectively could be seen to have caused the initial symptoms. Besides this implication there was also the suggestion that diagnosing hysteria indicated psychological difficulties on the part of the diagnoser almost as much as on the part of the patient.

While Slater ends his classic article with the admonition that the diagnosis of hysteria is a disguise for ignorance and a fertile source of clinical error, and as such both a snare and a delusion, this is not the whole story. In the 1969 edition of Slater and Roth's *Clinical Psychiatry* hysteria is presented in a very nuanced and balanced way. The term 'hysterical illness' is used widely. Its psychological origins are noted. The clinical features of trances, amnesias and splitting of the personality are described in detail. Therefore the marvellous piece of medical polemic that is the *BMJ* article stands somewhat apart from other views with which Slater's name can be associated. The impact of the *BMJ* article would seem to reflect a willingness of the general psychiatric establishment to receive a negative view of hysteria. One explanation that can be offered for this is that the generation of therapists who had most doubted the existence of hysteria could not afford to acknowledge its reality: as members of the war effort they could not afford to accept that war was psychologically damaging. Better dead than discharged from service was the medical position in the Second World War, as discharge to recover from nerves, it was thought, would increase the general level of disaffection with the war effort.

The contributions of psychiatrists to the war effort from both sides of the Atlantic, from a perspective of forty years' remove, read very naïvely indeed. That therapy during the war was a mask for social engineering is all too evident. This being the case it might be expected that such a generation would seize on apparent 'scientific' support of their position.

Slater's views should also be seen against a background of his own deeply held wish that psychiatry should become as scientific as other branches of medicine. Only physical treatments that could be adequately standardized and reliably delivered, he felt, could bring about such a scientific basis and allow the psychiatrist to 'cut the cackle'.

There was a dark side to this however. In line with the experience of modified insulin treatment of the war neuroses Sargant and Slater after the war in their best-selling *Physical Methods of Treatment in Psychiatry* advocated the use of insulin coma treatment for schizophrenia and prefrontal leucotomy for refractory conditions of all sorts. As they delivered their message it appeared that their advocacy was based solely on unimpeachable evidence. However within a few years of the appearance of this book insulin coma therapy had disappeared entirely and the supposed evidence for it had been shown to be worthless.[28] Prefrontal leucotomy followed almost immediately afterwards. While many psychiatrists trained in that generation are still wary of using the term hysteria there are others who can be found to wonder how they came to be conned into using the physical treatments advocated by Sargant and Slater.[29] This point is important, as much of the public support for the anti-psychiatry movement of the 1960s almost certainly came not from opposition to the theoretical tenets of orthodox psychiatry, as pilloried by R. D. Laing, but rather from deep-seated unease at the methods of treatment being used.

Crazy like a fox[30]

There are many other reasons why the present mental health establishment might have reservations about hysteria. I have suggested elsewhere that most bizarre behaviour is psychological in origin. Actual disturbances of neuropsychological functioning, when they occur, do not – except in a very small number of patients – give rise to truly bizarre behaviour. The lack of insight typically associated with a psychosis cannot be shown to be the result of cerebral dysfunction but rather is far more plausibly explained as a set of psychological *reactions* to underlying dysfunctions. It follows from this that a great many of the patients who become chronic psychiatric patients must do so for neurotic reasons rather than by virtue of having a severe psychosis. If so the appropriate treatment of such patients will embrace psychological approaches rather than simply rely on drug treatments alone. These issues go to the heart of the ambiguities inherent in the word psychosis.

Psychiatry appears to have a blind spot for this point. We are quite happy to claim that many 'gastro-intestinal' problems have no organic basis in gut disorder. We do not call this condition hysteria at present but rather Briquet's syndrome. Similarly we have been able to show that the commonest cause for cardiac investigations in *civilian* populations is effort syndrome/Da Costa's syndrome/cardiac neurosis. Again this is not called hysteria. But we do not seem to see that exactly the same point might apply to the mental disorders. We have no problems in seeing that 'hysterics' may simulate gut or cardiac problems or epilepsy, but we do not appear to expect any of them to simulate madness. This point was noted by Janet, who argued that most seemingly psychotic behaviour involves acting and should not be taken seriously. Supposedly psychotic patients, he claimed, often try to impress by the grandeur of their guilt, in which they themselves believe only half-heartedly or not at all.

Perhaps a reason for our being particularly blind to these aspects of madness today can be found in the fact that the dominant language and paradigm of psychiatry has for two decades now been solely biological. It is very difficult to fit notions of playfulness or inconsistency into formulations such as the dopamine hypothesis of schizophrenia or the catecholamine theories of depression. And yet all the evidence points to the fact that the presentation of hysteria adopts the illness language of the day.

A particularly dramatic example of what is involved has recently come to light in the case of Charcot's *grande hystérie*. With Charcot's death and the rise of the dynamic psychologies, neurology and psychiatry went separate ways. Neurologists were no longer interested in hysterical convulsions. At this time *grande hystérie* seemingly disappeared – so much so that many experts came to doubt that there ever really was such a clinical phenomenon. Charcot's patients must have been fooling him, it is hinted. However, far from disappearing completely, grand epileptiform hysteria was recently rediscovered in a Kentucky backwoods setting. It has been argued that the reason for this is because the modern myths of what are acceptable clinical presentations have not spread to such places.[31]

It may seem ironic, but any dispassionate reading of such evidence should suggest that there is nowhere better for modern hysteria to hide than in a psychiatric setting. The situation in psychiatry today is not unlike that of neurology in Charcot's day. We can reliably diagnose many conditions when they present in ideal forms. But our wards and practices are full of individuals who by force of diagnostic requirements get labelled atypical affective disorders or schizophrenics, who at best approximate to the criteria for these illnesses.

Hysteria and schizophrenia[32–3]

There is a further body of evidence that makes it likely that many of our chronic psychotic patients are in fact hysterical rather than anything else. As originally conceived by Kraepelin dementia praecox and hysteria had little in common. Dementia praecox was a chronic disorder characterized by delusions and hallucinations and commonly also by clear organic impairments of cognitive functioning. It occurred more often in males than in females. But in 1907 Eugen Bleuler postulated that the fundamental pathology in the disorder involved a splitting of cerebral functions, and accordingly rechristened the disorder schizophrenia.[34] The basis for this splitting according to Bleuler involved a physical loosening of associations.

Bearing in mind the reflex-associationist models of mental functioning outlined in Chapter 1 and conceptions of hysteria as involving aberrant reflexes and associations, this new disorder, while in severe cases looking quite different to hysteria, was conceptually almost identical to it. Added to this was the fact that, if loosening of associations was the basis for schizophrenia, there presumably would have to be milder forms of the disorder, as well as the severe forms that ended up in institutions. How different then would these milder forms look to hysteria?

Is it a coincidence then that the decline in the use of the term hysteria coincided with the introduction of the term schizophrenia? Just as hysteria had at one point subsumed a large part of all psychiatric disorder, so by the mid-1950s, especially in the USA, almost all psychiatric patients apparently had schizophrenia – and a great number of the general population seemingly had latent forms of the disorder. In part the reason for this was almost certainly the looseness of diagnostic criteria for schizophrenia, as it was conceived by Bleuler. Any splitting between thought, emotion and conduct was liable to lead to suspicions of schizophrenia. The very name implies a splitting of mental functions. And indeed the popular conception of schizophrenia appears to be of a disorder of multiple personalities, which for Janet in 1907 was actually an extreme form of hysteria.

There were attempts to resist the expansion of schizophrenia in this way. A number of investigators held out for the concept of an hysterical psychosis.[35–6] The term schizoaffective psychosis was introduced to cover disorders that did not quite seem like classic schizophrenia and yet were more complex than the usual cases of affective disorder.[37] This term was frequently criticized from a theoretical point of view but was also widely used. What few people realize was that one of the original criteria for a diagnosis was the occurrence of some precipitating trauma or failure in love. I would argue that the difficulties in resisting the expansion of schizophrenia, noted above, lay in a failure to distinguish between delusional disorders and psychoses.[38] This point will be picked up again in Chapter 10.

In the late 1960s there was a reaction to the loose use of the term schizophrenia and the number of schizophrenics dropped, particularly in the USA (with a corresponding expansion in the number of affective disorders). But even so a recent study, in which a rigorous version of Schneider's first-rank symptoms was used as diagnostic criteria for schizophrenia, found that only 20 per cent of those now being labelled as schizophrenic met strict criteria for the illness.[39] If not schizophrenia, what do the other 80 per cent have, and what is the cause of their symptoms?

POST-TRAUMATIC STRESS DISORDER[40-4]

After the Second World War American views on the traumatic neuroses remained heavily analytic in their orientation and geared towards overt social engineering in their implications. As late as 1975 reviews of traumatic neuroses based on Second World War material discussed the issues in terms of simple anxiety reactions occasioned, for example, by the need for the infantryman to keep quiet as he lay in wait for combat, thus inhibiting the natural aggressive responses of posturing and yelling. This could be allayed by the example of courageous generals, who if they led their men vigorously from the front (in the American style) had a much lesser incidence of traumatic neuroses among their troops. The troops it seems were often seen as meeting their passive dependency needs by the solidarity of battlefield company. This was shown by the fact that they usually broke down when it came close to going home, owing, it was claimed, to the potential loss of battlefield solidarity and the imminent need to stand adultly on their own two feet.[45]

While it was recognized that there were still some veterans who appeared to be having difficulty as a result of their war experiences, the problem was supposedly quite small. However there were a number of factors that meant that the traumatic neuroses engendered by the Second World War were not going to slip readily beneath the carpet. In the first place there were the concentration camp survivors, many of whom emigrated to the United States. These individuals could not all be dismissed as being disturbed before the event. Many remained disturbed indefinitely afterwards. There were also a number of ongoing wars such as the Korean war and the Arab-Israeli conflict. But above all there was the Vietnam war.

There were two unusual features to the Vietnam war. One was the extent to which the civilian population were aware of what was going on at the battlefront. The other was the extent to which it was possible to escape from active service by draft dodging, political influence or illness. Military psychiatrists blamed this public awareness doubly – in the first instance because of difficulties it posed to indoctrination, and in the second instance because not only was there not the unthinking acceptance necessary for indoctrination but also there was a positive public rejection of what the soldiers were doing. This more than anything else led to an atmosphere in which the difficulties that returning veterans were having were made salient. It led to the official recognition of a post-traumatic stress syndrome.

Furthermore, given that the Vietnam war did not require mass mobilization, the position of the psychiatrist was quite different. In the previous world wars there was a need to get the soldier back to the front line. As Grinker and Spiegel put it, the job of a psychiatrist was to provide a good relationship in the midst of all that was going on – but a good relationship which involved a return to duty.[46] This was as much a Catch 22 for the psychiatrist as for the soldier. Whereas in civilian life the therapist could avoid advising the patient on what to do, in the Second World War they had to take responsibility for 'stimulating the patient's motivation, set their goals and direct their sublimations'. None of this applied in Vietnam.

This led in 1980 to the establishment of post-traumatic stress disorder as a separate diagnostic category. As already mentioned in the Introduction to this book, this was the first time ever that a psychiatric diagnostic system recognized the possible existence of a wholly environmentally determined psychiatric disorder. This I am sure runs against the grain of popular expectation.

Previous editions of the American diagnostic manual (*DSM* I and *DSM* II) and the various versions of *ICD* all had sections for adjustment reactions. But as the term reaction implies these were not seen as autonomous disorders. If they became chronic the implication was that there must be something else wrong with the individual. Equally if one had a neurosis (an autonomous psychological disorder) under these systems it was implied that there must have been a pre-existent personality or biological abnormality, according to the orientation of the diagnostician.

The essential feature of PTSD, as defined in *DSM* III, was the development of symptoms following a psychologically distressing event that lies outside the range of normal experience. The event was not supposed to be just bereavement or a business loss but rather something like involvement in a combat situation, a hostage situation or some natural disaster for example. PTSD however has rapidly broken through these restrictions.

Of equal importance however *DSM* III goes on to describe the disorder in terms of the experiences of the sufferer. These typically involve:

[a subsequent] re-experiencing of the traumatic event, in the form of recurrent, intrusive recollections or dreams and nightmares or absences (dissociations) in which the event may be relived to the extent of the person acting as though they are once again present at the scene. Recurrent waves of emotion often precede overt recollection or may occur independently. There is usually an avoidance of stimuli associated with the event, which may even amount to an apparent amnesia for the occurrence of a trauma. Intense distress may be experienced, when reminders such as anniversaries are unavoidable or on exposure to events or objects that may symbolize some aspect of the traumatic experience.

Aside from the recognition that a disorder might be environmentally precipitated, this simple description of the disorder in terms of the experiences of the sufferer and especially the references to recurrent intrusive imagery and waves of emotions is almost unique in the psychiatric literature. Not since Freud in 1895 had psychological problems been described in this way.

DSM III goes on to note that very frequently subjects take to alcohol or drugs to blot out awareness of the distressing events. There is a concomitant increase in arousal, shown for example in a liability to be easily startled. Subjects may also find it difficult to get to sleep or to stay asleep. Commonly there are difficulties concentrating and increases in irritability. Alongside this there is a psychic numbing – a feeling of being detached from or removed from others.

The recognition of post-Vietnam PTSD has led also to an awareness of the enduring reactions of many Second World War soldiers, which in the absence of an appropriate framework had been all but invisible. It also became clear that many of the descriptions of the veterans of previous wars mapped readily on to the new criteria – such as intrusive nightmares and the occurrence of episodes of dissociation and the experience of reliving rather than just remembering past events.

Rape trauma syndrome[47]
If a trauma can in principle cause a relatively longlasting disorder in normal people, perhaps traumata less severe than the holocaust or natural disasters such as earthquakes may do something similar. At no point are criteria spelt out as to the severity needed to induce disorder in normal people. It is now accepted that rape is a potential precipitant. The term rape trauma syndrome was coined by Burgess and Holmstrom in 1974.

A good deal of work has now been done on this condition. In the course of a rape a variety of dissociative phenomena occur, in particular derealization – 'this is not happening' – along with depersonalization – 'this is not happening to me'. Immediately afterwards there may be amnesia for the event. In the course of a rape there is also a submissive quasi-paralysis. This play-dead reaction is a prewired autonomic response to stress, which leads for example a mouse to hang limply when a cat picks it up by the neck and to remain apparently dead when then deposited on the ground by the cat prior to playing with it. Submission however in the case of rape is invariably interpreted by the rapist as acquiescence – and sometimes also, it would appear, by the judge at a later trial. It may even be seen this way by the victim subsequently, who wonders why they put up no struggle, leading to self-blame or to the thought that they secretly did acquiesce.

Another feature of rape is that the victim may become very 'loving' towards their tormentor and very grateful when finally set free. This is a pattern of behaviour also found in hostage situations. It would appear to stem from the ambiguity inherent in the oppressor's being at the same time the only means of liberation.

There are marked similarities between the post-rape syndrome and the PTSD of war veterans. Victims in particular relive the rape in flashbacks. Those awakened from sleep by the rapist often end up waking up most nights close to the time of the event. A variety of physical symptoms set in, including headaches, insomnia or sleep with nightmares, appetite problems, startle reactions. Subjects often become afraid to go to various places on their own. They may change phone number or move house or generally attempt to put as much distance between them and the event as they can. They may begin drinking or taking drugs.

Burgess and Holmstrom contend that rape does not bring about rape trauma syndrome by virtue of the sexual act involved so much as the violence entailed. A common finding post-rape was a distrust of everything, even of formerly safe places, people or occupations, as though the world had turned hostile. This is noteworthy in the light of Freudian claims for a sexual basis for all neuroses.

In addition to the support for PTSD that has come from rape trauma syndrome, a variety of natural (earthquakes) and man-made (bombings and hijackings) disasters in recent years have led many psychiatrists to become convinced of the reality of the disorder. This in turn has led to the growth of disaster medicine and to the recognition that PTSD can occur after less than overwhelming adversity. This would seem to be a conclusion that must be drawn from studies in which disaster counsellors exposed to the survivors of disasters themselves may develop PTSD symptomatology, even though not exposed to any personal risk.[48]

Neurosis or malingering?

The orthodox nineteenth-century medical view of traumatic neuroses resulting from train crashes or accidents in the workplace and leading to insurance claims was that there must be a real physical pathology in these cases to cause the clinical picture, or else that subjects were dissimulating to gain a reward. The experience of war did not shake the dominance of such approaches and this remained the position until the mid-1980s. The study most cited in favour of this position was carried out by Miller in 1960.[49] He found that 90 per cent of his sample went back to work once a court case had settled their financial compensation. Despite the fact that this study became the odd one out of an increasingly large number of studies its findings were appealed to as orthodox until the mid-1980s. Exactly why this should have been so is unclear; what is clear is that there are considerable financial and insurance implications riding on any reversal of the orthodox view.

The majority of studies, in contrast to Miller's, indicate that if subjects with disabilities for which no organic cause can be found have not gone back to work before their court case they are unlikely to go back afterwards.[50] This is the case whether they receive large amounts of compensation, small amounts or no compensation at all. It also appears to be the case that poor outcomes do not stem from any prior personality abnormality, do not correlate with previous poor work records and do not depend on any family abnormality.

There has however quite recently been a dramatic sea change in these matters. In 1976 the US Supreme Court ruled for the first time that a disaster could cause a psychological disorder that should be compensatable. This followed after the Buffalo Creek disaster, in which a dam broke and flooded 1,200 homes. Over and above the compensation paid for loss of life and property and personal injuries the court ruled that the event had left a significant number of survivors psychologically disturbed and that the Tennessee Water Authority had to pay compensation for this also.[51-2]

The comparable benchmark disaster in Great Britain was the *Herald of Free Enterprise* sinking in 1988 – although compensation had been paid for 'nervous shock' as early as 1970.[53-4] In a recent ruling on the Hillsborough disaster the courts have decided that an individual may be financially compensated for PTSD even without being present at a disaster – if they had watched disaster befall their relatives on television.

The significance of these decisions is twofold. One is that the psychological disorder in question, being a matter of intrusive thoughts and disturbance of emotions, is diagnosed on the basis of the self-reports of those affected. The other is that for the first time the courts recognized that an autonomous psychological disorder can be precipitated entirely by environmental factors – hence my contention in the Introduction that in the 1980s the psyche and specifically psychological disorders have become 'real' in a way they weren't before.

SEDUCTION AND HYSTERIA

In the late 1950s, a hundred years after Tardieu's reporting of the physical and sexual abuse of children, the problem resurfaced through the work of Kempe and colleagues in the USA.[55] Much of the impetus for this work came from X-rays of injured children. These showed, in the case of some children, the presence of multiple healed fractures or deformities that were not suspected at the time of initial clinical presentation. It took several years for the issue to be taken seriously. It also took, as it so often seems to do, the coining of an apposite title for the syndrome – the battered baby syndrome.

As with Tardieu the initial descriptions of the syndrome were predominantly in terms of physical injuries. The behaviour of the child, if referred to at all, was described in terms that, it was hoped, might prove useful diagnostically. The children were said to be quiet, timid, miserable or sullen. What might have been going through their minds was nowhere discussed.

As in the 1860s the issue developed and investigators became aware of sexual abuse as well as physical abuse and that the sexual assaults were most likely to come from relatives, especially from fathers. The occurrence of incest was rediscovered. An incredulous scientific and lay community have since watched while the estimates for the frequency of both physical abuse and incest have soared. In Britain the problem was particularly highlighted by the Cleveland sexual abuse controversy. But arguably the United States is even more concerned with the problem, and concern there has resulted in extensive support networks for recent and former victims of sexual abuse and an intensive effort to raise public consciousness on the issues.

As in the late nineteenth century the possible occurrence of abuse preceded any recognition that it might have serious psychological aftereffects. As late as 1975, in the *Comprehensive Textbook of Psychiatry*, there was no discussion of the inner mental states of abused children. In this huge, 2,707-page book, written by the most eminent American psychiatrists, there is no serious treatment of this issue. The section on child-battering discusses the mental state of the parent who batters, with the blame being put on the mother; the rising number of cases were put down to the rising level of violence in society generally.[56] In the section on incest it is noted that there is little agreement that father–daughter relationships cause serious psychopathology. It is presumed that they do not because 'the liaison satisfies instinctual drives in a setting where the mutual alliance with an omnipotent adult condones the transgression'.[57]

It has only recently become clear that this is not so. Increasingly the after-effects of child abuse have been formulated in terms of a PTSD, with the added complication of interference with a developmental process. Abused children, it seems, are afterwards subject to intrusive flashbacks and to waves of emotion without apparent cause. They become nervous, withdrawn and generally less trusting of their environment. In later life there is a higher incidence of depressive disorders, as well as drug and alcohol abuse. There is also an increased incidence of suicide attempts, self-mutilating behaviour and further episodes of victimization.[58–62] Furthermore, as mentioned in the last chapter, MPD is thought to originate most commonly in childhood assaults. The diagnosis of MPD is at present largely confined to America. But in addition to the core criteria necessary for such a diagnosis there are a number of accessory criteria, the presence of which make the diagnosis more likely. These consist of third-person auditory hallucinations, absences, headaches, nightmares, depersonalization, derealization and a generalized misery. Subjects presenting with such symptoms in Britain, where specific enquiries about childhood abuse are not routinely undertaken at psychiatric clinics, would be likely to be diagnosed as suffering from either depression or schizophrenia.

Borderline syndromes[63–4]

Another syndrome recently legitimated by *DSM* III is pertinent here. This is borderline personality disorder, which is characterized by a pattern of unstable and intense interpersonal relationships, impulsiveness, recurrent self-mutilation or attempted suicide, frantic efforts to avoid real or imagined abandonment and marked and persistent identity disturbance and a generalized sense of boredom and emptiness. Overlaid on this may be transient 'psychotic' disturbances.

The above makes up many people's picture of an hysteric. It fits with a number of Janet's descriptions. It also fits a description of hysteria by Sydenham from 1681:

the very slightest word of hope creates anger . . . They have melancholy forebodings. They brood over trifles, cherishing them in their unquiet bosoms. Fear, anger, jealousy, suspicion and the worst passions of the mind arise without cause . . . there is no moderation. All is caprice. They love without measure those whome they will soon hate.[65]

This disorder entered *DSM* III in 1980 but its parentage differed from that of MPD and PTSD. Borderline conditions began life as borderline schizophrenia or pseudo-neurotic schizophrenia – a mild form of the disorder in which there was loosening of associations and episodic 'psychotic' behaviour but not the chronic deterioration or first-rank symptoms typical of schizophrenia.

These conditions were then taken over by Kernberg and the object-relations school of analysis in the mid-1970s. This post-Freudian school, whose leading lights have included Melanie Klein, Winnicott, Fairbairn, Kernberg and Kohut, have in common a downplaying of the importance of instinctual drives and an emphasis on the differentiation of self from others. The borderline conditions, in which such differentiation is poor, were their flagship.

In a supreme historical irony however it now appears from recent research that up to 80 per cent of subjects with a diagnosis of borderline personality disorder have been the victims of seduction or assault in their past. In one sense this should be good news for object-relations theorists. However, while trying to reconstruct Freudian theory from within, they have never shown any interest in going back to 1895 to start again. Their contention has been that the basis for all subsequent psychological difficulties is laid down during the primary relationship between mother and infant. Such a view does not encourage a focus on the nature of any subsequent environmental traumata.

The unfolding of events here has been instructive. With increased interest in trauma a number of studies were undertaken of the incidence of childhood trauma in chronic psychiatric disorders, especially schizophrenia.[66] The results revealed that, of a sample of women diagnosed as having 'schizophrenia', half were liable to have been victims of childhood sexual assaults. Bearing in mind that multiple personalities usually emerge only with the help of a therapist, that one has to be dynamically oriented to even suspect the existence of borderline pathology, and bearing in mind that typically fewer than half of those diagnosed as having schizophrenia actually meet strict as opposed to loose criteria for the illness, do all these patients have schizophrenia?

The answer would appear to be almost certainly not. If criteria for borderline personality are applied to the same samples, 80 per cent and more of subjects who meet these criteria are liable to have been abused.[67-8]

Aside from producing non-specific psychoses, borderline states, MPD and post-traumatic neuroses, sexual abuse during childhood leads to an increased incidence of physical symptoms (Briquet's syndrome) in later life. In a study of a group of patients with confirmed sexual abuse in childhood Arnold, Rogers and Cook found their patients had a mean of eighteen non-psychiatric consultant appointments and eight operations each.[69] In these latter there was a two-thirds rate of normal findings in tissue removed at operation. This level of morbidity had not however led to inquiries about emotional difficulties or past histories of abuse.

The hazards of interpretation

A central issue thrown up by the discovery of widespread physical and sexual abuse is the need to establish the truth of what has happened. There has been concern about the validity of children's statements, which has led to an effort to find some independent marker. In physical abuse X-rays will often do this. In sexual abuse this concern led in Cleveland to what seems to have been excessive reliance on the anal dilatation reflex. But where it has been possible to confirm children's statements it seems that their claims are right in over 80 per cent of cases. The likelihood of fabrication seems to increase when there are concomitant factors such as divorce and custody proceedings.

There have been attempts to devise a method that would allow a decision to be made on the weight to be put on the child's statement. These attempts involve content analysis of the structure, details and consistency of the child's statement or statements. There have been claims by a number of researchers that such analyses do sift out the true from the false. Whether these claims can be accepted or not is uncertain. But the issues involved touch on almost all the points raised in previous chapters.

In the first place the amount of detail given by the child seems to depend on how experienced the interviewer is. Paradoxically it appears that the naïve and not the experienced interviewer gets more detail. This appears to be because the child acts as though given a licence to embroider when with a naïve interviewer. The amount of detail given to a male as opposed to a female interviewer may also differ, and the story offered is influenced by whether the child is with its mother. The current emotional state influences it, as does the probable emotional state at the time of the abuse. Whether the story has been told before affects the way it will be told on subsequent occasions. The expectations of the interviewer, and any leads they provide, will all too often colour the account, as the recent wave of satanic abuse clearly indicates.

This is what would be expected if remembering were seen as a purposeful act, a creation, rather than just a neutral reading from some tablets of stone. The purpose, as in any action, is to some extent determined by the situation in which the subject finds themself. Telling the story at all however affects it for ever – in much the way that going into the local corner shop more than once affects our memory of the shop. The more we shop there, the more our memory of shopping there will be a composite of the many times we have been there, and the more difficult it will be to remember any one episode of being there. Similarly after a traumatic interview for a job we replay the scene and dialogue in our minds repeatedly afterwards, touching up bits as we go on an if-only-I'd-said-this basis. This can get to the point where it becomes difficult if not impossible to remember what actually was said.

Applying all these factors to the question of establishing what happened in situations of possible abuse leads us to expect that even if the abuse did happen the child's story is likely to be inconsistent and contradictory. This follows as the truth of the matter is in a sense as much a fabrication as any possible other version of events. This will apply even to those cases in which subjects appear to be reliving events rather than just remembering them. Indeed the wealth of concrete detail that some subjects provide may seriously mislead the unwary. Interpretation will therefore inevitably remain a hazardous enterprise. It is ever a matter of establishing a probable account of what happened rather than supposedly scientifically 'proving' a point.

The example of subjects who claim to have photographic memories brings out the issues well. When asked to remember a piece of text or the details of a picture such subjects report clearly seeing an image of the page in their mind's eye. However if it is suggested to them that some details of their memory are wrong the image in their mind's eye changes accordingly.[70] Freud was prone to illustrating the validity of his contentions with etymological examples, in which for example the word for some action could be shown to have a sexual origin. Borrowing a leaf from his book we can note that even photographic memory involves a potentially hazardous *re-cognition* of what happened, rather than just a simple reseeing.

To add to the hazards of interpretation, a surprising finding has been that sexual abuse sexualizes. Far from being sexually inhibited, children who have been sexually abused often become forward and sometimes quite shocking in their language and behaviour. They play seduction with interviewers. This seems to be part of the general process of re-enacting or reliving that happens after trauma. A similar phenomenon occurs in children exposed to violence, who become aggressive and assaultive towards their peers. These effects wear away if the child is able to recover for some months in a supportive environment.

Such effects might be taken by some as giving some grounds (mistaken) for believing that the child rather than the adult was responsible for the abuse. Freud and his contemporaries can perhaps be forgiven for wondering if some degenerative mechanism of some sort must not be operating to produce such seeming perversity so young.

THE ENVIRONMENTAL PRECIPITATION OF NEUROSIS

A great deal of recent research supports the contention that trauma may precipitate neuroses. A number of reviewers have noted the similarity of the emerging picture to Janet's original formulations.[71-2] But surely these events are not so common that they could account for the creation of all neuroses – in which case it might be asked, are the *remaining* neuroses the result of some degeneracy?

A central aspect of the studies reviewed above suggests otherwise. It would appear to be the act of violence rather than the specifically sexual nature of seductions that leads to subsequent problems. This has become clear from studies which have shown very similar outcomes in children subjected to physical violence alone, without sexual abuse. It has also been found that being the witness of violence may be as damaging as being its direct victim. Thus children who witness assaults on their parents by burglars or murderers or who are exposed to the physical maltreatment of a mother by a father also show PTSD, a tendency to the development of borderline syndromes and Briquet's syndrome.[73] Given this, it becomes much more plausible to suggest that a very large number of neuroses are environmentally determined.

At the time of writing the findings of a British survey have just been published in which it has been claimed that up to one in four women have been raped at some point in their lives – most often by husbands or boyfriends. This replicates an earlier American study which contained a number of other disturbing findings.[74] One was that women raped by men they know are not the victims of some quasi-crime but are in fact more likely to be significantly injured in the course of the rape than are women raped by a stranger. Raped women are eleven times more likely to be depressed in later life than women who have not been raped, seven times more likely to have a social phobia and three times more likely to have an obsessive-compulsive disorder.

At this point I have to interject a personal confession. Influenced by an orthodox psychiatric training, I, like many of my colleagues, have not until recently systematically asked for a history of possible childhood trauma. Where such trauma has come to light against a background of manic-depression or a supposed schizophrenia I, and I am sure others, have been liable to regard it as unfortunate but to dismiss it as coinciden-tally occurring in a disorder that was constitutionally determined. But in taking histories now in the light of the emerging findings on trauma, and indeed on thinking back on individuals I have treated – particularly the ones who have failed to respond to the antidepressants or neurolept-ics they were prescribed – I am all too aware of traumas that I have noted but not acted on before. However, far from finding a high incidence of sexual abuse or a history of physical assaults, it has seemed to me that an equally large number of subjects who have dissociative or borderline symptoms have been the *witnesses* of abuse or have been *mentally* tortured. Particularly common have been stories of children being locked in bedrooms or in either cloakrooms or outhouses, sometimes for two or three days, sometimes left in their own urine, faeces or vomit, and sometimes to be faced in later life with a parent who is pleased with themselves for never having hit their child.

However there is a further question that anyone who is committed to an environmental point of view must answer. Why, if the disorder is environmentally precipitated, does it become as chronic as Briquet's syndrome, MPD and the borderline disorders appear to be? The full answer to this will have to await an outline of possible psychotherapeutic manoeuvres that might be undertaken in such states. This will be developed in Chapter 9. For the present however we can note that current research suggests that the after-effects of trauma depend to some extent on the level of support available to the child. An unknown proportion of sexually abused children who attempt to approach their mothers for support for example are confronted by someone who has herself been assaulted in the past. The response to the child in these circumstances is often quite negative and may even involve the spectacle of the mother breaking down, which of course compounds the situation facing the child.[75]

Dissociation and repression

In the next chapter I will argue that the core pathology of PTSD cannot be one of banishing traumatic memories to some unconscious to be kept there by defences, as Freud claimed. It must involve a dissociation of some sort – a lying outside of focused awareness. In Chapter 9 I will argue that this happens because the traumas that precipitate PTSD and the borderline disorders cannot be interpreted in terms of events that can be integrated adequately into a working model of the self.

Patients with borderline disorders however provide some interesting clues to something else that goes on in these states. If asked why they slash their wrists or attempt suicide, they often say that they do so to get some release or to defend against something worse happening – about which they are often uncertain.

The following case may perhaps make clear both the kinds of torture that may give rise to borderline disorders and what is involved in episodes of self-mutilation. To preserve anonymity I will call the individual concerned Sarah. I first saw Sarah after she had taken several overdoses. The antidepressants and neuroleptics she had been prescribed in the past had done little good. I saw her for a few sessions in which I tried to do what Freud had been doing in 1895 – to get the person concerned to call up images to their mind's eye. Towards the end of one session the phone rang in the office and I answered it. While I was talking Sarah proceeded to break the office up. To understand why requires a brief detour.

In early puberty, when the girls at school began to talk about developing pubic hair and breasts, Sarah became aware that she had had pubic hair for years and did not seem to be developing breasts. She later began to produce facial hair and to spend hours each day plucking it – in the end she was sometimes spending up to three or four hours a day doing so. Afraid of men, she spent time with women and was referred as a consequence to a psychiatrist because of her sexual orientation. He was of no help. The situation dragged on for years until in her late twenties she was diagnosed as having a minor biochemical abnormality in the production of sex hormones, which could readily be treated.

During the session in my office Sarah had revisualized an episode that had taken place in the school swimming pool. The boys had their hour first and then they filed out past the waiting girls. On one such occasion they noticed, or it seemed to Sarah they noticed, her lack of breasts and prominent *mons veneris* and began sniggering. It was this scene she was 'in', with all its concomitant rage, when the phone rang in my office. Later, when 'out' of this state, she said that her previous overdoses had all been taken to bring to an end a train of comparable intrusive images or a sense of rising foreboding. This appears true of the majority of self-harming episodes of individuals with borderline disorders; many other examples can be found in Jerome Kroll's authoritative book on the condition.[76]

The significant point here is that Sarah's behaviour, and the behaviour of many other individuals in comparable situations, involves a very conscious attempt to 'repress'. Such repression is for the most part within awareness. This is quite different to the Freudian notion of defensive repression, which not only supposedly acts to keep things out of awareness but is also itself out of awareness. Freud inferred the existence of such a repressive mechanism *indirectly* from what patients said; the individuals themselves did not, he believed, have direct access to the phenomenon.

Do such individuals have direct access? In favour of this is the fact that we all often, purposefully and consciously, repress certain impulses or defend against shameful or painful memories. This is usually quite successful – and there is no evidence that it is not also healthy. But it seems that in the case of the borderline disorders or PTSD this form of defence is not as adaptive, presumably because the trauma involved has stretched the natural limits of adaptability.

7 Project for a Scientific Psychology

Everything we find by experience to be in us which we can see in inanimate bodies must be attributed to our body alone. Everything in us which we conceive entirely incapable of belonging to a body must be attributed to our soul. Descartes, *Passions of the Soul:* Article 3.

In the first six chapters I have outlined the slow development of the notion that environmental stress may precipitate psychological disorder. As the idea is relatively simple and in some senses intuitively obvious this must mean that its failure to take hold indicates that there are other potent factors at play. In the case of the PTSDs and the impact of such a notion may have on the interests of a nation at war, what is at stake seems clear-cut and easily understood. Once the question of childhood trauma and the role it might play in the later development of psychological difficulties is raised, the picture begins to cloud over.

Around 1880, when this narrative opened, hysteria encompassed all the neuroses. Are the lessons suggested by PTSD applicable to the other neuroses, which from 1880 onwards began to crystallize out of the body of hysteria? What about obsessive-compulsive disorder or agoraphobia? The issues begin to develop in complexity when it comes to applying what we have learnt to the other neuroses. For instance some still say there is only one general neurotic condition, but *DSM* III notes up to nine different neuroses, without including for example alcoholism and other substance-dependent states. Is alcoholism a psychological problem? Does the difficulty in deciding this or deciding on the number of neuroses have anything to do with the issue of environmental precipitation of the neuroses in general and the legal and financial implications this might have?

But even where hysteria is concerned the issues are more complex than may seem apparent at this juncture in the book. If PTSD, MPD and the borderline disorders are caused by trauma, why do these conditions not respond relatively straightforwardly to a psychotherapy aimed at establishing what actually happened?

At stake here is an issue larger than just the question of the individual neuroses. At stake is the nature of the psyche and of psychotherapy. I have noted the recent switch in focus from the dynamic unconscious to consciousness. Consciousness is radically social in a way that the unconscious or the nervous reflexes of behaviourism are not. But what is consciousness? How do events enter consciousness? How does consciousness interact with its subconscious or unconscious substrates?

At stake also is the traditional view of mental illness. While post-traumatic stress disorders may be relatively rare, it is conceded that they may be severe. These are not mild disorders. This runs counter to the orthodox view that the neuroses are a set of mild disorders and as a consequence are of no great strategic importance in the battles for possession of the mental illnesses. How many other severe clinical conditions are essentially neurotic rather than psychotic?

The second half of this book will take up these issues. It will do so by working backwards from the most recent developments in the neurobiology of the unconscious and the advent of computer modelling of the psyche in this chapter to Descartes' initial distinctions between mechanical brains and spiritual minds in Chapter 10. In so doing it will become clear that the ramifications of the American Psychiatric Association's formulation of the concept of PTSD extend far beyond the questions of legal rights or financial compensation for the victims of trauma.

THE DEMISE OF BEHAVIOURISM[1-3]

There is no easy way to avoid complexity at this point. The best option seems to be to go in at the deep end with some of the puzzling kind of observations that led to the overthrow of behaviourism. In Chapter 4 I noted the emergence of behaviourism as the dominant psychological model of mental functioning from the mid-1930s onwards. It rose to its position of dominance by gaining control of the strategic ground of physiological plausibility. Its simple model of the mind in terms of reflex functioning had no more psychology than physiologists could understand and not enough physiology to confuse psychologists. But for a theory that put so much store on being physiologically appropriate behaviourism paid remarkably little heed to the brain. This oversight was raised from the start by Karl Lashley. According to behaviourists all behaviour must be constituted by sets of stimuli and their reflex or associated responses. It was assumed that these reflexes must be stored in the cortex. One of the reasons therefore that man's behaviour was more complex than that of animals might be simply a case of his having more storage space. But Lashley found himself unable to cause animals to lose the skills they had acquired in behavioural experiments by removing sections of their cortex.

Attempting to replicate Lashley's findings some years ago David Oakley and colleagues put normal and decorticate rats through a range of problem-solving tasks. There was no difference between the two groups on tasks that required only the ability to acquire habits – indeed the decorticate rats were if anything better at these. But where the solutions required an ability to generate or refer to an 'internal map' rats with a cortex did clearly better.[4]

Similar findings began to emerge from a number of laboratories in the late 1970s and early 1980s. Richard Hirsh proposed that the implication was that rats (and humans) can acquire both habits and memories and that these are stored separately.[5-6] Habits, he argued, are the result of classical behaviourist learning. Memories are something that can be recalled to mind – a model. In the case of memory I can resee what has happened in my mind's eye.

Work on the phenomenon of blindsight by Weiskrantz, Humphrey and others sheds some more light on the implications of the distinction drawn by Hirsh.[7] Blindness can result from disorders within the eye or the nerve running from the eye to the occipital cortex, or it can result from disturbances to the cortex itself. Subjects with cortical blindness experience themselves as blind. But when placed in front of objects they claim to be unable to see they nevertheless manage to locate them and pick them up much more often than other subjects who are blind. Typically they account for their apparent blindsight by saying that they can 'sense' objects in front of them.

This makes sense because it is known that some visual processing goes on in relay stations along the optic nerve before it reaches the cortex. For example we often blink to keep something out of our eyes before we have a chance to 'see' it. It now appears that subcortical systems manage such reflex reactions while cortical visual systems do the 'seeing', and that this seeing involves building up images or models of the environment.

Memories are to habits as 'seeing' is to sensing. They appear to involve the constructing of models, the complexity and detail of which depend on the requirements of the task in hand. The models can usually be visualized – remembering typically involves a reseeing in one's mind's eye. This point can be illustrated by a feature of Alzheimer's dementia. This cortical dementia leads in its early stages to a loss of memory but not to a loss of the ability to acquire habits. For instance when introduced to me a patient with Alzheimer's will typically not be able to remember my name two or three minutes later. They may not remember me introducing myself, even though I may have done so on several occasions. But if I then show a list of names and ask them to pick out mine they will often plump for the right one, with an uncertain question, 'Could it be David Healy?' What seems to be happening is that the repetition of my name has *primed* them to picking it out from a pool of other strange names, even though they cannot replay in their mind's eye a scene in which I introduced myself to them.

A French physician, de Claperede, made similar observations on patients with Korsakoff's psychosis – an alcohol-induced amnesia. De Claperede introduced himself to a woman with Korsakoff's one day by shaking hands with a pin in his hand. The next day she refused to shake hands but could give no reason for her reluctance. In general even though patients with Korsakoff's cannot remember they can learn new skills, even though they will never remember how or when or where they learnt them. They cannot resee in their mind's eye the time and place of learning.

Alzheimer's disease also brings out the close links between perception and memory. For example when shown the letters of the alphabet in Figure 2 subjects with Alzheimer's will typically be unable to make them out. The point here is that if they are unable to perceive correctly quite simple shapes on a piece of paper it is not so surprising that a kind of memory that involves a *reseeing* in the mind's eye should also be failing.

Such findings, which appear to demand the existence of internal maps or images, return us to the position that Tolman found himself in in the 1930s, before he was swept away by the tide of behaviourism. Now however the tide is running the other way. This is due principally to the advent of computer modelling of mental processes, which began in the late 1950s. One might have expected that such a radically unconscious automaton as a computer would once and for all have permitted the scientific analysis of behaviour without recourse to mental imagery. Ironically however computers have indicated how psychological functions might operate through the genesis of models and images, and in so doing have provided a 'neurobiological' rationale for the further exploration of consciousness.

Fig. 2 These are degraded letters of the alphabet. Ordinarily, looking at them the individual will have little difficulty making out which letter of the alphabet is involved. Subjects with certain brain disorders however will be unable to make out the letters that are suggested in these series of dots. They will be unable to see the wood for the trees.

At roughly the same time as computers came into psychology there was also a set of significant developments in the neurobiology of the subcortical areas of the brain – the seat of habits. As will become clear, far from being a simple reflex system or some unitary psychoanalytic Id, current findings suggest that these brain areas comprise a multi-system structure, the various parts of which operate in different ways.

THE ANATOMY OF THE UNCONSCIOUS[8–9]

As early as the eighteenth century Winslow had observed that there was a network of ganglia running alongside the spinal column, from which nerves ran to the heart, lungs, gut and genito-urinary organs. This he termed the sympathetic nervous system. Another complementary system was subsequently identified and called the parasympathetic nervous system. In 1898 James Langley suggested that the sympathetic and para-sympathetic systems formed part of an autonomic nervous system – so called because of the relative autonomy or involuntary nature of its functioning. In contrast to the voluntary nervous system, which arises from the cerebral hemispheres and whose destruction in a stroke causes paralysis, the autonomic nervous system remains unaffected in its functioning on removal of the cerebral hemispheres.

By 1840, as noted in Chapter 1, the nervous system was well on its way to being seen as a mechanical system, driven by electrical activity. In 1904 Elliott in Cambridge suggested that the sympathetic system acted by releasing chemical neurotransmitters. He was ignored as the idea had too much the suggestion of a resurrection of animal spirits. But his work was confirmed by Walter Cannon in the 1920s, who showed that the stimulation of sympathetic nerves led to the release of a hormone that had previously been identified in the adrenal gland – adrenalin. This raised heart rate and blood pressure, leading Cannon to suggest that the sympathetic nerves and the adrenal glands acted as a system that was mobilized in response to stresses – whether pain, loss of blood or the sight of a threatening situation. Its mobilization put the organism on an action footing, in preparation as he put it for fight or flight. He proposed that the sympathetic system was central to fear and anxiety.

Vigilance[10]
Cannon's proposal involved the peripheral nervous system. Until 1960 no one appears to have believed that the animal spirits of chemical

neurotransmission might have a role in the central nervous system.[11] In 1954 Marthe Vogt discovered noradrenalin in brain cells. In 1964 it was shown that noradrenaline-containing neurones formed a system which had its roots in some of the oldest areas of the brain. It is central to vital functions such as breathing, cardiac activity and arousal. As the cells which contain noradrenalin stain blue, the 'nucleus' of noradrenalin-containing cells came to be known as the *locus coeruleus* (LC).

Current views are that the LC comprises part of a vigilance system involved in sensory biasing and feature extraction. When novel or fearful things appear in the environment this system switches on and orients the animal/man to what is going on. Orientation involves a heightening of figure-ground discrimination. This improves progressively with arousal up to a threshold, at which point hyperarousal leads to a fall off in discrimination. As figure-ground discrimination occurs subcortically it is unaffected in blindsight, and it is this that permits simple shape localization and discrimination and general orientation.

Those of us who still have our cortices intact can get some idea of what is involved by considering those senses that do not involve cortical modelling – when the threat comes from within. As anyone who has had a distended bladder or colon can testify, what happens is that one becomes aware of there being something not quite right. This awareness when heightened will help pinpoint which organ is involved but only in a very gross sense. When there is an inflammation of the large bowel or an obstruction of the small bowel the system will pick out the relevant organ from the ground of other viscera, but it does not localize the problem accurately within one organ.

An example may indicate a role for the vigilance system in the startle reactions of PTSD. I recently saw a woman in her mid-twenties who had been referred for anxiety. It transpired that she had been married for several years to a man who regularly beat her up to the point of knocking her unconscious. She had miscarried on several occasions, once after being pushed down the stairs. She left him and started a new life, one aspect of which involved joining a climbing club. One day out climbing she got stuck in a gully. The climber ahead of her extended a hand back to help and she panicked, almost certainly because her vigilance system was primed to register as a serious threat the figure of a male hand coming towards her, especially against a background of increased anxiety in the first instance.

Recent work by Svensson in Stockholm suggests that the LC is more responsive to internal threats than to external ones. It had long been known that the sympathetic system responds to pain, lowering of blood pressure or loss of blood; nevertheless there has been almost exclusive interest in the role it plays in adapting to external difficulties. While investigating LC function the Swedish group found that even the modest changes in blood pressure and volume that followed on changing posture were sufficient to activate the locus. Full bladders and distended colons clearly inhibited an animal's orienting response in a novel environment, indicating that the LC may even be biased toward internal threats.[12] This might seem to favour the psychoanalytic contention that the return of repressed endogenous material is of greater importance to anxiety levels than environmental factors. However the reality of what is involved seems far more prosaic than the proponents of psychoanalysis might wish for, as two examples may indicate.

It is frequently found that some elderly subjects who become confused or delirious have a urinary tract infection or severe constipation. In these cases activation of the LC against a background of diminished processing resources leads to something like the effects of extreme anxiety – confusion and disorientation. Using 1890s terminology, this gives us an actual neurosis. (Something similar happens in alcohol withdrawal.)

The other example concerns low-grade illnesses. These tend to make people edgy and irritable for probably very similar reasons. It is common to find that tension or sleeplessness precedes the onset of a viral infection. It is also known that many people who have silent cancers are vaguely aware that there is something wrong with them, often for considerable lengths of time, before diagnosis. It pays therefore to take some heed of bodily intimations. Elsewhere I have argued that depression is an illness which leads to a pervasive physical malaise[13]. The traditional psychiatric response to patients who insist that there is something physically wrong with them in the case of depression is not however to applaud their insight but to label them 'psycho'-neurotic and to accuse them of somatization.

Tolerance

When our cortices are intact and the threat is external being vigilant involves targeting the full battery of cortical processing resources in a particular direction. This is experienced in terms of heightened awareness, but it can come about only in the presence of tolerance to everything else in the environment. Tolerance is what happens when you live on a busy street or beside a train line apparently without hearing the noise after the first few days. It may be only when a particularly large truck roars past the front window or the noise stops that you become aware again.

Something that happened to me recently may illustrate one important point about both tolerance and vigilance. One of the casement windows in the bedroom where I was sleeping began to creak. It could be heard clearly while lying in bed at night. Over the course of a few weeks, far from becoming tolerant to it, I found the noise became more and more prominent. Why? Well, the house in which I was living was an old one, which looked like earning me a modest amount of money when it was sold. I had a private fear however that it was going to fall down. Cracks had begun to appear in the plaster. And the house next door had had to have piles driven into its foundations to counteract subsidence. Given this, the creaks could have been the result of shifts in the structure of the house rather than just a consequence of ill-fitting windows. When I finally got round to inspecting the window – something I put off, not wanting to know the worst – it turned out that it was strictly a window problem and not a house problem that was causing the noise. Almost immediately afterwards I 'stopped' hearing the noise.

This indicates that the issue involved in tolerance is one of survival. Organisms pay heed to novel events until they have assessed the threat that such events pose. When they are judged to be harmless less heed is paid to them. If it remains uncertain what is going on attention is maintained. The event however that is being reacted to is rarely something simple and of absolute salience. In the case of my creaking window the situation in which this noise was occurring was made up of a large number of personal circumstances which involved issues of 'survival'. Similarly in the wild animals faced with novel sounds, sights or smells react not just to those stimuli but to an entire environment. This is not simply a matter of deciding whether the beast that makes that strange noise is dangerous or not, but rather whether the environment in which such beasts occur is a safe one. Or alternatively: I thought I knew what was going on around here but it seems that I don't.

This is particularly the case with alcohol and drugs. Like loud noises or visual events they bring about change in the internal milieu. While the change is novel and its significance uncertain we react sensitively to it. If repeated administration proves harmless enough reactions will increasingly be blunted. Thus drinking in one single environment at one point of the day – at one's local in the evening – can lead to the development of an ability to handle quite large amounts of alcohol without becoming inordinately disco-ordinated or slurred of speech. However having a drink (or a fix) over a business lunch or in the morning may go to one's head much more quickly.[14]

The targeting of resources that can be brought about may be precise to the point of permitting vigilance to what is happening in one field of vision while being tolerant to what happens in the other. This we do on looking through a microscope for example. The example of operating a microscope was one that Eliot Slater was wont to offer in the apparent belief that it indicated the irrelevance of dissociation as a mechanism in the production of neurosis. However given that the system that enables us to function this way is not under voluntary control there would appear to be scope for things to go wrong.

Craving[15]

In 1959 the neurotransmitter dopamine was identified in the central nervous system. Cell bodies containing dopamine have since been shown to comprise part of a ventral tegmental system. From this some dopamine neurones run to motor areas of the brain and their loss causes Parkinson's disease. Others run to mid-brain and cortical areas and are centrally involved in what is termed incentive learning – the kind of learning that occurs when an animal encounters a *biologically* important stimulus such as food or a potential sexual partner.

In 1954 Olds and Milner discovered that there appeared to be pleasure spots in the brain.[16] Implanting electrodes through which a rat can give itself an electric current by pressing on a lever in most brain areas produces nothing of note. In some areas however the rats seem keen on the effects of self-stimulation and may even self-stimulate to the exclusion of food and drink. It was quickly proposed that these experiments indicated the existence of pleasure centres in the brain – a possibility that almost certainly would have found favour with both Freud and Skinner. (Where earlier behaviourists argued that behaviour consisted of clusters of stimuli and reflex responses Skinner argued that behaviours became established because of their rewarding qualities.) The ventral tegmental system seemed closely associated with these pleasure systems. But the picture has become far more complicated. The notion of pleasure centres has been diluted considerably and it now seems that, far from there being pleasure 'hot spots' in the brain, there are areas of the brain that respond to familiar signals pleasurably and unfamiliar signals with displeasure. Pleasure seems more a function of the familiarity of the message being relayed through the system than the result of any intrinsic property of the system that is capable of overriding all other aspects of behaviour.[17]

The operation of this system is now of central interest in the study of the addictions. It used to be argued that the terrors of going through withdrawal were what kept so many people addicted. But if the terror of withdrawal were such a significant factor in producing chronic abuse it might be expected that, once freed from the clutches of the demon drink/drug, anyone with the least bit of wit would keep well clear of further involvement. What perversity or degenerate impulse leads to further abuse?

The customary response to this problem has been to distinguish between physical dependence and psychological dependence. The former leads to clear-cut withdrawal symptoms when the drug is stopped, but the latter, a state of mind, is supposedly the real problem with the addictions. When asked why they return to their habits addicts and alcoholics often respond in terms of 'cravings' – a notion that seems to have the suitable intangibility of a psychological quality but that also conveniently suggests a depravity or perversity in keeping with the social opprobrium accorded to addicts. (The idea of craving was first introduced in 1878, in the heyday of degeneracy, by Edward Levinstein in a book entitled *The Morbid Craving for Morphia*.[18]) Current research suggests however that cravings are a physical dependence of another sort. Only some drugs of abuse – such as cocaine, the amphetamines, nicotine, alcohol and the opiates – cause cravings. LSD and the psychedelics do not. It appears that drugs that feed into the brain systems responsible for the generation and satisfaction of appetites, of which the ventral tegmental system outlined above is a part, are associated with cravings, and those that do not affect this system are not.

What appears to be involved is just the opposite to tolerance. This phenomenon has been called behavioural sensitization. Certain drugs induce it, others do not. Morphine is capable of inducing both sensitization and tolerance. Animals on morphine develop tolerance to its analgesic effects but sensitization to its appetitive effects. Given the complexities involved, awareness of this developed slowly.[19–20]

A moment's reflection should indicate that the last thing an appetitive system could do with is tolerance to the sight of food, drink or sex – rather just the opposite. In contrast to the effect of environmental cues in helping to bring about tolerance because they signal the non-threatening, or insignificant, nature of what is happening, one might expect environmental cues to take on significance where appetite is concerned. That is, animals will become increasingly sensitive to aspects of an environment that indicate the possibility of food or sex or drink. Such cues should lead to increased interest.

This seems to be exactly what happens to all of us where our appetites are concerned. Typically we do not notice the accumulation of environmental prompts pushing us towards the consummation of an appetite unless we have been removed from the environment artificially for a while. For example I saw someone recently who had been put on total intravenous nutrition for a bowel complaint and confined to a food-free environment. When liberated from this régime he went down to the hospital foyer and found himself assailed by food. On one side of the foyer was a sweetshop, on another a vegetable and fruit shop and on a third the hospital canteen and snack bar from which the aroma of an imminent mealtime was emanating. On all sides people were munching chocolate bars or eating sandwiches or fruit. These are cues we all take in our stride daily and pay little heed to but which are in reality powerful messages that are silently priming our appetites. Exposed to them for the first time after weeks this individual was overwhelmed, and panicked.

In a similar fashion public houses and the cultures surrounding both drink and drug-taking prime an appetite that has been created. This can extend to having one's appetite aroused by the sight of needles. Once stimulated, appetites have a way of grabbing attention. Shakespeare has captured the psychology involved better than anyone before or since:

Sonnet 129

The expense of spirit in a waste of shame
Is lust in action; and till action, lust
Is perjured, murderous, bloody, full of blame,
Savage, extreme, rude, cruel, not to trust;
Enjoy'd no sooner but despised straight;
Past reason hunted; and no sooner had,
Than past reason hated, as a swallowed bait,
On purpose laid to make the taker mad:
Mad in pursuit and in possession so;
Had, having, and in quest to have, extreme;
A bliss in proof, and proved, a very woe;
Before, a joy proposed; behind a dream.

All this the world well knows; yet none knows well
To shun the heaven that leads men to this hell.

It is natural to bend our minds to the satisfaction of our appetites when they require satisfying. As the weight of cues to indulgence build up we typically come closer and closer to behaving on automatic pilot. We less and less regard alternative cues in the environment. Thus the hacking cough is not registered as we light up a further cigarette, or the little soothing snack while we worry about our weight, and the children's Christmas presents get forgotten until the drink runs out. One way to put this is in terms of dissociation. In instances as extreme as these we seemingly fail to make what others would see as 'reasonable' associations. This blocking is something we may have little 'insight' on. Indeed in severe cases of substance dependence or appetite disorder the lack of insight, just as with hysteria in the last chapter, may be far greater than in the so-called psychoses, which are supposedly characterized by lack of insight.

PSYCHOANALYSIS, BEHAVIOURISM
AND THE UNCONSCIOUS

The developments we have outlined permit a number of points to be made.* One is that, common to the various forms of unconscious learning involved, there is a lack of autobiographical detail. There is no stamp of when, where or why the learning was acquired. Thus a number of the psychoanalytic criteria for the Id are met by these systems. But it would seem that there is no such thing as a homogeneous Id. Rather even the most primitive areas of the brain show considerable structure. These structures do not, it would seem, relate to each other in any readily characterized hierarchical fashion and none is exclusively concerned with erotic impulses.

The second point is that the operations of these systems seem to be a matter of primings and habituations rather than a question of imagery or symbols. There seem to be no models or representations of any kind in the old brain. Accordingly it would seem that this particular unconscious could not easily function as part of a dynamic unconscious, in the sense required by psychoanalysis.

A third point is that, even at this level of the psyche, functions appear to be geared towards anticipating the future rather than defending against the past.

Finally, while ordinarily subcortical and cortical systems appear to work in harmony, there also appears to be the possibility of disjunctions between these systems. When this happens we may become aware without being conscious of what we are aware of, for example, or we may

---

*There is at least one further unconscious system that is part of the old brain. This is the cerebellar system, which seems to function in the regulation of the automatic motor movements necessary for skills. Propensities to follow certain movements with others get primed in cerebellar systems and allow thereby for the rapid mobilization of movements without conscious reflection. There seems little evidence to support the notion that the laying down of skills requires the participation of the so-called pleasure centres mentioned earlier.

find that our pursuit of an appetite had involved the suspension of critical judgment. This suggests two things. One is that dissociation is possible. The other is that, equally, there is potentially more than one form of dissociation (with several more to follow on the cortical level).

The psychobiology of substance abuse

Superficially alcoholism and the various substance dependencies with their 'oral' qualities might be expected to fit in with the general psycho-analytic theory of stages of psychosexual development. Psychoanalysts after Freud certainly appeared to think so. Sandor Radó for example argued that it is not alcohol or drugs but the impulse to use them which is the core of the addiction.[21] The craving for pleasure the drug gives supposedly derives from an inability to handle frustration that would otherwise give rise to tense depression. The intervention of alcohol or drugs however, works not pharmacologically but supposedly by a magi-cal willing of the Ego, which cathects its problems out on the substance of abuse. Radó argued that this is effectively a form of masturbation.

Robert Knight argued in 1937 that the alcoholic's personality is characterized by excessive demands for indulgence which are doomed to frustration in an adult world, leading in turn to rage and hostile acts against those who are thwarting him.[22] The outcome of this is guilt and masochistic self-punishment, leaving the alcoholic in need of affection – and of course indulgence is one sign of affection. As affection becomes progressively less likely the circle tightens. Knight believed that such behaviours were first laid down by maternal responses to infantile dif-ficulties with oral pacifiers.

Later, more object-oriented approaches have put less emphasis on intrapsychic impulse control and more on interpersonal dynamics. Here drinking is seen as an incidental pleasure, aimed at bringing about psychological torment and a situation in which the subject will be scol-ded by authoritative others and will have to beg forgiveness. This game is indulged in as the alcoholic is classically afraid of intimacy and the dynamic of reproach and forgiveness at least provides for emotionally intense interactions.[23]

Taking a behavioural approach, substance abuse can be seen as a classic instance of aberrant habit (reflex) formation. It might be expected therefore to respond to behavioural interventions. It does not. Various régimes have been tried – reinforcing abstinent behaviour, punishing abuse behaviour and attempting to set up conditioned reflexes to alcohol. Neither behavioural approaches nor the insight-oriented psychoanalysis of alcoholic behaviour have had any better success rates than those reported in Chapter 5 in connection with LSD treatment.

The most obvious thing about these formulations of substance dependence is that they involve the transposition of ideological principles on to the problem rather than a creative attempt to come to grips with it based on the actual experiences of affected subjects. In marked contrast the therapy of substance dependency now aims to map out in detail the situation of the dependent individual and to base interventions on such details. This point is taken up in Chapter 9. A second point is that both analytic and behavioural approaches focus on the internal failings of affected subjects – their degeneracy – despite increasing evidence that the kinds of learning that form the basis of appetitive behaviour are context sensitive and in the face of considerable evidence that substance dependence problems are social creations. A third point is that these formulations are *biologically* naïve. They ignore distinctions between drugs of abuse that cause withdrawal as opposed to those that cause both withdrawal and cravings and a third group that cause neither withdrawal nor cravings.

THE REDISCOVERY OF THE PSYCHE

When the soul wishes to remember something, [it] makes the gland, inclining successively to different sides, drive the spirits toward different places in the brain, until they come upon one where the traces are which the object we will to remember has left there . . . The pores of the brain through which the spirits have previously made their way because of the presence of this object have thereby acquired a greater facility than the others for being opened again in the same way by the spirits approaching them. So these spirits coming upon these pores enter into them more easily than into others – whereby they excite a particular movement in the gland, which represents the same object to the soul and makes it understand that this is the one it willed to remember. Descartes, *Passions of the Soul*: Article 42.

But for its references to the pineal gland, Article 42 of the *Passions* could have been taken straight out of Freud's *Project for a Scientific Psychology*. Both straddle the growing distinction, outlined earlier, between memory and learning. Where habits and the old brain appear to deal in tendencies, propensities and intimations, remembering appears to be a reseeing, a matter of models, images and representations. As the question of emotional images in our mind's eye appears to be a recurring one throughout the book, the psychology and location of these images must be addressed.

Imagery[24-6]

Writing in 1883 Francis Galton, a cousin of Charles Darwin, took up the question of mental imagery – visual memory.[27] When he asked a number of his scientific colleagues to call a picture to their mind's eye and describe the details to him he was surprised that many of them claimed to be unable to do so. Some dismissed the notion of a mind's eye or even that of an image as merely a figure of speech. However he got the opposite reaction from a sample of non-scientists, who were quite amazed that anyone could possibly question the existence of internal imagery. He concluded that we all imagine but that women, children and more primitive peoples are particularly imaginative. Had he included internal monologues or dialogues along with visual imagery he would probably have obtained a higher overall incidence of internal events, as recent research suggests that some of us are visually and others verbally/aurally biased.*

There are two points here. One is that Galton sampled a hundred scientists to establish the range of the experiences people have. This is a point that will be taken up again in Chapter 10. The other is that for almost a hundred years, despite his study, psychologists have not been prepared to countenance the existence of any such internal events. The idea of treating the matter scientifically has often been ridiculed in terms of insubstantial images being flashed up on ghostly mental screens. As it is patently obvious that there are no screens in the brain it has been inferred that imagining must be just something we imagine.

However the notion that one cannot, in principle, be scientific about images because they are not accessible to objective verification only really holds water if one believes that human beings are congenitally mendacious. It is clear that there is a difficulty with the idea of being objective about internal, inaccessible, 'subjective' events. But wherein does the objectivity of perception of external events lie? Attempting to draw a scene is one sure way to wonder about the evidence of one's own eyes regarding external events. Anyone who tries usually finds that what they thought they saw before them was just a working copy, a model of reality. Certainly what gets produced at the end by the artist is no photograph. What about the perceptions we have when confronted with a series of dots or ambiguous smudges and we see shapes in them? Or again the so-called optical illusions, where we see figures that may

---

*As we are all right- or left-handed, but the world caters only for right-handers, I propose to restrict the discussion of internal events to imagery rather than to monologues or dialogues. Apologies to the left-handers.

be interpreted as either of two things – a vase or two faces for example.

Simple examples such as this illustrate that perception seems to involve an *internal* construction of working models and that my working models may not be the same as yours. So 'objectivity' isn't just a matter of looking at what's out there – it is something we arrive at by consensus. If so there seems no good reason to believe that one cannot be objective about percepts in the mind's eye. This is exactly what I suggest internal images are – perceptual models, produced by the very same constructive activities of the psyche that go into building the percepts we use to interpret the outside world. Once constructed they can then be scrutinized on an 'internal screen'.

Taking just such a naïve approach to images – seeing them as models flashed up on internal screens – has led a number of researchers, most notably Roger Shepard and Stephen Kosslyn, to model the act of imagining using the image-generating capacities of modern computers. The one appears to map on to the other extraordinarily well. Such work has allowed detailed predictions about what will happen for example if a subject is asked to imagine an object and then rotate it in various directions, or to imagine elephants standing beside dogs and then focus on one or other of the two animals. Predictions on questions such as these have been borne out time and again by rigorous testing in various laboratories.

On the basis of such data it can be argued that all perception is actually imagination. We hang on to some images and call them percepts if they are consistent with the further evidence we look for. Others we dismiss as just imagination because no further confirming evidence can be found. This can be illustrated by a thought experiment. Suppose, walking through a bedroom, you glimpse a tiger out of the corner of your eye lying in the corner. You can imagine walking out without paying any further heed and then wondering if you imagined what you think you just saw. The tiger is likely to be dismissed as imaginary because of the unlikelihood of a second glance providing confirmatory evidence – unless of course it does.

There is an important implication for the development of our argument that follows from any account of images that casts them as percepts with an internal reference or as the inner aspect of percepts. It is this. Percepts don't intrinsically involve symbolic reference. When I see a grain silo I primarily see a grain silo and not a phallus. I can see a phallus if I want, but doing so is a matter determined by social conventions rather than by the intrinsic nature of the percept. The symbolic transformation of percepts according to social conventions is not tied to any fundamental biological realities. Thus images of a lamb or a fish may, for Christians, stand for Christ.

As with percepts therefore the interpretation of images is in the first instance a matter of getting their constituent details right. They may have symbolic overtones, but if they do these will be relative and set by current social conventions rather than absolute and set by biological realities. Thus dreaming of scarab beetles now will probably refer to fantasies of exploration or of the exotic and will probably follow seeing a horror movie with not-quite-dead mummies in it, whereas in Egypt 3,000 years ago it would have had a significance set by then prevalent mythologies.

From this it follows that the interpretation of the symbolic aspects of an image will be a matter that any reasonably well-informed member of the society the imaginer comes from will be as likely to get right as any other. Spending some time at the interpretative game will tend to improve one's performance – in much the manner that repeatedly doing cryptic crosswords improves one's skill – but practice will not guarantee interpretative accuracy.

Demythologizing images in their manner does not however imply that they are 'simple' entities. In contrast to Huxley's analogy of the whistle of a locomotive, they are no more irrelevant to human functioning than are percepts themselves. Like percepts they are working models and may be very complex constructions depending on the task being modelled. The capacity to imagine lays the basis for memory, which now appears to involve 're-cognizing' the past. It also lays the basis for planning, or memory for the future, which involves an ability to imagine a sequence of events and to register at the appropriate time whether the proposed operation is proceeding according to plan.

For millenia imagery has been used as a mnemonic device. More recently cognitive psychology has discovered that the imageability of a stimulus shapes how well it is recalled later – abstract ideas are recalled poorly. One might imagine therefore that traumatic events might be indelibly imprinted into memory in an accurate and detailed form. In contrast however it seems that the witnessing of dramatic events may lead to serious problems in recalling those events accurately, partly, it seems, because the registration of images without full understanding of their significance, or a chance to analyse the events, leaves a subject open to the influence of post-event suggestions.[28]

Emotions[29–30]

One image in particular is liable to be an extraordinary creation of the psyche, the significance of which is always, at least in part, uncertain. This is the image or complex of images of oneself that float through the mind's eye repeatedly day and night. Far from being a simple representation this particular complex of images is one that is invested with emotions.

But what is an emotion? Ulric Neisser has suggested that emotions are to actions as images are to percepts. Just as we can construct perceptual models at will and flash them up on an internal screen, so also we model our actions and can detach these models from actual actions and can enact them instead on some internal stage. Just as images can have all the technicolour and textual detail of percepts, so also emotions will have all the sensations that go with actions. They will be felt.

Let me expand on this. Scanning internal imagery typically leads to one's eyes moving just as though one were scanning some external scene. Similarly if emotions are the inner aspects of actions being emotional should involve minimal movements or tendencies to movement. It does. These are often quite apparent to outsiders. For example, if I am angry you may stand a bit back from me. Why? Not necessarily because I have said I am angry; but because my general posture and physiognomy however may well indicate someone in whom particular action systems are primed. This is something I may or may not be aware of: most of us will know of someone who at some time has shouted in a belligerent fashion, 'I am not angry!'

This potential lack of awareness of what is obviously going on in us is important. But what *is* happening? One possible answer is that there is a clash between the way we wish to perceive ourselves and the way we are. We may not like the idea of images flashing through our mind that do not correspond with how we wish to see ourselves, but there is no doubt that our emotions and actions betray to others our intentions in a way that our imaginings do not. They can therefore potentially threaten our self-images by incurring the displeasure of others. Furthermore action involves an engagement with the world in a way that perception does not, but any engagement is likely to reveal as much about the actor as it is about the world.

It makes sense therefore that, just as the sympathetic system acts to prepare animals for fight or flight, so there should be a mechanism to switch off action and all semblance of action in certain dangerous circumstances. This third option is, as we have seen in the discussion of rape trauma syndrome, to play dead, as when a mouse or a bird hangs limply in the jaws of a cat. This freezing, it has been argued, is the prototype of a dissociative reaction.[31–2] While noting that there would appear to be more than one kind of dissociation, the association between emotions and actions outlined above does indicate why *this* kind of dissociation is liable to happen in emotional situations – situations in which the appropriate action or emotion may seriously compromise the individual involved. We have seen that such freezing responses are found commonly during the course of a rape or in hostage or other traumatic situations.

I have separated emotions and images, but they come together on the internal stage in the form of emotional imagery, in particular in images of ourselves in action or intending action. Everyone who has a sexual fantasy is well aware that images of ourselves in action have consequences in the appropriate action systems. But conversely, if actions in compromising situations are liable to be inhibited, the fact of emotional imagery introduces potential inhibition and censorship into our private fantasies. For example what happens if the image of ourself does things that we cannot countenance? This is the common experience of many who seek psychiatric help, from the mother who sees herself strangling her children in her mind's eye, to the man who sees himself picking up a little girl and wondering what prevents the realization of his worst fears, or the disaster survivor who imagines himself going back to help others and wonders why he didn't. Such images are the stuff of obsessional disorders. But where do they come from? Is there some buried source of distressing images – images that in some way reveal our true emotions?

Split brains and parallel processing[33–5]

Talk about images and emotions is apt today to lead many to think in terms of the right hemisphere of the brain. However as we saw in Chapter 5 the notion of locating psychopathology to one or other brain hemisphere or to the imbalance between them received a severe setback at the end of the nineteenth century. Such notions have resurfaced with recent work on split-brain research.

Splitting a brain involves sectioning the *corpus callosum*, which is a body of fibres connecting one hemisphere to the other. The first operations of this sort were undertaken in the 1950s in an attempt to control severe epilepsy, where abnormal electrical impulses spread from one hemisphere to the other. It proved beneficial in a number of cases. Initial impressions were that subjects whose *corpus callosum* had been split were no different after their operation; closer examination revealed more mysterious effects.

When one's eyes are kept fixed it is possible by suitably positioning objects to have them registered in one cerebral hemisphere before the other. In normal subjects this leads to the information almost instantly being transferred to the other hemisphere. In a subject whose *corpus callosum* has been sectioned information normally gets into both hemispheres because the eyes are not normally fixed. But by asking such subjects to fix their eyes and by suitably positioning objects it seems that information can be sent to one hemisphere that does not get to the other, and that each hemisphere can build up separate memories of what has been presented to them.

Furthermore the interpretations put on events by the separate hemispheres may differ. This has led to notions that each side has its own 'personality' and – in a curious echo of the 1880s – that the right side is supposedly the more emotional, creative and intuitive and the left side more analytic, logical and verbal. And just as in the 1880s there were movements aimed at teaching people to be ambidextrous in the hope that this would enable them to tap into the unused potential of their right hemispheres, so also today there are books written for the popular market purporting to offer techniques to tap into the more creative, artistic side of oneself: the suppressed right hemisphere. In 1880 it was proposed that hypnosis acted by accessing right-hemisphere processing. A current theory today is that LSD brings out its consciousness-expanding effects by facilitating a switch to right-hemisphere dominated processing.

While most of these ideas, then and now, belong in the realm of popular mythology, splitting brains has raised in a very acute form the question of localization of function. In the 1960s and 1970s it was widely argued that the operation yielded two disconnected but relatively normal hemispheres within one skull – in other words, two minds. This, it was argued, is obscured in normal people because the two minds run in perfect parallel and are completely intercommunicative. It was also argued that the left hemisphere, by virtue of its language capacity, appeared to construct a common personal myth to serve as an identity for both hemispheres, thereby further obscuring the presence of two minds. Thus if instructions were given to the right hemisphere to scratch, for example, and the left hemisphere were then asked why the scratching, it would never answer that it did not know but rather would come up with some explanation – such as, I had an itch.

However another view on brain functioning and localization has been gaining favour in recent years. This has been called the modular approach. It has been stimulated in part by the findings from split-brain work but it owes its primary inspiration to developments in computer programming. The relevant developments have been the progression from the notion of computer programs written in the form of discrete serial operations to programs operating on the basis of parallel distributed processing. Applying this to the psyche allows the proposal that, far from whole areas of the brain being given over to major psychological operations such as speech, imagery or emotions, much smaller areas carry out more specific functions. The functions required for normal speech are spread throughout the brain, both anterior and posterior and on both right and left. They combine in the production of speech. Many of them can be disconnected without the speech act being completely compromised. However there are some functions necessary to speech that are usually located on the left, which if damaged lead to serious difficulties – hence speech has seemed to lie on the left-hand side. In the case of images Kosslyn has proposed that the function that 'puts' details into the picture is located in the left hemisphere with other functions being located on the right.

Taking this approach it is possible to conceive of more than one consciousness within the skull. The localized functions are in general so small that they could not possibly be personalities in their own right. But they are also so numerous that a number of different psychological organizations may, as it were, avail of their services variously. Thus whereas the double-mind idea in the 1880s and the early split-brain work could not readily account for the seeming facts of MPD, a modular approach can. This fits in very well with Janet's contention that in hysteria and MPD it is psychological functions rather than neural operations that are split. For instance he argued that learning to ride a bicycle produces a psychological bicycle-riding centre. Subjects who end up unable to ride a bicycle by virtue of hysteria have a disorder of this psychological centre rather than of any anatomical structure. The development of such psychological centres, he conceded, must at some point have depended on the mobilization of brain functions. But once established bicycle riding can call on different modules on different occasions. A modular approach seems better equipped to meet these requirements than one that would hardwire bicycle riding to a single brain area. This perhaps is even more clear in the case of writing. Once the psychological centre has been established a subject may be able to write with their feet or holding a pen in their teeth, if deprived of the original executive mechanisms. In contrast in hysteria, if the idea of writing is compromised, then all subsidiary functions may operate normally – except when it comes to writing.

Taking the modular approach, there will be considerable amounts of potentially conscious processing of many different aspects of a situation going on simultaneously, of which some are selected based on appropriateness for the task in hand. Selection does not necessarily lead to awareness. For example one can drive a car while one's mind is a million miles away. It follows from this that things may be going on around us of which we are not aware but which we do process and of which we may become aware later on. It also follows that dramatic and comprehensive changes in psychological functioning may occur abruptly according to the requirements of the situation. One of the better examples of this is when a subject switches from one language to another. Switching in this case entails not only accessing different words but also different rules and indeed an entirely different mental set. What changes is not just a set of associative connections between certain words but rather a set of psychological operations, with an accompanying systematic dissociation from all the prompts that would activate the psychobiological structures appropriate to the first language. Given that such large-scale switching can be common and everyday, the idea of switching from one personality to another doesn't seem so impossible.

I will argue in the next chapter that these modular sub-units, unlike comparable units in a computer, are likely to be spontaneously active. This will inevitably lead regularly to the generation of internal imagery at variance with a subject's perception of themselves – battering their child for instance. Such images I will argue arise *accidentally* rather than as part of some subterranean revelation. Far from such fantasies revealing the hidden wishes of the subject they rarely reveal anything of great interest. It is an individual's reaction to such images that is likely to reveal that person's true nature, rather than the images themselves.

DISSOCIATION OR REPRESSION?

A modular approach to brain functioning envisages a great deal of processing going on in parallel the whole time. From this activity material is selected and becomes conscious based on appropriateness for the task at hand and integratability with the current model of the self. Other options are passively suppressed, in the sense of just not taken up, rather than actively repressed. One way of putting this is that we dissociate from these other options.

This can be applied to the post-traumatic disorders. The unique feature of the recent definition of PTSD is the presence of intrusive imagery and emotions which recur repetitively in both waking and dreams. The images, far from being disconnected from their emotional investment, are often accompanied by intense emotion, even to the point where subjects *re-enact* the events in question. These intrusions appear to alternate with episodes of numbness and amnesia. This formulation contrasts with the classic formulations of hysteria, which portrayed it as a state dominated by amnesia and one in which emotions have been suppressed or have become disconnected from their original object.

However, rereading the older texts, it becomes clear that world-war veterans and even hysterics from the last century had very similar intrusive experiences and that often it was the ability of the therapist to get into and manipulate the patient's imaginal world that promoted recovery. Thus Grinker and Spiegel described a pilot who had been hit on his last flight before going home. In the course of a hypnotic session he began to re-enact the incident at the point when he was losing blood and consciousness and was panicking, to the point of slumping and turning pale, his pulse racing as it would do with blood loss. The therapist however suggested that a pane of glass blew out of the cockpit and that refreshing air came blowing in. This led to a revival of both physical and mental state.[36] Janet recounts handling several cases similarly.

The writer who came closest to recognizing the presence of conscious recurrent imagery in his patients was Freud – the 1895 Freud. As we have noted he came to the conclusion that the images or clues to the trauma were within his subjects' consciousness in a great number of cases. The difficulty lay not in retrieving them so much as in expressing them.

The modern recognition of the role that imagery and associated emotion may be playing in this condition has only been possible in the last decade or so with the rehabilitation of imagery and introspection generally. The phenomenon of recurrent imagery suggests psychic work. That material that is difficult to integrate is being wheeled episodically across the stage of awareness.[37] Very similar findings can be reproduced experimentally by showing normal subjects film clips with a variety of material on them. The more distressing the material the more all subjects afterwards report recurrent intrusive flashbacks and episodes of numbing.[38] The significance of this finding is that it suggests that what happens in the post-traumatic disorders and hysteria does not happen because of some prior psychodynamic pathology.

Autobiographical memory[39]

The experience of recurrent intrusions of past happenings will almost certainly have occurred to most readers – after interviews for jobs they did not get, for example, or after situations where they have made a serious social blunder. A recently developed concept, termed autobiographical memory, seems relevant here.

Basically the proposal is that we do not organize our memories in some neutral filing system as can be found in a computer, with memories stored from A1, B1 to AZ 299, BZ 299 etc. Rather our filing systems are based on 'who we are', where this is defined as much in terms of our expectations, hopes, goals and values as in terms of our past. Changing who we are may completely change the contents of our store of easily retrievable memories.

Some idea of how this store of memories can change may be conveyed by the following scenario. Faced with the need to look for a new job one's image of oneself can become somewhat fluid over the course of a few weeks. It is common to find in this process that individuals who had sworn that it was not in them to do certain jobs or live in certain parts of the country adapt themselves to the realities of where the likely jobs will be. Over the course of a few weeks they may even do the unthinkable and become quite enthusiastic about the possibility of living in London for example. After all there is so much culture . . . ! It is quite possible then to swing to the opposite and to become very enthusiastic about rural life over the course of a few weeks if first one job and then another fails to materialize.

Facing the prospect of an interview most subjects will mentally rehearse the interview beforehand and create self-images (fantasize) about what will happen when they get the job. It may only be when they enter the interview room and get asked something unexpected that they realize that their *current* plans for themselves may not coincide with the plans of those on the opposite side of the table. In this case even a very simple but unexpected question, asked to put the interviewee at ease, may throw them completely. Commonly reported occurrences are of one's mind going blank or of the whole situation seeming unreal and the interviewers perhaps seeming far away, or of one leaving oneself and being able in some way to watch this bumbling idiot make a mess of an interview.

Similarly soldiers go to war not expecting to die but rather to be brave and to return home a hero to the girl they left behind, there to settle down with her and to raise a family. It may only be under enemy fire that it comes home to them that the plans the enemy has for them may not coincide with their own. In cases such as having a shell go off close by or being asked an awkward question at interview, the work that went on for several weeks before jobs that never materialized may need to be reworked in a few minutes. This and the radical nature of the appraisals involved can be expected to lead to a failure of autobiographical memory.

This modern concept of autobiographical memory overlaps considerably with the notion of personal consciousness developed by Janet at the turn of the century. The question of what comes into consciousness, he argued, was determined by its integratability with the existing 'I' whose consciousness this is:

When memories become subconscious it is because they conflict with the subject's other ideas and feelings. If we drag them back to a consciousness that will not tolerate them, they will soon be driven out again and we shall have to begin the whole process once more.[40]

Modern though the term autobiographical memory is, the methods of study – collecting memories in response to certain prompts and placing them in individualized reference frames – are old, dating back, along with the first systematic population-based study of mental imagery, to 1883 and Francis Galton.[41] It is only in recent years that the issues he raised have been taken up again and that his investigative approach to psychology has begun to emerge from the shadows of experimental psychology. Why this suspension of what is now termed an ecologically valid approach to psychology should have occurred is picked up in Chapter 10.

Amnesia

There seems at least one problem with this reformulation of Janet's proposal for hysteria. It seems probable that mild degrees of dissociative amnesia have been experienced by every reader of this book and are a common response to social stress. The cases of shellshock or of fugues in students, who just before their exams are found wandering miles away from home not knowing how they got there, indicate that a dissociative amnesia may even be far more comprehensive than any deficit of memory found in all but the most terminal cases of Alzheimer's dementia. This amnesia however seems to be the polar opposite to what appears to be a very valid remembering in the case of recurrent imagery and emotions.

A simple experiment reported recently by Bradley and Baddeley sheds some light on this.[42] They examined how well subjects remembered sets of words over a period of time, some of which were emotionally loaded and others not. Initially the emotional words were less well remembered but it seemed that with the passage of time they became more memorable than the neutral words. Extrapolating to the larger picture this seems to fit well with what happens after shocks or trauma. At first there may be a state of numbness or amnesia. This state of minimal awareness may even persist for years. But sooner or later it begins to resurface. When it does there may be a problem in expressing the feelings or images involved if they are incongruent with a current self-image. Indeed one reason for the neglect of the post-traumatic disorders, other than the more general neglect of consciousness for the past eighty years, has been that typically patients with PTSD have had difficulty articulating such material, despite its salience in their minds. Instead they have tended to repress the material – just as many of us do. In the case of a parent glimpsing an image of themselves *possibly* battering one of their children for example the immediate reaction is to repress the material. Such a repression, in contrast to the analytic usage of this word, suggests an active suppression of conscious material that is felt not to be politic either to dwell on or to make public. We all feel that such repression works, and furthermore there is evidence to show that indulgent fantasizing may lead on to murder or other unwelcome behaviours,[43-4] whereas putting thoughts out of one's mind is a normal method to control the malignant growth of a fantasy.

I have suggested above that repressed material does not reveal the true nature of the individual. In fact, in a cruel twist, the individuals who are most likely to be appalled by images of themselves harming their children are the ones least likely to do so. So abhorrent will they find the idea that they will attempt to 'over-repress' it – to make sure it is really gone. All too often this leads to a pushing of the offending image out to the edge of consciousness, although the feeling that there is a need to keep a check on it means it cannot be pushed completely out. It is therefore even more likely to recur. This kind of vicious circle is likely to get established if the wrong kind of image afflicts an individual at the wrong time – at a time when they are more vulnerable to the particular implications inherent in the image. This 'neurotic' round is likely to become established as much by accident as anything else, as I will argue further in Chapter 10.

When it comes to talking about recurrent intrusive imagery there is a further difficulty. Declaring ourselves verbally is essentially a univocal communication that, at any one point in time, can only abstract certain aspects of the stream of consciousness. In part therefore the difficulty in talking about recurrent imagery will be that there is always far more going on on our conscious stages than we can ever describe. The problem is like commenting on a football match. Sometimes the most important events happen on a different part of the pitch to that which you happen to have your eye on at that moment.

It would seem likely, from Freud's own descriptions, that both dissociation and relatively conscious repression, as well as problems in translating images into words, were all processes that were operative in those subjects in psychotherapy with him around 1895. What is not clear from his very vivid descriptions is whether any appeal to a dynamic unconscious, as it was later to become, was or is necessary.

Physical amnesia

While it seems that the hysterics of old may all have had recurrent intrusive imagery and emotions that were ignored in the general ignoring of the psyche, they also had blindness and paralyses. How can these be explained? I have suggested that remembering is in a sense re-perceiving. Equally however perceiving is remembering. The percepts or images we conjure up to interpret or model what it is that lies before us depend heavily on past experience with earlier percepts and our memory of the outcome of such experiences. Given this it may seem less surprising to the reader that if dissociative amnesia can occur in the face of stress so also might dissociative blindness.

Of course on this basis all of the physical manifestations of hysteria might be put down to dissociation – after all, movement also involves memory and hence paralyses could be seen as a form of amnesia. This in essence was Janet's argument. He claimed that at no point was the subject truly amnesic, paralysed or unable to sense normally but that there was a failure of personal perception. Sensations and movement were not integrated into a self.

A PSYCHOLOGY OF CONSCIOUSNESS

This raises the question of what integrates? What controls access into awareness? To answer this we must have a model of consciousness itself. Thinking about models of consciousness has however been even slower to get going, after the hiatus of behaviourism, than have studies on imagery and emotions.

There is a good deal of empirical research going on at the moment, which seems likely to lead to more detailed and powerful models. This includes the sampling of streams of consciousness – in William James's phrase the 'blooming buzzing confusion of consciousness' – to explore the internal monologues, reminiscences, rehearsals and speculative forays that constitute consciousness.[45] Another seam of investigative mining is a phenomenon which seems to be the opposite of recurrent intrusive imagery – recurrent momentary forgetting.[46] But the obvious point to make in the face of Freudian or other claims regarding consciousness or the unconscious is that we still simply have not got much of a clue about how consciousness operates.

At present there are broadly speaking two types of models of consciousness. Both argue that the bulk of cognitive processing is essentially non-conscious. By non-conscious here however I do not mean unconscious in the Freudian sense but rather subconscious in something closer to Janet's sense. The example of processing instructions or events while under anaesthesia, outlined in Chapter 5, indicates the existence of this subconscious processing or what is sometimes now termed the cognitive unconscious.[47] This appears to involve a form of priming that is distinct from the subcortical priming that forms the basis for the vigilance and appetitive systems, outlined earlier in the chapter (see Figure 2).

In the first model of consciousness, associated with the names of George Mandler and Tim Shallice among others, most processing even if complex and detailed occurs out of consciousness.[48] But it is argued that there are some operations that require awareness. These are operations such as choosing, appraising and comparing. Thus at points of decision-making or when learning a new skill one becomes conscious – even acutely conscious – of competing representations, and one monitors the evidence in favour of the various options. This also happens when there is a mismatch. Functions such as driving a car may be proceeding smoothly with minimal awareness, but if one's performance does not fit with expectations one will suddenly switch back to concentrated awareness.

A quite different model has been offered by Tony Marcel.[49] He has argued that it is not the case that representations compete and that the most appropriate ones enter consciousness. Rather non-conscious processing, while it may be elaborate and representational, does not contain images or emotions. Entry into conscious awareness happens

THE STRUCTURE OF CONSCIOUSNESS

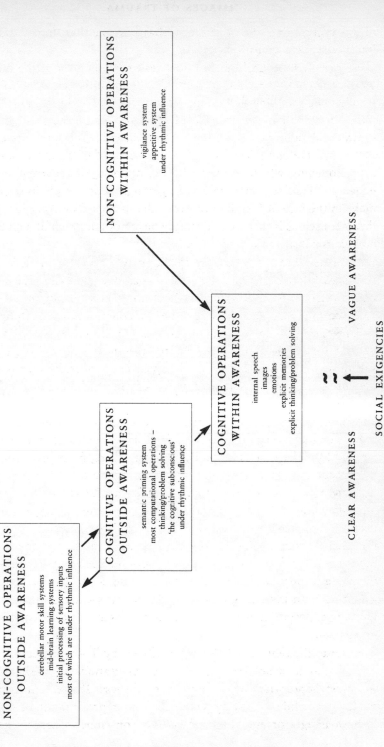

NON-COGNITIVE OPERATIONS OUTSIDE AWARENESS

cerebellar motor skill systems
mid-brain learning systems
initial processing of sensory inputs
most of which are under rhythmic influence

COGNITIVE OPERATIONS OUTSIDE AWARENESS

semantic priming system
most computational operations –
thinking/problem solving
'the cognitive sub-conscious'
under rhythmic influence

NON-COGNITIVE OPERATIONS WITHIN AWARENESS

vigilance system
appetitive system
under rhythmic influence

COGNITIVE OPERATIONS WITHIN AWARENESS

internal speech
images
emotions
explicit memories
explicit thinking/problem solving

CLEAR AWARENESS

VAGUE AWARENESS

SOCIAL EXIGENCIES

Fig. 3   Diagram outlining some components of consciousness.

147

only when such representations are further synthesized into the higher level models that we call images and emotions.*

Images on a computer screen provide an analogy for this. The greater part of a computer's processing is in non-image form. The creation of images enters information into a different mode – one shaped by external needs and suitable for further interaction with the outside. An important implication of this kind of model is that there would be no images lying completely outside of potential awareness – just as there are no images in the bowels of the computer. There are functions which colour and size and shape things, but there are not already coloured and sized and shaped images lying dormant.

Marcel has carried out some of the most widely cited experiments on consciousness. He has shown that subjects presented with key-words, under conditions in which they are unable to register seeing them, are still able to distinguish them and that their distinctions bias subsequent behaviour. For example presentation with either the word *money* or *river*, in a manner that leaves the subject unaware that they have seen anything, will significantly bias word associations to the word *bank* subsequently presented explicitly.

Such findings have interested the beleaguered defenders of psycho-analysis. Howard Shevrin, whose subject with a blood phobia, A.M., was briefly outlined in Chapter 2, applied a variation of Marcel's methods to this case.[50] Based on the clinical interpretation that A.M. had sadomaso-chistic impulses and that his phobia of blood had a symbolic relation with these impulses, Shevrin and colleagues presented A.M. subliminally with lists of words that they thought might be particularly liable to access the conflicts they proposed for his dynamic unconscious. Their findings were that the words they chose did seem to threaten A.M. as judged on EEG recordings of brain functioning. From this, and compar-able results in other cases, they concluded that modern neuropsychology was on the way to the rescue of psychoanalysis. But Marcel, in reply, has questioned why it should be supposed that giving a subliminal stimulus should access the dynamic unconscious any more than giving a supraliminal one.[51] Masking the experimental stimulus as he has done only prevents it entering conscious awareness; it doesn't necessarily

---

*A converse point may focus the issues here, which is that without images, emotions and memories we would not be conscious, in the normal sense of the word. In subjects with Korsakoff's psychosis or comparably profound amnesias, who are unable to recall to their minds' eyes anything of their past, there may be moment to moment awareness, but along with their loss of memory there is usually also the loss of a coherent sense of self – a loss of self-consciousness.

make for access to a dynamic unconscious. This is particularly clear if one takes a modular approach, which envisages a myriad of relatively autonomous processing units with probably not much leakage from one area of processing to another. Non-conscious entry into this means that processing is stimulated in some sub-units but not with the degree of intensity necessary for the results of processing to force their way into conscious awareness.

A further problem arises from recent neurobiological research. The analytic approaches generally have postulated Oedipal and pre-Oedipal conflicts in childhood and that it is these that give rise to the phenomenon of childhood amnesia. However since the early 1980s it has become clear that rather dramatic changes in cortical architecture take place in childhood, so that over the course of a child's first few years they lose up to half of their cortical cells and subsequently lose a great number of the nervous processes connecting one cell with another.[52] If there is any biological basis to memory this must mean that the circuits on which early memories may be laid down are being dug up and resurfaced repeatedly. It seems no surprise that memories during this period are liable to be scanty.

However if modern analytic notions seem without anatomical justification, the models of consciousness offered above seem to talk too much of computer processes and not enough of the contentless intimations and urges that the *locus coeruleus* and ventral tegmentum push into awareness. They do not seem dark enough or irrational enough to account for life in the raw. In its early years, the willingness of psychoanalysis to tackle the biological questions of lust and appetites found favour with many in the psychological community. In the next chapter I will return to biology and to a less mechanical model of psychological functioning in an attempt to bring the models of psychological functioning outlined above to life.

8 The Dynamic Unconscious and the Dynamics of Consciousness

In Chapter 7 the scope of the book was broadened from a historical study of the evolution of the concepts of hysteria and PTSD to take in recent work on the nature of the unconscious and the issue of consciousness. This chapter will take these issues further and in particular will pick up on the interaction between the unconscious and consciousness. In doing so it will return to the original mechanism that Freud envisaged as underlying the dynamism of the unconscious – rhythmicity. However I will argue that, far from having the inevitability of a mechanical operation as envisaged by Freud, both the dynamic unconscious and consciousness with which it interacts operate probabilistically in a manner aimed at anticipating the future rather than defending against the past.

There are good reasons for taking up these issues in terms of depression. The clinical picture of depression can be mapped on to that of a post-traumatic disorder quite well. Both involve a certain numbness, with recurrent waves of emotion. Both may involve little difficulty immediately after the trauma only to lead to an apparent resurfacing of the problem at a later date – seemingly triggered by innocuous events.

Janet, Breuer and Freud all argued for some version of this model. For Janet almost every hysteric was also depressed, and it was the lowering of mental energy brought about by the depression that permitted the development of hysteria. Breuer speculated that a single dominating unhappy idea, lying in the subconscious of depressives, could plausibly produce the clinical signs and symptoms of depression. For Freud this single dominating unhappy idea was the consequence of losing out in the Oedipal struggle. Further losses, he argued, cause depression by reawakening a primal loss. For the various object-relations theorists we all adopt 'a depressive position' even earlier in life than the Oedipal phase. This supposedly occurs in the process of negotiating independence from our mother and recurs at various different developmental stages when the question of independence arises. The occurrence of depression in later life then depends on the adequacy of our efforts to resolve the difficulties inherent in the balance between dependence and independence.

However intuitively plausible this last view is there are a number of difficulties with it. Many of the life events that trigger depression are not so traumatic – such as changing jobs because of promotion or moving to the house of one's dreams. In addition, where detailed investigation of subjects with borderline disorders and Briquet's syndrome has indicated an unrecognized history of physical or sexual abuse or gross disturbance of some sort in their past, this has not been the case for depression. Individuals who develop major depressive disorders appear to have no greater frequency of traumatic events in their childhood than those who do not become depressed. Furthermore Briquet's syndrome and the borderline disorders are relatively rare conditions but it now seems that most of us suffer a recognizable depressive disorder at some point in time.

More significantly perhaps, in contrast to post-traumatic disorders, the content of a depressive disorder is not dominated by the reliving of some prior unresolved event. This is also in contrast to grief reactions. In grief most normal subjects are consumed by recurrent intrusive imagery and emotions, often triggered by reminders of their loss. Some grief reactions, just like the post-traumatic neuroses, seem to go underground only to resurface later in a most painful and acute reliving of an earlier loss. In general grief reactions map far more closely on to the model of a post-traumatic neurosis than does depression.

Finally, unlike the post-traumatic neuroses, depressive disorders respond to anti-depressants and to ECT. This response to physical treatments rather than to 'talking therapies' has been a cornerstone in the medical argument that depression is an illness rather than simply a neurosis. It is for these reasons that depressions generally are subsumed under the category of manic-depressive psychosis – even where the subject may never have been manic, shown evidence of delusional beliefs or appeared to be hallucinating.[1]

The central importance of depression in this context lies in the accumulating body of evidence that this 'psychosis' is in most instances a mild disorder. When severe, depressive disorders are liable to be so by virtue of the neurotic responses they mobilize rather than by virtue of any intrinsic severity. When taken in conjunction with the potential severity of the post-traumatic disorders this 'mildness' points strongly to a need to undo the equation *severity = psychosis = biological disorder* that applies at present to psychiatric disorders and underpins the professional demarcation currently in place between psychiatrists and psychologists, to the detriment of both professions and of course those who seek help from them.

There is a further relevance in the case of depression which is that, as Janet argued, it may lay the basis for the later development of many neuroses. In so doing it opens up a new set of interpretive hazards, one of which is a liability to attribute recurrent images and emotions mistakenly to traumas that occurred in the past. The other is that the neuroses that develop in response to depression do not arise clearly from either endogenous or environmental sources alone. They arise rather in a fashion that may be termed accidental. The implications of this will be addressed further in Chapter 10.

RHYTHMICITY

The enchainment of past and future
Woven in the weakness of the changing body
Protects mankind from heaven and damnation
Which flesh cannot endure
T. S. Eliot, 'Burnt Norton'

In attempting to come to grips with these issues it is worth while to return to the problem Freud had in writing the Project for a Scientific Psychology. He was faced with a need to postulate an observer, within the brain, to account for the ability of a neuronal network to screen incoming information and detect what was likely to be acceptable and what was not. He was forced to conclude that some biological experience, probably innate, must be involved. It was this turn to the innate that led later to the development of his ideas about the Id and a switch from a psychology of consciousness to psychoanalysis.

Very similar problems faced the behaviourist psychologists some years later. Postulating a mechanical model of the mind, very similar to that in Freud's Project, behaviourists were faced with some awkward facts. In essence the various forms of behaviourism postulate that behaviour is a complex set of habits, whether these are established by simple association or reward-reinforced learning. Yet when asked to recall a name we are able to do so on some occasions but not on others. When shooting or bowling or engaging in any other activity we perform variably. Some days are good, others are not. Some times of the day we feel sharp, at other times we lose our edge.

As noted by Hull, the leading behaviourist of the 1930s, humans simply are not like computers or robots who, once programmed, mechanically repeat the performance.[2] Rats, the favourite experimental animal of the behaviourists, seem to be frustratingly like humans in this regard also. For many years behaviourists persisted with efforts aimed at getting rats to sleep or eat on cue, as learning theory suggested that all significant behaviour should be cue-based.[3] However it is not possible to condition a rat to fall asleep when and only when the clock in its cage shows twelve o'clock. When it comes to sleeping, eating and drinking, and indeed most of the behaviours that really count, as opposed to running mazes or pressing levers, rats seem to follow some internal *dynamic* of their own. Not only that, but when rats are taught intricate tasks or when their emotions are conditioned to certain stimuli the learning shows up best at the same time of day as they were taught. At other times of the day the experiments just work less well.

Such experimental findings do not apply only to rats. There are easily observable cycles of many of our behaviours, whether sleeping and waking or eating and drinking or remembering and learning. And these easily observable rhythms are only the tip of an iceberg. It has been said that to have life is to have rhythmicity. But even this underestimates the extent of the phenomenon. Ilya Prigogine discovered that even non-living collections of chemicals may start oscillating synchronously.[4] Far from being a source of instability such oscillations bring an order into what would otherwise be chaos. This order has been central to the development of life itself. There is not a living cell or system that has not built an organized system of oscillations into its functioning. Typical examples are the cascade systems in enzymes or the feedback regulation of enzyme activity. Adjacent cells in an organ end up oscillating in synchrony and there are typical rhythms in all our organ systems, from heart-rate variations during the day to rhythms in visual acuity, characteristic pulsatile outputs for each of our hormones, rest-activity rhythms and rhythms in deep body temperature.

Apart from the long-term controls on behaviour that such a system sets up, oscillatory systems lead to the phenomenon of pacing and the existence of pacemakers. Nerves are not just wet wires along which electrical impulses travel; they are cells, and accordingly are composed of a multitude of enzyme systems and other components, all of which are intrinsically oscillating. As these systems are geared towards the generation and transmission of impulses it is inevitable that such generation should occur *spontaneously*.[5] Spontaneous firing can even be demonstrated in nerve cells grown in culture and isolated from all other influences.

An interesting consequence of this is that nerve cells never constitute some *tabula rasa* on which an environment may write as it wishes. Rather environmental influences may act in one of two ways – either to add to or to damp down what is happening spontaneously. Thus the vagus nerve slows the heart from its spontaneous rate, while sympathetic nerves speed it up, but neither are responsible for the spontaneous baseline rate. Similarly with the brain. Our organs of balance discharge spontaneously; turning one way causes the discharge rate to speed up, turning the other way causes it to slow down.[6]

Circadian rhythms[7–9]

The first recorded observations on rhythmicity were made by a French astronomer, De Mairan, in 1729. He noted that plants raised their leaves to the sun even before it rose. Not only that, but they still raised their leaves even if removed to sunless caves. This suggested some active organizing process rather than a passive response to the environment.

Darwin later recognized daily, weekly and monthly cycles in behaviour and argued that these must stem from a common descent from tidal-dependent marine organisms. Living on the water-line would lead to the development of weekly and daily cycles. In general the existence of rhythmicity allows an organism to avail of temporal changes. This offers a wider variety of evolutionary niches for organisms. They are not limited to the spatial opportunities offered by the environment but can share the space with other occupants, for example, if they can manage to confine their active utilization of the space to a different time-frame. Despite this identification as a potentially important factor in evolution the study of rhythmicity has never attained full scientific respectability.

Some responsibility for this, ironically, may lie with Fliess, who first convinced Freud of the ubiquitous nature of rhythmicity and of its significance for mental life. Fliess developed a system centred on the presence of innate 23-day (male/physical) and 28-day (female/emotional) rhythmic cycles. In the 1920s Alfred Teltscher, an Austrian engineer, proposed a further, 33-day, cycle based on work done on the intellectual performance of students at school and university. This 'biorhythm' model of rhythmicity has tended to discredit all scientific study of rhythms.* But there are a number of other difficulties as well. Firstly scientists are concerned with regular and predictable phenomena and have not had the inclination, or, up until now, the necessary statistical tools, to take on the study of life as a pulsing, highly variable phenomenon. Secondly the pulses in question have not always been so obvious. This is because not everything beats in synchrony but, commonly, different rhythms are loosely co-ordinated with each other. This leads to a masking of many rhythms by others so that there appear instead to be conditions of calm stability rather than of dramatic variability. Thirdly the idea of dramatic variability seems to go against one of the oldest principles in biology, the principle of homeostasis. This principle, first propounded by Claude Bernard in 1865, states that living systems aim at maintaining constant conditions. For example arrangements are made to excrete waste products if they build up past a certain point, or to counterbalance shifts in blood pressure or acidity in the blood should either of these vary beyond fairly narrow limits. This principle would on the surface appear to militate against any dramatic variability in vital functions.

The situation is now changing however. The necessary statistical tools to investigate rhythmicity are now available. Where they were once seen as being in contradiction with the principle of homeostasis, circadian rhythms are increasingly being seen as a three-dimensional example of homeostasis. Rhythmicity allows the priming of physiological functions for imminent use and shuts down functions that are no longer needed. This priming and shutting down makes more gradual the degree of variation that occurs at times of physiological activity. For example there are rhythms in eating but also anticipatory rhythms in the brain cells responsible for appetite, in the hormones necessary for efficient digestion and in the intestinal enzymes necessary for processing the food load. This complex network is primed before we are even aware of

*During the 1950s a biorhythm model of behaviour with intersecting cognitive, emotional and vital rhythms and critical days at the points of intersection was proposed. A recent popularization of this can be found in Thommen's *Is This Your Day?*[10] Many readers will have seen charts or calculations claiming to be able to decode where one is in one's emotional, intellectual or physical cycle. Most will realize that this is an amusing party game but no more.

In contrast to biorhythms an acceptably scientific approach to the issues of rhythmicity began with the establishment of the International Society for the Study of Biological Rhythms in 1937. Because of confusion with biorhythms this society was renamed in 1971 the International Society for Chronobiology and the term circadian rhythm came into use to distinguish a rhythm with a sound empirical basis from a biorhythm.

wanting to eat, so that once we start eating the digestive physiology will smoothly handle the task with the minimum of excessive variation. Following digestion all these systems shut down. This arrangement permits the efficient mobilization of resources and permits functions that are not needed to lie quiescent.

Clocks and rhythms[11–12]

Rhythmicity in the nervous system is paced, just as in the heart. This function is carried out by a 'clock'. Initially this was thought to be the pineal gland but it is now known to lie in the suprachiasmatic nucleus, in an area of the brain that regulates appetite, fluid balance, temperature and hormonal secretion. The clock pacemakes and by this means 'organizes' internal rhythms. It also synchronizes external routines and internal rhythms. Synchrony with environmental rhythms does not just happen as one might expect, given two adjacent oscillating systems. Totally free from environmental influences rhythms continue to hold their shape but that shape becomes extended to a 25-hour or longer cycle rather than a 24-hour one. Given an internal tendency to a 25-hour rhythm there is always a need for adjustment.

There is a consequence of this organization for the culture of nervous problems. From antiquity observers had noted that there seemed to be a periodicity in episodes of nervous disorder. This seemed most clear in manic-depressive illness, as subjects often cycled regularly between depression and mania or had recurrent illnesses, of about the same length and often at the same time each year. This led to efforts to determine the period of the illness, or the period between episodes of the illness – with Fliess's biorhythm theory being a high point in these efforts. The implication was that there was some internal clock marking time until the next episode, which would happen regardless of what else might be taking place in the life of the individual at the time. Such a view reinforced notions that depression and mania are endogenous illnesses, whose onsets have little to do with social factors and more to do with some sort of degenerate reflex. But the discovery that the period of the internal clock is *circa* one day puts paid to such ideas. Far from circadian rhythms following Fliessian harmonics that roll on despite what may be going on in the environment, the clock seems to be reset several times a day by environmental factors. This opens up a quite different perspective on depressive disorders, which is that they might arise by virtue of a mismatch between internal rhythms and external routines – as for example happens in jet-lag and shift work.

THE RHYTHMIC UNCONSCIOUS

Rhythms can be entrained by environmental factors. Two of the most important factors are the light–dark and the temperature cycles. Entrainment to such cycles leads to considerable structuring of internal physiological functions. Thus for a sleep–wake cycle to run efficiently in parallel with the light–dark cycle there must be programmes that turn off the need for micturition or defecation during the night. All physiological functions are structured in this way so that those needed at particular points of the 24-hour cycle are primed at the pertinent times. In this way the organism both maximizes its chances of *mastering* its particular environment and *knows* something about the environment.

For Freud and thinkers of his day physics and physical concepts, in particular the concept of energy, provided the ultimate paradigm. Theories were respectable in so far as they appeared to conform to the principle of the conservation of energy or to the second law of thermodynamics. However today, at least in biology, the notion of information is the core reference point. Circadian rhythms embody biological information that antedates even the evolution of DNA. The capacity for anticipating needs based on internalized knowledge of the environment can be seen in plants which raise their leaves to the sun even before it has risen. It can be seen in the dramatic changes in hormone levels, nervous system activity and cardiovascular tone that takes place in us before we wake, which prepares us to face the stresses of the waking day. It can be seen in animals who live underground and emerge only after dark has fallen, when predators have gone. Putting their noses out of doors to check on whether it is safe to come out would be dangerous. Rhythms provide a means of knowing without taking these risks.

While light and temperature cycles are of some importance in human beings social cycles are of much greater importance to the organization of human rhythmicity. We appear to structure our internal biologies in accordance with the routines of significant others in our lives. We take our cues from them for waking, eating and sleeping, regardless of whether it is bright or dark outside. The attempt to isolate subjects from social influences has proved to be very difficult. Even sending people down into caves with no apparent contact with the outside world may not succeed.

This structuring of our biologies in response to social signals provides us with some knowledge of our social situations – an unconscious knowledge. But it is important to specify more closely what kind of knowledge is involved.

Life evolves in progressively more complicated forms on the basis of bets – the bet being that the latest species has incorporated (in the literal sense of built into the body) ever better strategies for survival in the face of uncertainty. Survival involves managing the future rather than defending against the past.

All plant and most animal species operate on the basis of fixed bets. In response to certain important stimuli there are fixed reactions. Recent evolution has taken a gamble of introducing flexibility into this system of fixed reaction patterns. Corticate animals, especially the higher mammals, can model their environment rather than just respond automatically. But even in these cases the form of modelling that is perception is a bet. We fill in lines or dots that are not there to see squares and rectangles, on the basis of what seems like a good bet from the available evidence. We can adjust our bets with a little practice – given a few days' practice we can cope with a world seen through upside-down spectacles.

In order for this conscious modelling to take place most physical and mental functions must happen automatically. This is necessary in order for the organism to have enough time left over to play with the complex predictive models that are perceptions. Circadian rhythms are one of our most fundamental sets of bets aimed at achieving just this. They follow the best bets in our social environment. Like perceptions they stay programmed to what seems like the best bet until the inevitable force of circumstance or repeated failures of prediction lead to a reversal. When entrainment to the environment breaks down the consequences are twofold. One is a decreased efficiency of adaptation to external circumstances. The other is a decreased internal efficiency as the structure built up in relation to environmental order tends to collapse. This failure of adaptation and decreased internal efficiency can be seen in outline in states of jet-lag or when shift work becomes disruptive. These changes affect cognition, motivation and mood.

Rhythms and cognition[13–14]

As noted, behaviourist psychologists found that their animals did not learn like automata. One recently recognized reason for this involves state-dependent learning. This depends on the idea that the brain, unlike a computer, can be influenced by things other than the input from the keyboard. The brain's hardware is turning over quite apart from any inputs from outside.

What is involved becomes clear in the case of drugs and fevers. By drinking a small amount of alcohol, for example, we alter our brain state. What we register thereafter must alter an already altered brain state. The combined effects of both alterations will be most easily reproducible again when I next have a similar amount of alcohol. It is this that underlies the experience that many people have had of having conversations over a drink that they appear later unable to recall. Based on this, if I leave my car somewhere because I have had too much to drink and cannot remember where it is the next day, I am more likely to remember if I have another drink. In the same way fevers change brain state. As a result it may be very difficult to remember much more than in a hazy way the few days spent lying in bed feverish. If we get to the stage of delirium we may remember nothing.

Circadian rhythms provide an encompassing source of brain-state changes. Everything in the brain is rhythmically turning over – hormones, neurotransmitters, receptors and other neurobiological elements. It is not surprising therefore to find that time of day influences cognitive functions such as learning and remembering.

This happens in two ways. One is through what is called the basic rest–activity cycle. This is a 120- to 180-minute rhythm which can be seen most clearly in infants, who wake and sleep on a three-hour cycle. In later life this is subsumed into a 24-hour framework, but it is still recognizably present dictating a pattern of varying energy levels during the day and our entries to and exits from the various stages of sleep. This cycle operates to alter the tone of the *locus coeruleus* such that levels of arousal and vigilance fluctuate rhythmically. In this manner during both day and night we pass, willy-nilly, through a sequence of stages of consciousness, each with its predominant set of associations. This in part may account for the recurrent rather than the constant nature of intrusive imagery and emotions in the post-traumatic disorders – it certainly seems to account for those recurrent intrusive images we call dreams.[15]

There is a second way in which rhythms affect our thoughts. This follows as the very stuff of thoughts and memories is constantly changing, whether or not we are actively thinking and remembering. As you the reader sit there reading you are probably aware of images and thoughts coming to mind unbidden and on the other hand of finding it difficult to consistently keep your mind on some aspect of the text that you might want to think about. These seemingly unprompted images and fantasies have long been of interest to psychodynamically oriented theorists, who argue that such fantasies are far from unprompted. It is this that has led to claims that, lurking behind their seeming unconnectedness, is a royal road to a dynamic unconscious whose contents may be brought into consciousness by the careful scrutiny of associations.

However if circadian change means anything it means that the very stuff from which images are made is turning over like everything else in the brain. This has two consequences. One is that our images of things don't last long. Short-term memory typically lasts only thirty seconds before the original impression of something that we register decays. The other is that images must be suggesting themselves the whole time, as the stuff of which they are made is reconfiguring itself constantly. This should give rise to something like what happens when we look at clouds or fires. Images suggest themselves from the changing shapes. The images we see in such situations will depend on the current concerns of what can be called the ego or personal consciousness. But if this is the case then it would seem that the Id does not push images up into consciousness, against which egos defend, but rather that the images the ego sees, or is not prepared to see, all lie within consciousness.

Rhythms and motives[16-17]

Those basic motives we call appetites, operating through the ventral tegmental system, are obviously under rhythmic control. But the influence of rhythmicity on motivation extends much further than this. For example working with chaffinches Rutger Wever found that exposure to constant bright light leads eventually to a state of sustained sleepless activation. An implication of his experiments is that much of our normal behaviour stems simply from the strategic necessity of organic systems to be in harmony with their environment. For humans this means being in harmony with social periodicities. Given such harmonization we fall asleep in part not because we want to but because everyone else does. The weight of what everyone else is doing, as well as environmental factors such as light and temperature cycles, feeds through and determines a great deal of our behaviour by affecting our physiology – leaving us with little effective choice in the matter.

Mania is characterized by a state of sustained sleepless activation, quite comparable to that found by Wever in chaffinches. From armchair distance it is sometimes assumed that in mania the subject is feigning their hyperactivity. However the analysis outlined above suggests the possibility that they are being driven. This accords with what many subjects say – that their activity is involuntary.

In depression there is the reverse. Subjects are sapped of energy or have the wind taken out of their sails. Again they usually say that this fatigue is an affliction rather than something they can control. Commonly they are bewildered at their inability to summon up the energy to do things they want to do. But the only reason they can come up with for this lack of energy is that there must be something wrong with their will-power. Those supposed to be helping them often fail to point out other more benign possibilities, and indeed often bring about further demoralization by suggesting that the person is truly at odds with themselves and will not get better until they face up to some unpleasant truths.[18]

Rhythms and the Id[19]

On the one hand unconscious and rhythmic inputs to cognition and motivation come close to comprising Freud's original Id. On the other hand they also return us to the type of psychology of the unconscious that was articulated first by Janet and James but which has seen little further development, until recently. It was William James who first proposed that habits play an important role in mental life. Since so much of what we do appears to occur automatically and unconsciously, yet we are not reflex-dominated automata, James argued that associations based on mental imagery could not be the whole story. Habits must be far more important than we often concede.

According to James habits arise spontaneously. They are not necessarily linked to pleasure and pain but grow in the soil of our lives like wild flowers, in whatever circumstances we happen to be. Even in prison, with no material pleasures or pains, we get into routines. Rather than depending on pleasure, habits grow because they confer advantages. Once acquired, the behaviour that is habitual occurs effortlessly, thus freeing attention to focus on the unforeseen; there is also an economizing of memory, constant repetition of a skill until it becomes habitual freeing us of the need to store as memories all of the various times we carry out the particular operation. So much needs to be stored in memory as it is that this economy offered by habit is not an insignificant one.

There are two important aspects to this arrangement. One is that, in the case of highly routinized behaviours, conscious awareness may be a hindrance – consciously remembering how to ride a bicycle for example can actually get in the way of riding it. The other point is that typically habits bear no mark of their origin. They are eternally present. As opposed to conscious memories they are impersonal. In contrast the act of conscious remembering involves the experience of 'this is part of my past I am remembering'. Memories are autobiographical in a way that habits are not.

If we extend the notion of habits to include a set of deeply ingrained habitual ways to handle impulses – impulses that are established in early childhood, at a time when we may be totally unaware that this is happening – such an Id would, like the Freudian Id, be timeless and impersonal. If we then embed the notion of habits in the larger context of routines we produce a dynamic Id that is predicated on circadian functioning. Like habits, routine suggests an organization of knowledge. It suggests that within particular frameworks much of what *will* happen has already been anticipated, already been faced, already been sorted out, so that when recurring it can be handled automatically, apparently even without thought. Routines overlap with habits. They make the acquisition of habits possible (as in state-dependent learning) and are in turn structured by habits. They have a neurophysiological foundation in circadian rhythms and in turn act to maintain particular circadian organizations.

We master large amounts of our lives by virtue of the social routines we engage in, therefore, literally by incorporating the information into our physiology. Who I am and the routines in which I live overlap. Familiar routines give me a sense of who I am. Unfamiliar ones may confront me with the sense of not being sure about who I am. In other words, much of who we are or what we feel ourselves to be gets buried in our activities. This sense of who I am may be totally at odds with any account of myself I am able to give. Giving an account of myself is another skill – one not easily routinizable, as any serious account will need constant updating. But the notion that I do not know who I am just because I cannot give some analyst a good account of myself does not hold up. Simply surviving indicates an 'ecologically valid self-knowledge'.

This proposed Id therefore would be a repository of unconscious knowledge which shapes the later acquisition of conscious associations – all of which would help to meet some of the problems faced by Freud in the Project. There are two clear differences however between the unconscious as conceived here and that proposed by Freud. The rhythmic unconscious, outlined above, is radically unconscious. It does not contain symbols or images. It does not contain inherited knowledge – although the capacity to be structured in a manner that will assist adaptation is inherited.

There is a second difference. Even if I am skilled at dissecting my own motives and well used to giving an account of myself, there is much that no one can put into words and be confident about. This is partly because a certain amount of meaning is literally buried in each act and partly also because all acts have at least a certain amount of incompleteness to them. All are performed in the face of uncertainty. Rather than being the repository of primal truths the unconscious proposed here is composed of fallible anticipations of the future. Depression provides one instance of what happens when unconscious predictions go wrong. It also illustrates how the operations of consciousness are predicated on anticipating the future.

RHYTHM AND BLUES[20-1]

While it has always been believed that depression is consequent on adversity, for decades there were a group of depressions known as the endogenous depressions which were supposed to come out of the blue. These were said to involve a chemical imbalance and accordingly they were seen as a medical illness appropriately treated with pills. However starting from the late 1960s, a series of studies has shown that the endogenous depressions are precipitated by life events. The conventional view is that the life event is traumatic and precipitates a PTSD of some sort. As we have noted earlier in this chapter there are problems with this view. An alternative is that, while life events may be traumatic and produce grief, they also involve a disruption of routines. This leads to a loss of clear signals to internal rhythmicity, with a consequent break-down of the kind that happens in jet-lag or after shift work – a life-event lag.

It may often be weeks after a death, a birth, a house move or a change of job – weeks after one has got over the initial reactions – before the depression strikes. Subjects are often amazed at becoming depressed some time after they thought they had come to terms with the change in their life. This delayed onset is not unlike the delay of several weeks that it takes for the rhythms of subjects in isolation experiments to drift out of phase with the environment. It is a necessary consequence of a system which is designed to track environmental change but not each and every change in the environment.

Circadian rhythms track environmental order. Accordingly we can completely change our environment – go on holidays – without ill effects. But moving jobs, even within the same building, may be an entirely different affair. Personal order and the efficient functioning of one's entire body in response to that order may be disorganized. All the cues that one had built up in the old environment, which were reliable indicators of what was likely to happen next, may be gone, and with them go important signals to internal processes of what to prepare for next. This is analogous to what happens when two pendulums are swinging side by side; if one is interfered with the period of the second also changes – with time. Disruption of circadian rhythms in this manner leads to a loss of vitality – as in shift-work maladaptation syndrome. There is a considerable amount of evidence that the majority of depressions are rather like what happens to us after shift work. They are noticeable but not disabling. They involve the same core complaints – disturbances of behaviours that have significant automatic and rhythmic components, such as sleep, appetite and libido as well as energy levels and concentration. Most run a brief self-limiting course, as do shift-work disturbances. This would be predicted of a rhythm disorder as rhythms must inevitably reharmonize with environmental periodicities.

Depression in this context is being taken to mean not sadness, guilt or hopelessness, but dysphoria, lethargy and apathy. This may run against the grain of common expectation of what is meant by depression but current evidence would suggest that, far from having intrusive imagery or a clear psychological problem, depressed subjects, if they go to their general practitioners, present with flu-like complaints of pain and lethargy, so much so that they are typically not diagnosed as having a psychological problem unless *in addition* they start talking about guilt or sadness.[22]

And of course the problem is improved by a physical treatment – antidepressants. These have the rather curious property of being neither euphoriant nor tranquillizing. And, unlike tranquillizers, euphoriants, tea, coffee, neuroleptics and every other agent which acts on the brain, they do not work immediately. They take up to two weeks to make much difference – a time period consistent with the resolution of a rhythm disorder.

Mood and emotion[23]

I am proposing that a disruption of circadian rhythms is at the heart of a mood disturbance. But what is a mood? For most of us the word usually seems to mean some sort of extended emotion. However closer scrutiny of the two terms and their usages suggests that moods and emotions are not the same kind of thing. Moods appear to be something more like climate, in contrast to emotions, which may find an analogy with the weather. Given a particular climate certain weather conditions are more likely, but sustained weather conditions of one sort does not indicate that the basic climate has changed. Put another way, mood is like the pedal functions of a piano whereas emotions are like the individual keys. Depressing the pedal colours the overall tone but does not produce melodies. The combination of emotional melodies may be all that is audible to the undiscriminating ear but the texture of a piece can be substantially influenced by use of the pedals.

As noted in Chapter 7 there do seem to be something like pleasure spots in some of the oldest brain areas. But pleasure seems to be something derived from the patterning of inputs through these pathways; familiar patterns are pleasant and unfamiliar ones less pleasant.

A striking feature of the brain is that, in contrast to the centres for vision, hearing, movement and touch, there are no pain centres. So how do we *register* pain? The answer seems to be that, when firing in unusual, or unfamiliar, patterns, the stimuli that carry touch or sound or whatever sensation are painful. Noise that is too loud is painful. Pressure on my arm that is too intense is painful. Stimuli that I do not normally have, such as the ones from the chemicals liberated in the tissues around the wound on my hand, are painful.

There are good grounds, based on this understanding of pain, to suggest that rhythms provide the substrate for what we call mood. When functioning normally they are by definition the patterns of familiarity. When out of joint, as in jet-lag or with shift-work disturbances, there is dysphoria bordering on the painful. Significantly many depressed subjects complain of pain and malaise rather than or underlying their emotions of sadness, hopelessness and guilt.

It has been notoriously difficult to put the dysphoria of depression into words. The model being offered here may help explain why this should be, proposing as it does that mood is to emotion as habits are to memories. Just as habits in contrast to memory are an inarticulate process, of which there is dim awareness rather than clear recall, so also we can expect mood changes to be difficult to put into words. This difficulty in expression, it should be noted, does not arise because of conflicts about our image of ourselves of the kind that inhibit us from expressing our emotions.

Depressed subjects classically find it difficult to articulate their state. They know they feel out of joint and at odds with themselves but are usually unable to convey what the state feels like. But while this central difficulty is similar to that experienced by jet-lag sufferers and those with shift-work disturbances these latter are able to convey their state by reference to the experience they have been through. The same is true when it comes to articulating our experience of pain. We depend on being able to point to a wound, thereby getting across our meaning. When the pain is internal and not localizable we classically have much greater difficulties.

If depression involves, at its core, something like the disorder outlined here, then it is an environmentally precipitated psychosis rather than an environmentally precipitated neurosis. One of the many senses of the word 'psychosis' is to indicate a disorder in which the core symptoms result from an alteration beyond the normal range in an aspect of brain functioning.[24] In this sense depression, as outlined above, is both a psychosis and an illness. But in this sense of the word there is no implication that a psychosis is a more severe psychological disturbance than a neurosis. One does not have to infer any *abnormality* of brain functioning to account for the recurrent intrusive images and emotions found in PTSD or obsessive-compulsive disorder. But these neuroses in some cases lead to much greater distress than depression.*

THE DYNAMICS OF CONSCIOUSNESS

Disruptions of circadian rhythms will lead to an irruption of the unconscious into consciousness. Things that had been done automatically before will not now be done as efficiently. Things that had not to be thought about before now have to be thought about. Unfortunately while some behaviour can be sorted out by thinking, some must be automatic or it will not occur at all. Thinking about automatic behaviours will in general only make the problem more salient without leading to a remedy – but where there is a problem it will be impossible not to think about it. Thinking about such things as how to stay asleep or how to be interested in something will in turn decrease the amount of attention available for the kind of environmental demands that thinking can have an impact on. Having to cope with the kind of problems that thinking cannot solve reveals a great deal about the dynamics of consciousness.

*In this sense depression would be a neurosis in the older, pre-1895, use of this term – although one that is environmentally precipitated rather than the result of any degeneracy. Prominent recurrent intrusive imagery and emotions would, in contrast, have qualified pre-1895 as a psychotic disorder. Confusingly, and as a direct result of Freud's influence, the term neurosis, at least in American psychiatry, is now banned totally and psychosis is restricted to disorders which involve delusions and hallucinations. The confusion in these terms is brought out nicely when one finds shift-work disturbances being referred to as 'pseudo-neuroses'.[25]

Dynamic psychology reborn[26-8]

One of the more recent advances in psychology concerns the reactions of individuals who are called upon to make judgments under uncertainty. This field has developed around the issues of the assessment of risk or the making of diagnoses, whether these assessments/diagnoses are made by stockbrokers, doctors or simply experimental subjects put in situations where they have an incomplete possession of the relevant facts but are nevertheless forced to make choices.

This has led to a recognition of the strategies (heuristics) that we bring to such situations. We all it seems behave with the 'logic' of a gambler rather than that of a logician retrospectively analysing a problem. We have hunches regarding what to 'go with'. We base our hunches on information to hand rather than on a rational assessment of the probabilities (availability heuristic). We go by stereotypes, such as 3 and 7 are lucky numbers but 13 isn't (representativeness heuristic). Despite this we often hang on to our hunches in the face of mounting evidence – sometimes increasingly firmly (anchoring heuristic). Or if we change we do so abruptly and discontinuously.

The study of such illogicality appropriately belongs to dynamic psychology. It seems that in situations of uncertainty we all bring 'biased' strategies to the management of uncertainty. There is a sense in which talk of systematic biasing in the estimates we make is redolent of the claims of psychoanalysis, but what is involved in the management of uncertainty is a question of heuristics rather than one of defences – a method of handling incoming data rather than a method of avoiding home-truths. Our knowledge of such dynamics have, furthermore, arisen from studies of the ways in which *we all* estimate probability rather than from studies in which *a few* analysed subjects handle their difficulties.

However while illogical these heuristic strategies are not irrational. Perception also involves the construction of biased probability estimates. Thus when faced with ambiguous pictures or scenes we opt in just the same way for images of the obvious and familiar and are biased by things we have seen recently. This is dramatically clear when we fall in love and think we see our lover in passing strangers.

These heuristic strategies do not apply in jet-lag or shift work as it is clear what has gone wrong and what the likely outcome will be. But depressed subjects, faced with a change in themselves and uncertainty regarding the outcome of the change, operate as all subjects do when called on to make judgments under uncertainty. Their opinions of what is happening to them tend to the stereotypical. They are coloured by other things that have recently happened to them. They also tend to hold on to particular views of what is wrong, in a manner that may not be easily shifted despite convincing evidence that they are mistaken.

In the case of depression the stereotypes that best account for the available evidence are those that emphasize personal failings. The rationale for this is roughly: 'I don't know what's wrong with me but I'm not up to par. All the available evidence is that I'm not able to pull my weight. People who do not pull their weight are useless, worthless people. Therefore I must be a useless, worthless person.'

This has a number of consequences. One is that the conclusion that current poor performances indicate personal worthlessness will necessarily be demoralizing. This demoralization amplifies the original disturbance. At this point also subjects will begin to talk of personal worthlessness rather than just of malaise or dysphoria, leading GPs to recognize the condition as a 'psychological' problem. This produces the label of depression, with all the problems and expectations that this brings.

There are other options for the resolution of this uncertainty. There is the 'spiritual' outcome, for example. Disturbances of rhythms can lead to a drying up of image flow, a sense of lethargy – that everything is a struggle. This, accompanied by guilt and hopelessness, gives a picture close to a dark night of the soul experience, where the spiritual pilgrim feels deserted by God and has no joy from living or taste for life. This type of outcome is likely if such a possibility is available to the depressed person – if one of their available stereotypes is that of the soul abandoned by God. Increasingly in our culture today individuals are less likely to come to such conclusions. But they must have been all but inevitable in many communities in the past.[29]

The operation of these biases in all of us has been described in detail elsewhere.[30] The point behind raising the issue here is threefold. One is to indicate that this dynamic is likely to lead to the emergence of hysteria. A second is that it produces a set of notable interpretive hazards. The third is that depression offers us a window on the operations of consciousness.

The dynamics of hysteria

I have argued that, in attempting to account for changes in how we are functioning, we are liable to base our judgments on evidence readily available to us rather than to wait until we have sought out all possible evidence. We are liable to be over-influenced by stereotypes. And we are also liable to anchor on some often inappropriate view of what is wrong with us. This amounts to saying that we are likely to become hysterical, as defined by Janet. He proposed that hysteria is a disorder in which subjects operate under the influence of fixed ideas that do not correspond with organic pathology.

Depressed subjects regularly override the evidence of what is actually physically wrong with them in favour of their idea of what is wrong. They are encouraged in this by the myriad of minor physical symptoms that accompany depression, such as a dry mouth, dry skin and hair, constipation, anorexia, insomnia, anergia etc. The very fact that nothing is dramatically wrong is a hindrance, rather than a help, to getting the answer right, in that where something is grossly disturbed the affected subject usually gets a much fuller data set on which to operate.

Such a dynamic accounts for example for why an elderly woman I saw recently, who was clearly depressed, claimed that she had a tumour of the throat, and that it was this that was making eating impossible for her. Closer examination revealed that she had indeed a dry throat and that eating was probably uncomfortable. It also revealed that she had a husband who died of a tumour of the throat, making tumours of the throat available to her in a way they would not be for the rest of us.

This kind of 'inappropriate' clinical presentation is today termed abnormal illness behaviour rather than hysteria.[31-3] However, as illness behaviour is behaviour that is as it were superimposed on a real illness, the notion of abnormal illness behaviour causes almost as much medical discomfort as does that of hysteria. All too often abnormal illness behaviours seem to function to real illnesses as grins do to Chesire cats – something that may unfortunately be left behind after the illness has gone.

In medical and surgical outpatient clinics it is now recognized that abnormal illness behaviour gives rise to a greater amount of consultation time than does actual active pathology – as the examples of Da Costa's and Briquet's syndrome discussed in Chapter 6 illustrate. In psychiatry however grins without cats have the kind of insubstantial quality that we associate with ghosts in the mind's machine. They spook us. This creates a situation in which other doctors turn to the psychiatrist for advice on what they would think is a clear psychiatric problem – illness behaviour in the absence of an illness – only to find the psychiatrist frustratingly difficult to engage.

There is a further irony in that psychiatrists, in their efforts to make of manic-depression and schizophrenia real illnesses, have in recent exclusively biological hypotheses taken away the possibility of one of the features of all other medical illnesses – their halo of illness behaviours.[34]

In addition to the 'semi-hysteria' that is abnormal illness behaviour it is common clinical experience that depressed patients may be frankly hysterical – in the sense of going off their feet, losing their memories or voices. Half of the cases cited in the preamble began in depression. This hysteria usually clears up when antidepressant treatments cure the underlying depression and thereby take away the stimulus to the hysteria. (This rather than the crude idea of repatterning probably accounts for the usefulness of ECT in the war neuroses.)

What applies to hysteria is also true for the other neuroses. If not somewhat hysterical, the depressed subject is highly likely to be phobic or obsessional. In general all of these disorders clear with effective treatment of the underlying depression, if the core disorder has not been too severe or allowed to persist for too long. In a proportion of all these cases however the neurosis will persist after the underlying disorder has cleared up, necessitating a further and specific intervention. This has not been a problem for the phobic and obsessional states since the introduction of effective behavioural methods. But it is a problem in cases of hysteria, particularly if there are social factors maintaining the hysterical position.

The hazards of interpretation

Depression, therefore, can act directly as a trauma to initiate a neurosis. It can also, by lowering competence and generally increasing anxiety levels, make more likely a neurotic response to what would have otherwise been relatively minor environmental problems.

In attempting to account for what is happening to them depressed subjects commonly come to the stereotypical conclusion that they must be useless, worthless people. While the initial conclusion will be based on current poor levels of functioning they will then trawl through their past for confirmatory evidence. In the nature of things they will find it. We all have shameful events of some sort locked away – consciously repressed. These are liable to become the focus of attention and may be elaborated into events of major significance. This of course may lead to the impression that what is involved is a post-traumatic neurosis of some sort.

The phenomenon of state-dependent memory, mentioned earlier, will tend to reinforce this. Many people who become depressed for a second time find the memories and preoccupations they had during the first episode come flooding back as though it were yesterday, even though it might have been decades before. At least part of the basis for this seems to lie in the actual alterations in physical state brought about by the depressive episode.

The combined weight of these two factors is liable to create the impression of an unresolved post-traumatic neurosis – indeed a particularly 'neurotic' neurosis, in that the subject will seemingly be caving in over quite minor issues. However far from being particularly weak-minded or degenerate the individuals who in my experience are most likely to go down this path are those who have up to the onset of their depression been particularly go-getting or have had the highest standards for themselves. Often the problem lies in the determination to hunt down the psychological cause for what is not a psychological problem.

Rhythmicity is unconscious in the true sense of something that can *only* function unconsciously, not in the sense of something that is not available to consciousness through inattention or repression or that can potentially be brought into consciousness with training. When rhythms go wrong however the results do irrupt into consciousness. They enter in the way that a knock in the engine of your car or a sudden loss of power when you put your foot on the accelerator enters into consciousness. This is not another way for the car to work. This is the car not working. The *it*, rather than a semi-personalized sexual Id, has gone wrong.

Psychotherapies in general have advocated becoming aware of what one is not normally aware of, whether it be one's emotions, or buried problems, or neglected areas of one's psyche. However the unconsciousness that is buried in rhythmicity is not the source of more vital truths or a repository of past repressions. Coming face to face with one's inner working as in depression does not lead to an advance in self-knowledge and does not guarantee health. Becoming aware of the wheels of one's brain turning ever more slowly or a drying up of image flow is no dark night of the soul. Neither is getting better predicated on accepting some truths. Accordingly the traditional role for insight is not operative in the psychotherapy for such a disorder.

The constitution of consciousness[35-6]

One of the major surprises of recent years has been the finding that *biological* depressions respond reliably to talking treatments, most notably to cognitive therapy. There are two ways this could happen. One, which is indirect, applies whatever one conceives the biological basis of depression to be. This is that recovery can be brought about by removing blocks to recovery, in much the way that reducing anxiety levels in the case of someone who has an ulcer promotes recovery.

An additional direct mechanism may apply if depression involves a disturbance of circadian rhythms. This is that cognitive therapy and the other therapies shown to be useful for biological depression have in common encouragements to structured and motivated activity, and this can be expected to lead to a re-entrainment of disturbed rhythms.[37]

The response of biological depression to cognitive therapy has had implications for one of the original tenets of cognitive therapy, which was that subjects who became depressed were somehow being more illogical than the rest of us, as evidenced by their making incorrect inferences from everyday events. They were, it was argued, somehow psychologically degenerate compared to the normal. In contrast the model of cognitive biasing outlined above envisages the cognitive super-structure of depression arising by a process of normal irrationality acting on a subtle and difficult to interpret basic disorder.

But aside from disputes about why cognitive therapy might work there is the nature of its practice, which will now concern us. In theory subjects who are depressed come to their therapist and make statements such as, 'I am a useless, worthless person,' to which the appropriate response is to ask them for the evidence for this assertion, to get them to assess whether the evidence entirely supports the assertion, to help them to look around for any other ways to interpret the evidence or for other evidence that they have neglected and which when considered might provide the basis for a reinterpretation.

In practice what this means is that the subject provides the details of a scene that has happened recently, such as an encounter with a friend, that has caused them to feel bad. They might say for example that while they were there saying something their friend seemed to be paying no heed to them. The first point to note here is that what is involved is a reading of an image in the mind's eye or a replay of some internal dialogue.

The second point regards what happens next, which is that the thera-pist is unlikely to ask for a cold assessment of probabilities, as to whether this really means that their friend thought they were not worth paying any heed to. Rather they will be asked to do two things. One is to give a much fuller context for the incident – to rewind their mind's-eye reel and replay the scenes before and after the episode in question. The other is to get hold of the images that flashed through their mind when they became aware that their friend was paying no heed to them.

The subject's conscious experience is often something like having a sideshow playing in parallel to the main performance, and the job of the therapist is to get them to focus on what is happening in the sideshow

– what the plot of that show is. Frequently the sideshow will feature a performance in which the subject as central actor is standing in one spot with people circling round apparently oblivious of their existence, or in which they may be left crying in one spot after everyone has left. These images will have flashed through the subject's mind, ordinarily almost unnoticed. These private images are not ones that subjects imagine are of importance in the process of negotiating with the outside world. But it would seem they are registered enough to cause a wave of sadness, anger or frustration to wash up on to the deck of consciousness – apparently almost from nowhere.

The earlier discussion of heuristic strategies was somewhat abstract. The latter example brings home what actually happens. The stereotype of the useless, worthless person is not some paper fiction. Rather it actually becomes incarnate on the mental stage. Early in a depression this interloper, new to his role, may be somewhat two-dimensional, but in due course he cloaks himself in the garments and gestures of past performances until he becomes a player who 'in a fiction, a dream of passion, could force his soul so to his whole conceit, that from her working all the visage wann'd; tears in his eyes, distraction in his aspect, a broken voice, and his whole function suiting with forms to his conceit'. A player capable of reducing many a Gilbert Ryle to the status of a rogue and peasant slave.

There is an important lesson here regarding the mechanisms that control entry into consciousness. The images that cognitive therapy deals with ordinarily are a mixture of truth and fantasy, of what has happened, what could have happened and what might happen – 'if things keep going the way they are, I can literally see people ignoring me'. In attempting to grapple with this cognitive therapy aims at getting a full picture of what is going on in the mind of the subject, but for the purpose of persuasion rather than in order to abreact some trauma. From the point of view of therapy this points to the need to make different calculations on different occasions regarding the balance of truth and fantasy incorporated in mental imagery.

On a broader front however the evidence from depressed patients would appear to suggest that these heuristic strategies are not simply some biased calculation of probabilities but rather are intrinsic to the workings of, if not entirely constitutive of, the very mechanism that governs what enters consciousness. We don't consciously make calculations or balance probabilities. We have images of possibilities or of options. The calculations are done earlier and govern what images we see.

This is analogous to what happens when we perceive. Prior to perceiving a range of stimuli are used as depth cues from which the probable sizes and distances from us of elements of the scene before us are judged. A considerable calculation of probabilities based on available cues, with undue weight being given certain representative features of the scene, goes on all the time, the outcome of which are the percepts we anchor on.

If this is the case it follows that consciousness is not a stage from which most of the important actors are missing. What enters consciousness is not the result of a compromise between defensive forces and unconscious instinctual drives. Rather the images that consciousness contains are models of current projects and their likely outcomes or future options. Consciousness anticipates the future rather than defends against the past. This is consistent with the findings of altered consciousness noted by Gregory in Chapter 5 and also of the operations of the systems subserving vigilance and appetites outlined in Chapter 7 and the circadian rhythm system in this.

There are a number of surprising things about cognitive therapy. One is that with its development, for the first time, a major psychotherapy has turned to a focusing on imagery in the management of psychological disorder. The other is that this therapy has been endorsed, pretty well unreservedly, by the medical establishment. These two issues will form the themes of the next chapter.

9 The Passions of the Soul: their Politics and their Management

All the things that the soul perceives by the mediation of the nerves may also be represented to it by the haphazard course of the spirits . . . [which can give] a picture that sometimes happens to be so similar to the thing it represents that one can thereby be deceived. But one cannot be deceived in the same manner in connection with the passions, inasmuch as they are so close and so internal to our soul that it is impossible that it should feel them without their being truly such as it feels them. Descartes, *Passions of the Soul*: Article 26.

The subject matter of the eight chapters so far has been the issue of images in the mind's eye or discourses on the mental stage and what these may reveal about our state of mind. Along with Descartes and Freud we have found reason to doubt the relation between these events and what happens or has happened in the 'real' world, although our conclusions about the consequences of this uncertainty differ to those of both Descartes and Freud.

The passions of the soul appeared for both Freud and Descartes to escape the taint of uncertainty. For Descartes the immediacy of their experience could not sensibly be gainsaid. For Freud, whatever the cognitive uncertainties of analysis, there was an erotic undertow which provided the ultimate legitimation of psychoanalysis. The recourse to symbols that we have noted derived its validity from the almost tangible reality in analysis of what came to be called the transference emotions. These are emotions which develop in analysis. They supposedly derive from Oedipal or primal complexes and are 'transferred' on to the analyst.

While the phantasma of mental imagery have unnerved philosophers the 'healer' has traditionally been charged with channelling the passions of the soul to the benefit of the individual and society. Success in this has traditionally been thought to involve an intuitive ability to plumb the erotic depths and discern there the movement of forces making for recovery or relapse. It was this intuitive ability that the analysts sought to bring into the scientific realm with their analysis of transference reactions. The history of the depth of psychotherapies since Freud has been a history of ever deeper plumbing of these depths. However it is not clear that any bottom has ever been found against which soundings, of the kind that modern science demands, can be taken.

There has been a further problem in that the established scientific order has not appeared willing to support this exercise. It has appeared that, implicit in the notion of the erotic, is a potential subversion of the moral order. The analytic contention has roughly been that the established sciences do not wish to open this Pandora's box to find out whether this is the case or not.

It is not possible therefore simply to analyse consciousness and attempt to pinpoint the dynamics governing the entrances and exits on the stage of consciousness. The question of 'transference' between therapist and patient as well as the exchange between psychotherapy and orthodox medicine must also be faced.

THE ORIGINS OF PSYCHOTHERAPY[1-3]

Part of the mythology of psychoanalysis has been that Freud created dynamic psychotherapy *de novo*. The focal point of the mythology is that the history of psychotherapy really began with Freud's self-analysis and his discovery of the dynamic unconscious. This analysis provided the stem from which other therapies have been derived.

However it was not psychoanalysis that discovered the erotic depths of the healing act or that first engendered a medical reaction to a form of healing that explicitly sought to mobilize such reactions. One hundred years before Freud Mesmer charted these waters. I would argue that it has been from hypnotherapy rather than psychoanalysis that all other psychotherapies have been derived. Of pertinence to the larger argument of this book is the contrast between analysis and hypnosis. Where analysis has proceeded ever deeper into the unconscious the trajectory of development in hypnosis has been from an initial focus on the unconscious to an ever clearer focus on consciousness.

Magnetism[4]

It has been conventional, since Ellenberger, to note that hypnosis had antecedents in a variety of ancient practices and rituals, including shamanism and exorcism. Textbooks list a number of charismatic healers such as Paracelsus, Gochenius, Valentine Greatraks and Gassner. However these therapies differed critically in their world view to modern psychotherapies.

The first steps on the road to modernity were taken by Franz Anton Mesmer in the 1770s. Mesmer's initial method of treating patients was to sit in front of them, trapping their knees between his and holding both their thumbs. He might then massage a patient in some part of their body, depending on impressions that developed during his encounter with the patient. This typically led to a crisis which commonly involved a convulsive episode followed by a lethargic state. This seemingly brought about cures in convulsive disorders, blindnesses, paralyses and a host of other disorders.

This procedure differed little from what exorcists had been doing before him, but in contrast to the exorcists Mesmer saw the disturbances afflicting his patients not as possession by some spirit or as some loss of their soul but as a physical disturbance within them. The breakthrough came when he undertook to treat a Fraülein Osterlein, who was suffering from a profusion of physical complaints – probably quite like Anna O. Aware of current treatments using magnets, Mesmer got her to swallow water containing iron filings. He then had magnets placed around her and by means of these was able to cause something that felt like a fluid to move around within her. This proved therapeutic. Far from putting the success of the treatment down to the use of magnets however some aspect of the encounter led him to believe that there was a corresponding fluid in him and that it was the disposition of his fluid which, aided by the magnets, brought about a therapeutic realignment of hers. This fluid he termed animal magnetism. He went on to conceive of the body as a system containing numerous small magnetic dipoles and the entire system as one large magnet with one pole at the head and the other at the feet. Illness resulted from blockages to the flow of magnetic fluid through the body. Contact with the magnetism of Mesmer himself was designed to remove the blockage.

Mesmer left Vienna, where he had been practising, for reasons that are not clear, and arrived in Paris in 1778. His practice grew so large so fast that he had to resort to a form of group therapy. The therapy room was curtained and dim and music was played during sessions. Clients linked hands in a chain, which was supposed to facilitate conduction of the magnetism, and Mesmer moved among them provoking crises. In an era of great enthusiasm he became the rage. He made several efforts to present his findings and theories to the respectable academic bodies of the day but was initially rejected. Finally, in March 1784, a commission was established to investigate the validity of his claims.

When the commission came to see the proceedings however Mesmer was out of town and they investigated instead the practice of a competing magnetizer, D'Eslon. It had been claimed that crises could be provoked by touching magnetized trees or drinking magnetized water. D'Eslon was asked to magnetize one of a number of glasses of water and one of a number of trees. Subjects when then asked to drink some water or approach the trees were thrown into crises, but unfortunately by the wrong trees and the wrong glasses of water. The commission's conclusion was that the phenomenon of animal magnetism consisted of the conjunction of the overheated imaginations of both the magnetizers and their patients. No attempt was made to assess the response rate of various disorders to being magnetized, even though there appears to have been a clear response rate.

In a secret report submitted to the academies it was also noted that there appeared to be a marked erotic element to these magnetic procedures. It was noted that the crises usually involved a fluttering of the eyelids, shorter, quicker and shallower breathing, heaving of the chest and convulsive movements, and was followed by a languorous state. What was this but orgasm? Typically also the magnetizer was an older man and the magnetized were young and impressionable women. The possibility of sexual malpractice was thought to be highly likely.

Medicine and magnetism[5]

This verdict, along with increasing dissent among his followers and what may have been an episode of depression, led to Mesmer's withdrawal from Paris and to a decline in the movement there. But there is another side to the story that bears examination. Although they had to spend a considerable amount of time afterwards defending against charges of sexual malpractice the magnetizers were not, it would seem, unduly distressed by this problem. Their concern at least initially was with the politics of the report.

It was argued that the commissioners were seeking to suppress a popular movement aimed at benefiting mankind. What right did the commissioners have to decide on this question? Should not the people decide? The doctrines of magnetism were almost identical with the medical doctrines of the time in proposing an imbalance of some vital fluid. The medical approach however sought to correct the imbalance by purgings, bleedings, sweatings or blisterings. These procedures were generally carried out as a matter of principle, without much regard to what we would now consider as the obvious physical state of the patient. The results of such processes were often to leave the patient more enervated and to hasten death.[6] In contrast magnetism could do little harm and often did great good.

Furthermore, although Mesmer charged great sums of money for his services, subsequent therapists often offered their services free, especially to the poor. This was in marked contrast to medical practice. The philanthropic thrust of the magnetist movement can be deduced from the name given to its official body – the Society of Harmony – and also from the fact that many of its initial members were later prominent movers in the French Revolution. Whether the commissioners were aware of the revolutionary potential of magnetism or not, the early magnetizers argued that orthodox medicine was a political body whose interests coincided with those of the state. Why else would 12,000 copies of the report condemning magnetism be circulated free?

THE EMERGENCE OF HYPNOSIS[7–9]

As early as 1784 the Marquis of Puységur, a follower of Mesmer, discovered that one of his farmhands could be magnetized without a crisis being provoked. The farmhand went, rather, into a deep trance resembling sleep but in which he could carry out instructions – an artificial somnambulism. It was the production of this state, rather than that of crises, which came to be called mesmerizing. After coming out of the trance the farmhand was amnesiac for what he had said and done during it but could remember what had happened if remesmerized. He also appeared to be somewhat more lucid, and even intelligent, when mesmerized. Puységur felt that the state depended on the will of the mesmerizer, as it did not seem to take as well if the mesmerizer did not want to help his client. Puységur's discovery marks the first hint of a therapy that might be neither a spiritual process nor the physical one conceived by Mesmer but rather something that would later be called psychotherapy. Following Puységur an increasing number of mesmerizers aimed at inducing somnambulism rather than crises.

Subsequently the Abbé Faria argued that the mesmerized state was one of lucid sleep in which subjects became increasingly susceptible. Whereas Puységur had thought that the state was induced by the will of the mesmerizer, Faria argued that there existed different degrees of susceptibility to being mesmerized and hence the condition must depend more on the subject than on the inducer. Deleuze put forward the idea that what was involved was fixed attention on a single idea. Bertrand demonstrated the production of hallucinations and negative hallucinations in the mesmerized state as well as what are now called post-hypnotic behaviours. Dupotet produced anaesthesia under mesmerism and pioneered its use for surgery. He also noted that while sensation might be reduced perception could at the same time be heightened so that the subject might be anaesthetized but extraordinarily lucid.

During the period between 1815 and 1845 the idea of rapport began to develop. Observers noted that there appeared to be a very subtle interaction between the mesmerizer and their subject, a state of recipro-cal influence. It seemed that the subjects became especially sensitive to subtle nuances on the part of the mesmerizer.

At the time interest in mesmerism in England appears to have been minimal. Its principal proponent was John Elliotson, who lost his place in the medical establishment as a consequence. A James Esdaille while in India found that operations conducted upon patients in the mesmeri-zed state had better cure rates and a lesser degree of post-operative infection. The reception of their ideas led both to postulate a medical conspiracy against mesmerism.

In 1841 Elliotson invited the French mesmerist Lafontaine to tour England. On tour he was seen by James Braid, who attended as a sceptical observer but came away convinced there must be something to the phenomenon. Braid noted that susceptibility varied in the population and proposed that the condition was similar to the state that affects animals exposed to danger, where they can become frozen in apparent fascination before a predator. (Being mesmerized still connotes a state of fascination.) In an effort to break with the unsavoury associations that mesmerism had by 1845 Braid proposed naming the process hypnosis, in recognition of its affinities with the sleeping state.

Braid thought that fixity of gaze was essential to the induction of these states until the discovery that blind men could be hypnotized led to a shift in thinking and the proposal that what is involved is instead exclusive concentration on one idea. Just as the optic nerve fatigues when a subject stares fixedly at one thing, so also, he supposed, the will might fatigue through the effort of sustaining attention on the hypnotist, and might collapse to yield the passivity of hypnosis.

Regarding the ease with which hypnotic states could be induced in groups he pointed to the phenomenon of empathy and emotional con-tagion. When one person in a room starts yawning so too do the others. This, Braid noted, could even extend to the dog lying on the floor. This empathy combined with the fact that ideas can bring about behaviours without much conscious intervening – for example thinking about food produces salivation or the thought of a child can produce lactation in a nursing mother – led to the notion that the hypnotic state involved expectations. Such expectations might, he thought, act through the recently discovered reflexes, whereby it had been shown that actions could be stimulated that bypassed conscious awareness.

Medicine and parapsychology[10-11]

From about 1840 mesmerism began to find a niche for itself in parapsychology. Mesmer had, from the start, claimed that being magnetized liberated the sixth sense. It was noted also that some subjects apparently had visions while in trance. Others seemingly became able to see their own insides and to diagnose complaints they might have, as well as predict when their disorders would clear up – a potentially illegal practice of medicine! Surgery under hypnosis implied that almost anyone could claim a place in the newly developing operating theatres, something the medical profession was never likely to tolerate.

These phenomena were expanded into regular visionary seances and clairvoyancy. Central to this development was the apparent possession in 1845 of the Fox home by spirits of former residents. A communication was set up with these spirits by Mrs Fox and her daughters, at first hesitantly and by knocking and later with greater facility and more publicly in the form of seances. Seances brought to light the existence of mediums – subjects who are particularly able to contact spirits. With the development of seances came techniques such as automatic writing, crystal gazing and age regression. Initially intended as a *reductio ad absurdum* age regression came to be seen as providing evidence in favour of reincarnation and the transmigration of spirits.

All of these techniques were later used by Janet, James and Prince in the exploration of consciousness. However they also provided material for the proponents of scientific orthodoxy to damn the entire enterprise. A damnation, it should perhaps be noted, in which both scientific and clerical orthodoxy lined up on the same side.

FROM HYPNOTHERAPY TO PSYCHOTHERAPY[12-13]

Between 1784 and 1880 successive applications to the Académie des Sciences for official recognition of hypnosis met with rejection. Ellenberger has argued that these rejections were inevitable as the submissions invariably attempted to demonstrate the scientific validity of phenomena such as foreseeing the future. Against this background Charcot's success in getting hypnosis restored to the scientific agenda is a testimony to his standing and the force of the arguments he used.

Perhaps Charcot's most important finding was his discovery of the effects of hypnosis on the traumatic neuroses. Following exposure to shocks subjects might be paralysed, struck dumb or lose their memory. Until Charcot investigated these states it was assumed that these traumatic disorders did not differ from other aphasias, paralyses or memory disturbances. But he was able to show that, under hypnosis, such subjects could often recover their lost functions, and that hypnotized subjects, told that they had lost the use of an arm or leg for example, would display a paralysis of the type found in subjects whose disorders came on after trauma. Under hypnosis patients with post-traumatic amnesia could recount what had happened to them during the period of apparent amnesia. Treatment of post-traumatic disorders therefore became a matter of hypnotic abreaction. Despite the 'psychological' nature of the phenomena under investigation hypnotherapy remained for Charcot essentially a physical treatment.

Bernheim and psychotherapy

The Nancy school of hypnosis, in contrast to that of Charcot, originated with the practice of a country doctor called Liébault. Bernheim, who was then professor of medicine at the nearby university of Nancy, came in 1882 to observe Liébault's practice and, convinced that there was something to it, and in collaboration with Liébault, attempted to refine the principles of its operation. In the first place Liébault seemed to have no great inductive procedure but rather merely suggested the idea of sleep to his clients. Hypnosis often appeared to take, whether or not the subject closed their eyes. Even with their eyes open and apparently unaffected suggested cures were sometimes brought about. This led to the isolation of suggestion as the key component of the hypnotic process.

Liébault's therapy was, it seems, one of imperative suggestion – it was simply suggested to the subject that whatever ailment they had would clear up. Bernheim evolved to a position of persuasion. Seeing a patient over several sessions, he would negotiate their recovery. This he was later to claim was the first explicit 'psychotherapy', a claim made in spite of the abreactive nature of Charcot's handling of traumatic neuroses. For Charcot, as we have mentioned, hypnosis was an experimental neurosis – implying that the physical operation of the nerves was being affected. The Bernheim view was that it was an experimental psychosis – implying that the operations of the psyche, not of the nerves, were being affected.[14]

To appreciate what Liébault and Bernheim were up to it is useful to consider the question in terms of imagery. In essence Liébault conjured up an image of the patient as cured and simply insisted on this vision. Bernheim in contrast appears to have spent time getting to know his patient and then persuading them that the image he had of them corresponded with what was possible for them. We can surmise that in so far as these images took hold in patients' imaginations, and in so far as their illnesses were psychologically remediable, they got better. The method of ensuring that the desired image took root differed. These two therapies have roots as far back as the Stoics and later Descartes.[15] Bernheim's emphasis on persuasion falls somewhere in between the modern practice of cognitive therapy, where patients are encouraged to grasp images that may flit through their mind's eye and assess how well these correspond to a possible objective reality, and neurolinguistic programming, where images are focused on and actively manipulated to produce other mental states.[16]

The Nancy school triumphed over that of the Salpêtrière, in part perhaps simply because Bernheim outlived Charcot, who died in 1893. Following Charcot's death many of his more notable disciples switched camps and ridiculed the notion that there might be anything more to hypnosis than persuasion. His method of using several gifted hysterics, and ignoring as a consequence the more subtle states that are the norm for hypnosis, was criticized. Bernheim in contrast based his ideas on seeing hundreds of clients hypnotized. But in great part Bernheim's victory was more a matter of not being quite so completely obliterated as Charcot by the medical backlash to hypnosis that came about at the turn of the century.

Medicine and hypnosis

As well as the scientific rejection of mesmerism before Charcot there was a rejection based on the continuing identity between mesmerists and the forces of social reform. One implication that could be drawn from mesmerism was that the entire social order itself was to some extent suggested – that the reason the poor were so poor was not any nervous degeneracy but rather the inertial weight of the social system. This possibility led to close links between the mesmerists and the emerging anarchists.[17]

The mesmerists also managed to fall foul of organized religion. Spiritism was obviously a problem. But even more so was the finding that under hypnosis a number of subjects had what appeared to be visionary ecstasies, in which stigmata might be produced. These could range from the seemingly mundane production of blisters under hypnosis to full-scale stigmata of the crucifixion and passion of Christ. That such phenomena are possible is confirmed by cases like that of Steven in the preamble. Such findings however had unsettling implications for the assessment of the lives of many saints.[18] Janet in particular fell foul of the Catholic Church on this matter.

Many of these tensions crystallized in 1892 around a trial with notable similarities to that of Kenneth Bianchi, the Hillside Strangler. A Paris prostitute, Gabrielle Bompard, had been an accomplice to the murder of a bailiff by her boyfriend Michel Eyraud but pleaded innocent, claiming that she had been under Eyraud's hypnotic influence when the crime took place. This murder of a lowly functionary by a prostitute and common thief captured the front pages of French newspapers for several months, indicating that the issues were more profound than might have appeared on the surface.[19]

During the trial the dangers of hypnosis were aired. It was claimed that unscrupulous practice could lead to shady practitioners assaulting young women, who were referred to them for minor medical matters requiring hypnotic anaesthesia. It was also thought it seems that there was quite a risk of male servants or travelling salesmen hypnotically influencing bourgeois housewives and having their way with them thereafter. Such rapes would also conveniently be accompanied by posthypnotic amnesia. A number of cases were cited of women who had seemingly inexplicably left their husbands and whose infidelities were put down to hypnotic influences.

The teachings of both Charcot and Bernheim on hypnosis were a cause for concern. For Charcot only a latent hysteric could be hypnotized. The use of hypnosis on such a latent condition would enhance the tendency to degeneration, leading to increases in the strength of automatic urges and bestial tendencies – which could then be inherited. For Bernheim, Bompard could have committed the crime while under hypnotic influence. Furthermore Bernheim suggested that the effects of hypnosis could be likened to the manipulation of crowds to produce mass hysteria. As France had only a few years beforehand had the experience of the Paris commune and then that of a former army general, Boulanger, setting himself up as a latterday Napoleon, riding around the provinces on horseback and being greeted with adulation as he went, this was a politically sensitive comparison.

The significant upshot of the trial was that the legal practice of hypnosis was restricted to the medical profession and that the Catholic Church banned it altogether – a ban that stayed in place until 1955.

The practical lessons drawn from the trial were that women should not travel alone. They also should not stare at strangers.

The rather obvious point to make here is that it was almost certainly vastly more common for middle- and upper-class men to be responsible for the rape of working-class or servant girls than for working-class men to have their wicked ways with the flower of bourgeois feminity. Thus in the course of a few years hypnosis was rejected doubly, once in 1892 as a possible socially undermining force that might corrupt morals, and again in 1895 when it revealed significant moral corruption by leading to the unearthing of evidence pointing to the widespread existence and damaging effects of incest and child abuse. In both cases it was rejected by members of the class, sex and age group who were likely to have been most responsible for the abuses in question.

There is a further irony. One might have imagined that the demonstration of the possibility of surgery under hypnosis by Esdaille and others would have been embraced by the medical profession. It wasn't. Part of the reason for this probably had to do with the introduction of chloroform in 1845. This, and subsequently nitrous oxide, was embraced wholeheartedly by the medical profession. The occasional scandals of sexual interference with patients while under anaesthesia were either not believed or else simply had little impact. Neither did the fact that orthodox anaesthesia was a more dangerous enterprise than patients were ever aware of, with a considerable number of fatalities, detract from its adoption. Histories of these developments to this day eulogize the discovery of anaesthetics, the agents of therapeutic sleep. Little or no regard is paid to side-effects or to scandals surrounding their use.

FREUD AND TRANSFERENCE

While the erotic possibilities of the special rapport between magnetizer and magnetized had long been noted it still came as a considerable surprise, it would seem, to both Breuer and Freud when they were actually faced with the issues in the flesh. Freud however went on to develop out of this his notion of transference, which in turn was used as evidence in favour of the validity of psychoanalysis.

Freud's initial practice of hypnosis was very much in Liébault's mould, with imperative suggestions being offered patients. Reading his case histories it seems that every possible memory from the past that could cause any distress was summoned up and dismissed, in a manner that now seems very superficial. However as he began to move towards a traumatic model of hysteria he needed something more in the line of abreaction to unearth pathogenic memories. This he took from Charcot. But unlike the accidents that lay behind Charcot's traumatic neuroses he became convinced that the events he was pursuing were ones that involved shame or guilt, which no one would particularly want to remember. This gave rise therefore to a defence against the memory.

As regards where the memory had been 'sent' Freud found time and again that it was actually *in consciousness*, but couldn't easily be got hold of. As outlined in Chapter 3 this led to the procedure of placing his hands on the patients' foreheads when it came to asking them to remember things they appeared to have difficulty with, and instructing them to say the first thing that came into their mind. Regarding this he commented:

It would be possible for me to say by way of explaining the efficacy of this device that it corresponded to a 'momentarily intensified hypnosis'; but the mechanism of hypnosis is so puzzling to me that I would rather not make use of it as an explanation. I am rather of the opinion that the advantage of the procedure lies in the fact that by means of it I dissociate the patient's attention from his conscious searching and reflection . . . The conclusion which I draw . . . is as follows. The pathogenic idea which has ostensibly been forgotten is always lying close at hand and can be reached by associations that are easily accessible. It is merely a question of getting some obstacle out of the way. This obstacle seems once again to be the subject's will.[20]

The therapeutic problem therefore was transformed. It was not simply one of extirpating a foreign body but rather one of melting a resistance. To do this the therapist had to create the motives that would overcome the resistance. One motive could be simply the appeal of becoming like the physician who takes part in the process as 'a representative of a superior or freer world view'. Another could be the possibility of engaging the 'intellectual interest of the patient'. Once the patient got the hang of solving riddles by reading their own text some of them could be expected to pursue further solutions out of interest − 'to regard themselves with the objective interest of an investigator'.

The discovery of transference[21]

Freud considered that by far the most important motivation was some form of love. The importance of this was such, he noted, that difficulties in an analysis went hand in hand with difficulties in the relationship between patient and therapist. Thus if a patient appeared to be resisting remembering it was often as much if not more because of feelings towards the therapist as it was because of any difficulties in the material to be remembered. For example they might be feeling neglected, or insufficiently appreciated, or worried if the material to be presented would cause the therapist to lose interest in them. (Does the difficulty we all have in saying the first thing that comes to mind lie in the nature of the material or in the potential reaction of whoever is going to hear it?)

A particularly important complicating factor arose from the patient's transferring ideas or emotions arising from the analysis on to the therapist. This insight came about after a patient declared her passion for Freud. Subsquently, in analysis, she remembered another man and a scene where she was talking to him while wishing that he would take the initiative and sweep her up into his arms. This Freud interpreted in terms of the analysis bringing this feeling back to the surface before it revealed its historical context, thereby leading to the lady in question transferring these emotions on to Freud himself. It was from this kind of incident, if not this one in particular, that he went on to postulate that the relationship between the analysand and the therapist mirrors the past. Present distress or ambiguity in the therapeutic relationship mirrors past distress and ambiguity in some other relationship. Reminiscence was therefore not the only necessary way forward. A reintegration could be approached by looking at how things were or were not fitting together now, rather than just looking for how they had fallen apart in the past.

This is a claim that most modern schools of psychotherapy would probably accept. However in post-1896 Freudian hands it became a means of escaping from present awareness. Just as with the analytic recourse to symbols, so the interpretation of transference became a means of aborting the process of fully exploring the present contents of consciousness in favour of explaining certain aspects of these in terms of past events. It subverted the claims of the present by a recourse to past determinants.

It is at this point, for example, that Gestalt and encounter therapies diverge from the depth psychologies. Seeing how the now fits together in preference to analysing the past became their therapeutic method.[22-3] For both these forms of therapy present feelings and present erotic tensions are taken to derive very much from present situations. A focus on the past is seen as just one more attempt to evade an encounter with the present. Therapy is a process of encouraging the individual to get hold of the images or awarenesses that flit momentarily through consciousness. Ordinarily these may seem so transient or evanescent that they are assumed perhaps not to be of much significance and hence are not taken into account. Often however they will also be somewhat at odds with convention, habits or routines and hence it becomes a matter of strategic convenience not to pay much heed to them. Why such a focus on the present might be therapeutic is dealt with later in the chapter.

Transference and hypnosis[24-5]

Deep emotional rapport and therapy by negotiation were all integral aspects of hypnotherapy, as practised by Janet for instance; it is not clear that Freud had done any more in 1896 than to abandon Liébault's method. However with the collapse of the seduction theory of hysteria the need for an abreactive form of hypnotherapy also vanished. The subsequent development of psychoanalysis was to put a very particular construction on the past events that determined present feelings in the therapeutic encounter.

With the general discrediting of hypnosis after 1900 psychoanalysts almost of necessity had to claim that they practised something more rational and scientific than hypnosis. The triumph of psychoanalysis in turn cemented the demise of hypnosis – apart from its use for abreaction during the world wars. Far from asking whether analysis was just another modified form of hypnosis the central issue after the First World War became one of explaining, in analytic terms, what happens in hypnosis. Concepts such as regression were put forward to account for the findings of hypnosis. The 'delightful' sense of fatigue found in hypnosis was taken to indicate its truly libidinal quality, as were the fears and fantasies that most people have about hypnosis. To the hypnotist, as opposed to the psychoanalyst, were ascribed unconscious wishes for magical power and sexual domination. Ernest Jones saw hypnosis as an essentially narcissistic state in which all the critical faculties of the super-ego were suspended. Freud argued that hypnosis facilitated a patient's concentration of attention on the therapist in a way that led to the rapid development of transference reactions but that the inability to work through these were the drawback to the state. It was therefore the analysis of transference and its analysis in terms of an invariable primal template that differentiated psychoanalysis from hypnotherapy. But was this really the case?

In analytic therapy attention is focused on specific material. External stimuli and material are progressively excluded – just as happens in an hypnotic induction procedure. The process of free association may be a slow way to build up expectancies but it is also a rather certain way to do so if the therapist is always going to interpret the material in terms of fixed ground rules. There is a further ambiguity in that the love of such a wonderful person, whose *suggestions* cannot be wrong, depends to an unknown extent on coming up with the right kind of material. This is a powerful incentive to the forms of reciprocal sensitivity found in hypnosis.

Freud was later to tie down transference emotions to emotions appropriate to the Oedipal period translated into the analytic encounter and seemingly taking the analyst as their object. But all the ambiguities of analysis come to the fore here. As it becomes clear to a patient that 'Oedipal' material is required, so it seems Oedipal material is forthcoming – in a way that it is not in Jungian or other therapies. Patients may even in therapy sessions begin to act childishly. Is this not an hypnotic age regression?

The issue is made more complicated, rather than solved, by the question of transference. Transference, in its strictest analytic sense, consists of feelings towards the therapist specific to therapy, which supposedly reflect primal emotions for parental figures. But do such emotions reflect the feelings that arise from a true appreciation of either a parent or a therapist apart from their role, or are they part of the ecology of childhood? In childhood, for example, one is fearful and respectful towards all authority figures. As the number of authority figures diminish later in life so too these feelings and submissive attitudes diminish. They may resurface only when called in to see the head of department or the bank manager, when all of a sudden powerful feelings established in childhood may erupt. Or they may resurface when faced with a moody therapist. But is this what Freud meant? If so analysis reduces itself to a form of behaviourism, where present behaviour is dominated by habits established earlier. Perhaps he meant feelings for the person of the parent rather than their role, in which case, is it really possible for a child reliably to differentiate feelings for the person of their father from feelings created by his role? And if that is possible will the adult they later become reliably be able to recapture the particular differentiations made by the child? This recapturing it must be remembered will have to take place in the context of also trying to differentiate these childhood feelings from feelings for the person of the analyst and feelings peculiar to the roles of therapist and patient. It will also have to take place against a background of the analyst's almost certainly insisting on collapsing these various differentiations.

Medicine and the depth psychologies

It is not my concern to detail here the medical reaction to psychoanalysis, which analysts since Freud have been at pains to point out has been astonishingly vituperative. I have argued that much of the practice of modern psychiatry is predicated on a profound opposition to psycho-analysis.[26] This opposition, like the Western 'capitalist' reaction to 'com-munism', has gladly embraced a policy of mutually assured destruction, with patients unfortunately being the losers.

While the arguments of modern psychiatry have centred on the scien-tific credibility of psychoanalysis, and while this book has argued that psychoanalysis is indeed radically flawed in this regard, I do not believe that the opposition can simply be explained in terms of a debate about scientific matters. Rather there has been, from the start, a political and social agenda to psychoanalysis which has, I would argue, aroused opposition from both the medical and social establishments to a greater extent than any details surrounding analytic practice or its scientific procedures. Freud was quite clear on this, and on the reason for it. As he saw it the proper acceptance and adoption of psychoanalysis would lead to radical changes in society.

The reaction to psychoanalysis is so well known that I propose, in order to bring out the full extent of medical antipathy to the depth psychologies, to focus instead on one set of reactions to *Jungian* thought. At first blush Jungian psychotherapy would seem neither to have fallen foul of the establishment in quite the same way as psychoanalysis nor to have within it comparable material for offence. In safe contrast to Freud, who claimed to have read a dark and brutal message in the unconscious, Jung found religion and God. Out of the Jungian uncon-scious, there seemingly arise archetypal images common to all cultures and all times, suggesting a transcendent reality and a religious base to human striving. Where Freud found incestuous sexual fantasies and impulses Jung found the almost desexualized anima, and went on to proclaim the psychological importance of the Catholic Church's recog-nition of the Immaculate Conception. Where Freud saw in war a proof of his thesis about humanity Jung saw in chivalry many of the eternal concerns of mankind.

While this seems to be the case for mainstream Jungian thought there has been a revolutionary aspect to the Jungian approach which has led to as vigorous a suppression as was ever visited on the mesmerists. In contrast to psychoanalysis the symbols and motifs of Jungian therapy resemble the material found after taking consciousness-expanding drugs, such as LSD and ketamine. Recent work on the culture of these drugs has invoked Jung as the depth psychologist whose writings are most in sympathy with findings from the use of these drugs – a shaman for our times.

As outlined in Chapter 5 the effects of these drugs depend on the setting in which they are taken and appear to involve the induction of suggestibility – effects that resemble hypnosis. This dependence on setting led a number of academic investigators during the 1960s, most notably Timothy Leary, to advocate that LSD should be taken in private among friends, as its taking was as much a religious event as a scientific one. The experiences and their significance were held to overlap with the mysticism of many oriental religions. The Tibetan Book of the Dead, in particular, became the gospel of the psychedelic movement and the taking of psychedelics was seen by many as a time-saving and effortless way to achieve effects that would otherwise need several years of hard work at yoga.[27]

The similarities between the psychedelic movement and mesmerism extended also to the political sphere. Around the use of these drugs a number of communes were set up, the members of which advocated peace, love and a dropping out of conventional society and the rat race. It is almost impossible to evaluate these communes, as they quickly attracted the disaffected and casualties of American society, whose entry brought an increase in crime and lawlessness.

In the late 1960s a reaction to the use of the psychedelics set in. Although there are no well-documented cases of adverse reactions to LSD, and although it had been used widely by clinicians without ill effects, even in physically debilitated populations, in a manner that suggested that it was at least physically benign, a number of scare stories began to circulate. It was claimed that LSD caused damage to chromosomes and that the offspring of takers would be likely as a consequence to be handicapped or might even be monsters. There is no evidence that this is the case. A story also circulated that users of LSD might be attracted to look at the sun and, being unable to look away, would be blinded. Other stories related how users jumped to their death from the upper floors of buildings. The psychedelics were grouped with the opiates as narcotics, although they produce neither physical nor psychological dependence, and in 1966 severe legal restrictions were placed on their use and on research into their effects. Their demise came swiftly thereafter and it echoed the orthodox medical response to mesmerism. The psychedelics, and with them untrammelled Jungianism, have seemingly been obliterated. One searches in vain in even the most comprehensive of orthodox textbooks of psychiatry for a section on the psychedelic drugs – just as one does for a section on hypnosis – even though these quite remarkable agents should be of great interest to workers in the mental health field.

However, while resisted on the level of scientific orthodoxy, the depth psychologies, and psychoanalysis in particular, have been adopted on another. In many circles 'analysis' of one sort or another has in the second half of the twentieth century replaced religion. We are living through what Phillip Rieff has termed 'the triumph of the therapeutic',[28] and William Barrett 'the death of the soul',[29] a time in which analysts and other depth psychologists have replaced philosophers as the arbiters of what is important in human affairs.

The examples of mesmerism and the depth psychologies suggest that an occupational hazard of psychodynamic psychotherapies has been for their proponents to develop messianic tendencies. In Chapter 10 I will suggest that Descartes' division of human behaviour into spiritual and mechanical components was in great part responsible for this.

THE REDISCOVERY OF TRANCE[30–2]

While these cultural battles have raged a more experimental approach to hypnosis has come to the fore, in which two schools of thought have been pitted against each other. One has been behaviourally oriented and has argued that there is nothing to hypnosis but a state in which one person attempts to meet the perceived wishes of another – if necessary by outright simulation. Theodore Barber has been a leading exponent of this school and more lately Nicholas Spanos. The other school of thought has argued that hypnosis brings about distinctive psychological changes. Its best-known representatives have perhaps been Ernest Hilgard and Martin Orne.

The question has been pursued in the laboratory rather than in psychiatric clinics. One consequence of this is that the link between hysteria and hypnosis has been severed. The laboratory subjects have been typically young and healthy college students. A further finding has been that there are no improvements in mental performance when the subject is in hypnosis. The significance of this is twofold. On the one hand there has been an impression that hypnotized subjects can be made more intelligent or can somehow get in touch with other truths, and this has supported the political or messianic agenda of mesmerism. The other is that therapists from Breuer and Freud to today have been impressed with the astonishing detail of their subjects' reminiscences. This has regularly been put forward as one argument in favour of the veracity of the accounts of trauma they elicited. But when put to the test hypnotized subjects asked to remember the number-plates of cars involved in crimes do no better than non-hypnotized subjects, even though they may be subjectively sure that they are doing well. They may even seem to be reading the number-plate in their mind's eye.

Proponents of the theory that there is a neuropsychological change specific to hypnosis point to phenomena such as trance logic and hidden observers. Trance logic is where hypnotized subjects are asked to look at the experimenter and then close their eyes. The experimenter, unknown to them, leaves. They are then instructed to open their eyes and see the experimenter – which they do. But when asked to describe what they see many see a transparent experimenter. Subjects who are simulating hypnosis do not spontaneously report such transparent images. Trance logic is also shown when age-'regressed' subjects use words that they could not have possibly known when they were the age in question, or when subjects who are told they cannot see something in a room agree but nevertheless walk around it rather than through it.

The hidden observer phenomenon was described first by Hilgard. What happens is that a subject, made analgesic under hypnosis, is asked if there is some part of them registering pain. They seem able at one and the same time to demonstrate apparent analgesia and to report on the quality, intensity and location of the pain. This dissociation led to Hilgard formulating what has become known as the neo-dissociationist theory of hypnosis.

Against such findings Spanos and others have produced a considerable amount of evidence that there is nothing that happens in hypnosis that cannot be simulated by well-motivated but unhypnotized subjects. Of particular interest here is that he has shown that using coping strategies such as focusing attention on unrelated imagery can lead normal unhypnotized subjects to tolerate many of the pains that are supposedly the hallmark of hypnotic analgesia.

Spanos has also argued that there is a 'social' reason why some subjects are not hypnotizable – that this has to do with ambiguities in the instructions they receive rather than because they lack any special brain reflex. Thus when told that amnesia will set in under hypnosis the instruction may be taken to mean that the memory in question will just vanish or else that the subject will pay less heed to it. It seems that those who interpret it to mean that the memory vanishes do poorly, whereas those who take the instruction to mean that they should direct attention away from something, which they will nevertheless be at least partly aware of, do well. The same holds for hypnotic analgesia.

Regarding the hidden observer phenomenon Spanos has shown that, whatever is involved, there is no observer neutrally observing the 'reality' of some situation that the hypnotic subject is apparently missing. If it is suggested to the hidden observer that he is buried so deep that he is even less likely to feel pain than the hypnotized subject then the observer reports that this is the case.

What then, if anything, is hypnosis? The laboratory hunt for a unique marker of hypnosis appears to have come to an impasse. In great part this hunt has been for some evidence of altered physiological functioning – a hunt for evidence of some altered reflex. The present conclusion must therefore be that hypnosis is not a physiologically distinctive state.

Trance

It is increasingly common to find the hypnotic state referred to as a trance state. By trance here is meant not so much the external appearance of not being fully present but rather an internal absorption – a state of reverie. In contrast to postulating a neural reflex or to saying that hypnosis involves doing what is suggested to one, which is difficult to distinguish from saying that hypnosis involves an abnegation of responsibility, the word trance, I believe, refers to a psychological phenomenon in a way the other two do not.

This is brought out for example by the phenomena of trance logic. Both seeing an unreal experimenter and making mistakes when age-regressed are readily explicable in terms of imaginative involvement in a project. Also, as noted above, involvement in imaginative exercises without an explicit hypnotic induction procedure appears capable of bringing about considerable analgesia. More telling perhaps has been the recognition of the phenomenon of auto-hypnosis. It seems that children in particular are liable spontaneously to go into trances/fantasies/daydreams, and it is argued that this is the prototype of the hypnotic state. The increasing use of the term trance coincides with the return to respectability of research on imaging and imagination that has come about in the wake of the recent cognitive revolution in psychology.

A recognition of the reality of imagery, the importance of consciousness and the autonomy of the psyche provides a defence against the claim that hysteria or the neuroses generally are simply aberrant forms of social protest. In the case of hypnosis, while there are social inputs into hypnotizability, it seems too much to suggest, as earlier social psychologists did, that the reason why individuals tolerate major surgery under hypnosis is in order to please their hypnotist or in order to maintain the identity that they have built up for themselves of being good hypnotic subjects. Imagery however is radically social. We construct our images from common external material and in accordance with common cultural possibilities. It is this that allows the social psychologist to manipulate the hypnotic state. It also points to the social constitution of consciousness, from which it follows that changes of consciousness can be expected to follow on social events as much as on the prompts of some internal subconscious dynamic, such as diurnal rhythms affecting all of us.

A further possibility emerges out of a recognition of a distinction between psychological operations and either mental/social influences on the one hand or neurophysiological processes on the other.[33] In ways that are not yet fully understood imagination can be expected to influence physiological functioning. A good example of this has been described by Luria in the case of a man with hypermnesia. This individual could make his heart rate increase and other physical functions alter at will by imagining some scene in real life that would normally have brought about the required change. Thus he could increase his heart rate by imagining himself running after a bus.[34] A similar mechanism operating in the case of both hypnosis and hysteria could provide an alternative explanation to the psychoanalytic explanation of altered physical functioning in terms of its symbolic relation with earlier conflicts. When it comes to a case like that of Steven, cited in the Introduction to this book, such an explanation in terms of symbolism breaks down. What is involved seems more like a re-enactment; symbolism explains nothing. The alternative is that particularly intense imaginative involvement in the course of dreaming could produce these effects. This is plausible, if it is borne in mind, as Luria's experiments would seem to indicate, that some of us appear to have a greater facility than others for translating imaginative absorption into physical effects.

There is one further point to note. Applying the logic of a psychological autonomy of trance states to the various therapies predicated on altered states of consciousness, we would have to argue that the compelling nature of the experiences involved should not be taken as evidence regarding external or social reality. On this basis *valid* experiences suggesting reincarnation or an ultimate meaning or purposefulness to the universe do not provide compelling evidence for beliefs in either of these possibilities. This is not to say however that these experiences may not be used fruitfully for therapeutic purposes.

Such a position, in a number of ways, brings us back to Janet. He took over techniques such as automatic writing, age regression and the creation of other personalities, which had been developed by the spiritist movement, in order to explore consciousness rather than to plumb an unconscious. But he did not believe that the 'spiritual' nature of the experiences implied that he was in any way dealing with a spirit world. From Charcot he took the notion of abreacting traumatic events and from Bernheim the idea of a psychotherapy by negotiation. But he argued in each case for an autonomy of the psychological process involved. While doing so he argued repeatedly for the interpenetration of personal consciousness with social meanings. The hypnotized subject, he pointed out, has to learn to be hypnotized. Over the course of a few sessions both the subject and the hypnotist learn what they need to do to get to where they both want to get.[35]

Finally the imagery of trance states is not simply cognitive – it is also emotional. In a study of those spontaneous trance states we call day-dreams Susan Aylwin describes the imagery involved as feelings dressed in the underwear or pyjamas of thought, not yet having knotted the ties and put on the respectable overcoats that thoughts are required to wear before they go out in public.[36]

Article 46 of Descartes' *Passions of the Soul* hints at why such emotional imagery can lead to the dissociation found in hypnosis, and can also potentially produce the out of control trance states found in borderline disorders:

There is one particular reason why the soul cannot readily alter or check its passions, which [is] that they are not only caused by but also maintained and strengthened by some particular movements of the spirits. They are almost all accompanied by some excitation taking place in the heart, and consequently also throughout the blood and the spirits, so that until this excitation has ceased they remain present to our thoughts. And as the soul, in becoming extremely attentive to something else can keep from hearing a little noise or feeling a little pain but cannot in the same way keep from hearing thunder or feeling the fire burning the hand, so it can easily overcome the lesser passions but not the most vigorous and the strongest, until after the excitation of the blood and spirits has abated.

THE DYNAMICS OF ORDINARY EXPERIENCE

In recent years there has been a fragmentation of the therapies on offer, with in 1980 over 200 different 'psychotherapies' listed in *Time Magazine*. As we have seen, many have commented that psychotherapy has in some sense taken the place of religion in modern experience. It does so both on the grander theoretical side and in the mundane realm of convenience inspiration, on sale in a thousand airport and railway bookshops.

In contrast to this diversity a group of therapies has begun to appear which does not seem to have a 'religious' character. These therapies I propose to refer to as the cognitive-behavioural therapies even though they also include interpersonal therapy and the motivational interviewing techniques derived from encounter therapies, neither of which would see themselves as simply behavioural or cognitive in orientation. As a group however these therapies seem more tied to the process of effecting specific clinical changes and less to the reconstruction of personalities according to some preordained mould. And they set about effecting change in ways that have much in common.

In order to bring out the salient and common aspects of these new therapies I will look at how they handle imagery and at the questions of concrete details and of competence. As will become clear, it is quite arbitrary to cut the material up in this way – these three aspects overlap with each other to a great extent.

Focus on imagery[37–8]

In the last chapter I dealt with the current practice of cognitive therapy. While in theory cognitive therapy aims to get at and challenge a subject's personal 'schemata', in practice, as we have seen, what happens is that their internal imagery or monologues are explored. These are taken as being representative of where the subject is 'at' at any one point in time.

Perhaps the most striking instance of the new focus on internal imagery comes from a most unlikely souce – behaviour therapy. Behaviour therapy began life as an offspring of behavioural learning theory. As such its ideological commitment was to an analysis of the outward aspects of behaviour. In contrast to psychoanalysis behaviour therapists eschewed all investigation of internal mental events – until, that is, such a procedure was shown to work. This came about first of all in the case of phobias. The usual procedure had been gradually to desensitize subjects to a feared stimulus by having them get slowly closer to it. For example someone with a fear of mice would be asked to look at a picture of a mouse; then they might be invited to step into a room in which there was a mouse in a cage; subsequent steps might involve going over to the cage and picking it up, with a final step of picking up the mouse. But one of the findings was that it was often sufficient to get subjects to imagine a mouse or a feared situation. They were encouraged to dwell on the image while learning to relax at the same time.

Such approaches have been adopted even more widely in recent years. For example in the case of flying phobias, rather than involving the steps of going to airports, boarding planes and subsequently flying, treatment now may be almost entirely imaginary. Subjects will be encouraged to imagine themselves on a plane which crashes. They are invited to imagine the chaos and destruction – to see in their mind's eye bits of bodies flying through the air, perhaps even bits of their own body. Similarly individuals with recurrent intrusive fears of harming their children may be asked to imagine themselves skewering their child with a knife or throwing the child out of the window. These are highly distressing procedures. The fact that they are distressing points to the emotional potency of imagery and suggests strongly that images cannot simply be superficial features of mental life. The object of the exercise is to get the individual to the point of being able to live comfortably in the presence of their own images – to stop being frightened of their own mind.

Focus on details

Prior to its more recent recourse to imagery the most notable feature of behaviour therapy was its focus on details, with success often being thought to hinge on whether all the relevant stimulus and reinforcer details had been elicited. Cognitive therapy has equally had an interest in detail. It aims to get all the details of an individual's current images or cognitions. No attempt is made to dig deeper or to analyse hidden motives. Indeed no attempt is made to impute motives at all. What happens rather is that the subject is encouraged to provide ever further examples and ever further details.

This approach has recently had a notable triumph. In some anxiety states there appears to be no obvious trigger. These are called panic attacks. Individuals become highly anxious, seemingly out of the blue. It has accordingly been difficult to do therapy with them and there has been a recourse to drug therapy instead. Treatment with antidepressants that have an anxiolytic profile brings about improvement in 50–60 per cent of cases. But a recent modification of cognitive therapy has been claiming a response rate of 90–100 per cent.[39–40]

The modification in question developed out of an attention to detail. Subjects were noted to become anxious for no apparent reason. But what, it was asked, went through their mind *after* they began to panic. Unnoticed in almost all cases of pure panic disorder it seems are images or cognitions in the mind of the affected person that they are having a heart attack or a stroke or seriously losing control in some way or other. They then take the appropriate action. If they believe they are having a heart attack, for example, they sit or lie down and take things as easily as possible. This course of action however maintains the whole process because they are left glad to be alive but unclear as to whether they are alive *because of* the evasive action they took. The circle is broken in subsequent panic attacks by doing the opposite to what the person has been doing in order to avoid disaster. Thus if the fear is of heart attacks they are encouraged to exercise or generally to do all the things they ought not do if they actually were having a heart attack.

In the case of alcoholism and drug dependency a variety of different therapies from various theoretical backgrounds have recently begun to converge on the need for greater detail than has traditionally been sought.[41-4] The best-known approaches are Miller's motivational interviewing technique and Cox and Klinger's motivational structure questionnaire. In both it is acknowledged that the problem with therapy is not any lack of motivation on the part of the substance misuser but rather a failure on the part of the therapist fully to understand the problem from within. It is not sufficient to establish the facts of an individual's substance consumption or to make sure they understand the hazards of abuse; rather the interviewer needs to know what the user gets out of their habit. The aim is to establish as fully as possible the nature of the trade-off being done between the risks and benefits of misuse. The hope is that a full articulation of the model of the self the individual is operating with will enable them to modify it. Even slight modifications may be all that are needed to generate significant change downstream.

In treating subjects with borderline disorders Jerome Kroll has recently highlighted the traditional neglect of detail and the adverse consequences this may have.[45] Commonly such subjects during the course of a therapeutic session will have an episode of disorientation or confusion or will have periods when they experience derealization, depersonalization or other odd experiences. While both subject and therapist may be vaguely aware of this it has not been customary to establish exactly what is happening, what its triggers are, when it began happening first and whether it can be forestalled. Establishing such details would potentially allow the subject to become more competent. The aim of promoting competence is a further point of convergence between therapies.

Focus on engagement and competence

A salient aspect of the therapies under discussion here is their focus on testing things out in practice. This is in marked contrast to the traditional approach of the depth psychologies, in which therapy is a private transaction between two individuals and an almost exclusively verbal enterprise.

The most notable exponent of this approach is perhaps Isaac Marks. In a series of reformulations of the theoretical bases for behavioural approaches to therapy he has argued that exposure is a common element of effective treatments. Affected individuals must, he argues, confront the object, or image, of their fears. Exposing themselves to the usually avoided stimulus for a sufficient length of time effects significant change – whether the feared stimuli are the mental images that may haunt a person with an obsessional or phobic disorder or even the delusions of someone who has a delusional disorder.

Similarly in the case of cognitive therapy for depression the focus of therapy is not simply an analysis of the material that is specific to a therapy session. There are two other commonly used strategies. One is to get the subject to keep a diary of things that happen between sessions that cause them distress. The other is to give them tasks to do between sessions which they then report back on. In the case of interpersonal therapy for depression or anxiety a similar approach is taken, in that an interpersonal problem is identified in the therapy session and the subject is then encouraged to take on the issues raised between sessions.

Why should engagement make a difference? One reason is simply the benefit that we all get from mastery of a feared stimulus, whether or not the stimulus is one about which we are neurotically anxious. But there is another aspect to this. Engaging in the world always has consequences for the actor. This is the clear basis on which Gestalt and encounter therapies were formed.

I noted earlier that, whereas Freud subverted the significance of present awareness and impulses, the Gestalt and encounter approaches aim at facilitating an appropriation of such material. In the normal course of events it is extremely difficult to get hold of the here and now. It just does not seem possible to start saying all the things that go through our mind's eye – all the irritations with or fantasies about others. Why not? It commonly turns out that it is a certain view of oneself, a view of what one spontaneously is, that blocks the expression of the material in question. This view is socially rather than Oedipally determined. For example the presence of attractive members of the opposite sex will inhibit me from saying certain things depending on how I wish to portray myself, as will the presence of a potential employer. The first things that come to mind are often not well integrated into our idea of others' ideas of us. Getting hold of them then necessarily goes hand in hand with a potential transformation of our conceptions of ourself – an experience like having the rug pulled out from under you or having the seeming solidity of things dissolve in front of you. Engagement therefore runs the risk of self-transformation. This I would argue is in part what underlies the therapeutic effectiveness of exposure and homework in both cognitive and interpersonal therapies.

Far from being simply a rational exercise engagement of this sort is a highly emotional encounter. What is involved is not experienced as a cool reappraisal of ourselves but rather as an emotional experience – or, to go back to the definition of emotions given in Chapter 7, an experience that a range of other actions have suddenly become possible. Engagement also raises the question of competence. When dealing with phobias or obsessional states Janet took the approach that insight was almost irrelevant, that what was required was to get the subject functioning again. This he did by means of what would now be seen as behavioural techniques, such as thought stopping, response prevention and a deliberate scheduling of personal actions to ensure competence.

Taking a very similar approach to the borderline disorders Kroll has recently argued that whatever we do for patients we should at least at the end of the day leave them in some way more competent than they were before – and not less competent, as is a common side-effect of the pursuit of 'insight'. It is this that underlies his appeal to recognize the occurrence and details of cognitive disorganization in subjects so that a management strategy can be implemented. These strategies depend in the first instance on good and detailed descriptions of what is happening. As he puts it, the heart of understanding lies in the details of what actually has been or is being experienced.[46]

RESISTANCE?

A situation has not been satisfactorily liquidated, has not been fully assimilated, until we have achieved, not merely an outward reaction through our movements, but also an inward reaction through the words we address to ourselves, through the organisation of the recital of the event to others and to ourselves and through the putting of this recital in its place as one of the chapters of our personal history . . . Strictly speaking, one who retains a fixed idea of a happening cannot be said to have a 'memory' of the happening. It is only for convenience that we speak of it as a 'traumatic memory'. The subject is often incapable of making with regard to the event the recital we speak of as a memory; and yet he remains confronted by a difficult situation in which he had not been able to play a satisfactory part, one to which his adaptation has been imperfect, so that he continues to make efforts at adaptation. Janet, *Psychological Healing*.[47]

There is increasing evidence from the cognitive therapy of panic disorder and behavioural management of phobias and compulsive thoughts that establishing as precisely as possible all of the details of a person's experience opens the way to effective therapy. This, I have argued elsewhere, is a coherent goal of psychotherapy and one that can be pursued scientifically.[48]

When some sort of traumatic event has precipitated the disorder then an attempt to determine the nature of the event and assistance at working through its personal meanings would seem indicated. However the conventional wisdom is that simply uncovering the past does not, as Freud found, necessarily transform a present neurosis. As has been pointed out, despite what may be intense reliving experiences on ketamine, affected subjects may not be cured or may relapse shortly after apparent cure. This striking demonstration of the hazards of straightforward interpretation was one of the main factors that led Freud to abandon the seduction theory and with it to abandon a form of psychotherapy that was not unlike the model I have just outlined.

Simply getting the correct interpretation may not be sufficient in cases with the complexity of childhood seduction or trauma. This is almost inevitable, given the account of what is involved in remembering outlined in Chapters 6 and 7. Memories, in this instance, are of distinctly autobiographical events. The need is not to uncover a set of concrete details but rather to reconstruct an autobiography. Almost inevitably successful reconstruction will require the reconstruction of a number of linked autobiographies rather than just one target autobiography. But it seems to me that a necessary step on this pathway would be at some point to establish an agreed version of certain key events in the past.

Establishing these events and promoting competence are laudable goals of therapy, but can more be done? Why do subjects relapse? Does the occurrence of relapse not put a serious question mark against the theory underpinning a particular therapy, as Freud felt in 1897? Some light can be shed on this issue by considering another recently developed therapy that also focuses on detail and competence but does so from another perspective: family therapy.

Family therapy

In subjects with schizophrenia or affective disorders there has been increasing interest in recent years in the idea of mobilizing the individual's own resources to help them manage their illness.[49] There has also been a movement to engage the family of the individual as one such resource. This stands in marked contrast to previous approaches in which the family has all but been seen as the cause of the illness. There is an emerging body of evidence that such approaches decrease morbidity and enhance the quality of life. In the psychoses generally and in many cases of the neuroses this I believe is a most helpful development.

However there is another role for family therapy which I wish to highlight here. There is a story told about Mesmer that brings out the issues involved.[50] While still in Vienna he was called upon to treat an eighteen-year-old girl, Marie-Theresia de Paradis, who had been blind since the age of three. Despite this handicap she had taught herself to play music exceptionally well. Many treatments had been tried but none had helped. After being magnetized by Mesmer her sight returned, but only it seemed when he was there. Other physicians contested the cure and Mesmer ended up in dispute with her family. Subsequently she remained blind even when magnetized by him. He put this down to her family having too much interest in her remaining blind – upon which depended a considerable income and trips to the homes of the wealthy and famous.

There has been speculation that it was his failure in this case which precipitated Mesmer's departure from Vienna. There has been speculation that Marie-Theresia became too attached to him and he to her. Certainly after this case he became depressed and then left for Paris, leaving his wife behind. In 1784, shortly after the encounter between the magnetic movement and the Académie des Sciences, Marie-Theresia and her family came to Paris, where she gave a concert. He attended. The story of his 'failure' began to circulate Paris, perhaps because the Paradis family stayed six months. Mesmer again seems to have become depressed. Later that year he left Paris and effectively walked out of history.

The point behind this story is that the involvement of the Paradis family and their interests in this case should probably not be taken as a case of conscious contrivance but rather as an instance of the need to be prepared sometimes to renegotiate the identities of several people if enduring change is to take place in one. It is on such premises that family therapy for refractory neuroses is based. Of the cases cited in the Introduction to this book all bar two had significant family involvement which probably contributed to chronicity. The social component of such a therapy should not be taken to imply that what is involved is a case of social engineering and that accordingly hysteria is a manifestation of social repression. What is involved is rather a case of manoeuvring a group of people to a point where all can imagine other possibilities for each. Such imagining will be highly emotional, in that what is being imagined are other courses of action.

There are a number of old sayings from many cultures to the effect that if you want to hide something you should put it under the nose of the person who is looking for it. When living together, especially in families, it is all too obvious that, as Tennessee Williams put it in *Cat on a Hot Tin Roof*, we live under 'the thundercloud of a common experience'. In traditional analytic and depth therapies, with their focus on the verbal exchanges between two individuals in an artificial setting, this obvious point has been missed. In contrast it would seem to be something that cannot be avoided by therapies that aim at establishing what the details of a situation may be, what the constraints on individual imagination are and that aim at promoting competence in settings outside of the consultation setting.

10   The Genesis and Significance of the Neuroses

On seeing that all dead bodies become devoid of heat and movement, people have imagined that it is the absence of the soul that made the movements and the heat cease. So they have groundlessly believed that our natural heat and the movements of our body depended on the soul. Whereas they ought to think on the contrary that the soul departs when someone dies only because the heat ceases and the organs used to move the body disintegrate. Descartes, *The Passions of the Soul:* Article 5.

I have argued elsewhere that a great deal of the current difficulties in psychiatry stem from Descartes' distinctions between a spiritual mind and the material brain.[1] This particular dualism had three consequences. One was that it became difficult to distinguish between psyches and minds. A second and allied problem was that of appreciating that there might be a set of specific psychological disorders. This has led to difficulties with the idea of a neurosis. Is it a disease or is it just bad behaviour? A third consequence was the mechanistic and determinist view of man it fostered, which led to the determinist view of man found in psychoanalysis and to the notions of degeneracy and endogeneity. These issues are interlinked but will be handled in turn during the course of the chapter.

My contention is that the significance of the neuroses is that they point to the existence of a set of psychological operations that are distinct from both mental operations and brain functioning and that their precipitation by environmental events runs counter to the received notion of endogeneity. By implication this forces us to look again at the question of what is the human mind – or what it is to be human.

PSYCHES AND MINDS [2-3]

Prior to Descartes it had been the norm to distinguish between three levels of the soul. The lowest level, which involved the appetites and drives and was found in all animals, was called the vegetative soul. An intermediate level involving perceptions, emotions and memory was found in higher animals and was called the psyche. The highest level was thought of as the distinctively human part of the soul, the part that would survive death, the nous, or as it would now be called the mind. There had been little concern about the location of the mind.

The reason was as follows. Until the mid-seventeenth century the cosmos had been something that was kept in existence by the deity's constant fiat. Renaissance science pointed to the possibility of its being a machine which the deity had at some point wound up and started going but had since left to run its mechanical course. The successes of Copernicus and Galileo established the possibility that the workings of the machine should be open to investigation, without the investigators operating under the fear of being seen as sacrilegious. In a similar fashion investigators began systematically to probe the workings of the human body. Where once had been seen the mysterious portals and vital fluids of the soul, developments laid bare a variety of machine parts – a pump, bellows and lenses. Writing shortly after Galileo's trial Descartes could not have claimed that a human being was wholly and entirely a machine. Nor would he have been personally inclined to go this far, even if he had nothing to fear from the ecclesiastical authorities. While a human being might be a machine for the most part it seemed that there must also be something in humans that remained in constant, or at least potentially constant, communion with the divine. To deny this would have been to do away with the possibility of religion.

The resolution of the dilemma was to propose a mechanical body, of which most of the brain was potentially a part, and a non-mechanical soul. A great deal of philosophical effort has since gone into working out how such an arrangement might work in practice. In the midst of this attempt to distinguish two sides of a philosophical mobius strip one important aspect of thinking about the mind prior to Descartes has been lost. This was the notion that there were three distinct layers to the soul. The demands of science in the seventeenth century required a division of the soul into two entities, but this division was dictated by strategic necessity rather than by virtue of its being either a good or an obvious description of how things actually are. It required the sacrifice of one of the traditional layers of the soul.

One set of faculties, the lowest, containing the appetites and instincts, could conceivably operate mechanically. Another set, the highest, containing the spiritual and mental faculties, obviously could not be readily mechanized. It became the ghost in the machine. But what of the intermediate set? What of consciousness, memory, emotion and imagination? Where once there had been three possible locations for these there were for Descartes effectively only two. Faced with the faculties of consciousness, imagination and emotion he opted to locate them within the soul.

This had two effects. One was to hinder their subsequent scientific investigation by contributing to the impression that there is something insubstantial about consciousness, imagination and emotion. The other was to set the seal on what had been a progressive degeneration of our ideas about the mind. For the Greeks the mind was the part of us that was responsible for the human striving for personal coherence and consistency, the drive for authenticity, the part that was not found in animals. However so complete was the success of Aristotle and Plato in articulating a vision of what it was to be human that the terms they used to explain their position – psyche, nous and soma – became reified. From the mind being a *striving* to find coherence and a right course of action, using all the human faculties of insight, judgment and rational argument, it *became* the faculties of insight and judgment.

One consequence of this is that, as work on the psychology of animals has progressed and has revealed them to have insights, consciousness and emotions and to be capable of making judgments of sorts, it has seemed that they also must have 'minds'. This has led to confusion about what is distinctive about the human state. Another consequence has followed on the invention of the first calculating engine by Babbage in the nineteenth century. This put the ultimate localization of the logical or rational engine clearly on the scientific agenda. A problem with this research programme however is that, despite the claims that Aristotle characterized man as the rational animal, neither Aristotle nor Plato would have agreed that the distinctive feature of human beings is their possession of a logical or rational engine as such.[4]

In the nineteenth century the interest of this mechanical research programme coincided with that of evolutionary theory. One of the fundamental concerns of the early evolutionary theorists – Darwin, Spenser, Huxley, Romanes, Wallace, Baldwin and James – was to account for the human mind in evolutionary terms; by this however they did not mean the capacity for solving problems but rather the moral faculty in humans. If the moral faculty could not be accounted for then

God must have intervened at some point in the process and the whole of evolutionary theory as a consequence would be trivialized.[5]

But how could a moral faculty evolve? There were two options, which were effectively determined by Descartes – one romantic and the other 'rational'. The romantic approach was that some universal mind, supra-personal consciousness, wisdom or panpsychism is in some way inherent in matter. This idea had first been put forward in 1760 by Julien Offray de La Mettrie, who proposed that matter harbours active properties of motion and sensation, which achieve expression as mental activity when matter is combined to the level of complexity found in humanity. Somewhat later Romanes and Wundt both claimed to be able to detect manifestations of the mind in single-celled organisms. Clarke and Jacyna in their monumental work on the origins of nineteenth-century neuroscientific concepts have argued that a great deal of the progress in this area owed its inspiration and driving force to the romantic pro-gramme of finding intelligence, as opposed to just intelligible mechan-isms, in material entities.[6]

The 'rationalist' alternative was that the mind was a consequence of sensations from outside. This was the Humean view. Ideas were held to be copies of sense impressions; thinking was a matter of associating these images. This approach had two implications. One was that humans potentially were reflex automata driven by the environment, which after all is the source of all sensations. The other was that the source of clear ideas must lie in refined sensory impressions. Upbringing, therefore, would be important to the production of the enlightened individual.

Both of these models would permit minds to evolve. The romantic one did so in so far as minds were inherent in matter anyway and that evolution involved nature revealing herself. The rationalist alternative did so since if reason were just an amalgam of sensations then animals would have to be able to reason, in a kind of fashion, and humans just did more of it. Both models however, in their lack of a clearly articulated and differentiated model of the mind, were prone to derail.

The pitfall for rationalism has been the risk of making mental oper-ations purely reflex and automatic. This thrust has led to the physiologi-cal and behaviourist approaches to mental functioning that have in general subverted the idea of an intending 'I' and have made of humans automata. The romantic approach, in contrast, with its failure to make differentiations, has given itself little control over meaning. Meaning wells up from below as it were, uncontrollably. This approach underlaid the programme of the depth psychologies and in particular of psycho-analysis. For this reason they have always been prone to derail from psychological issues into the realm of the mental. This derailing has been all but irresistible when, for example, exploring the psyche has thrown up evidence in favour of reincarnation and metempsychosis, a sense of *presque vu*, out of body experiences and white lights on the edge of consciousness, as outlined in Chapters 5 and 9.

Evolutionary theory straddled the divide between romantics and rationalists. Observations as early as the second century AD by Galen on goats learning to take milk from their mothers suggested that animals have a wisdom that is untutored, that is not just environmentally determined. Darwin's position was that the inherited structure of the brain must in some way cause instincts. These were passed on because habitual behaviours modified structure and the modified structure was then inherited. This could be interpreted simply in terms of evolution producing a better adapted machine. But time and again evolutionary theorists and the psychologists who operated on the fringes of evolutionary theory appear to have interpreted human behaviour as simply a manifestation of what is inherent *ab initio*. This tendency, together with findings such as out of body experiences, has led to the heady mixture that is spiritism and to the belief of many depth psychologists that they are dealing with the fundamental questions of human existence, a belief that has sought political expression from the involvement of magnetizers in the French Revolution onwards.[7]

What seems needed here is a distinction between a philosophy of mind and a *psychology* of 'transcendent' experience as first put forward by William James[8] and more recently by Andrew Neher.[9] But to locate this body of knowledge convincingly as a psychology rather than as a science of ultimate human meanings will need the articulation of a differentiated model of human functioning in which psyches and minds are distinguished. The existence of the neuroses, I believe, points strongly to the necessity for such a distinction.

THE NEUROSES

As the body was desacralized in the course of the scientific revolution so also were its afflictions. Where formerly illness, disease and disfigurement were taken to indicate something about the spiritual essence of the individual, in the course of the scientific revolution they became increasingly seen as mechanical disorders – mechanical because, in line with the distinctions between mechanical brain and spiritual mind, the only effective options in the case of behavioural disturbances were moral disorders or mechanical breakdown.

In the case of the nervous disorders we have seen, in Chapter 1, that the breakthrough was made in the early years of the nineteenth century with Gall's discovery of the hierarchical structure of the nervous system and Magendie and Hall's discovery of the reflex. This led to an intensely physical conception of the neuroses, where previously some vague disturbance of vital spirits was supposed. All of this changed in 1895 when the work of Freud and Janet pointed to a third possibility. In describing the clinical features of the psychoneuroses they pointed to the existence of a group of disorders, involving disturbances of memory, emotion, imagination and consciousness, that involved neither physical/mechanical breakdown nor moral failing. The problem with this was that there was effectively no other option.

One attempt to solve this problem has been to define the neuroses as mental illnesses, along with schizophrenia and manic-depressive illness. This attempt has arguably led to a discrediting of the notion of a psychiatric illness. Manic-depression and schizophrenia (dementia praecox) were defined as illnesses by Kraepelin on the basis that some of their symptoms must stem from biological disorder of some sort.[10] But the neuroses lack the stigmata of biological disorder. How then are they to be classified? In attempting to answer this we must decide how many neuroses there are, what causes them and what happens in a neurosis.

How many neuroses?

This book began with hysteria as the pre-eminent neurosis. However a process of dissecting neurotic syndromes out of the body of hysteria had begun with Benedikt's description of Planschwindel (dizziness in public places) in 1870, renamed agoraphobia by Westphal in 1871. In 1873 Lasègue in France and Gull in England described anorexia hystérique, or anorexia nervosa. In 1878 Westphal described a syndrome he named obsessive-compulsive disorder (Latin *obsidere*, 'to besiege') in which individuals are besieged by repeated intrusive senseless acts and ideas. Around 1895 Hecker, Wernicke and Freud all distinguished anxiety neurosis. At the same time a number of paranoid states were described by Janet, Freud and Kraepelin, which they saw as psychological problems rather than illnesses.

Today's classificatory systems distinguish between generalized anxiety disorder, phobic anxiety, social phobia, panic disorder, obsessive-compulsive disorder, hypochondriasis, PTSD and a variety of dissociative and somatizing disorders. But there has always been a claim that there are far fewer core neuroses – perhaps even only one general neurosis. The various neuroses would be distinct, it is argued, if they had separate aetiologies, natural histories and responses to treatment. But the neurotic disorders co-occur more often than would be expected by chance.[11–12] And a cognitive-behavioural approach seems effective for phobic disorders, obsessive-compulsive disorder and panic disorder.

However, while panic disorder, agoraphobia and obsessional disorders are associated, these neuroses are no more closely associated with hysteria and the dissociative states outlined in Chapter 4 than would be expected by chance.[13] These findings fit with Janet's contention that there are broadly speaking only two neuroses – hysteria, which he saw as being triggered by environmental trauma, and psychaesthenia.

Janet saw psychaesthenia as being more constitutional in origin. The term literally means a weakness of the psyche, and the evidence pointed, for Janet, to a weakness that was manifest very early in life, although it could also appear later in life following stress or fatigue. His descriptions of the state first appeared in 1903 in *Les obsessions et la psychaesthénie*, which described 300 cases.[14] To this day it is praised as containing the best descriptions of obsessional states but it remains untranslated.[15–16]

For Janet psychaesthenia involved three stages. In stage 1 the individual has an inner sense of incompleteness and torment. No satisfaction is gained from any undertaking. This leads to agitation and doubt, indecision and continual mild amnesia. In stage 2 ruminations, phobias and generalized anxiety appear. A developing compulsion for order and perfection leads to constant checking. Uncertainty leads to defensive rituals. Obsessions with homicide may lead to a knife phobia. Obsessions involving weight may lead to a food phobia and dieting – anorexia nervosa. Stage 3 is dominated by forbidden thoughts of a sacrilegious, violent or sexual nature. A parent may develop images of themselves cutting off their child's head and throwing it in boiling water. Janet described the case of a woman troubled by thoughts of a priest inserting a wafer into her anus and that of a man with an impulse to rape a woman in a church pew. This kind of clinical picture, which is characteristic of obsessive-compulsive disorder, was he thought only the final stage of a process and not the core of the disorder. Other possibilities on this level were a range of paranoid disorders that until recently would more commonly have been diagnosed as schizophrenia.

I suggest that it makes sense to work with the idea that there are four neurotic syndromes. One would be what was hysteria but now comprises the complex of PTSD, borderline disorders and MPD. Its distinctiveness derives from its origin in trauma of one form or another. This is shaped by the developmental stage at which the trauma occurs. Its symptoms are in part distinctive, involving as they do in one way or another the rehearsing of a past event, but the mechanisms that maintain it are not distinctive, as will become clear below.

A second syndrome would involve the phobic and obsessive disorders. This also, I will argue, owes its origins largely to environmental factors. In large part the mechanisms that maintain it are also implicated in the post-traumatic disorders, as the next section will illustrate. Disorders in this complex respond well to cognitive-behavioural interventions. While it seems that similar interventions might offer the best hope for PTSD, they do not at present appear as beneficial as they do in the phobic and obsessional disorders.

A third syndrome comprises some anxiety states and paranoid/hallucinatory disorders. Traditionally in psychiatry the presence of delusions has led to a diagnosis of psychosis, with the implication that the subject is therefore ill rather than just psychologically distressed. This tradition stems from the received belief that Kraepelin distinguished two mental illnesses, and only two – manic-depression and schizophrenia, both of which are psychoses because of the occurrence of delusions in both.

It is true that Kraepelin proposed that there were two distinct mental illnesses, but he also claimed that there were three psychoses, with paranoia being the third.[17] This, according to Kraepelin, was a delusional disorder that had its origins in personality vulnerabilities – it was a psychological disorder. Freud writing in 1896 endorsed this view, including paranoia among his neuro-psychoses of defence, along with hysteria and obsessive-compulsive disorder.[18] Janet also endorsed this view, including paranoid states among the obsessional disorders.

In part the difficulty in accepting that neurotic disorders could involve delusions seems to come from our belief that the neuroses are not severe disorders, and that they could not therefore evolve to delusional 'intensity'. But this is a modern view. Rereading the older texts it is clear that many of the patients Freud and Janet diagnosed as hysterical had episodes of florid 'madness'. Also, as noted in Chapter 6, there have always been some in the world of English-speaking psychiatry who have seen the need to keep open the idea of an hysterical psychosis. The French have not had this problem, in that French classification permits a diagnosis of *bouffée délirante*, a short-lived 'psychotic' state that is neither manic-depression nor schizophrenia. I have also argued elsewhere that the perceived severity of the psychoses is in most instances determined by a set of neurotic reactions to an underlying disturbance.[19] In favour of the notion of a paranoid neurosis are an increasing number of reports of the efficacy of cognitive therapy in a number of chronic delusional states.[20-1] There is also some emerging evidence that deluded subjects have an attributional style liable to predispose them to the generation of beliefs that are likely to be seen as delusional.[22-23] Thus there are good grounds for undoing the equation of severity = psychosis = illness. Undoing it however would leave us with a set of potentially severe disorders that reason demands we should be able to categorize but which do not fit very well into the ill–immoral dichotomy we have at present.

The fourth syndrome is that of substance abuse. This will be picked up in greater detail later in the chapter to illustrate by contrast some of the points being made about the other neuroses. In brief, it also falls uneasily into the categories of disease or of simple badness. It may also be extremely severe.

What happens in the neuroses

States of paranoia, or florid obsessionality, Janet argued, couldn't arise out of an otherwise normal mind. There must have been some weakness there beforehand which showed itself in a general difficulty with action and in particular with personal relationships. In contrast to the hysteric, who either loves or hates intensely, the psychaesthenic doesn't know whether he loves or hates. This, Janet proposed, was because they lacked sufficient psychological tension, although exactly what psychological tension was supposed to be was never made entirely clear.[24] It was something that physical illness, fatigue or emotional stress all could lower. Janet suggests that it at some point corresponds with a degree of physical tension. These ideas however were never developed, as by the time he moved from describing cases of psychaesthenia to speculating on its origins in 1920 the psychological debate had passed him by.

What might the psychic weakness be, and is it constitutionally determined? The first point to make is that Janet saw overt psychaesthenia as commonly having its onset during an episode of depression or low morale. He actually appears to have seen depression as just one more manifestation of psychaesthenia. This is a position that it would be difficult to defend today, with current research criteria clearly differentiating depression from phobias and obsessional disorders. What is clear today, as outlined in Chapter 8, is that depression appears to generate neurotic responses, either hysterical, obsessive-compulsive or phobic, and that in a substantial number of cases these neuroses survive the underlying depression.

There are further possibilities. Approaching the issue of the genesis of phobias and obsessional disorders from a learning theory perspective Isaac Marks has recently argued for a biological input.[25] He notes that evolution appears to build certain propensities into organic systems. Why else would we be so afraid of sharks and snakes but not of cigarettes and cars? In all species certain stimuli can be shown to trigger anxiety or avoidance reactions. Eyespots are a good example. Many species of moth appear to have developed wing markings that look like a pair of eyes when the wings are opened out, and this appears to produce avoidance reactions in predators.

In a recent study Watts and Wilkins found that subjects with agoraphobia react with headaches and panic to visual stimuli such as fluorescent lights, glare of sunlight on water, bright sunshine and stroboscopic lights.[26] The same stimuli trigger headaches in a large number of otherwise normal subjects, but not the sense of panic. As noted in Chapter 4 another stimulus which can potentially have anxiogenic effects is hyperventilation, the effects of which may, if the hyperventilation is sustained, be comparable to low doses of LSD or ketamine. Why should such stimuli lead to a neurosis? A possible explanation of this is that in subjects who have a neurosis certain prodromal symptoms may lead to maladaptive cognitive reactions.

Watts has listed a number of reactions that can be observed in phobic and other subjects, the varying combinations of which may produce differing clinical pictures.[27] One possible reaction is to cope with anxiety by suspending active perceptual processing. In favour of this are findings that spider phobics can't distinguish spiders they have seen before from ones they haven't. There are three ways in which this could come about. One is that in the presence of spiders they actively avert their gaze. Another is that they also seem to enter a state of poorly focused attention: they become glazed. The third is that, even if asked to look at the spider and describe it, they show poor recognition afterwards. This suggests that a set of distraction strategies are being employed, such as pretending to be somewhere else, distorting the feared image or concentrating on non-feared elements of a situation. These lead to the feared stimulus not being processed.

Watts suggests that such mechanisms may underlie depersonalization and derealization, which are such a feature of PTSD. It is known that phobic subjects, who have symptoms of derealization at a bus stop for instance, find that if they are joined by a therapist the environment comes back into focus. Such strategies permit the subject to manage but, like the reactions of panic-disorder patients who think they may be having a heart attack and sit down, they are essentially counterproductive and maintain the maladaptive behaviour in place.

A further cognitive reaction that may lead on to a neurosis and that may play some part in all psychaesthenic states, and certainly does in panic disorder, is to misinterpret the symptoms of anxiety. In all cases such a formulation depends on the essentially normal workings of physiological systems. The problem is psychological rather than mechanical or moral. This is brought out by the common finding that phobic and obsessive subjects, when called to do things without prior warning, often have little trouble. Central to the development of neurotic difficulties therefore is anticipation and a set of cognitive management strategies that are essentially counterproductive.

What causes neuroses?

Regarding the origin of those neurotic states that do not result from trauma Marks also notes that there are lessons from evolutionary biology that may be significant.[28] While learning theory has always been associated with experiments on animals and extrapolations from these to humans, often of dubious significance, Marks notes that all too often learning theorists have been using laboratory rats as experimental machines rather than animals. A concern with them as animals might have led to greater interest in ecologically valid learning paradigms.

In such paradigms social learning appears to be important, with the role of conspecifics assuming much greater importance than early learning theorists would have expected. For example if birds are shown for the first time an animal that would otherwise not make them anxious, in the company of other birds that are clearly made anxious by this animal they too will display anxiety. This anxiety generalizes to other settings and they can in turn be shown to transmit it to further conspecifics. A dramatic example has also come from herds of African elephants in which some members were shot several generations earlier. Although it is known that younger members have never been exposed to adverse consequences at the hands of humans they still flee from humans. This suggests that learning is being transmitted effectively from one species member to another.

The importance of this kind of learning is that the possibility of unlearning anxiety is blocked. In the case of a mother and daughter faced with a mouse, for example, the mother's reactions of anxiety will lead to the daughter being anxious. Where a child who falls off her tricycle is likely to get back up on it quickly, thereby forestalling the development of a neurosis about tricycles, this option is often blocked when a child learns anxiety from a parent.

Thus prepotent responses, such as the anxiety reaction to hyperventilation or glaring sunlight, might predispose to neurosis and the influence of significant others may determine the outcome one way or the other. However this is true for all of us. The process can be overridden either if the subject is introduced to the stimulus, in the first instance, while in the presence of someone who handles it competently, or, subsequently, by cognitive and behavioural techniques. These appear to tackle the issues quite successfully and lead to a subject's learning to override what before had incapacitated them.

Thus even if not precipitated by trauma there is considerable scope to argue that the neuroses owe their origins to environmental events. In the section on the mechanization of science I will argue for the possibility of an 'accidental' origin for most neuroses rather than one that is endogenously determined and inevitable. The case of substance dependence brings this out and shows further how social factors can significantly shape the course of events.

Substance dependence[29–31]

Substance dependence provides an instructive counterpoint to the issues raised here. In the case of alcohol, the opiates and cocaine there are clear physiological changes induced but no biological disorder other than side-effects such as cirrhosis. Just like the hysteric, there may be nothing that clearly differentiates the alcoholic from the rest of us other than a pattern of behaviour. There is no such thing as a substance-abuse proneness. The majority of drinkers and drug users are not addicts, nor is there any clear amount of these agents that makes a consumer an addict. Indeed the goal of getting the alcoholic or drug user to remain abstinent often seems to be the only thing that gives these disorders their shape. If the drinker were to return to social drinking, for example, they would be indistinguishable from the rest of us.

Where Eliot Slater took up arms single-handedly against the 'snare and delusion' that is hysteria, many have railed against the folly of seeing substance dependence as other than a problem of living. There has in addition been a long tradition of seeing substance abusers as degenerate, and just as with hysteria this has helped focus attention away from the environmental precipitants of the condition. Nevertheless, just as with hysteria, no amount of inspired polemic can get away from the existence of a vast problem.

Consider first the political dimension. Despite having been the first nation to legislate against opium use, in 1729, the Chinese found their domestic market being flooded with opium imports by the British in the 1830s, owing to a British attempt to balance their trade deficit with the Chinese. This led to the destruction of opium cargoes in Canton in 1838, which precipitated the opium wars – fought by the British in the name of Free Trade. Complete cynicism is not warranted, as it was only after 1868 that opium began to be viewed as a problem in the UK. But at present the most vigorous advocate of Free Trade has all but been at war in one country and has invaded another in an attempt to stamp out trade in cocaine. This despite the fact that one drug of addiction, tobacco, that is a cause of greater morbidity than cocaine, has in the past been the biggest foreign currency earner in the USA and that in the nineteenth century taxes on another, alcohol, regularly formed up to half of the revenue of the US administration.

In trying to square such circles the hitherto dominant therapeutic focus on the degeneracy of substance-abusing individuals rather than on the management of appetites in the treatment of substance dependency has a convenient effect, in that the need to question the role of society in the problems of substance dependency is avoided. Were the arguments that are often applied to substance abuse applied to food, which is reasonable in that both operate through common appetitive mechanisms, one might come up with the formulation that the current overweight state of Western populations generally represents a collective flight from reality. While there is a sense in which this argument has germs of truth in it, it seems unlikely that we are collectively more removed from the truth, neurotic or out of touch with ourselves than we were as a society a hundred years ago. What has changed rather is the availability of food.

In the case of alcohol repeated surveys show that the amount of alcohol abuse reflects the relative cost and availability of drink. This holds true for smoking also. Similarly the current escalation of cocaine abuse is more likely to be predicated on an increase in its availability than any degeneration of society. Yet we as a society appear able to ignore the evidence of social inputs to this neurosis.

If we do away with the spectre of degeneracy implied by the notion of cravings and say that classic substance dependence involves the management of appetites, what about LSD, PCP and the recent designer drugs that do not cause either withdrawal or cravings? These are also abused, despite increasing evidence that abuse may even be fatal. Why? Such abuse cannot on the face of it be accounted for by invoking physical mechanisms. The only explanation seems to me to be that underlying drug use there is a certain amount of playful activity. This has two aspects to it. Firstly there is our innate curiosity which leads us to try something new simply because it is there, just as some of us will climb unclimbed mountains or run across continents. Secondly playfulness is a means to handle boredom. For want of something better to do humans will turn to virtually anything, no matter how dangerous it may be. Even Russian roulette, as Graham Greene confessed, may be a way of livening things up or structuring them.

From this perspective it is simply a matter of accident that some of the activities available to be sampled cause physical dependence and others cravings, just as it is an accident that some of the pursuits available, such as motor-bike riding, have a high fatality rate. Just as with motor-bikes it seems that if one can get through a stage between the ages of fifteen and twenty-five without having been involved in high-risk pursuits or having suffered as a consequence, then one is much less likely to be accidentally killed or to end up substance dependent. It is not that playfulness diminishes after this age so much as that commitments and responsibilities restrict for most of us the opportunities to participate.

This perspective throws the spotlight back on the social factors that contribute to substance abuse. Where there is a restricted range of social outlets it is much more likely that any one outlet will be indulged in to a greater extent. Where the outlets available are unstimulating it is much more likely that dangerous alternatives will be resorted to. The question of what is perceived as unstimulating is however very much a question of education and culture. Putting these factors together loads the gun barrel with more live bullets in the case of certain social classes and environmental situations. But such implications can be avoided by adhering to the notion that drug use stems from individual perversity or the overwhelming potency of certain agents.

The issues in question are brought out by recent references to a new 'neurosis' suffered by 'women who love too much' who are supposedly *addicted* to being beaten up and ending up in unsatisfactory relationships. While there is certainly a small group of individuals with borderline disorders who may be said to precipitate repeatedly their own victimization[32] the vast majority of women (or men) who are beaten up or psychologically tortured do not in any meaningful sense of the word bring this on themselves. The reality is that social relations are such that they often cannot easily get out of damaging relationships. This reality and the need to do something about it can be all too conveniently ignored by blaming the problem on some endogenous masochistic impulse.

The significance of neuroses

The structure of the neuroses, outlined above, points to a set of disorders that can neither be put down to mechanical breakdown in the biological machine nor accounted for in terms of individual evil or inauthenticity. Individuals with a neurosis are no more or less inauthentic than the rest of us. They have a circumscribed problem that cannot in any meaningful sense be said to be the result of lack of self-knowledge. But equally they cannot reasonably be said to have a disease. I am not saying that there are not neurobiological correlates to the neuroses but rather that there is no evidence from them of any physiological disorder.

An alternative is to accept that the neuroses are neither instances of inauthenticity/moral failing nor of disease; but that they are autonomous psychological disorders, a different category of event to the other two. Taking this option however requires some clear distinction between psyches and minds. At present this is blurred. Until the issue is tackled the problem of categorizing the neuroses will remain.

A further aspect of the neuroses to emerge from the above analysis is their accidental quality. There seems to be nothing inevitable about them. Their occurrence and course depend it would seem on a conjunction of factors. They seem embedded in the environment, so much so that in cases in which family therapy is appropriate their resolution may be a matter of changing the environment. This does not fit the picture of a machine or mechanical breakdown that has been the dominant metaphor of man and his physical afflictions since Descartes.

THE NEUROSES AND THE MECHANIZATION OF SCIENCE

A further implication of Descartes' division of humans into a mechanical body investigable by scientific means and a non-mechanical spirit was the impetus that he thereby gave to a mechanistic approach to science. Henceforward the objects that science would investigate, from the macro to the microcosmos (humans), were seen essentially as machines whose working parts had to be anatomized. Science became experimental, in the sense of taking the machine apart to see how it works, rather than investigative, in the sense of hunting for the range of different machines there might be that could do the same job. Success was being able to take the machine apart and put it back together again in a way that worked. Such an approach favoured a philosophy of science that empha- sized logic rather than heuristics. This follows as all machines are logical; they do not work if they are not logical.

In the mid-seventeenth century the notion of probability was discovered. By the end of the eighteenth century many of the developments that would later lay the basis for statistical science were in place. The earliest developments of this approach were sustained by the needs of the insurance industry. But there gradually grew up a body of data on populations and life-spans, morbidity and mortality and, more important, a familiarity with the notions of a normal distribution of values and the idea of correlating the incidence of one thing with that of another. These developments were later to assume greater significance with the emergence of evolutionary theory, for which the idea of a normal distribution of qualities around a mean was a *sine qua non*.[33]

These developments intersected with the idea of a mechanical science only in the first half of this century. The idea that science might not be the logical exercise it had been thought to be and might instead be something more investigative, aiming at probable or best possible descriptions, took shape under the influence of evolutionary theory but more significantly in response to the development of quantum mechanics and Mendelian genetics.[34]

The idea that science might be a non-mechanical, investigative enterprise was resisted strenuously in psychology, almost certainly owing to insecurities about scientific status. In psychology the earliest experiments by Wundt and others were seen as only necessarily involving one subject. Taking measures from more than one subject, or repeated measures in one subject, were taken in essence to be replications of the original experiment. Unfortunately Fechner, Wundt and all others found considerable intra- and inter-individual variation. This was put down as measurement error round the true mechanical value. The development of the t-test and Fisher's analysis of variation in the 1930s capitalized on this. These approaches permitted the results of studies, in which there were a large amount of variables, to be mechanically fed through a calculator which would then churn out 'significant' findings. This allowed what was essentially a mechanized form of inductive logic based on experimental results. It supposedly removed experimenter error from the scientific equation.[35] It became the norm for psychology journals to insist on conformity to these statistical models; nothing else was considered scientific.

It is only in recent years that both psychology and physiology have realized that this variation is not error around some true mean but an indication that biological and psychological processes are inherently variable.[36–37] The application of other statistical techniques in physiology in recent years has revealed the existence of stable frequencies in neurotransmission and of electrical events in the brain. In this case statistics are being used not to prove something is 'significant' but rather to get a best possible description of a phenomenon. Similarly the techniques now applied to circadian rhythms aim at getting the correct description of the rhythmicity in question, rather than proving 'significance'. The recent development of chaos theory has taken all this one step further, in allowing for multidimensional, customized descriptions of events.

Oddly enough however, as noted in Chapter 7, as early as the 1880s Francis Galton was doing population surveys of mental imagery and autobiographical memory. This method of investigation, which aimed at establishing an existing distribution of qualities, is now termed an ecological approach. It derived its rationale from evolutionary theory rather than from physics. The statistical basis for this approach was provided by Pearson who developed the correlational methods to *describe* the data being generated. These laid the basis for an understanding of neuropsychological assessments of subjects – the most notable of which form the basis of what are now intelligence tests.

However the Galton/Pearson programme clashed with the perceived scientific needs of psychology in the early years of the century and was effectively suspended. Pearson's correlations of functioning were reified by Spearman. It was inferred that the distribution of IQ scores indicated a distribution in a very physical amount of intelligence in subjects. In essence intelligence quotients became indices of mechanical efficiency. These were subsequently put to distinctly political uses.[38]

In recent years a probabilistic revolution has been emerging in psychology as part of the more general cognitive revolution. Along with a recognition that the physiological bases of psychological processes operate probabilistically there is an increasing awareness that on the psychological level we operate no less probabilistically. There has been a recognition of man as an intuitive statistician. This in turn has prompted a turn to more ecologically valid investigations of cognitive functioning, as the example of perception may show.

Far from being a simple mechanical act it is now clear that perception is a sequence of best possible guesses based on uncertain cues, such as distance or brightness. As there is an irreducable uncertainty between such cues and the object to be perceived we all ordinarily use multiple cues and take a best possible reading. Natural selection ensures that we will probably end up with a 'useful' outcome. All of this happens subconsciously. We are not aware of the calculations involved and the objects we perceive seemingly stay relatively constant in the process.

Experimental psychology has traditionally approached the investigation of perception and other psychological operations by attempting to isolate one variable and vary it systematically, while holding other variables constant, in order to reveal a causal relationship. This was the method derived from classical mechanics. But it is now accepted in psychology that, as we normally use multiple cues, this approach is un-ecological, which perhaps explains why the results of such experiments have never generalized very well to the real world. The reason why this should be the case becomes more clear once it is revealed that not only do we use multiple cues but population surveys indicate that different individuals use different perceptual strategies.

As Egon Brunswik, the originator of the notion of humans as intuitive statisticians, put it: 'while God may not gamble, animals and humans do . . . they cannot but help gamble in an ecology that is only partly accessible to their foresight.'[39] It took over forty years for psychology to begin to pick up on Brunswik's initial vision. In recent years James Gibson[40] has put the ecological approach to perception on a sound footing and Ulric Neisser[41] and others are attempting the same for memory. This approach involves leaving the laboratory and going back to the world of everyday life in order to get as full as possible a description of the phenomena under investigation.

The probabilistic revolution and the neuroses

Applied to the neuroses this approach would mean that a research programme should involve going out to investigate the range of phenomena that are being experienced by individuals. It is remarkable that after a century of psychotherapy with subjects having borderline-type conditions one of the foremost experts on the disorder, Jerome Kroll, should have to claim that the principal stumbling block to progress is our lack of knowledge of the details of these individuals' experiences.[42]

As with the study of perception and memory in ecological settings such a research programme cannot go ahead without enlisting the experimental subject as a co-investigator.[43-4] In this regard it is probably significant that we have recently had the publication of a history of insanity from the point of view of the sufferers and the incarcerated, the details of which to this author at least appear to bear out the contention that enlisting the experimental subject is a *sine qua non* of fruitful research.[45] It is probably equally significant that perhaps the most comprehensive review of this book in the most orthodox of journals was bitterly critical of the whole enterprise.[46]

In Chapter 8 I outlined how probability assessments now appear to enter into the most intimate areas of our personal functioning, shaping the cast of characters and the dialogue on our mental stages. Predictions made from what we know of the judgments of normal individuals in situations of uncertainty account, I would argue, rather well for the neurotic/illness behaviour superstructure of depression and schizophrenia. So far no attempt has been made to map this kind of model on to the neuroses that arise independently of episodes of depression, although the recent cognitive models of panic would appear capable of being formulated in these terms.

Taking a probabilist approach to the neuroses would bring out their 'accidental' origins. This is of significance when interpreting the neuroses, particularly those whose genesis has not involved significant trauma. It would emphasize that these disorders are not an inevitable Freudian story, or the necessary outcome of a constitutional psychaesthenia, but rather have their roots in a series of real events, many of which could have happened otherwise.

As a brief outline of the kind of precipitation I have in mind, consider the following. Janet has been criticized for neglecting the element of conflict in psychaesthenic states. In contrast Freud saw these states as originating in a conflict over the expression of aggression or sexuality. Both however saw obsessional subjects plagued by images of murder or perversion as usually being timid and unassertive. But in discussing the role of circadian rhythms in cognitive functioning it was suggested that images to some extent must arise accidentally by virtue simply of a turnover of their material parts. This brings the spectre of unwelcome possibilities rather than unwelcome impulses into the centre of the personal stage.

Borrowing from Kraepelin (and Ernst Kretschmer) the idea of individual vulnerabilities we can postulate that the wrong possibilities at the wrong time in particular individuals may cause problems, depending on their understanding of what is happening or the support they can call on. Obviously there are a lot of conditions here that must be fulfilled if a neurosis is to develop, and whether they are fulfilled or not will be a matter of accident rather than the result of inevitability. This accidental quality to a neurosis, its being a result of interactions between an individual and their environment, is my reason for claiming that what is involved is not any degenerate weakness of the psyche but rather something that could potentially happen to any of us.

Furthermore an attempt to manage possibilities appears to be central to the neuroses. From the post-traumatic startle reactions in response to apparently innocuous stimuli to the phobic's derealization reactions, the obsessional's rituals or the paranoid's over-conclusive judgments, all neurotics display a fear of the future – what might happen. They have a loss of tolerance for ambiguity.

Such a vision of the neuroses stands in complete contrast to that of Freud, who was the complete determinist. In psychoanalysis nothing is ever probable or possible. All is determined, down to slips of the tongue. There are no accidents. The classic 'joke' about analysis is that someone who is late for therapy is resisting insight, even if they were held up by an earthquake or a robbery on the way.

Degeneracy

Machines break down because of internal design flaws, not because of the environment. Granted the machine may break down because it has been left out and has rusted, but even in instances such as these the implication is that the design was at fault – the designer forgot to rust-proof it adequately. On this basis the ultimate outcome of a strictly mechanistic approach to human disease is that, to have broken down, the machine in question must have been degenerate in some way.

This mechanical approach interacts destructively with romanticism. For the romantics, as noted, intelligence was immanent in the original primal stuff. It was not something that resulted afterwards as a product of evolution. Claiming that our ends are in our beginnings inevitably means that when attempting to account for unfortunate outcomes the romantic approach has had to have recourse to some version of original sin – the failings of humanity are also immanent in the primal stuff. Some elements of this conception appear always to have tinged the mechanical notion of degeneracy, leading to the heady cocktails in which degenerate physical functioning has been held responsible for degenerate behaviour.

Over the last nine chapters the various ways in which the machines that are neurotic individuals might be degenerate have been reviewed, from the idea of an aberrant reflex to the psychoanalytic contention that the cognitive moorings of the impulsive engine are inadequate for the job. In all instances it is the individual's constitution that is in some way being blamed. In all cases this process of blame seems to fit conveniently with the interests of certain social groups.

Since the Second World War the dominant mechanical metaphor has been genetic. There has been an intensive search over recent years to find the genetic faults responsible for both the neuroses and psychoses. There is however a radical flaw in this research programme which stems from the original romantic idea that evolution involves the development from a blueprint.[47–8] According to this view the design of the organism is laid down *ab initio*. It then unfolds, and the flaws apparent in the final product are ones that were present in the original design. With the impact of Mendelian genetics little, in many respects, actually changed. The popular view became the idea that one gene codes for one trait – that the overall blueprint was broken down into little bits of blueprint. Aberrant individual traits then ultimately resulted from aberrant genes.

It is now known that this is not the case. There are a multitude of genes that do not code for traits at all. Some regulate the developmental programme. Others may or may not be expressed. In a number of recently recognized cases the environment appears to determine which genes are expressed and which are not. This is a phenomenon called genomic imprinting, in which the usual process of genetic expression happens only following an environmental input.[49]

More generally however genes are ingredients of a recipe rather than bits of blueprint. They are the yeast or the spice rather than bits of a freeze-dried preparation, the addition of water to which produces the final cake. There is no master plan pre-existent anywhere that determines what the final outcome will be. Rather the outcome hinges on the fact that the mixing takes place under preset environmental conditions – a uterus at a certain temperature, with an initial supply of ingredients, most of which on a weight basis are not parts of the genetic code, and with a constant stream of other ingredients being added. The expression of any trait requires the co-operation of a large number of genes and the presence of a large amount of already mixed material.[50]

In a process such as this genes can only rarely be said to cause disease. Certainly they will contribute to the range of variation in the qualities that we each possess. Particular combinations of qualities exposed to particular sets of accidental circumstances may lead to unfortunate out-comes but this is quite different to saying that there is a design fault.

Some examples may bring this out. In the case of depression there is evidence that the levels of both steroid and thyroid hormones influence the outcome. It is quite likely that a number of other factors do also. The genetic input to such factors is therefore liable to contribute to the resolution of the disorder or otherwise. But significantly in these genetic instances the products of an original genetic input are shaping the out-come of the disorder rather than determining its cause. Such inputs however will lead to there being a genetic component to the affective disorders, a finding which seems to lead many to conclude that these disorders are not really environmentally precipitated but rather arise endogenously.

In the case of the neuroses the only established fact affects alcoholism.

Some races produce less of an enzyme, alcohol dehydrogenase, than others. This means that one of the breakdown products of alcohol accumulates in the blood – a product that in high concentrations produces nausea and headache. The result of this is that alcoholism is far less common among the Chinese than among Caucasians. In this instance a genetic input positively protects against the disorder rather than provides its ultimate degenerate basis.

Commenting on this kind of view of genetics, in which the older dichotomy of nature and nurture is sidelined in favour of a probabilist view of development, Susan Oyama has emphasized that it will be difficult to give up the idea of genetic determinism, as we will then have to face the future and the past without the excuses of original sin or the comforting certainties of either a divine plan or a set of inevitable laws that would allow us to predict with certainty what is going to happen next.[51] Given the ambiguous lack of determinism implied in the new genetics Robert Plomin and colleagues have argued that the field at present provides a Rorschach test for psychiatry, often revealing more about a researcher's biases than about the nature of the disorder under investigation.[52]

IMAGES OF UNCERTAINTY

I have repeatedly adverted to the need for a view or definition of the mind that would distinguish it from the psyche. The psyche has been characterized in terms of internal representations, of which images are a good symbol. The operations of the psyche appear to be based on probability assessments carried out in situations of uncertainty. But the first and central image of uncertainty in the book is that neither I nor anyone else can, at present, offer a clear-cut idea of what the mind is.

It is clear I believe that the human mind differs from that of animals. Something else has evolved. But trying to pin down what is distinctive about the mind is no easy task. Just as with some of the images in our mind's eye most of us have some idea of what it is that is needed but cannot guarantee that the details will add up. What is involved is not just attempting to define what the mind is but rather what it is to be human.

Before Descartes the issue of relating whatever it was that the mind was proposed to be to its substrates did not arise to confound the picture. Descartes sorted the problem out by locating anything that we feel to be distinctly human – such as consciousness, emotions and a capacity for language – in the soul. In this scheme of things animals were mindless automata. Current evidence points strongly to the unacceptability of this view. Animals appear to possess consciousness, emotions, skills and memory. I have proposed elsewhere that the higher animals possess a highly developed psyche.[53] Virtually everything that we think of as being distinctively human can be found in animals in at least rudimentary form.

What is distinctive to us? There are two bodies of thought and one piece of evidence that can be invoked in support of a contention that the mind is the human faculty that subserves a striving for moral coherence or authenticity. One body of thought is contained in the original Greek formulations of the issue, in which the mind is clearly not a calculating engine but rather is referred to as the 'light' of reason, with the clear implication that the proper pursuit for mankind is self-discovery through doing the right thing.[54] The other body comes from the early evolutionary theorists who were concerned to pinpoint how the mind evolved. Their writings make it clear that the issue they were grappling with was not how intelligent problem-solving evolved but rather how morality evolved.[55] The piece of evidence, of course, is the existence of the neuroses, which involve poor problem-solving, aberrations of the emotions, memory and perceptual processes but clearly do not involve issues of authenticity.

Based on such considerations, I proposed that the mind is an organization of psychological faculties aimed at authenticity. I have in mind here a strictly material mind – one in which there is nothing other than physical elements and chemical compounds organized according to biological possibilities and conforming also to psychological realities, but equally one that is not determined by such a constitution: one that can operate as a recognizably autonomous entity over a range of chemical, biological and psychological conditions.

One implication of this formulation is that the study of psychology can be only a part of the study of humans. It is important to research human psychology, just as it is to study human biology, and in particular perhaps the psychology of dissociative experiences so that, as Andrew Neher has put it, humans do not pay the price of psychological ignorance with their sanity, happiness and lives.[56] But of equal importance is the study of history, economics, law and the social sciences. It is these that tell us what we have been, shed light on who we are and point us towards what we might be. The study of psychology, even of a depth psychology, cannot replace these other studies, as it has tended to do in the recent past, becoming in the words of Hans Kung 'no longer merely a therapeutic procedure but an instrument of universal enlightenment'.[57]

Another implication is that neurotic disorders and inauthenticity will be two entirely different things. This returns us to Freud and the mesmerists, who when they failed to correct neurotic disturbances turned instead to programmes to change society. One of the pressing needs we have, I believe, is to get back the notion of a distinctively psychological disorder that does not involve one person pontificating on the adequacy or authenticity of another. The replicable successes of cognitive and behaviour therapies have brought this possibility much closer. What seems needed to complement this is the development of a philosophy of the human subject and their drive for authenticity.[58]

There are further, legal, implications in that traditional insanity defences have rested on the notion of mental disease. If the neuroses, and with them the most bizarre and serious disturbances of behaviour such as the borderline disorders or MPD, are not to be considered diseases but rather psychological disorders, then the notion of responsibility for criminal actions needs reformulation. It is clear from cases such as that of Kenneth Bianchi in this century and Gabrielle Bompard in the last, as well as the handling of shellshock in two world wars and any attempt to formulate a rational justification for American interference in the affairs of other countries in order to eradicate drug trafficking, that such a reformulation will be no easy matter.[59]

Dialectics and uncertainty

This view of the mind is one that entails a post-romantic complexity, in that the human striving for authenticity is not something that is held to be inherent in the primal stuff but rather something that has evolved with humans. This stripping away the blueprints of what we are supposed to be leaves us unsettlingly alone. It also puts out the light on Rousseau and Kant's vision in which 'what is permanent in human nature is not any condition in which it has once existed or from which it has fallen but rather it is the goal for which and toward which it moves'.[60] Evolution, far from providing a clear indication of where we are heading, has produced a situation in which it is up to us to determine what we will be.

In situations of uncertainty such as this progress and decline will inevitably interplay dialectically. The dialectical process appears to have brought us to what seems like a focal point in history. There is a growing awareness of our responsibility for the environment. There is an increasing recognition of environmental causes of what were formerly thought to be endogenous diseases, such as cancer. There have also in recent years been significant attempts to grapple with the issues of our responsibilities for each other, with statutory and non-statutory efforts to highlight the question and early treatment of child abuse and even more recently the question of marital rape.

All too often our interventions and discoveries appear to compound the problems. Throughout the book we have seen biological discoveries used to excuse social arrangements. This has been true of notions of a degenerate reflex as well as asymmetries of the cerebral hemispheres. The notion of intelligence testing has been perverted from its original purpose of assessing the competences of individuals in order best to tailor an educational programme to their needs, to a programme that has been held to indicate important aspects of the biological make-up of individuals, based on which their fitness to breed or to receive education at all could be determined. Most recently sociobiologists have read entire social structures into the genetic code, with E. O. Wilson arguing for the existence of conformer genes and upwardly mobile genes.

A particularly striking instance of this was the psychoanalytic programme which envisaged man as having only recently contained a basic animality within the slender restraints of civilization. These barely repressed impulses are supposedly always liable to erupt into the conflagrations of war or indiscriminate and unbridled sexuality. However the truth of the matter on closer inspection seems far more complex. The animal kingdom in no way presents a uniform picture of bestiality, whereas humans in their dealings with others seem capable of distinctive acts of savagery and cruelty.

The psychoanalytic story, as well as illustrating the maxim that a little biological knowledge is a dangerous thing, also illustrates the necessity for such knowledge. It has been ecological studies of incest in animals and the development of genetics that most tellingly reveal the flaws in psychoanalysis. The recent discovery of the extensive remodelling of connections between cortical cells in the first few years of life sheds light on the question of childhood amnesia. And closer attention to learning in animal species in ecological settings, as Isaac Marks has indicated, provides clues to the genesis of the neuroses.

Dialectics and medicine

We know that the mechanisms of the psychoses are in essence no different from those of the neuroses, but we do not have at our disposal the quantitative stimulation necessary for changing them. The hope of the future here lies in organic chemistry or the access to it through endocrinology. This future is still far distant, but one should study analytically every case of psychosis because this knowledge will one day guide chemical therapy. Freud, Letter to Maria Buonaparte, 15 January 1930.[61]

Modern medicine seems particularly subject to dialectical influences. An increasing proportion of the illnesses we treat are caused by previous drug treatment, while every new drug produced potentially changes attitudes cumulatively in favour of a mechanized medicine, thereby pushing us one step further towards a medical nemesis. The issue of drug treatments should remind us that in order to understand any dialectical process we must consider the interplay between what is known and whose interests are involved. This returns us to the question first posed by the mesmerists, when magnetism was proscribed by the French Academie des Sciences: whose interests does medicine serve?

While both Freud and Janet anticipated the development of biological therapies for psychiatric disorders,[62] the full relevance of this question to the issue of the neuroses has begun to become apparent only since the start of the mass tranquillization of distress with pharmaceuticals during the 1950s. The most recent stimulus to the categorization of the neuroses into an ever greater number of disorders has come from Donald Klein, who in 1964 suggested that panic disorder was a distinct entity to agoraphobia. He made the claim on the apparent lack of cognitive features to the disorder. On this basis he suggested that it would be particularly likely to respond to drug treatment. Subsequent studies have demonstrated an effectiveness of imipramine and other antidepressants in subjects with panic disorder.

Panic disorder has swept to a position of prominence among the neuroses today. In part this must be because of the vast amount of research done on it over the past decade. This research however has not been done out of a pure disinterested scientific desire to map out the boundaries of a new condition. Rather it has been drug company sponsored, with rather clear commercial interests at stake.[63]

In the 1970s the Upjohn pharmaceutical company produced a new benzodiazepine – alprazolam. By the end of the 1970s benzodiazepines looked an increasingly uncertain marketing prospect. It was at this point that the debate about panic disorder had begun in earnest, as in response to Klein's suggestions one of the committees responsible for drafting DSM III had to consider whether panic disorder merited a separate entry into the new classification. The conjunction of this medical debate and Upjohn's interest led Upjohn to sponsor a series of very large research studies on panic disorder, comparing alprazolam to other drug treatments. This was well funded research, with extensive provision for conferences and workshops – in fact it was so well funded that it became a standing joke among associated investigators in the mid-1980s to refer to panic disorder as 'Upjohn Illness'.

What seems to be involved here is a process of drug companies listening out for market opportunities and moving in on them. I have referred to this as a 'Luke Effect' and believe that it is playing a progressively larger part in medical science.[64] The notion of a Luke Effect is adapted from Robert Merton's Matthew Effect. Merton has argued that while scientific ideas may be adopted on their merits, all things being equal they get taken up based on the eminence of their proposers or on whether the work comes from Cambridge rather than North Wales for example. The Matthew Effect was so named after the parable of the talents in the Gospel according to Matthew, which ends with the moral that to him who has more shall be given but from him who has not, even that which he has will be taken away. The Luke Effect is modelled on the parable of the sower in the Gospel according to Luke, in which seeds are distributed. Some fell on stony ground, some fell on fertile ground but springing up were choked by weeds, while others fell on good soil and yielded up a bountiful crop. The parable ends with the exhortation to those who have ears to listen – which is what drug companies do very well.

Another example may bring home the point. In 1964 Ciba Geigy produced clomipramine, a modified version of their then best-selling antidepressant, imipramine. They were left with a marketing problem as clomipramine was no more effective than imipramine but it had substantially more severe side-effects. They sponsored a series of studies in which clomipramine was given intravenously in high doses. It was found that it appeared to be in some way anxiolytic, proving of some benefit in phobic and obsessional states. Since the market for drugs for phobic anxiety was at this stage targeted for other compounds Ciba Geigy targeted clomipramine for obsessional disorders instead. All of the research that was subsequently done on drug treatment of obsessional states between roughly 1977 and 1987 in Europe involved clomipramine. Noting this Isaac Marks has commented that as a consequence the impression has built up that clomipramine is in some way specific to obsessional states. There is no direct evidence that it is.[65-6]

In the first instance there simply have not been sufficient studies of other agents. In the second there is clear evidence that clomipramine is useful in other anxiety states, suggesting that it is a non-specific anxiolytic rather than a specific treatment. And in the third instance, while it is of some benefit, the benefits in question are limited. Neither it nor the subsequent 5HT uptake inhibitors modelled on it cure the disorder. They appear rather to make the subject less distressed about their condition, acting in many ways like atypical neuroleptics.

This process goes beyond the simple marketing of drugs. I have argued elsewhere that at present the marketing of psychotropic drugs is increasingly constraining psychiatric research and shaping the very concepts we use.[67] Jerome Kroll has taken this one step further and made a case that the categories adopted by *DSM* III have been significantly influenced by the requirements of the American pharmaceutical and insurance industries.[68] This particular dialectic appears to have had its origins with the establishment of a recognizably modern pharmaceutical industry in the middle of the last century. Before this there was an increasing degree of therapeutic nihilism in the medical profession as the older humoral theories of disease broke down, taking with them both the rationale for medical interventions *and* a common language shared by both physician and patient.[69–70] Far from this leading to a deterioration in health, starting from roughly the same period there was a dramatic improvement in public health.[71] This however did not result from advances in medical technology but rather largely from improved nutrition and housing and public health measures. Most of the improvements had taken place by the time specific drug therapies were introduced. Nevertheless the belief appears to have developed that it is the high technology achievements of modern medicine that are responsible for the improvements in our health.

This point is of particular relevance when it comes to psychotherapy. Isaac Marks has suggested that, although clomipramine has effects in obsessional disorders which, applying statistical techniques, can be called 'significant' when compared to exposure therapy, its true worth is of marginal significance.[72] Behaviour therapy however does not have the advertising or the marketing clout of Ciba Geigy. This clout is reinforced by the general belief that if a drug helps there must be some underlying biological abnormality that it is mechanically correcting. This is likely to change in the short term only if drug companies acquire the rights to psychotherapy and perhaps even the health services. This variation on the Galbraithian New Industrial State has come within the bounds of possibility given the development of focused and effective psychotherapy packages and the increasing industrialization of medicine.[73] In the meantime, despite the controversy surrounding the benzodiazepines, the mechanization of the neuroses proceeds apace.

It would have been easy to say the *medicalization* of the neuroses proceeds apace but this is strictly speaking not the case. As noted, the other consequence of the demise of the humoral theories of illness has been the loss of a common language shared by doctor and patient. The increasing mechanization of medicine is seen by many as threatening the fundamental basis of medical therapy, which traditionally has involved in the first instance an empathic witnessing of the existential situation of another and a proscription to do no harm rather than an injunction to be an effective technician.[74-5] This possibility is seriously compromised by the loss of a common language. One of our most urgent tasks is the recovery of such a language; such a recovery I believe will require some attempt to put in place a modern definition of what it is to be human.

This is not a polemic against modern medicine or the pharmaceutical industry, whose achievements have been more substantial than many of their radical critics care to admit, but an attempt to illustrate how uncertainty leads to a dialectical process. There is no unambiguously right or wrong position. This is brought home perhaps by William Osler's definition of the human at the end of the last century, before the development of the modern medico-pharmaceutical complex. He distinguished us as a species not by our possession of rationality or language but by our propensity to self-medicate. This said it can be noted that the medico-pharmaceutical complex probably also stands at a focal point in the current dialectical cycle. We are close to being able to intervene in our own genetic make-up. The next generation of drugs will be products derived from human genome engineering. Given our record at interventions thus far the outcome of this particular dialectic is unlikely to be an end to history. This potential development symbolizes the hazardous nature of the human enterprise. Who are we, what will we be? The dangers are caught by George Oppen's poem, 'Carpenter's Boat':[76]

> The new wood as old as carpentry
>
> Rounding the far buoy, wild
> Steel fighting in the sea, carpenter,
>
> Carpenter,
> Carpenter and other things, the monstrous welded seams
>
> Plunge and drip in the seas, carpenter,
> Carpenter, how wild the planet is.

Appendix: Dissociation Checklist

The following is a checklist of dissociative symptoms. Many of them happen to most of us some of the time. They are commonest in conditions when our physiology is altering rapidly – such as when we are falling asleep or waking up or if we have fevers etc. For this reason they are also common in anxiety states, particularly if a shock or reminder of some trauma causes a sudden surge of anxiety.

While the checklist has been compiled from symptoms that are particularly common in individuals with borderline or multiple personality states, scoring positively on a number of symptoms in no way indicates that you have a borderline personality organization or that there are buried childhood traumata that need attending to.

0 = never   2 = monthly   4 = weekly   6 = several times a week
8 = daily   10 = several times a day

1) *I feel things are not real, as though what's happening is part of a TV programme rather than real life.*
0 ... 1 ... 2 ... 3 ... 4 ... 5 ... 6 ... 7 ... 8 ... 9 ... 10
Does it bother you?   No ... A Bit ... A Lot

2) *I feel I'm not real. I have to pinch myself to see if I'm really here.*
0 ... 1 ... 2 ... 3 ... 4 ... 5 ... 6 ... 7 ... 8 ... 9 ... 10
Does it bother you?   No ... A Bit ... A Lot

3) *When I am dozing off or falling asleep I see very vivid images. (These may be either frightening or fascinating.)*
0 ... 1 ... 2 ... 3 ... 4 ... 5 ... 6 ... 7 ... 8 ... 9 ... 10
Does it bother you?   No ... A Bit ... A Lot

4) *When I am dozing off or falling asleep I hear what sound like real noises or voices.*

0 . . . 1 . . . 2 . . . 3 . . . 4 . . . 5 . . 6 . . . 7 . . . 8 . . . 9 . . . 10
Does it bother you?   No . . . A Bit . . . A Lot

5) *I have the experience of leaving my body and looking back at it from outside.*
0 . . . 1 . . . 2 . . . 3 . . . 4 . . . 5 . . 6 . . . 7 . . . 8 . . . 9 . . . 10
Does it bother you?   No . . . A Bit . . . A Lot

6) *I have the experience of somehow looking at myself doing things stupidly or making a mess of things.*
0 . . . 1 . . . 2 . . . 3 . . . 4 . . . 5 . . 6 . . . 7 . . . 8 . . . 9 . . . 10
Does it bother you?   No . . . A Bit . . . A Lot

7) *I find that I cannot remember parts of what happened earlier in the day.*
0 . . . 1 . . . 2 . . . 3 . . . 4 . . . 5 . . 6 . . . 7 . . . 8 . . . 9 . . . 10
Does it bother you?   No . . . A Bit . . . A Lot

8) *I get the feeling that there are parts of my life that I cannot remember at all.*
0 . . . 1 . . . 2 . . . 3 . . . 4 . . . 5 . . 6 . . . 7 . . . 8 . . . 9 . . . 10
Does it bother you?   No . . . A Bit . . . A Lot

9) *I find myself in places without knowing how I got there.*
0 . . . 1 . . . 2 . . . 3 . . . 4 . . . 5 . . 6 . . . 7 . . . 8 . . . 9 . . . 10
Does it bother you?   No . . . A Bit . . . A Lot

10) *I get told by my family or friends that I don't seem to recognize them.*
0 . . . 1 . . . 2 . . . 3 . . . 4 . . . 5 . . 6 . . . 7 . . . 8 . . . 9 . . . 10
Does it bother you?   No . . . A Bit . . . A Lot

11) *I look in the mirror and do not recognize myself.*
0 . . . 1 . . . 2 . . . 3 . . . 4 . . . 5 . . 6 . . . 7 . . . 8 . . . 9 . . . 10
Does it bother you?   No . . . A Bit . . . A Lot

12) *I feel that there is a fog or haze between me and the real world.*
0 . . . 1 . . . 2 . . . 3 . . . 4 . . . 5 . . 6 . . . 7 . . . 8 . . . 9 . . . 10
Does it bother you?   No . . . A Bit . . . A Lot

13) *I remember some things from the past so vividly that it feels as though they are actually happening again.*

0 . . . 1 . . . 2 . . . 3 . . . 4 . . . 5 . . . 6 . . . 7 . . . 8 . . . 9 . . . 10

Does it bother you?   No . . . A Bit . . . A Lot

14) *I go into trances.*

0 . . . 1 . . . 2 . . . 3 . . . 4 . . . 5 . . . 6 . . . 7 . . . 8 . . . 9 . . . 10

Does it bother you?   No . . . A Bit . . . A Lot

15) *I get the feeling that I am more than one person.*

0 . . . 1 . . . 2 . . . 3 . . . 4 . . . 5 . . . 6 . . . 7 . . . 8 . . . 9 . . . 10

Does it bother you?   No . . . A Bit . . . A Lot

16) *I get so absorbed in doing something (e.g. watching TV or reading a book) that I am unaware of things happening around me.*

0 . . . 1 . . . 2 . . . 3 . . . 4 . . . 5 . . . 6 . . . 7 . . . 8 . . . 9 . . . 10

Does it bother you?   No . . . A Bit . . . A Lot

17) *A voice inside my head comments on things I do.*

0 . . . 1 . . . 2 . . . 3 . . . 4 . . . 5 . . . 6 . . . 7 . . . 8 . . . 9 . . . 10

Does it bother you?   No . . . A Bit . . . A Lot

18) *I feel things are not real, as though what's happening is staged with other people acting parts rather than living them.*

0 . . . 1 . . . 2 . . . 3 . . . 4 . . . 5 . . . 6 . . . 7 . . . 8 . . . 9 . . . 10

Does it bother you?   No . . . A Bit . . . A Lot

19) *On waking from sleep or a snooze I see very vivid images or scenes.*

0 . . . 1 . . . 2 . . . 3 . . . 4 . . . 5 . . . 6 . . . 7 . . . 8 . . . 9 . . . 10

Does it bother you?   No . . . A Bit . . . A Lot

20) *On waking from sleep or a snooze I hear voices or sounds as though they are really there.*

0 . . . 1 . . . 2 . . . 3 . . . 4 . . . 5 . . . 6 . . . 7 . . . 8 . . . 9 . . . 10

Does it bother you?   No . . . A Bit . . . A Lot

21) *I wake up and do not know where I am.*

0 . . . 1 . . . 2 . . . 3 . . . 4 . . . 5 . . . 6 . . . 7 . . . 8 . . . 9 . . . 10

Does it bother you?   No . . . A Bit . . . A Lot

22) *My mind goes blank.*

o ... 1 ... 2 ... 3 ... 4 ... 5 ... 6 ... 7 ... 8 ... 9 ... 10

Does it bother you?   No ... A Bit ... A Lot

23) *I get the feeling of having been somewhere before.*

o ... 1 ... 2 ... 3 ... 4 ... 5 ... 6 ... 7 ... 8 ... 9 ... 10

Does it bother you?   No ... A Bit ... A Lot

24) *I have the experience of not recognizing somewhere or someone I should be very familiar with.*

o ... 1 ... 2 ... 3 ... 4 ... 5 ... 6 ... 7 ... 8 ... 9 ... 10

Does it bother you?   No ... A Bit ... A Lot

25) *I find during the day that disturbing images flash into my mind.*

o ... 1 ... 2 ... 3 ... 4 ... 5 ... 6 ... 7 ... 8 ... 9 ... 10

Does it bother you?   No ... A Bit ... A Lot

26) *I hear voices in my head.*

o ... 1 ... 2 ... 3 ... 4 ... 5 ... 6 ... 7 ... 8 ... 9 ... 10

Does it bother you?   No ... A Bit ... A Lot

27) *I hear voices that sound as though they are coming from outside when there is no one there.*

o ... 1 ... 2 ... 3 ... 4 ... 5 ... 6 ... 7 ... 8 ... 9 ... 10

Does it bother you?   No ... A Bit ... A Lot

28) *I feel as though everyone is looking at me – maybe waiting for me to make a mistake.*

o ... 1 ... 2 ... 3 ... 4 ... 5 ... 6 ... 7 ... 8 ... 9 ... 10

Does it bother you?   No ... A Bit ... A Lot

29) *I get emotional and don't know why.*

o ... 1 ... 2 ... 3 ... 4 ... 5 ... 6 ... 7 ... 8 ... 9 ... 10

Does it bother you?   No ... A Bit ... A Lot

30) *I get physically numb to the point where I can injure myself or cut myself without feeling any pain.*

o ... 1 ... 2 ... 3 ... 4 ... 5 ... 6 ... 7 ... 8 ... 9 ... 10

Does it bother you?   No ... A Bit ... A Lot

31) I get nightmares.

o . . . 1 . . . 2 . . . 3 . . . 4 . . . 5 . . . 6 . . . 7 . . . 8 . . . 9 . . . 10

Does it bother you?   No . . . A Bit . . . A Lot

*32) I get the feeling that there is someone or something nearby, when
there doesn't appear to be.*

o . . . 1 . . . 2 . . . 3 . . . 4 . . . 5 . . . 6 . . . 7 . . . 8 . . . 9 . . . 10

Does it bother you?   No . . . A Bit . . . A Lot

References

INTRODUCTION

1 Moody, R. A. Bodily Changes During Abreaction, *Lancet*, 934–5, 1946.
2 Taylor, D. C. Hysteria, Belief, and Magic, *British Journal of Psychiatry*, 155, 391–8, 1989.
3 Janet, P. *Major Symptoms of Hysteria*, Macmillan, London, 1907/1920.
4 Showalter, E. *The Female Malady: Women, Madness and English Culture, 1830–1980*, Virago Press, London, 1987.

ONE *The Historical Origins of Hysteria*

1 Diethelm, O. *Medical Dissertations of Psychiatric Interest before 1750*, Karger, Basel, 1971.
2 French, R. K. *Robert Whytt, the Soul, and Medicine*, Wellcome Institute for the History of Medicine, London, 1969.
3 Pinero, J. M. L. *Historical Origins of the Concept of Neurosis*, trans. D. Berrios, Cambridge University Press, 1983.
4 Hippocrates, *Complete Works*, Paris, 1849, vol. 8, p. 329.
5 Plato, *Timaeus*, Penguin Books, Harmondsworth, Middlesex, 1977.
6 Shorter, E. *A Short History of Women's Bodies*, Penguin Books, Harmondsworth, Middlesex, 1985.
7 Rosenberg, C. E. The Therapeutic Revolution, in *The Therapeutic Revolution: Essays in the Social History of American Medicine*, ed. M. J. Vogel and C. E. Rosenberg, University of Pennsylvania Press, Philadelphia, 1979, pp. 3–25.
8 Sneader, W. The Prehistory of Psychotherapeutic Agents, *Journal of Psychopharmacology* 4, 1990, pp. 115–19.
9 Willis, T. *Cerebri anatome*, 1664, p. 124.
10 French, op. cit.
11 Pinero, op. cit.
12 Drinka, G. F. *The Birth of Neurosis*, Simon & Schuster, New York, 1984.
13 Healy, D. *The Suspended Revolution: Psychiatry and Psychotherapy Re-examined*, Faber & Faber, London, 1990, Chapter 2.
14 Descartes, R. *The Passions of the Soul*, Hackett Publishing Company, Cambridge (1659/1989), translated by Stephen Voss.

15 Clark, E. and Jacyna, L. S. *Nineteenth Century Origins of Neuroscientific Concepts*, University of California Press, Berkeley, CA, 1987.

16 Hall, T. S. *History of General Physiology*, University of Chicago Press, vols 1–2, 1969.

17 Boakes, R. *From Darwin to Behaviourism: Psychology and the Mind of Animals*, Cambridge University Press, 1984.

18 Wright, J. P. Hysteria and Mechanical Man, *Journal of the History of Ideas* 41, 233–47, 1980.

19 Whytt, L. L. *The Unconscious Before Freud*, Longwood, London, 1978.

20 In Dewhurst, K. *Hughlings Jackson on Psychiatry*, Sandford Publications, Oxford, 1982.

21 Boakes, op. cit.

22 Richards, R. I. *Darwin and the Evolutionary Theories of Mind in Behaviour*, University of Chicago Press, 1987.

23 Changeux, J. P. *Neuronal Man: The Biology Of Mind*, Oxford University Press, 1985.

24 Drinka, op. cit.

25 Healy, op. cit., Chapter 1.

26 Dowbiggin, I. Degeneration and Hereditarianism in French Mental Medicine 1840–90: Psychiatric Theory as Ideological Adaptation, in *The Anatomy of Madness*, ed. F. F. Bynum, R. Porter and M. Shepherd, vol. 1, Tavistock Publications, London, 1985, pp. 188–232.

27 Pick, D. *Faces of Degeneration: A European Disorder 1848–1918*, Cambridge University Press, 1989.

28 Drinka, op. cit.

29 Freud, S. Charcot, in Standard Edition of the Complete Psychological Works of Sigmund Freud, ed. J. Strachey, vol. 3, Hogarth Press, London, 1893, pp. 9–23.

30 Freud, S. Preface to the translation of Bernheim's suggestion, in ibid., vol. 1, 1888–9, pp. 75–85.

31 Sulloway, F. J. *Freud, Biologist of the Mind*, Fontana paperback, London, 1980.

32 Harrington, A. *Medicine, Mind and the Double Brain*, Princeton University Press, Princeton, New Jersey, 1987.

33 Ellenberger, H. F. *The Discovery of the Unconscious: The History and Evolution of Dynamic Psychiatry*, Basic Books, New York, 1971.

34 Harrington, A. Metals and Magnets in Medicine: Hysteria, Hypnosis and Medical Culture in fin-de-siècle Paris, *Psychological Medicine* 18, 1988, pp. 21–38.

35 Drinka, op. cit.

36 Sulloway, op. cit.

37 Masson, J. M, *The Assault on Truth, Freud's Suppression of the Seduction Theory*, Penguin Books, Harmondsworth, Middlesex, 1984.

38 In ibid., pp. 41, 44, 46.

TWO   *The Emergence of the Psyche*

1   Janet, P. *L'automatisme psychologique*, Paris, Alcan, 1889.
2   Janet, P. *The Major Symptoms Of Hysteria*, 2nd edn (1920), Macmillan Company, New York, 1907.
3   Ellenberger, H. F. *The Discovery of the Unconscious: The History and Evolution of Dynamic Psychiatry*, Basic Books, New York, 1971.
4   Nemiah, J. C. Janet Redivivus: The Centenary of L'automatisme psychologique, *American Journal of Psychiatry* **146**, 1989, pp. 1527–9.
5   Ellenberger, op. cit.
6   Sulloway, F. J. *Freud, Biologist of The Mind*, Fontana paperback, London, 1980.
7   Freud, S. and Breuer, J. *Studies On Hysteria*, Penguin Books, Harmondsworth, Middlesex, 1895/1986.
8   Ellenberger, op. cit.
9   Sulloway, op. cit.
10 Freud and Breuer, op. cit.
11 Masson, J. M. *The Assault on Truth, Freud's Suppression of the Seduction Theory*, Penguin Books, Harmondsworth, Middlesex, 1984.
12 Freud, S. The Neuropsychoses of Defence, in Standard Edition of the Complete Psychological Works of Sigmund Freud, ed. J. Strachey, vol. 3, Hogarth Press, London, 1894/1962, pp. 45–61.
13 Masson, op. cit.
14 Freud, S. The Aetiology of Hysteria, in Standard Edition, vol. 3, 1896/1962, pp. 191–221.
15 Freud, S. The Psychotherapy of Hysteria, in Freud and Breuer, op. cit.
16 Ibid., p. 380.
17 Freud, S. Project for a Scientific Psychology, in Standard Edition, vol. 1, 1895, pp. 295–391.
18 Sulloway, op. cit.
19 Clark, E. and Jacyna, L. S. *Nineteenth Century Origins of Neuroscientific Concepts*, University of California Press, Berkeley, CA, 1987.

THREE   *The Hazards of Interpretation*

1   Masson, J. M. *The Assault on Truth, Freud's Suppression of the Seduction Theory*, Penguin Books, Harmondsworth, Middlesex, 1984.
2   Masson, J. M. *The Complete Letters of Sigmund Freud to Wilhelm Fliess: 1887–1904*, Harvard University Press, Cambridge, MA, 1985.
3   Sulloway, F. J. *Freud, Biologist of The Mind*, Fontana paperbacks, London, 1980.
4   Healy, D. *The Suspended Revolution: Psychiatry and Psychotherapy Re-examined*, Faber & Faber, London, 1990, Chapter 2.
5   Masson, J. M. *The Assault on Truth*, p. 186.
6   Freud, S. and Breuer, J. *Studies On Hysteria*, Penguin Books, Harmondsworth, Middlesex, 1895/1986, pp. 354–6.

7 Esquirol, J. E. D. *Mental Maladies: A Treatise on Insanity*, Hafner Publishing Company, New York, 1845/1965.
8 Sulloway, op. cit.
9 Masson, *The Assault on Truth.*
10 Masson, *Complete Letters of Sigmund Freud to Wilhelm Fliess.*
11 Sulloway, op. cit.
12 Shevrin, H. Unconscious Conflict: A Converging Psycho-dynamic And Electro-physiological Approach, in M. J. Horowitz, *Psycho-dynamics and Cognition*, University of Chicago Press, 1988, pp. 117–67.
13 Hunter, R. C. On the Experience of Nearly Dying. *American Journal of Psychiatry* 124, 1967, pp. 84–8.
14 Klawans, H. L. *Toscanini's Fumble*, Headline Book Publishing, 1990.
15 Darnton, R. *The Great Cat Massacre*, Peregrine Books, Harmondsworth, Middlesex, 1985.
16 Healy, op. cit.

FOUR *The Eclipse of the Psyche*

1 Sulloway, F. J. *Freud, Biologist of The Mind*, Fontana paperback, London, 1980.
2 Richards, R. I. *Darwin and the Emergence of Evolutionary Theories of Mind and Behaviour*, University of Chicago Press, 1987.
3 Gould, S. J. *Ontogeny and Phylogeny*, Harvard University Press, Cambridge, MA, 1977.
4 Ibid.
5 Sulloway, op. cit.
6 Healy, D. *The Suspended Revolution: Psychiatry and Psychotherapy Re-examined*, Faber & Faber, London, 1990, Chapter 3.
7 Freud, S. *Case Histories 1: Dora and Little Hans*, Penguin Books, Harmondsworth, Middlesex, 1977.
8 Arens, W. *The Original Sin*, Oxford University Press, 1986.
9 Ibid., p. 83.
10 Ibid., p. 102–21.
11 O'Donnell, J. M. *The Origins Of Behaviourism: American Psychology 1870–1920*, New York University Press, 1985.
12 Lyons, W. *The Disappearance of Introspection*, MIT Press, Cambridge, MA, 1986.
13 Boakes, R. *From Darwin to Behaviourism: Psychology and the Mind of Animals*, Cambridge University Press, 1984.
14 In ibid., p. 225.
15 Ibid.
16 Healy, op. cit., Chapter 4.
17 Ryle, G. *The Concept of Mind*, Penguin Books, Harmondsworth, Middlesex, 1949/1983.
18 Boakes, op. cit.
19 Mayr, E. *The Growth Of Biological Thought*, Harvard University Press, Cambridge, MA, 1982.

20 Mendel, J. Versuche über Pflanzen-hybriden, *Versuche Natur. Vereins Brünn* **4**, 1866, pp. 3–57.

21 Healy, op. cit., Chapter 3.

22 Gould, op. cit.

23 Richards, op. cit.

24 Caporael, L. R., Dawes, R. M., Orbell, J. M. and Van der Kragt, A. J. Selfishness Examined: Co-operation in the Absence of Egoistic Incentives, *Behavioural and Brain Sciences* **12**, 1989, pp. 683–739.

25 Bruner, J. *Actual Minds, Possible Worlds*, Harvard University Press, Cambridge, MA, 1986.

26 James, W. *The Varieties of Religious Experience: A Study in Human Nature*, Penguin Books, Harmondsworth, Middlesex, 1902/1986.

27 James, W. *Psychology, the Briefer Course*, ed. G. Allport, University of Notre Dame Press, Notre Dame, Indiana, 1892/1985.

28 Humphrey, N. *Consciousness Regained*, Oxford University Press, 1984.

29 Humphrey, N. *The Inner Eye*, Faber & Faber, London, 1986.

FIVE *Consciousness and its Vicissitudes*

1 Nemiah, J. C. Janet Redivivus: The Centenary of L'automatisme psychologique, *American Journal of Psychiatry* **146**, 1989, pp. 1527–9.

2 Nemiah, J. C. Depersonalisation Neurosis, in *Comprehensive Textbook of Psychiatry*, ed. A. M. Freedman, H. I. Kaplan, B. J. Sadock, Williams & Wilkins, Baltimore, 1975, pp. 1268–72.

3 Mesulam, M. M. Dissociative States with Abnormal Temporal Lobe EEG: Multiple Personality and the Illusion of Possession, *Archives Neurology* **38**, 1981, pp. 176–81.

4 Mavromatis, A. *Hypnogogia: The Unique State of Consciousness between Wakefulness and Sleep*, Routledge & Kegan Paul, London, 1987.

5 LaBerge, S. *Lucid Dreaming*, J. P. Tarcher, New York, 1985.

6 Kenneally, T. *A Family Madness*, Hodder & Stoughton, London, 1985.

7 Moody, R. A. *Life After Life*, Bantam Books, Atlanta, 1985.

8 Zaleski, C. *Other World Journeys: Account of Near Death Experience in Medieval and Modern Times*, Oxford University Press, 1987.

9 Roberts, G. and Owen, J. The Near-death Experience, *British Journal of Psychiatry* **153**, 1988, pp. 607–17.

10 Bierce, A. 'An Occurrence at Owl-Creek Bridge', in *The Collected Writings of Ambrose Bierce*, Citadel Press, Secaucus, NJ, 1946, pp. 9–18.

11 Janet, P. *The Major Symptoms Of Hysteria*, 2nd ed. 1920, Macmillan Company, 1907.

12 Ellenberger, H. F. *The Discovery of the Unconscious: The History and Evolution of Dynamic Psychiatry*, Basic Books, New York, 1971.

14 Harrington, A. *Medicine, Mind and the Double Brain*, Princeton University Press, Princeton, NJ, 1987.

15 Clarke, B. Arthur Wigan and the Duality of the Mind, *Psychological Medicine Monograph*, 1988, supplement 11.

16 Boakes, R. *From Darwin to Behaviourism: Psychology and the Mind of Animals*, Cambridge University Press, 1984.

17 Yaroshevsky, M. G. *Ivan Sechenov*, trans. M. Beuroff, MR Publishers, Moscow, 1986.

18 Changeux, J. P. *Neuronal Man: The Biology Of Mind*, Oxford University Press, 1985.

19 Dewhurst, K. *Hughlings Jackson on Psychiatry*, Sandford Publications, Oxford, 1982.

20 Prince, M. *The Dissociation of a Personality: The Hunt for the Real Miss Beauchamp*, Oxford University Press, 1905/78.

21 Bliss, E. L. *Multiple Personality, Allied Disorders and Hypnosis*, Oxford University Press, 1986.

22 Dell, P. F. Professional Scepticism about Multiple Personality, *Journal of Nervous and Mental Disease* 176, 1988, pp. 528–31.

23 Humphrey, N. and Dennett, D. C. Speaking for Ourselves, *Raritan* 9, 1990, pp. 68–98.

24 Rosenhan, D. L. and Seligman, M. E. P. *Abnormal Psychology*, W. W. Norton & Co., New York, 1989.

25 Nemiah, J. C. Hysterical Neurosis: Dissociative Type, in *Comprehensive Textbook of Psychiatry*, ed. A. M. Freedman, H. I. Kaplan and B. J. Sadock, William & Wilkins, Baltimore, 1975, pp. 1220–30.

26 Rycroft, C. Foreword to Prince, op. cit.

27 *Diagnostic and Statistical Manual of Mental Disorders*, 3rd edn, American Psychiatric Association, Washington, DC, 1980.

28 Prince, op. cit.

29 Hilgard, E. R. A Neodissociation Interpretation of Pain Reduction in Hypnosis, *Psychological Review* 80, 1973, pp. 396–411.

30 Bonke, B., Fitch, W. and Millar, K. *Memory and Awareness in Anaesthesia*, Swets & Zeitlinger, Amsterdam, 1990.

31 Rosen, M. and Lunn, J. N. *Consciousness, Awareness and Pain in General Anaesthesia*, Butterworths, London, 1987.

32 Dobkin De Rios, M. and Winkelman, M. Shamanism and Altered States of Consciousness, *Journal of Psycho-active Drugs* 21, 1989, pp. 1–128.

33 Masters, R. E. L. and Houston, J. *The Varieties of Psychedelic Experience*, Turnstone Books, 1966.

34 Neil, J. R. 'More than Medical Significance': LSD and American Psychiatry 1953–1966, *Journal of Psycho-active Drugs* 19, 1987, pp. 39–45.

35 James, W. *The Varieties of Religious Experience*, Penguin Books, Harmondsworth, Middlesex, 1902/1986.

36 Huxley, A. *The Doors of Perception* and *Heaven and Hell*, Grafton, London, 1954/1989.

37 Hansen, G., Jensen, S. B., Chandresh, L. and Hildent, T. The Psychotropic Effect of Ketamine, *Journal of Psycho-active Drugs* 20, 1988, pp. 39–45.

38 Gregory, R. L. Consciousness in Science and Philosophy: Conscience and Con-science, in A. J. Marcel and E. Bisiach, *Consciousness and Contemporary Science*, Oxford University Press, 1989.

SIX *The Traumatic Neuroses*

1 Erichsen, J. in M. R. Trimble, *Post Traumatic Neurosis: From Railway Spine to the Whiplash*, John Wylie & Son, Chichester, 1981.

2 Page, H. in ibid.

3 Sulloway, F. J. *Freud, Biologist of The Mind*, Fontana paperback, London, 1980.

4 Nemiah, J. Anxiety Neurosis, in A. M. Freedman, H. I. Kaplan and B. J. Sadock, *Comprehensive Textbook of Psychiatry*, 2nd edn, Williams & Wilkins, Baltimore, 1975, pp. 1198–207.

5 Masson, J. M. *The Complete Letters of Sigmund Freud to Wilhelm Fliess: 1887–1904*, Harvard University Press, Cambridge, MA, 1985.

6 Freud, S. On the Grounds for Detaching a Particular Syndrome from Neurasthenia under the Description 'Anxiety Neurosis', in Standard Edition of the Complete Psychological Works of Sigmund Freud, ed. J. Strachey, vol. 3, Hogarth Press, London, 1895/1966, pp. 90–115.

7 Stone, M. Shellshock and the Psychologists in F. F. Bynum, R. Porter and M. Shepherd, *The Anatomy of Madness*, Tavistock Publications, London, 1985, pp. 242–71.

8 Hudson, C. J. The First Case of Battle Hysteria? *British Journal of Psychiatry* 157, 1990, p. 150.

9 Mott, F. W. *War Neuroses and Shell Shock*, Hodder & Stoughton, London, 1919.

10 von Monakow, C. Diaschisis, excerpted in *Mood, States and Mind*, ed. K. H. Pribram, Penguin Modern Psychology, Harmondsworth, Middlesex, 1914/1969, pp. 27–36.

11 Stone, op. cit.

12 Brown, W. The Revival of Emotional Memories and its Therapeutic Value, *British Journal of Medical Psychology* 1, 1920, pp. 16–19.

13 Myers, C. S. The Revival of Emotional Memories and its Therapeutic Value, *British Journal of Medical Psychology* 1, 1920, pp. 20–22.

14 McDougall, W. The Revival of Emotional Memories and its Therapeutic Value, *British Journal of Medical Psychology* 1, 1920, pp. 23–9.

15 Fenichel, O. in Trimble, op. cit., p. 49.

16 Freud, S. Psychoanalysis and the War Neuroses, in Collected Papers 5, Hogarth Press, London, 1919/1949, pp. 83–7.

17 Freud, S. Thoughts for the Times on War and Death, in Collected Papers 4, Hogarth Press, London, 1915/1949, pp. 288–317.

18 Sargant, W. *Battle for the Mind: A Physiology of Conversion and Brainwashing*, William Heinemann, London, 1957.

19 Sargant, W. and Slater, E. *Physical Methods of Treatment in Psychiatry*, 3rd edn, E. & S. Livingstones, London, 1954.

20 Slater, E. *Man, Mind and Heredity: Selected Papers on Psychiatry and Genetics*, ed. J. Shield and I. I. Gottesman, Johns Hopkins Press, London, 1971.

21 Grinker, R. R. and Spiegel, J. P. *Men Under Stress*, J. A. Churchill, London, 1945.

22 Sargant and Slater, op. cit., p. 9.

23 Slater, E. and Roth, M. *Clinical Psychiatry*, Balliere & Tindall, London, 1969.

24 Slater, E. Diagnosis of 'Hysteria', *British Medical Journal* 1, 1965, pp. 1395–9.

25 Slater and Roth, op. cit.

26 Sargant and Slater, op. cit.

27 Baker, S. L. Military Psychiatry, in Freedman, Kaplan and Sadock, op. cit., pp. 2355–67.

28 Shepherd, M. The Neuroleptics, *Journal of Psychopharmacology* 4, 1990, pp. 131–5.

29 Rollin, H. The Dark before the Dawn, *Journal of Psychopharmacology* 4, 1990, pp. 109–14.

30 Healy, D. *The Suspended Revolution: Psychiatry and Psychotherapy Re-examined*, Faber & Faber, London, 1990, Chapters 2 and 6.

31 Critchley, E. M. R. and Cantor, H. E. Charcot's Hysteria Renaissant, *British Medical Journal* 289, 1984, pp. 1785–8.

32 Healy, op. cit., Chapters 2 and 5.

33 Micale, M. S. Hysteria and its Historiography: The Future Perspective, *History of Psychiatry* 1, 1990, pp. 33–124.

34 Bleuler, E. *Dementia Praecox or the Group of Schizophrenias*, trans. J. Zinkin, International Universities Press, New York, 1907/1950.

35 Langness, L. L. Hysterical Psychosis: The Cross Cultural Evidence, *American Journal of Psychiatry* 124, 1967, pp. 143–52.

36 Hirsch, S. J. and Hollender, M. H. Hysterical Psychosis: Clarification of the Concept, *American Journal of Psychiatry* 125, 1969, pp. 909–15.

37 Kasanin, J. The Acute Schizoaffective Psychoses, *American Journal of Psychiatry* 13, 1933, pp. 97–126.

38 Healy, op. cit., Chapter 5.

39 Taylor, M. A., Abrams, R. The Prevalence of Schizophrenia: A Reassessment Using Modern Criteria, *American Journal of Psychiatry* 135, 1978, pp. 945–8.

40 **Diagnostic and Statistical Manual of Mental Disorders**, 3rd edn, *American Psychiatric Association*, Washington, DC, 1980.

41 Horowitz, M. J., Wilner, N., Kaltreider N. and Alvares, W. Signs and Symptoms of Post-Traumatic Stress Disorder, *Archives General Psychiatry* 37, 1980, pp. 85–92.

42 Brett, E. A. and Ostroff, R. Imagery and Post-Traumatic Stress Disorder: An Overview, *American Journal of Psychiatry* 142, 1985, pp. 417–24.

43 Brett, E. A., Spitzer, R. L. and Williams, J. B. W. DSM-III-R Criteria for Post-Traumatic Stress Disorder, *American Journal of Psychiatry* 145, 1988, pp. 1232–6.

44 Green, B. L., Lindy, J. D. and Grace, M. C. Post-Traumatic Stress Disorder: Towards DSM–4, *Journal of Nervous and Mental Disease* 173, 1985, pp. 406–11.

45 Baker, S. L. Traumatic War Neurosis, in Freedman, Kaplan and Sadock, op. cit., pp. 1618–23.

46 Grinker and Spiegel, op. cit.

47 Burgess, A. W. and Holmstrom, L. L. Rape Trauma Syndrome, *American Journal of Psychiatry* 131, 1974, pp. 981–6.

48 McCarthy, A. Surviving a Disaster – the Counsellor's Perspective, Abstracts, Spring Quarterly Meeting Royal College of Psychiatrists, 1990.

49 Miller, H. Accident Neurosis, *British Medical Journal* 919–25, 1961, pp. 992–8.

50 Tarsh, M. J. and Royston, C. A Follow-up Study of Accident Neurosis, *British Journal of Psychiatry* 146, 1985, pp. 18–25.

51 Titchener, J. L. and Cap, F. T. Family and Character Change at Buffalo Creek, *American Journal of Psychiatry* 133, 1976, pp. 295–9.

52 Stern, G. M. From Chaos to Responsibility, *American Journal of Psychiatry* 133, 1976, pp. 300–301.

53 Napier, M. The Attitude of the Courts to Post-Traumatic Stress Disorder, *Personal and Medical Injuries Law Letter* 5, 1989, pp. 28–31.

54 Napier, M. Post-Traumatic Stress Disorder: The Zeebrugge Arbitrations, *Personal and Medical Injuries Law Letter* 5, 1989, pp. 37–42.

55 Kempe, C. H., Silverman, F. N., Steele, B. F., Droegmueller, W. and Silver, H. K. The Battered Child Syndrome, *Journal of the American Medical Association* 181, 1962, pp. 17–25.

56 Fontana, V. J. Child Maltreatment and Battered Child Syndromes, in Freedman, Kaplan and Sadock, op. cit., pp. 2284–91.

57 Henderson, D. J. Incest, in ibid., pp. 1530–38.

58 Eth, S. and Pynoos, R. S. *Post-Traumatic Stress Disorder in Children*, American Psychiatric Association Press, Washington, 1985.

59 Breiere, J. and Runtz, M. Symptomatology Associated with Childhood Sexual Victimisation in a Non-clinical Adult Sample, *Child Abuse and Neglect* 12, 1988, pp. 51–9.

60 Friedrich, W. N. and Reams, R. A. Course of Psychological Symptoms in Sexually Abused Young Children, *Psychotherapy* 24, 1987, pp. 60–170.

61 Edwards, P. W. and Donaldson, M. A. Assessment of Symptoms in Adult Survivors of Incest: A Factor Analytic Study of the Responses to Childhood Incest Questionnaire, *Child Abuse and Neglect* 15, 1989, pp. 101–10.

62 Wolfe, V. V., Gentile, C. and Wolfe, D. A. The Impact of Sexual Abuse in Children: a PTSD Formulation, *Behaviour Therapy* 20, 1989, pp. 215–28.

63 Kroll, J. *The Challenge of the Borderline Patient*, W. W. Norton & Co., New York, 1988.

64 Hamilton, N. G. A Critical Review of Object Relations Theory, *American Journal of Psychiatry* 146, 1989, pp. 1552–60.

65 Sydenham, T. cited in O. Diethelm, *Medical Dissertations of Psychiatric Interest before 1750*, Karger, Basel, 1681/1971.

66 Carmen, E. H., Rieker P. P. and Mills, T. Victims of Violence in Psychiatric Illness, *American Journal of Psychiatry* 141, 1984, pp. 378–83.

67 Chu, J. A. and Dill, D. L. Dissociative Symptoms in Relation to Childhood and Physical Sexual Abuse, *American Journal of Psychiatry* 147, 1990, pp. 887–92.

68 Herman, J. L., Perry, C. and Van der Kolk, B. A. Childhood Trauma in

Borderline Personality Disorder, *American Journal of Psychiatry* 146, 1989, pp. 490–95.

69 Arnold, R. P., Rogers, D. and Cook, D. A. G. Medical Problems of Adults who were Sexually Abused in Childhood, *British Medical Journal* 300, 1990, pp. 705–8.

70 Finke, M. *Principles of Mental Imagery*, Bradford Books, MIT Press, Cambridge, MA, 1989.

71 Van der Kolk, B. A. and Van der Hart, O. Pierre Janet and the Breakdown of Adaptation in Psychological Trauma, *American Journal of Psychiatry* 146, 1989, pp. 1530–40.

72 Putnam, F. W. Pierre Janet and Modern Views of Dissociation, *Journal of Traumatic Stress* 2, 1989, pp. 413–29.

73 Pynoos, R. S. and Nader, K. Children who Witness Sexual Assaults on their Mothers, *Journal of American Academy of Child and Adolescent Psychiatry* 27, 1988, pp. 567–72.

74 Kilpatrick, D. G., Best, C. L., Saunders, B. E. and Verona, L. J. Rape in Marriage and Dating Relationships: How Bad is it for Mental Health? *Annals New York Academy of Science* 528, 1988, pp. 335–44.

75 Friedrich, W. N. and Reams, R. A. Course of Psychological Symptoms in Sexually Abused Young Children, *Psychotherapy* 24, 1987, pp. 60–170.

76 Kroll, op. cit.

SEVEN *Project for a Scientific Psychology*

1 Boakes, R. *From Darwin to Behaviourism: Psychology and the Mind of Animals*, Cambridge University Press, 1984.

2 Schacter, D. L. Implicit Memory: History and Current Status, *Journal of Experimental Psychology* 13, 1987, pp. 501–18.

3 Gardner, H. *The Mind's New Science*, Basic Books, New York, 1985.

4 Oakley, D. *Brain and Mind*, Methuen Press, London, 1985.

5 Hirsh, R. The Hippocampus, Conditional Operations and Cognition, *Physiological Psychology* 8, 1980, pp. 175–82.

6 Mishkin, M., Malamut, B. and Bachevalier, J. Memories and Habits: Two Neural Systems, in *Neurobiology of Learning and Memory*, ed. G. Lynch, J. L. McGaugh and N. M. Weinberger, The Guildford Press, New York, 1984.

7 Weiskrantz, L. Some Contributions of Neuropsychology of Vision and Memory to the Problem of Consciousness, in A. J. Marcel and E. Bisiach, *Consciousness and Contemporary Science*, Oxford University Press, 1989, pp. 183–99.

8 Clark, E. and Jacyna, L. S. *Nineteenth Century Origins of Neuroscientific Concepts*, University of California Press, Berkeley, CA, 1987.

9 Changeux, J. P. *Neuronal Man: The Biology Of Mind*, Oxford University Press, 1985.

10 Koella, W. P. A Modern Neurobiological Concept of Vigilance, *Experientia* 38, 1982, pp. 1426–37.

11   Carlsson, A. Early Psychopharmacology and the Rise of Modern Brain Research, *Journal of Psychopharmacology* 4, 1990, pp. 120–26.

12   Svensson, T. H. Peripheral Autonomic Regulation of Locus Coeruleus Noradrenergic Neurones in Brain, *Psychopharmacology* 92, 1987, pp. 1–7.

13   Healy, D. *The Suspended Revolution: Psychiatry and Psychotherapy Re-examined*, Faber & Faber, 1990, Chapter 8.

14   Baker, T. B. and Tiffany, S. T. Morphine Tolerance as Habituation, *Psychological Review* 92, 1985, pp. 78–108.

15   Jaffe, J. H. Addictions: What does Biology have to Tell? *International Review of Psychiatry* 1, 1989, pp. 51–62.

16   Olds, J. and Milner, P. Positive Reinforcement Produced by Electrical Stimulation of Septal and Other Regions of Rat Brain, *Journal of Comparative Physiology and Psychology* 47, 1954, pp. 419–27.

17   Gloor, P. Inputs and Outputs of the Amygdala, in *Limbic Mechanisms*, ed. K. E. Livingstone and D. Hornykiewicz, Plenum Press, New York, 1978, pp. 189–209.

18   Parssinen, T. M. *Secret Passions, Secret Remedies: Narcotic Drugs in British Society 1820–1930*, Manchester University Press, 1983.

19   Hand, T. H. and Franklin, K. B. Associative Factors in the Effects of Morphine on Self-stimulation, *Psychopharmacology* 88, 1986, pp. 472–9.

20   Stewart, J., de Wit, H. and Eikelboom, R. Role of Unconditioned and Conditioned Drug Effects in the Self-administration of Opiates and Stimulants, *Psychological Review* 91, 1984, pp. 251–68.

21   Radó, S. Narcotic Bondage, *American Journal of Psychiatry* 114, 1957, p. 165.

22   Knight, R. P. The Psychodynamics of Chronic Alcoholism, *Journal of Nervous and Mental Disorders* 86, 1937, p. 538.

23   Berne, E. *Games People Play*, Penguin Books, Harmondsworth, Middlesex, 1964.

24   Finke, R. *Principles of Mental Imagery*, Bradford Books, MIT Press, Cambridge, MA, 1989.

25   Kosslyn, S. M. *Ghosts in the Minds' Machine: Creating and Using Images in the Brain*, W. W. Norton & Co., London and New York, 1983.

26   Neisser, U. *Cognition and Reality*, W. H. Freeman & Co., San Francisco, CA, 1976.

27   Galton, F. *Inquiries into Human Faculty and its Development*, Macmillan, London, 1883.

28   Berkerian, D. A., Conway, M. A. and Mingay, D. J. Imaging and Being Misled: When Imagery Does Not Aid Memory, in *Imagery: 2*, ed. D. G. Russell, D. F. Marks and J. T. Richardson, Human Performance Associates, Dunedin, New Zealand, 1986.

29   Neisser, U. *Cognition and Reality*, W. H. Freeman & Co., San Francisco, CA, 1976.

30   Aylwin, S. *Structure in Thought and Feeling*, Methuen, London, 1985.

31   Bliss, E. L. *Multiple Personality, Allied Disorders and Hypnosis*, Oxford University Press, 1986.

32 Kretschmer, E. *Hysteria: Reflex and Instinct*, Peter Owen & Co., London, 1961.

33 LeDoux, J. E. Brain, Mind and Language, in *Brain and Mind*, ed. D. A. Oakley, Methuen Press, London, 1985, pp. 197–216.

34 Harrington, A. *Medicine, Mind and the Double Brain*, Princeton University Press, Princeton, NJ, 1987.

35 Kosslyn, S. M. Aspects of a Cognitive Neuroscience of Mental Imagery, *Science* 240, 1988, pp. 1621–6.

36 Grinker, R. R. and Spiegel, J. P. *Men Under Stress*, J. A. Churchill, London, 1945.

37 Horowitz, M. J. Unconsciously Determined Defensive Strategies, in M. J. Horowitz, ed., *Psychodynamics and Cognition*, University of Chicago Press, 1988, pp. 49–79.

38 Horowitz, M. and Wilner, N. Stress, Films, Emotions and Cognitive Response, *Archives General Psychiatry* 33, 1976, pp. 1339–44.

39 Rubin, D. C. *Autobiographical Memory*, Cambridge University Press, 1986.

40 Janet, P. *Psychological Healing*, Alcan, Paris, 1925.

41 Galton, op. cit.

42 Bradley, B. P. and Baddeley, A. D. Emotional Factors in Forgetting, *Psychological Medicine* 20, 1990, pp. 351–5.

43 MacCullough, M. J., Snowden, P. R., Wood, P. J. and Mills, H. E. Sadistic Fantasy, Sadistic Behaviour and Offending, *British Journal of Psychiatry* 143, 1983, pp. 20–29.

44 Kroll, J. *The Challenge of the Borderline Patient*, W. W. Norton & Co., New York, 1988.

45 Singer, J. L. Sampling Ongoing Consciousness and Emotional Experience: Implications for Health, in M. J. Horowitz, ed., op. cit., pp. 297–345.

46 Luborsky, L. Recurrent Momentary Forgetting: Its Content and its Context, in ibid., pp. 223–51.

47 Kihlstrom, J. F. and Schacter, D. L. Anaesthesia, Amnesia and the Cognitive Unconscious, in B. Bonke, W. Fitch, and K. Millar, ed., *Memory and Awareness in Anaesthesia*, Swets & Zeitlinger, Amsterdam, 1990.

48 Shallice, T. *From Neuropsychology to Mental Structure*, Cambridge University Press, 1988.

49 Marcel, A. J. Phenomenal Experience and Functionalism, in *Consciousness and Contemporary Science*, A. J. Marcel and E. Bisiach, ed., op. cit., pp. 121–58.

50 Shevrin, H. Unconscious Conflict: A Converging Psychodynamic and Electrophysiological Approach, in M. J. Horowitz, ed., op. cit., pp. 117–67.

51 Marcel, A. J. Electro-physiology and Meaning in Cognitive Science and Dynamic Psychology, in ibid., pp. 169–89.

52 Carlsson, M., Earls, F. and Todd, R. D. The Importance of Regressive Changes in the Development of the Nervous System: Toward a Neurobiological Theory of Child Development, *Psychiatric Developments* 6, 1988, pp. 1–22.

EIGHT   *The Dynamic Unconscious and the Dynamics of Consciousness*

1   Healy, D. *The Suspended Revolution: Psychiatry and Psychotherapy Re-examined*, Faber & Faber, London, 1990, Chapter 7.
2   Hull, C. L. *Principles of Behaviour*, Appleton-Century-Croft Inc., New York, 1943.
3   Brown, F. M. Rhythmicity as an Emerging Variable for Psychology, in F. M. Brown, R. C. Graeber, ed., *Rhythmic Aspects of Behaviour*, Lawrence Erlbaum, Hillsdale, NJ, 1982, pp. 3–38.
4   Prygogine, I. and Stengers, I. *Order out of Chaos*, Fontana, London, 1985.
5   Changeux, J. P. *Neuronal Man: The Biology of Mind*, Oxford University Press, 1985.
6   Ibid.
7   Minors, D. S. and Waterhouse, J. M. *Circadian Rhythms and the Human*, J. Wright, Bristol, 1981.
8   Brown, op. cit.
9   Sulloway, F. *Freud: Biologist of The Mind*, Fontana, London, 1980.
10 Thommen, G. *Is This Your Day?* New York Crown Publishers, 1973.
11 Healy, D. and Waterhouse, J. M. The Circadian System and Affective Disorders, *Chronobiology International* 7, 1990, pp. 5–10.
12 Healy, D. and Waterhouse, J. M. Reactive Rhythms and Endogenous Clocks, *Psychological Medicine*, 21, 1991, pp. 557–64.
13 Healy, D. and Williams, J. M. G. Dysrhythmia, Dysphoria and Depression, *Psychological Bulletin* 103, 1988, pp. 163–78.
14 Healy, D. Rhythm and Blues, *Psychopharmacology* 93, 1987, pp. 271–85.
15 Koukkou, M. and Lehmann, D. Dreaming: the Functional State-shift Hypothesis, *British Journal of Psychiatry* 142, 1983, pp. 221–31.
16 Wever, R. A. Circadian Rhythms of Finches under Bright Light: Is Self-sustainment a Precondition of Rhythmicity? *Journal of Comparative Physiology* 139, 1980, pp. 49–58.
17 Healy, D. and Williams, J. M. G. Moods, Misattributions and Mania, *Psychiatric Developments* 7, 1989, pp. 49–70.
18 Healy, *The Suspended Revolution*, Chapter 5.
19 James, W. *Psychology: The Briefer Course*, ed. G. Allport, University of Notre Dame Press, Indiana, 1892/1985.
20 Healy, Rhythm and Blues.
21 Healy and Waterhouse, Reactive Rhythms and Endogenous Clocks.
22 Blacker, R. and Clare, A. Depressive Disorder in Primary Care, *British Journal of Psychiatry* 150, 1987, pp. 737–51.
23 Healy and Williams, Dysrhythmia, Dysphoria and Depression.
24 Healy, *The Suspended Revolution*, Chapter 2.
25 Carpentier, J. and Cazamian, P. *Night Work*, International Labour Office, Geneva, 1977.
26 Kahneman, D., Slovic, P. and Tversky, A. *Judgement Under Uncertainty: Heuristic and Biases*, Cambridge University Press, 1982.
27 Healy, *The Suspended Revolution*.
28 Williams, J. M. G., Watts, F. N., Macleod, C. and Mathews, A. *Cognitive Psychology and the Emotional Disorders*, John Wiley, Chichester, 1990.

29 Jackson, S. W. *Melancholia and Depressions: From Hippocratic to Modern Times*, Yale University Press, New Haven, 1986.
30 Healy, *The Suspended Revolution*, Chapter 5.
31 Mechanic, D. M. The Concept of Illness Behaviour: Culture, Situation and Personal Pre-disposition, *Psychological Medicine* 16, 1986, pp. 1–7.
32 Pilowsky, I. A General Classification of Abnormal Illness Behaviours, *British Journal of Medical Psychology* 51, 1978, p. 131–7.
33 Waddell, G., Bircher, M., Finlayson, D. and Main C. J. Symptoms and Signs: Physical Disease or Illness Behaviour? *British Medical Journal* 289, 1984, pp. 739–41.
34 Healy, *The Suspended Revolution*, Chapter 5.
35 Beck, A. T. *Cognitive Therapy and the Emotional Disorders*, International Universities Press, New York, 1976.
36 Healy, *The Suspended Revolution*, Chapter 7.
37 Healy and Waterhouse, Reactive Rhythms and Endogenous Clocks.

NINE *The Passions of the Soul: their Politics and their Management*

1 Sulloway, F. J. *Freud, Biologist of The Mind*, Fontana, London, 1980.
2 Roazen, P. *Freud and his Followers*, Penguin Books, Harmondsworth, Middlesex, 1971.
3 Ellenberger, H. F. *The Discovery of the Unconscious: The History and Evolution of Dynamic Psychiatry*, Basic Books, New York, 1971.
4 Ibid.
5 Darnton, R. *Mesmerism and the End of the Enlightenment in France*, Harvard University Press, Cambridge, MA, 1968.
6 Rosenberg, C. E. The Therapeutic Revolution, in *The Therapeutic Revolution: Essays in the Social History of American Medicine*, ed. M. J. Vogel and C. E. Rosenberg, University of Pennsylvania Press, PA, 1979, pp. 3–25.
7 Bliss, E. L. *Multiple Personality, Allied Disorders and Hypnosis*, Oxford University Press, 1986.
8 Ellenberger, op. cit.
9 Kravitz, N. M. James Braid's Psychophysiology: A Turning Point in the History of Dynamic Psychiatry, *American Journal of Psychiatry* 145, 1988, pp. 1191–206.
10 Ellenberger, op. cit.
11 Darnton, op. cit.
12 Ellenberger, op. cit.
13 Drinka, G. F. *The Birth of Neurosis*, Simon & Schuster, New York, 1984.
14 Sulloway, op. cit.
15 Descartes, R. *The Passions of the Soul*, trans. S. H. Voss, Hackett Publishing Co., Indianapolis, 1649/1989.
16 Bandler, R. *Using Your Brain for a Change*, Real People Press, Moab, Utah, 1985.
17 Darnton, op. cit.
18 Wilson, I. *The Bleeding Mind*, Weidenfeld & Nicolson, London, 1988.

19 Harris, R. Murder under Hypnosis in the Case of Gabriella Bompard: Psychiatry in the Courtroom of Belle Epoque, Paris, in *The Anatomy of Madness*, ed. Bynum, Porter and Shepherd, Tavistock Publications, London, 1985, pp. 197–241.

20 Freud, S. and Breuer, J. Psychotherapy of Hysteria, in *Studies On Hysteria*, Penguin Books, Harmondsworth, Middlesex, 1895/1986, pp. 354–5.

21 Ibid.

22 Perls, F., Hefferline, R. and Goodman, P. *Gestalt Therapy*, Pelican Books, Harmondsworth, Middlesex, 1951.

23 Rogers, C. *Encounter Groups*, Pelican Books, Harmondsworth, Middlesex, 1973.

24 Brenman, M. and Gill, M. M. *Hypnotherapy*, Pushkin Press, London, 1947.

25 Chertok, L. Pyschotherapy, Suggestion and Sexuality, *British Journal of Psychotherapy* 5, pp. 94–104, 1988.

26 Healy, op. cit., Chapter 3.

27 Evans-Wentz, W. I. *The Tibetan Book of the Dead*, Oxford University Press, 1927/1988.

28 Rieff, P. *Triumph of the Therapeutic: Uses of Faith after Freud*, University of Chicago Press, 1987.

29 Barrett, W. *Death of the Soul*, Oxford University Press, 1986.

30 Orne, M. T. What Must a Satisfactory Theory of Hypnosis Explain? *International Journal of Psychiatry* 3, 1967, pp. 206–11.

31 Hilgard, E. R. *Divided Consciousness: Multiple Controls in Human Thought and Action*, Wylie & Sons, New York and London, 1977.

32 Spanos, N. P. Hypnotic Behaviour: A Social–Psychological Interpretation of Amnesia, Analgesia, and 'Trance Logic', *Behavioural and Brain Sciences* 9, 1986, pp. 449–502.

33 For a detailed model of how mind, psyche and brain relate to each other, see Healy, op. cit., Chapter 1.

34 Luria, A. R. *The Mind of a Mnemonist*, Harvard University Press, Cambridge, MA, 1987.

35 Janet, P. *Psychological Healing*, Alcan, Paris, 1925.

36 Aylwin, S. *Structure in Thought and Feeling*, Methuen, London, 1985.

37 Beck, A.T. *Cognitive Therapy and the Emotional Disorders*, International Universities Press, New York, 1976.

38 Marks, I. *Fears, Phobias and Rituals*, Oxford University Press, 1987.

39 Clark, D. M. A Cognitive Approach to Panic, *Behaviour Research and Therapy* 24, 1986, pp. 461–70.

40 Michelson, L., Marchione, K., Greenwald, M., Glanz, L., Testa, S. and Marchione, N. Panic Disorder: Cognitive-behavioural Treatment, *Behaviour Research and Therapy* 28, 1990, pp. 141–51.

41 Bennett, G. *Treating Drug Abusers*, Tavistock Press, Routledge & Kegan Paul, London, 1989.

42 Miller, W. R. Motivational Interviewing with Problem Drinkers, *Behavioural Psychotherapy* 11, 1983, pp. 147–72.

43 Miles Cox, W. and Klinger, E. A Motivational Model of Alcohol Use, *Journal of Abnormal Psychology* 97, 1988, pp. 168–80.

44 Prochaska, J. O. and Diclemente, C. C. Transtheoretical Therapy: Towards

a More Integrative Model of Change, *Psychotherapy: Theory, Research and Practice* 19, 1982, pp. 276–88.

45 Kroll, J. *The Challenge of the Borderline Patient*, W. W. Norton & Co., New York, 1988.

46 Ibid.

47 Janet, op. cit.

48 Healy, op. cit., Chapters 3 and 7.

49 Ibid.

50 Ellenberger, op. cit.

TEN *The Genesis and Significance of the Neuroses*

1 Healy, D. *The Suspended Revolution: Psychiatry and Psychotherapy Re-examined*, Faber & Faber, London, 1990, Chapter 1.

2 Popper, K. R. and Eccles, J. C. *The Self and its Brain*, Routledge & Kegan Paul, London, 1983.

3 Voegelin, E. *Plato*, Louisiana State University Press, Baton Rouge, 1966.

4 Voegelin, E. Reason: the Classic Experience, in *Anamnesis*, University of Missouri Press, London, 1989, pp. 89–115.

5 Richards, R. I. *Darwin and the Emergence of Evolutionary Theories of Mind and Behaviour*, University of Chicago Press, 1987.

6 Clark, E. and Jacyna, L. S. *Nineteenth Century Origins of Neuroscientific Concepts*, University of California Press, Berkeley, 1987.

7 Darnton, R. *Mesmerism and the End of the Enlightenment in France*, Harvard University Press, Cambridge, MA, 1968.

8 James, W. *The Varieties of Religious Experience: A Study in Human Nature*, Penguin Books, Harmondsworth, Middlesex, 1902/1986.

9 Neher, A. *The Psychology of Transcendence*, Dover Publications, New York, 1990.

10 Healy, op. cit., Chapter 2.

11 Andrews, G., Stewart, G., Morris-Yates, A., Holt, P. and Henderson, S. Evidence for a General Neurotic Syndrome, *British Journal of Psychiatry* 157, 1990, pp. 6–12.

12 Pittman, R. K. Pierre Janet on Obsessive Compulsive Disorder, *Archives of General Psychiatry* 44, 1987, pp. 226–32.

13 Ibid.

14 Janet, P. *Les obsessions et la psychaesthénie*, Alcan, Paris, 1903.

15 Toates, F. *Obsessional Thoughts and Behaviour*, Thorsons Publishing Group, London, 1990.

16 Pittman, op. cit.

17 Healy, op. cit., Chapters 2, 5.

18 Freud, S. Further Remarks on the Neuropsychoses of Defence, in Standard Edition of the Complete Psychological Works of Sigmund Freud, ed. J. Strachey, vol. 3, Hogarth Press, London, 1896/1983, pp. 162–83.

19 Healy, op. cit., Chapter 5.

20 Chadwick, P. D. J. and Lowe, C. F. Measurement and Modification of

Delusional Beliefs. *Journal of Consulting and Clinical Psychology* 26, 1990, pp. 225–32.

21 Lowe, C. F. and Chadwick, P. D. J. Verbal Control of Delusions, *Behaviour Therapy* 21, 1990, pp. 461–79.

22 Bentall, R. P., Kaney, S. and Dewey, E. Paranoia and Social Reasoning: An Attribution Theory Analysis, *British Journal of Clinical Psychology* 30, 1991, pp. 13–23.

23 Kaney, S. and Bentall, R. P. Persecutory Delusions and Attributional Style, *British Journal of Medical Psychology* 62, 1989, pp. 191–8.

24 Janet, P. La tension psychologique, ses degrès, ses oscillations, *British Journal of Medical Psychology* 1, 1920–21, pp. 1–15, 144–64, 209–24.

25 Marks, I. *Fears, Phobias and Rituals*, Oxford University Press, 1987.

26 Watts, F. N. and Wilkins, A. J. The Role of Provocative Visual Stimuli in Agoraphobia, *Psychological Medicine* 19, 1989, pp. 875–85.

27 Watts, F. N. Attentional Strategies and Agoraphobic Anxiety, *Behavioural Psychotherapy* 17, 1989, pp. 15–26.

28 Marks, op. cit.

29 Bakalar, J. B. and Grinspoon, L. *Drug Control in a Free Society*, Cambridge University Press, 1989.

30 Room, R. Drugs, Consciousnes and Self-control: Popular and Medical Conceptions, *International Review of Psychiatry* 1, 1989, pp. 63–70.

31 Parssinen, T. M. *Secret Passions, Secret Remedies: Narcotic Drugs in British Society 1820–1930*, Manchester University Press, 1983.

32 Kroll, J. *The Challenge of the Borderline Patient*, W. W. Norton & Co., New York, 1988.

33 Hacking, I. *The Emergence of Probability*, Cambridge University Press, 1975.

34 Healy, op. cit., Chapter 3.

35 Gigerenzer, G. Probabilistic Thinking and the Fight Against Subjectivity, in L. Kruger, L. J. Daston and M. Heidelberger ed., *The Probabilistic Revolution*, MIT Press, Cambridge, MA, 1987.

36 Ibid.

37 Gigerenzer, G. Survival of the Fittest Probabilist: Brunswik, Thurstone and the Two Disciplines of Psychology, in Kruger, Daston and Heidelberger, op. cit.

38 Gould, S. J. *The Mismeasure of Man*, Penguin Books, Harmondsworth, Middlesex, 1981.

39 Gigerenzer, G. Survival of the Fittest Probabilist.

40 Gibson, J. J. *The Senses Considered as Perceptual Systems*, George Allen & Unwin, London, 1968.

41 Neisser, U. Nested Structure in Autobiographical Memory, in *Autobiographical Memory*, ed. D. C. Rubin, Cambridge University Press, 1986, pp. 71–81.

42 Kroll, op. cit.

43 Healy, op. cit., Chapters 4, 7.

44 Healy, D. A New Science of Insanity, *New Scientist* 1737, 1990, pp. 34–7.

45 Porter, R. *A Social History of Madness: Stories of the Insane*, Weidenfeld, London, 1987.

46 Roth, M. Nobly Wild, not Mad? *British Medical Journal* 296, 1988, pp. 1165–9.

47 Gould, S. J. *Ontogeny and Phylogeny*, Harvard University Press, Cambridge, MA, 1977.

48 Oyama, S. *The Ontogeny Of Information*, Cambridge University Press, 1985.

49 Hall, J. G. Genomic Imprinting: Review and Relevance to Human Diseases, *American Journal of Human Genetics* 46, 1990, pp. 857–73.

50 Rosenberg, A. *The Structure of Biological Science*, Cambridge University Press, 1985.

51 Oyama, op. cit.

52 Reiss, D., Plomin, R. and Hetherington, E. M. Genetics and Psychiatry: An Unheralded Window on the Environment, *American Journal of Psychiatry* 148, 1991, pp. 283–91.

53 Healy, D. *The Suspended Revolution*, Chapter 1.

54 Ibid., Chapter 1.

55 Richards, in op. cit.

56 Neher, op. cit.

57 Kung, H. *Freud and the Problem of God*, Yale University Press, 1980.

58 Lonergan, B. J. F. The Subject, in *A Second Collection*, Darton, Longman & Todd, London, 1974.

59 For a review of this minefield see Stone, A. A. *Law, Psychiatry and Morality*, American Psychiatric Press Inc., Washington, DC, 1984.

60 Ibid., p. 234.

61 Freud, S. Letter to Maria Buonaparte, 15 January 1930, in *The Life and Work of Sigmund Freud*, ed. E. Jones, vol. 3, Basic Books, New York, 1957, p. 480.

62 Ellenberger, H. F. *The Discovery of the Unconscious: The History and Evolution of Dynamic Psychiatry*, Basic Books, New York, 1971.

63 Healy, D. The Psychopharmacological Era: Notes Toward a History, *Journal of Psychopharmacology* 5, 1984, pp. 152–67.

64 Ibid.

65 Marks, I. M., Lelliott, P., Basoglu, M., Noshirvani, H., Monteiro, W., Cohen, D. and Kasvikis, Y. Clomipramine, Self-exposure and Therapist Aided Exposure of Obsessive-compulsive Rituals, *British Journal of Psychiatry* 152, 1988, pp. 522–34.

66 Healy, D. What do 5HT Reuptake Inhibitors do in Obsessive-compulsive Disorders? *Human Psychopharmacology* 6, 1991, pp. 325–8.

67 Healy, D. The Marketing of 5HT: Depression or Anxiety? *British Journal of Psychiatry*, 158, 1991, pp. 737–42.

68 Kroll, op. cit.

69 Rosenberg, C. E. The Therapeutic Revolution, in *The Therapeutic Revolution: Essays in the Social History of American Medicine*, ed. M. J. Vogel and C. E. Rosenberg, University of Pennsylvania Press, PA, 1979, pp. 3–25.

70 Pellegrino, E. D. The Sociocultural Impact of Twentieth Century Therapeutics, in ibid., pp. 245–66.

71 McKeown, T. *The Role of Medicine*, Blackwell, Oxford, 1979.

REFERENCES

72 Marks, I. The Gap between Research and Policy in Mental Health Care, *Journal of Royal Society of Medicine* 82, 1989, pp. 514–17.

73 Bittner, T. E. The Industrialisation of American Psychiatry, *American Journal of Psychiatry* 142, 1985, pp. 149–54.

74 Pellegrino, op. cit.

75 Kleinman, A. *The Illness Narratives*, Basic Books, New York, 1988.

76 Oppen, G. *Collected Poems*, New Directions Publishing Corporation, New York, 1975.

Index

Page numbers in italics refer to figures and illustrations